My FOREVER GIRL

My FOREVER GIRL

USA TODAY BESTSELLING AUTHOR
LAURA PAVLOV

Entangled Publishing, LLC
644 Shrewsbury Commons Ave., STE 181
Shrewsbury, PA 17361
rights@entangledpublishing.com

Amara is an imprint of Entangled Publishing, LLC.
Visit our website at www.entangledpublishing.com.

Edited by Sue Grimshaw
Cover and edge design by LJ Anderson
Cover and edge images by timonko/Gettyimages and
CSA Images/Gettyimages
Interior design by Toni Kerr
Interior original illustration by Kait Bethune

ISBN 978-1-68281-721-6

Manufactured in the United States of America

First Edition June 2026

10 9 8 7 6 5 4 3 2 1

ALSO BY LAURA PAVLOV

BLUE SKY BAY

My Forever Girl

ROSEWOOD RIVER

Steal My Heart
My Silver Lining
Over the Moon
Crazy In Love
In a Heartbeat
Whisper Sweet Nothings

HONEY MOUNTAIN

Always Mine
Ever Mine
Make You Mine
Simply Mine
Only Mine

"The only dream that I'm chasing is right in front of me.
She's been in front of me my whole life."
—Cutler Heart

CHAPTER ONE

Cutler

"Damn, business is booming." I took a long pull from my beer and leaned my elbows on the counter of Four Clovers. The wood was warm from the afternoon sun, and the salty breeze drifting in from the bay carried the smell of grilled shrimp and fried cheese. From where I sat at the bar at the far end of the property, I had a clear view of the whole container park: the wide grassy courtyard in the center, dark wood picnic tables scattered across it, and the ring of food trailers circling like a bright, colorful horseshoe. Laughter and the hum of conversation rolled across the space, blending with the low thump of country music coming through the speakers.

"Summer has arrived, boys, along with all the tourists." Brody leaned over the bar and waggled his brows.

He owned the Down by the Bay Container Park—this whole open-air setup of trailers, turf, and string lights that had somehow become the town's hottest hangout, especially on warm nights like this when the air buzzed with heat and everyone seemed a little more laid back. He owned the bar, Four Clovers, where me and my boys met up weekly.

"Well, let me tell you what else has arrived with summer," Phoenix grumped. "All the damn teenagers who don't know how to handle their booze while they party down by the beach. These assholes don't have the decency to put out the damn bonfires that they start. We've gotten a call at the firehouse every fucking night this week."

Brody laughed as he looked at his brother. "Dude, do you not remember doing that exact same thing when we were dumb-ass teenagers?"

"No. I never fucked around with fire, hence the reason I'm a fucking firefighter now."

"It'll calm down in a little bit," I said, clapping him on the shoulder. "It's the beginning of summer break, so they just got out of school. I found a bunch of teens partying behind that property I'm working on for my family."

"Yeah, I heard you scared the shit out of them," Brody said with a laugh.

I shrugged. "I had a little fun with one of the cocky little shits who tried to tell me that his father owned that land, which was obviously not true, seeing as my family owns it."

"Good. Those fuckers need to learn some respect," Phoenix hissed before rubbing his face. "I swear this town is growing too damn fast. I don't like it."

Phoenix and Brody grew up here, and we actually met when I was a kid living back in Magnolia Falls. My dad loved to bring me out to Blue Sky Lake, as they had the best hikes around, and it wasn't too far from home. And then I'd decided to go to college not far from here, and we'd been friends for a long time now.

"Stop complaining. It's good for business." Brody held his fist up for me, and I gave him a pound. He was right. ROD Construction was booming, and I had more jobs than I could handle at the moment.

"I agree," I chuckled. "And at least it's not boring at the firehouse right now."

Phoenix rolled his eyes. He was a grumpy fucker, but I loved the dude.

"So, you leave tomorrow for Paris, right?" he asked, knowing I was relieved as hell that Gracie had finally agreed to let me go help her pack up and get her ass back home. She'd come live with me and work here for a few months until she took her new job back in New York.

Gracie Reynolds was my best friend. I'd even go as far as to say that she was my better half, because I didn't really do serious relationships, so she was my girl.

Always has been.

Gracie and I met when we were young, and we'd grown up together. We shared secrets and inside jokes that no one else understood and spent many summers together with our families. She was the person I counted on the most to tell me the truth, even when I didn't want to hear it. And she was the only person who could drag me out of my own head when life got messy. We'd never dated, never crossed that line—but she was hands down my person.

My girl.

"Yep. I leave in the morning. I'm glad she finally decided to call it done there. I hated that fucker, and I'm glad she kicked his ass to the curb."

I'd hated Gabriel, the guy she'd moved to Paris with, from the first time I'd met him. He oozed arrogance, and I never felt like Gracie was herself around him.

"Gee, we couldn't tell you hated the guy at all," Brody said with a laugh. "Have you ever noticed that you don't like anyone she's dating?"

"Listen. She deserves the fucking moon. That dude was an arrogant asshole. I don't know what she was doing with him." I took the last pull from my beer and set the bottle down. "But I'm glad she finally agreed to come here and stay with me. She doesn't make it fucking easy to help her."

I was looking forward to having my girl back in the same country and on the same time zone. And the fact that she'd be staying with me meant we'd have a lot of time together, which I was looking forward to.

I'd missed her.

"She's always been independent, and she's got her pride. You've got to let her figure things out on her own sometimes." Phoenix shrugged. "You can be a bit of a bull in a china shop when it comes to Gracie."

He wasn't wrong.

"I knew in my gut something was wrong. She hadn't been herself. And to finally have her admit that she'd been struggling… She'd dumped his ass two months ago and didn't want to tell anyone." I shook my head in disbelief. "She has no idea how much we all despised the dickhead."

I was close with Gracie's parents, and we'd had several conversations about it. I knew they weren't happy when she'd given up her entire life, her car, her job, her apartment, all to go live in Paris with Gabriel Laurent.

I actually had a physical reaction when she left for Paris. I had this pit in my stomach that truly didn't leave until the day she told me she was coming home.

I wasn't sure if it was my gut instinct about Gabriel not being the right guy for her or just the loss I felt when she'd left. Even when she was living in LA and I was here in Blue Sky Bay, we'd talk multiple times a day.

We always had.

And we'd see each other at least once a week, either for lunch or dinner, or she'd come stay with me for the weekend.

And when she left, I'd felt her absence in a way that I couldn't begin to explain.

I wasn't too proud to admit that I'd felt completely lost in the months she'd been gone.

I considered myself a very independent man. I'd intentionally set my life up that way.

But everything was different with Gracie, and being separated from her had proved more difficult than I'd expected.

"I'm not surprised. You know her better than anyone." Brody held up another beer, but I shook my head no. I had some work to do back at home tonight before I left.

"Hey, Cutler. What's a guy like you doing in a place like this?" Chloe purred as her arm came over my shoulder and she spoke against my ear.

"Well, this is the only place in town to go, so what option do I have?" I chuckled and tossed Brody a smirk. He rolled his eyes, and I turned in my chair to face her. "How are you doing, Chloe? And how's that husband of yours?"

She was a flirt, and everyone knew it. Personally, I found it to be disrespectful to her husband, Roy, who I happened to like—even if he always laughed it off.

She came on strong, but she was probably just a little starved for attention.

But I didn't mess around with married women, and I'd made that very clear with her on multiple occasions.

"You love to bring up my husband, don't you?" She giggled as she played with the ends of her long blonde hair.

I glanced over my shoulder at the blue-and-white trailer with the large sign that read Blue Sky Pizza, which sat just a few feet away. She and her husband owned it, so she was always here, as was Roy.

"Just reminding you that Roy's a good guy. But you know that, don't you?" I said playfully as I tossed her a wink.

"Well, you're no fun, Cutler Heart," she pouted.

"Said nobody ever," Phoenix said under his breath, which made me laugh.

"Fine. I'll see y'all later." She turned and walked away.

"She doesn't give up, I'll give her that." Brody shook his head.

"Nah, it's harmless. She just wants some attention," I said as my phone vibrated on the bar. I glanced down to see a text message from Gracie.

Gracie: *I get to see you tomorrow.*

Me: *Can't wait. I'll get you packed up in no time.*

Gracie: *I'm so ready to be home.*

Me: *Me too.*

Phoenix leaned over my shoulder, reading the text, because we clearly had no boundaries with one another.

"I can't believe you convinced her to come here for a few months. You are one persuasive motherfucker, Heart."

"I'm not surprised at all. You two just have a very close—*friendship*." Brody raised an eyebrow as he looked at me.

Most people didn't understand my relationship with Gracie Reynolds.

And honestly, I didn't give a fuck who understood it and who didn't.

"Hey. It works for us. That's all that matters."

"I've been in serious relationships before, and I didn't talk to my girlfriend as much as you and Gracie talk," Brody cackled.

"Maybe that's why they didn't last, huh?" I smirked.

He flipped me the bird.

"I remember that first time Gracie ever got drunk with us, and I was giving her a hard time about how codependent you two saps were," Phoenix said, trying to hide the goofy grin on his face. "And she went into this elaborate story about how you both got cell phones at the same time, as if that made it more acceptable."

"Yep. It was the Christmas that we turned thirteen. She lived in Cottonwood Cove, and I was in Magnolia Falls. We started texting and talking every day way back then. So we know when one of us is off. She calls me out for it, and I call her out for it. And she's been off ever since she moved to Paris."

"You two do have that sick sense, I guess." Phoenix took a pull from his bottle.

"It's 'sixth' sense, you dipshit," Brody bellowed out in laughter, and Phoenix gave him the finger.

I tapped a few times on the bar top as I stood. "I'm going to head home and get some work done, and then get packed up."

"Bass and Cannon are heading over in a bit. You don't want to stick around a little longer?" Brody asked, because all five of us usually met on Wednesdays for a beer, and we'd catch up on our week.

"I've got to get shit done before I leave. Tell them I'll see them when I get back."

"I think he's going home to wait by the phone like a little pussy," Phoenix said with a wicked grin on his face. "How about you bring me back a baguette. I hear they're fabulous, and a hell of a lot better than the shit my brother has us eating here."

"Fuck off," Brody said. "And who asks someone to bring them back a fucking baguette from Paris? How about you bring me back a hot Frenchwoman who wants a no-strings-attached relationship and is open to having sex in the back of the bar on my breaks. Preferably multiple times a day."

"I'll do my best," I said, laughing.

I had other things on my mind.

Starting with bringing my best friend back home.

CHAPTER TWO

Gracie

I was a total cliché.

It was my worst nightmare.

I felt like a complete failure.

Like everything I'd been warned about had happened.

And now I had to clean up the mess I'd made.

My parents had been suspicious that something was off, but Cutler was impossible to fool.

He was that guy.

He'd called me out several times, because he knew something was up, and I'd finally told him everything.

So of course, I started at the only place that felt right.

Cutler Heart was not only my best friend—he'd always been my safe place as well.

I pushed the door open, relieved to be home after a long shift at Le Café, the restaurant right below my apartment where I currently worked.

I glanced around the small space, reaching for the pink heart sitting on my nightstand.

CH + GR

Cutler Heart plus Gracie Reynolds. My best friend had made it for me when we were just kids, and I'd always kept it with me. It was like having a piece of home with me. I held it against my chest as I took in a couple of boxes that I'd packed up to ship back home.

Home.

Where even was that now?

I'd had an amazing apartment in Los Angeles, and a fabulous job at J&J Interiors.

And Gabriel Laurent had been a client of the firm's. I hadn't worked with him directly, but he'd been at several events we'd thrown, and he always found his way over to me.

The man oozed charm and sex appeal. At least initially he did.

He was older than me, and his perfectly coiffed salt-and-pepper hair definitely worked for him. He was always impeccably dressed in designer suits, and he carried himself with an abundance of confidence.

I was flattered that he'd been so relentless about taking me to dinner after we'd met. We dated for several months—he had a home in Los Angeles and a home in Paris.

It was a whirlwind romance, one that had me ignoring everyone's advice and throwing caution to the wind.

I'd never been impulsive, but it felt like the right time to follow my heart.

I made decisions that were so out of character for me.

And at the moment, I regretted every single one of them.

Which was why I was struggling so much with my current situation.

I'd always had a plan.

I'd always been independent and driven.

But Gabriel was so convincing. He'd encouraged me to start my own business. He'd told me about all the contacts he had back in Paris, and that it was a perfect place to start a design business of my own.

To work for myself, which was what I'd always wanted.

We were both going to support one another.

He was a talented artist, very well known in Paris, and he had a collection that would be coming out early next year. He wanted to be here, and he wanted me with him.

He'd said we could both chase our dreams in la Ville Lumière, as the locals called the City of Lights.

And hello, who wouldn't want to be an interior designer in a city with so much history and beauty?

This city epitomized my love for design with its endless character.

It'd taken some convincing, but once I'd agreed to go, I'd defended my choice to everyone I loved.

Everyone who thought I was making a mistake.

And it had been a disaster from the moment we'd arrived here six months ago.

My business plan had gone absolutely nowhere, and my relationship had completely changed shortly after we arrived in Paris.

Luckily, I didn't feel actual heartache or sadness at the realization that it wasn't going to work with Gabriel, but I was embarrassed that I'd put all my eggs in one basket—one crappy basket that everyone had warned me about.

So I was going to try to learn from this and move forward.

My phone rang, and I smiled when I saw my dad's name flash across the screen. It was late afternoon in Paris, so I knew they were just waking up. I dropped to sit on the bed in my tiny studio apartment and answered the FaceTime call.

"Hey, guys," I said as he and my mom appeared. She was wearing her bathrobe and sipping her morning coffee.

I loved my parents so much, and all I wanted to do was make them proud of me.

But I'd come to Paris and fallen flat on my face.

"Hi, sweetheart," Mom said with a big smile on her face as my father waved. "Are you getting packed up?"

"Yes. I mean, the place is the size of a postage stamp, so it's fairly easy."

"Well, I'm still grateful that Cutler is coming there to help you. You fly back to the States in three days, right?" Dad asked.

"Yes. I'll have a little time to show Cutler around Paris before we leave."

"We spoke to him yesterday, and he's so happy you agreed to go back to Blue Sky Bay for a few months," Mom said. "The home the Chadwicks are building sounds amazing. That'll be a good project for you to dive into." She reached for her glass of water where they were sitting at the kitchen table.

In the home where I'd grown up.

I loved that house.

I missed that house.

"Yeah, I think it's a good idea for now," I said. My parents had wanted me to come home to Cottonwood Cove until I got back on my feet, but I was not going to run home to Mom and Dad and ask them to rescue me, though I knew they happily would. It was mortifying that I was twenty-eight years old and barely had enough money in my bank account to buy a plane ticket back to the States. I'd been surviving on ramen noodles for the last few weeks, as I was barely bringing in enough money to make ends meet while I was working at the café. I'd gone through most of my savings, and I didn't want my parents to know how bad things were.

How far I'd fallen.

"I think it's great you're going there for a while before you head to New York. Sounds like a very exciting opportunity, but are you sure you want to live that far away?" my father asked.

Johnny was one of the owners of J&J Interiors, where I worked before throwing caution to the wind and moving to Paris. Thankfully he'd offered me a position back at the firm, but it would be in New York City. The opening wouldn't be available until the end of September, as Beth, another designer, would be leaving on maternity leave, with no plan to return.

So, instead of staying in Paris and barely surviving, I would move to Blue Sky Bay for the next three months, and Cutler had a few design jobs for me while I was there.

"I want to go back to doing what I love. I miss it. And Johnny is the best boss a girl could ask for. I'm just grateful they found a position for me."

A wide smile spread across my mom's gorgeous face. "Of course they want you back. And you'll still come home for Christmas this year, right?"

I'd moved to Paris the week before Christmas last year, my first holiday away from my family. I was miserable and I knew they were sad I wasn't there.

"Yes. Of course. I will never willingly miss a Reynolds holiday again."

My family was close. My brother, Burke, was a junior in college back in California, but he'd recently moved to Italy. He was doing a semester abroad in the fall, and he wanted to explore for a few months before he started the program. He and my parents had come to visit me in Paris not that long ago.

"We can't wait to see you, sweetheart. FaceTime us when you're with Cutler tomorrow so we can say hello," Dad said.

"You've got it. I'll talk to you soon. Love you."

"Love you more, Gracie girl," they said at the same time, just as we ended the call.

I spent the next hour organizing and cleaning before there was a knock on my door.

I groaned when I saw Gabriel through the peephole. We hadn't spoken since we'd broken up, aside from a few messages he'd left for me, which I hadn't returned. I pulled the door open.

"Hey. What are you doing here?" I said, my voice ice cold. This man didn't deserve my time or my energy. He had some nerve showing up here.

"I came to say goodbye to you, my love."

I tried not to physically show my repulsion as my hands fisted at my side, anger coursing through my veins.

My love?

He didn't even know what the word meant.

He'd lied to me. Betrayed me. And I'd hoped I'd never have to see his face again.

I looked at him as I blocked the doorway. "I'm guessing you stopped in the café and heard I was leaving?"

"Yes. I gave you some time to cool down and thought maybe you'd be ready to talk about it, and then I found out that you're leaving. Your age is showing, Gracie."

He loved to pull the age card on me. He was a decade older than me, and anytime we disagreed about anything, he'd say it was due to my age, not the fact that he was an arrogant prick.

"And your ignorance is showing, Gabriel." My lips formed a flat line.

"You broke up with me before you found out about the affair. So obviously we weren't happy. We both weren't happy. But we should have talked about it, not broken up." He crossed his arms over his chest, his crisp white dress shirt buttoned down low enough to show a little chest hair.

Gabriel was physically attractive, there was no arguing it—but now that I knew who he was, I didn't look at him the same way.

He'd changed so much from the moment we'd arrived in Paris, only to follow it up with broken promises and deceit.

We had nothing to discuss.

"Why do you care? You were sleeping with another woman." I sighed. "And as shitty as I think that is, you are correct—we weren't happy. This move was a huge mistake, and I'm ready to make it right."

"Perhaps if you'd moved in with me like I'd suggested, and not chosen to live in this..." He flung his arms around as his temper started to show again. Anytime he didn't get his way, he would find something to whine about. "This shit shack."

"How eloquent of you." I glared at him. "The only decision I'm proud of since moving here is that I trusted my gut about getting my own place. Otherwise, I would have felt trapped."

"Trapped?" he scoffed. "I live in a goddamn penthouse in a neighborhood most people dream of living in. 'Trapped' is a bit dramatic, Gracie."

"Listen, we've had time to cool down, so I'm going to speak plainly." I cleared my throat before continuing. "I romanticized our relationship, along with this move. You made me promises that you did not keep, and I pulled away from you because I wasn't happy. So let's cut our losses, and just say goodbye."

"And what promises didn't I keep, Gracie?"

Was he for real? Did he think I wouldn't call him out?

"Well, for starters, you were going to help me start my design business. But from the moment we arrived here, you did everything in your power to keep me from doing what I love. You guilted me daily about needing my help with your career. We were supposed to support one another. But I think you moved me here to make me your personal assistant. You had no intentions of helping me start my own business. You knew I didn't know anyone here, and you did what you could to force me to be dependent on you. But here I am, Gabriel, putting my life back together all on my own," I said, tipping my chin up as the words left my mouth.

His jaw clenched, and it was obvious that I'd struck a nerve. "Do you know how long the list of people is who want to be my assistant? Yet you didn't appreciate the opportunity I gave you."

"An opportunity that I didn't ask for. I have my own dreams. I can support yours and still pursue mine. You want a partner who supports yours and has none of her own. So, it was never going to work."

"My plan was always to help you after my next exhibit. But you were impatient. Young. Too quick to jump ship."

"Gabriel. You were having an affair. I'm certainly not the only one who jumped ship." I chuckled, but there was no humor in it.

"Has it ever occurred to you that I fucked someone else because I wasn't fucking you?" he hissed, showing that side of himself that had had me running for the hills the first time I saw it the night I'd ended things. "We hadn't had sex in months. I'm a man who has needs. You're a woman who doesn't bring much to the table sexually."

Ouch. That one is going to leave a mark.

I straightened my features, doing my best to act unaffected, while all my insecurities reared their ugly heads at the insult.

I'd made a lot of mistakes when I agreed to move here, but from the moment I saw this man's true colors, I'd left the relationship and never looked back.

I was proud of myself for that.

I hadn't known many people here, as the only friends I'd made had all been through Gabriel.

But I'd rather be lonely and broke than allow a man to disrespect me.

"You are the most narcissistic man I've ever met. You were unfaithful, and instead of apologizing, you double down and blame the other person for your actions. For the record, we weren't having sex because we weren't happy. We were miserable," I reminded him.

"Well, that doesn't change the fact that you're young and inexperienced. I don't feel like being a teacher." I noticed the way his shoulders tensed, teeth clenched.

"I wasn't looking for a teacher. I was looking for a partner. And I did not find one." I shrugged casually, because it was the truth. "I have nothing more to say to you, Gabriel. It's time for you to leave."

"Let me guess. Your best friend is swooping in to save the day." His face was bright red now, and the veins on his neck were bulging.

"You'd be correct. He's on his way here now. So you'd best get going because he won't be as cordial to you as I've been." I reached for the door handle and then smirked. "Remember, I told you he'd be the first one to hide the body."

I was referencing a night after we'd first moved here. We'd gotten together with a few of his friends and played this game. The group asked a question, and everyone went around and answered it. One of the questions was who our first call would be to if we'd murdered someone and we needed help hiding the body.

It was ridiculous, and we all laughed, aside from Gabriel, who'd refused to answer the question. He stated that he would never rely on someone else to cover his mess.

Did I really find him to be sexy at one point?

I'd answered the question without hesitation.

Cutler Heart would be my first call.

He'd hide the body, destroy the evidence, and agree to be my alibi.

Everyone found it comical, as I was the only one in the group who didn't have to even stop to think about it.

"I think you'll be happier in your small town and your small life." He pursed his lips. "Not everyone can handle my fame, and I do believe that was a struggle for you. But I do wish you well."

His fame? I had no problem with him being a well-known artist. I thought it was amazing. My problem was not with his fame—it was with the man himself.

He certainly did have a talent for insulting you and then following it up with a compliment, leaving you confused, as if you'd misunderstood something.

But I wasn't misunderstanding anything that came out of this manipulative, pompous asshole's mouth.

Things were crystal clear.

So, I pushed the door closed on him without saying a word.

Sometimes no response was the only fitting response.

This chapter of my life was closed.

And I was looking forward to the future.

CHAPTER THREE

Cutler

Bass: *Did you make it to Paris?*

Cannon: *Bonjour, bitches.*

Me: *Just landed.*

Brody: *Glad you're there. It's time for her to come home.*

Phoenix: *Hopefully you'll stop being a moody bastard.*

Bass: *Says the moodiest bastard of all.*

Phoenix: *Correct. I like riding solo. Heart is the life of the party. He isn't supposed to be mopey.*

Cannon: *He's not mopey. He's taking a look at his inner self.*

Brody: *The fuck are you talking about? Did someone steal Cannon's phone?*

Phoenix: *No. He hooked up with a woman who wrote a self-help book, and now he's being all philosophical.*

Cannon: *Listen up, boys. It's all about inner reflection. This shit is life-changing.*

Bass: *So are you going to see her again, seeing as she changed your life.*

Cannon: *Nope. She's a tourist and she already left town. But she left me with a lot to think about.*

Brody: *She left you with a boner and deep thoughts? That's quite the one-night stand.*

Phoenix: *He has a perpetual boner.*

Me: *That's not a bad thing. People pay good money for boners.*

Cannon: *Thanks, brother. You've always got my back.*

Phoenix: *Sounds like he's got more than your back. <eggplant emoji>*

Bass: *I've got to get to work, just wanted to make sure you made it there.*

Brody: *See you in a couple days.*

Cannon: *Bring our girl home. Tell her we miss her.*

Phoenix: *You're all so sappy lately.*

I'd arrived in Paris and grabbed a taxi, and I was immediately taken with the architecture, the cool mix of old and new. I cracked my window to let the breeze in, taking in the streets bustling with people as we drove past local shops and cafés. I craned my neck to get a view of the Eiffel Tower in the distance, making small talk with my driver before we pulled up at her building.

I swiped my card, thanked him for the ride, and stepped out of the car before climbing three flights of stairs to her apartment.

The door swung open, and there she was.

My girl.

Gracie Reynolds.

She looked thinner than usual, her face a bit gaunt, but her dark brown eyes still sparked the way they always had. Her long brown hair fell around her shoulders in waves, and even though I could tell it had been a tough couple of months, she was always the most beautiful girl I'd ever laid eyes on.

It was difficult for me to see her in pain. It always had been. When Gracie hurt—I hurt. I never could stand to see her struggling. So my rage for Gabriel ran deep.

I had this weird mix of anger and relief as I took her in.

I wanted to put my fist through Gabriel's face—but at the same time, I was so damn happy to see her.

I'd made the right decision insisting she come home and stay with me until her big move to New York. No sense staying here and suffering when we could have the summer together.

There was no hesitation. I pulled her into my arms and wrapped her up.

"I'm so glad you're here, Bear," she said, her cheek settling in the crook of my neck.

She'd given me the nickname when we were young. Everyone else had called me my self-given nickname at the time, "Beefcake," which still made me laugh. Because that shit had stuck, and it was a name I went by for most of my childhood.

But Gracie started calling me “Bear” when we were just nine years old, one summer when our families had gone camping. She said that I hugged like a bear.

As if she’d been hugged by a bear before.

She looked relieved to see me. Gracie had always been strong. She’d been there for me at my darkest moments, and I was happy to return the favor. I’d always known I was the lucky one in this friendship.

She was the best person I knew.

“There’s nowhere else I’d rather be.”

“Come in and see what I’ve done with the place,” she said, her voice teasing as she stepped back and motioned for me to come inside.

It was a small studio apartment, with just a bed and a small kitchenette.

“It’s really something,” I said, not making any attempt to hide the humor from my voice.

“Well, there were cute curtains and some peel-and-stick wallpaper on the walls, but seeing as we’re about to blow this popsicle stand, I’ve taken the little bit of décor that I had down.”

“It’s charming. And you have the one tiny window at least.” I moved to glance out at the view of another tall building and chuckled. “But I think my favorite part is the bathtub in the middle of the room.”

She shrugged as a wide grin spread across her face. “You know a bathtub is my deal-breaker. I can’t go without my baths.”

I pulled her back into my arms, because I’d fucking missed her. Her laugh and the smell of her strawberry and coconut hair.

“Well, you know there are multiple bathtubs at my house,

because you designed it. So you can bathe as many times a day as you want to. And the view from the bathroom looks at the mountains, and the guest room has a nice view of the bay."

"I can't wait. And I'm sick of eating ramen noodles, so cooking in your kitchen will be a treat."

"No more brick buildings and ramen noodles for you. You need a steak and some bread. You're dwindling away."

"You sound like my mother," she said with a sigh as she stepped back. "Speaking of food, you must be starving. Let's go downstairs and get something in your stomach. They insisted I come for a farewell meal on the house." She chuckled.

Her long dark hair fell in waves down her back, and she adjusted the strap on her yellow sundress whenever it slid down her shoulder. She looked like she hadn't seen the sun in a while, and normally her skin was a golden brown.

She clearly wasn't getting out much.

Gracie was an outdoorsy girl. She loved the mountains. She loved the water. She loved to ride horses. Hell, the girl grew up with a pet pig. What in the hell was she doing in this tiny apartment all by herself?

It was time to get her home.

"I am starving. But you know me, I'm always hungry." I chuckled as she leaned her head against my shoulder and blew out a breath.

"I'm so happy you're here. You did not need to come, but I'm so glad you did."

"Me too."

She took my hand and led me out of her apartment and down the three flights of stairs to Le Café.

"Gracie! I still can't believe you're leaving me!" A woman who appeared to be around our age hurried toward her and gave her a hug.

"I'll miss you, Maribel." Gracie motioned to me. "This is my bestie, Cutler."

"The infamous Cutler, a.k.a. Bear," Maribel said with a mischievous grin on her face.

I smirked more at the fact that she knew about me than the mention of my nickname.

"He's my Bear for sure." A wide grin spread across Gracie's face.

"Best friends, huh? She insists you two never dated, but I've never heard of a man and a woman being as close as you two are and not dating."

People always gave us a hard time about why we'd never dated. Why we'd never crossed the line.

Hell, I was surprised myself.

But at the end of the day, the timing had never been right for us. Once we were teenagers, the friendship had grown so strong that neither of us ever wanted to mess with a good thing. And then I had a brief time where I lost my way. Gracie got a boyfriend, and she stayed with him for years.

I became a serial dater when I joined her our second year of college, and it became clear that we were best off as friends.

Hell, it was probably for the better.

But I'd be lying if I didn't admit there were moments—occasional moments—when I'd catch her laughing, her head tipped back, her dark brown eyes sparkling, and something in my chest would tighten.

I never allowed myself to think about it for too long.

I always buried those thoughts as quickly as they'd come.

My relationship with this girl was the most important one in my life.

She was the closest person to me, and I wouldn't ever want to do anything to fuck that up.

"I think she likes it this way," I said to Maribel. "And this allows her to complain about all of her boyfriends to me, and I get to stay the good guy."

"All of my boyfriends?" She gaped at me. "All two and a half of them? You've got quite the more extensive list, Bear."

I chuckled as I took her in. Damn, she was pretty. Gracie Reynolds always managed to be the most beautiful girl in the room.

Always had been.

"You two are so funny. I've heard so much about you," Maribel said as the front door opened again and a group of four people walked in. "Pick any table you want. I'm guessing Collette will want to wait on you. You've always been her favorite."

Gracie chuckled. I'd heard about this place ever since she moved here. We settled in chairs across from one another on the patio, tucked beneath a red awning, and she reminded me that Collette and her husband owned the place. They'd hired Gracie a few months ago after she and Gabriel had broken up.

There were black flower boxes sitting on all four window ledges, filled with white and pink flowers. Sunlight bounced off the weathered wood tables, and the rich aromas of espresso and baked pastries floated around us.

"I'm glad you had this place to fall back on after you left that asshole. I'm just sorry that you lost so much time supporting him, while he did nothing to support you." I leaned back in my chair as the space around us was filled with the chatter of locals in hushed French and the occasional clink of porcelain cups.

She rolled her eyes. "I can't believe that I got myself in this position. That's why I didn't want to even tell anyone that we'd broken up."

"I'd wondered why you weren't getting your design business off the ground, and you just kept saying you were busy helping Gabriel at his office. It makes sense now." I blew out a breath.

"What does?"

"I knew something was off. The guys gave me a hard time and said it was because you were living so far away, but you were so distant, and I just had a feeling something wasn't right."

"You know me well." Her gaze softened. "He made all these promises about helping me get my career going here, and he never did a single one of them. I had no contacts, I don't speak the language, and every day he just kept coming up with things he needed help with."

"That fucker thought he could get you here and make you his puppet," I grunted, my hands fisting on the table. "So tell me the truth. All of it. I'll know if you're holding back, so just put it all out there."

"It happened pretty quickly." She exhaled and glanced away for a beat before turning back to look at me. "Once we arrived in Paris, it bothered him that I wouldn't move in with him. I reminded him that at the time, we'd only been dating for six months. Which, looking back, makes me question myself. Who gives up their job and their life for a six-month relationship? That's on me."

"You were in love, or at least you thought you were," I said, my voice tight even to my own ears. "He made all these promises about helping you build your own company. Paris is a beautiful place, and you've always been inspired by French design. So you looked at this as the opportunity of a lifetime. I understood why you wanted this—even though I couldn't shake the feeling that he was full of shit. Part of me thought maybe I was just being overly protective, and maybe I was reading him wrong. He never seemed genuine to me. I just hate that he hurt you, and I hate that I couldn't do anything to stop it."

Her gaze was wet with emotion. "Always my knight in shining armor."

I cursed to myself.

Not this time.

A woman with short blonde hair who was probably a few years older than us approached the table. "Bonjour, Gracie, and who do we have here?"

"Bonjour, Collette." Gracie moved to her feet and hugged her, and I stood up as well. "This is Cutler."

"Ahhh… We've heard so much about her American bestie. The teddy bear, right?" Her voice was teasing as she extended a hand to me. "You came to help her pack and take her home?"

Gracie and I both returned to our seats.

"Yes, happy to be getting my girl back home." I winked at Gracie.

"I clearly talk about you a lot," she said with a laugh.

Collette raised an eyebrow and chuckled. "She talked about you daily. I'm just glad she ended things with the turd."

Now it was my turn to laugh. "You and I are on the same page, Collette."

"I'm glad she's going back with you. She needs to be surrounded by good people, because she's the best." Collette placed a hand on Gracie's shoulder. "I'm sad you're leaving, ma chérie, but this isn't the right time for you and Paris. You'll be back when the timing is right."

Gracie smiled and nodded. It was clear that she'd been suffering here in Paris, without letting me or her family know what was going on.

I wasn't completely shocked. I mean, I was surprised she hadn't told me.

But she was a proud person.

A perfectionist and an overachiever.

We'd always balanced one another.

I'd lightened things for her, and she'd taught me how to look forward, how to plan and dream and all of those things.

I'd always known I was a lucky man to call Gracie Reynolds my best friend.

My girl.

She'd brought far more to my life than I'd brought to hers.

"I wish I could have come here under different circumstances, but I'll definitely be back," Gracie promised.

"I'll miss you. And your Bear sure did show up for you when you needed him, didn't he?" She winked before taking our orders and walking away.

"I still can't believe what a mess I've made of everything." Gracie shook her head and shrugged.

"None of this is on you. You haven't done anything wrong. You recognized things weren't right and ended it with that asshole, and that's all that matters." I reached for my water and took a sip.

"I'm done with relationships, Bear. I think I need to try something different. Nothing serious. You know, sort of like what you do."

I barked out a laugh. "And what is it that I do, Jeege?"

"You don't get that invested in people. I've never really just dated. I always seem to be in a long-term relationship. And look at where that's gotten me. I'm not investing in anyone other than myself for a while. All relationships are off-limits. So, teach me how to date casually, please." She chuckled.

This was not a conversation I ever expected to be having with Gracie. I didn't like the way she was now questioning herself. None of this shit was on her.

"Listen, we just have different ideas about relationships," I said, reaching for my wine glass as Collette set down our drinks and a charcuterie board between us. "There's no right or wrong way."

"My way is definitely flawed. I'm seriously done with it. I've been thinking about it, and I really want to try your way for a while. I've had three serious relationships, and they were all kind of a bust." She covered a cracker in apricot jam, placed some salami and cheese on it, and handed it to me, which made me laugh, because she always knew what I needed.

"There's nothing wrong with your way, Jeege."

"Gabriel hated that you called me Jeege, by the way," she said as she took a sip of her wine. My gaze tracked the movement, lingering on her mouth.

On her plump pink lips.

I forced myself to look away and rubbed my eyes. Maybe I could chalk it up to jet lag.

Okay, here's the deal.

Gracie Reynolds is my best friend.

We've never crossed the line.

But I'm human, and she's sexy as fuck.

And…she doesn't have a clue.

"I know," I said. "He asked me not to call you that, which I completely ignored."

"He did?"

"Yep. I think he just hated our relationship, and that was another red flag. And what was his fucking deal with the name? Why did he care? We have a history. You were always my Gracie girl." I chuckled. "And then I started calling you 'GG' for short, which just turned into 'Jeege.' The dude acted like I was calling you 'lover.'"

Her head fell back with a laugh. "He was very threatened by our relationship. I think he was happy that it was more challenging to talk to you with the time difference when I was living here. But I made it clear that we're a package deal."

"Well, we always make it work, don't we? But I'd be lying if I didn't admit I was a little worried about this one." I shifted in my chair, looking away for a second at the thought.

"How so?" she asked, popping a grape in her mouth.

"I figured if you married the dude, I'd slowly be cut out." I rubbed a hand down the back of my neck as two plates of pasta were set down in front of us.

"Never going to happen, Cutler Heart." She smiled as she forked her rigatoni, then looked up at me before she ate it. "Everything is always better when you're here."

"Of course it is. That's my job. So, we'll head home in a few days, and you'll stay there until you move to New York at the end of September. That'll give us the whole summer together."

"Yes. It'll be great. And you're going to teach me your dating ways." She wriggled her brows and reached for her wine glass. I watched her hand hover over the glass, taking in the way her fingers curled around it. A faint scar on her wrist, from when she fell out of a tree we were climbing when we were kids, caught the light, and I noted it instantly. Like some mental checklist of our shared history. The way I'd jumped down when I saw her fall, breaking my own ankle in the process. We'd been through so much together.

Keep it together, Cutler. She's your best friend.

Your best fucking friend in the world.

"I'll teach you whatever you want me to, Jeege," I said, careful to keep my tone casual.

"Good. I mean, we've always been able to talk about everything, right?" Her eyes had that spark again—the one that always made me notice details that I shouldn't. Just like the tiny crease at the corner of her mouth when she smiled.

"Absolutely. Why do you think I'm here? We don't keep secrets. We can always tell each other anything. That's the deal we made years ago. There's nothing you can't say to me."

She sighed and sat back in her chair, chewing on her lip, deep in thought. I sipped my wine, noting the way her shoulder shifted, and how her hair fell slightly over her collarbone.

Then she leaned forward, glancing around, her voice dropping to a whisper. "Okay. There's something I want."

I set my glass down and straightened in my chair, giving her my full attention. "Tell me."

"I want to be a better lover." Her gaze locked with mine.

Boom.

Mic drop.

I felt it immediately, a rush I wasn't supposed to feel, blood pulsing in my ears, pounding to…other parts of my body. My imagination was spinning, but I held myself rigid, forcing my face into a neutral mask.

"Really?" I said, trying to keep the edge out of my voice.

"Yes. I think that's step one of my fresh start. I'm definitely lacking in that area. And, according to every woman who's ever slept with you and then cried to me when things ended—you're quite talented in the bedroom."

There was a time when I'd enjoyed that lifestyle, casually dating and having a good time, but that hadn't been the case for a while.

I had a feeling it had a lot to do with Gracie.

Her leaving.

Her coming back home.

Things were about to get interesting.

CHAPTER FOUR

Gracie

Everything had changed in a matter of seventy-two hours.

I'd packed up my failed life in Paris and flown to Blue Sky Bay, a town that felt like a second home to me. It was where Cutler lived, and about an hour out of the city, so I spent a lot of time here. He lived in a ranch-style house in walking distance of the quaint downtown. His lot sat on the edge of Blue Sky Lake, with views of the water and the mountains in the distance. There was a peacefulness here, similar to where I'd grown up in Cottonwood Cove.

And right now, this was what I needed.

"I'm so happy we're here," I said as we pulled into Cutler's garage. It had been a long flight.

I wanted a hot bath and a good night's sleep.

"Me too. And I want you to make yourself comfortable. My home is your home, you know that, right?" he said before getting out of his truck as I unbuckled myself.

He'd left his truck at the airport when he'd flown to Paris, and seeing as we'd arrived home in the middle of the night, I was grateful we hadn't had to ask anyone for a ride.

"Thanks. I really appreciate it, Bear. It's good to be home," I said when he pulled my door open. I was tired and jet-lagged and moving slowly, which of course he'd picked up on. When I started to climb out, his large hands moved to my waist, and he lifted me out of the truck. The smell of sandalwood and cedar flooded my senses as he set me down. I glanced up, taking in his dark, slightly disheveled hair and his sleepy eyes under the dim lighting in his garage. He tilted his head to the side when he realized I was staring at him.

"You okay?" he asked, and my fingers itched to rake across the scruff peppering his jaw.

"Yes." I shook my head and smiled. "Just a little jet-lagged."

He nodded and moved to the back of the truck, and I followed before he shooed me away. "I've got it."

We went inside, and he stopped in the kitchen and grabbed us each a bottle of water from the fridge. He leaned against the island and handed one to me.

My best friend was tall, with broad shoulders. He was easily the best-looking man I'd ever laid eyes on.

He had more sex appeal than any one man should be allowed.

He also had the personality to go along with it. He was charming and funny and flirty by nature.

Women loved him.

Men loved him.

Kids loved him.

Adults loved him.

Cutler Heart was pure magic.

Always had been.

I'd been drawn to him from the first time I met him.

He'd always made me feel safe and loved and—special.

I reached for the bottle, his fingers grazing mine as I took it from him.

"Are you hungry?"

"No, I'm too tired to eat. Do you care if I take a bath before I go to bed?" I asked.

"Jeege. What did I say?"

"Your home is my home." I chuckled, my voice sounding slightly hoarse. Probably due to all the talking we'd done on the flight home, mixed with a lack of sleep.

"Exactly. Let's get these suitcases to your room, and you can take a bath and get some sleep." He set his water bottle on the counter and wheeled my bags down the hallway, stopping at the room beside his. I'd stayed here many times before, and I'd decorated the place, so I was more than comfortable at Cutler's home.

"I forgot how much I loved this room," I said as I plopped down to sit on the bed, and he moved to sit beside me.

Rustic wood floors ran throughout his home. He'd given me free rein on the interior design, which was modern farmhouse. He'd drawn this house on a pad of paper one night when we were still in college, and years later, he'd built it. Cutler had expanded his father's construction business here in Blue Sky Bay, and he was the architect on all their projects here as well as back in Magnolia Falls. He'd been written up in several architecture magazines and had a brilliant eye for design.

"It's your room. Always has been." He tilted his head to the side as a wicked grin spread across his handsome face. "Although, if memory serves, there was a time when we'd have sleepovers when we were young, and we'd sleep in the same bed because you were afraid to sleep by yourself."

"You were the only friend my parents ever let me have sleepovers with, and you were such a cuddly boy back then. You always ran hot, which I loved, because I was always freezing." I chuckled.

I'd known this boy—this man—most of my life.

"Yeah, and I loved warming up my girl," he said as he lunged forward, tipping me back on the bed. He hovered above me after rubbing his scruff against my neck as I fell back in a fit of giggles.

"You still run hot," I whispered as my fingers traced along the scruff on his jaw, the way they'd been dying to.

"Welcome home, Jeege. I missed you."

"I missed you too. And I'm happy I'm here," I said, sounding a little breathless. "And I'm not kidding about this, Bear. I really do want you to teach me some of your sexy tricks while I'm here, okay?"

"You don't need any tricks, Jeege. You're sexy as hell exactly how you are." He chuckled as he pushed up in one swift movement, almost abruptly, as he moved to stand at the foot of the bed.

I propped myself up on my elbows. "I want to have the kind of power that you have, you know? Like I just make one move, and the other person is all flustered. You've definitely got it, and I'm just asking for you to pass on your expertise."

He tipped his head back as he laughed, then shook his head and smiled. "You've got it—you just don't realize it. And I think that makes you even sexier."

"Listen, I'll just be straight with you. Gabriel basically said that I'm boring in the sack. Personally, I found him to be very unexciting. We hadn't had sex for months before we even broke up, but it's not like I have much to compare him to. So that's why I'd like to learn some things before I even consider entering my next relationship."

And who better to teach me than the man I trusted most in the world? He was experienced and sexy, and he'd never do anything to hurt me.

We were best friends, and I felt safe with him.

There was no risk of things getting complicated because it wasn't like Cutler would ever look at me as more than a friend.

It wasn't his thing.

But he could teach me plenty, and I was ready to learn.

"He said what to you?" His hands fisted at his side, and his jaw clenched. "Fuck this guy, Jeege. Don't let that fucker get in your head. You're perfect exactly how you are."

"I just want some tips, and you're the perfect guy to help me. I mean, who else could I ask to do this?" I smirked. "Come on. We're best friends. It wouldn't be that big of a deal. And this is a perfect time for me to get a bit more—educated."

He rubbed his face and blew out a breath. "You've been back in the States for an hour, and you're already tasking yourself with things to accomplish while you're here."

"What can I say, Bear. I'm a number one achiever—it's sort of my thing."

"Is this that Strengths test thing you made me do?" he asked.

"Yes. I'm a number one achiever and you're a number one woo, which makes a lot of sense."

He arched a brow. "How about you let your overachieving self have a little break for a few days, yeah? You can become a sexy diva once you get settled."

"I'll make you a deal," I said, my voice teasing as I moved to my feet. "I do all the cooking while I'm here, and you teach me how to be a sexy diva."

He smiled. "You're a damn good cook, so how can I turn that offer down?"

"Great. We can start tomorrow."

"Fine. Good night, Jeege. Let's get some sleep. I'll see you in the morning." He leaned forward and I closed my eyes, feeling that warmth and familiarity coming from him. I stayed still, letting the moment linger, enjoying the feel of his hand as it hovered at my shoulder, and the quiet weight of his nearness as he kissed the top of my head.

His presence had always been my safe place.

I sighed softly. "Good night, Bear. Love you."

"Love you more." He winked before walking away, pulling the door closed behind him.

A sense of excitement settled in my chest that I hadn't felt in a very long time. I was out of that tiny apartment and putting my life back together.

I had three months to work on an amazing project with my best friend.

I could hike in the mountains again, and swim in Blue Sky Lake.

I was going to get my mojo back, and Cutler Heart was going to help me do it.

I couldn't ask for a better teacher.

I made my way to the bathroom and turned on the water in the bathtub.

After undressing and tying my hair in a knot on top of my head, I sank beneath the warm water.

It felt good to be here.

This was exactly what I needed.

• • •

I'd helped Cutler design this kitchen a few years ago when he built this place, and I was silently patting myself on the back as I moved around the enormous space. It was so well thought out.

A chef's dream.

I'd been cooking noodles in a four-hundred-square-foot studio for the last few months.

This was a massive upgrade.

And his refrigerator was well stocked, of course, because my best friend enjoyed a good meal.

I'd woken up before the sun rose because my inner clock was all messed up. I went for a walk and did some stretching exercises, and now I was making pancakes, eggs, and bacon.

I was feeling much more like myself.

I was amazed at what a couple of days with my best friend had done for my mental state.

Like he'd breathed life back into me.

I normally cooked with music on, but Cutler was still sleeping, and I didn't want to wake him up.

I dropped a few handfuls of blueberries in the batter and gave it a few quick stirs before checking on the sizzling bacon. I made a little extra because he'd told me that one of his closest friends, Bass, was stopping by this morning to see me. I was close with all of Cutler's friends, and I couldn't wait to see everyone.

"Damn, my stomach started growling in my sleep," his deep voice said as he came around the corner, and I turned around and took him in.

I tried to keep my expression unaffected.

But hot damn. He wore a pair of gray joggers, hanging low on his hips, and nothing else. His chest was a mix of golden skin and chiseled muscle. Just the right amount. His abs were defined and cut, and my eyes trailed down to the deep V that clearly led to places I shouldn't have been looking at.

This was Cutler, after all.

I forced myself to turn away and cleared my throat. "Good morning. I hope I didn't wake you. I just thought I'd start cooking breakfast because I know you've got Bass dropping by this morning, and you wanted to take me to see the house after. There's so much to do. So. Much. To. Do."

Why was I rambling?

I looked at the batter in the bowl.

Focus.

I should be counting blueberries, not my best friend's abs.

A deep, husky laugh rumbled from behind me as his strong arms came around my shoulders. He kissed my cheek and held me there for a few beats. "Damn, it's nice having my girl back."

"Do we always walk around in no clothing?" I asked, peeking over my shoulder as he made his way to the coffeepot.

I got a glance of his back and smiled as I took in his tattoo. The one I'd gone with him to get right after he turned eighteen. It was a tribute to his father and godfathers.

Ride or die.

"I mean, I sleep naked, so I put on pants just for you." He winked.

I wondered what lay beneath that layer of gray fabric.

I'd had a teaser last night, and I couldn't stop thinking about it. The erection he'd pressed against my lower belly was something I'd thought only belonged in the pages of fiction.

What was wrong with me?

It had been a while since I'd had sex, or any affection for that matter.

Maybe it was my newfound desire to liven things up in my romantic life.

I was no longer looking for a partner.

No. I was looking for a lover and nothing more.

The new me was not an overthinker. She wasn't looking for forever. She was looking for a good time.

A good damn time.

Because when was the last time I'd had a good time?

"Well, thank you for that." I tried to hide my smile as he topped off the coffee in my mug. "I hope you're hungry."

"Always."

"Yo, yo, yo!" a voice called from the door to the garage. Obviously Bass had the code, and of course he'd just walked in. "I hear our favorite girl is back in town."

He came around the corner, and before I could react, he was pulling me into his arms, lifting me off the ground, and spinning me around. "Glad you're back, Gracie girl. Our boy has been a miserable shit without you."

He was tall, just like Cutler, with brown hair that was longer on top and shorter on the sides. He'd always had a good amount of scruff, but he was sporting a full beard now.

He set me back down on my feet, and Cutler chuckled. "That's a bit dramatic, yeah?"

"Are you claiming you haven't been a sad sack these last few months?" Bass moved toward the stove and turned off the flame to the bacon.

Always the chef.

"Damn, this looks perfect. I forgot how good you were in the kitchen," he said. It was a huge compliment, considering he'd recently been named one of the most talented chefs on the West Coast by a very prestigious cooking magazine. He owned a well-known steakhouse in town called Bennett's on the Bay. People were willing to drive a great distance to eat there too, just to experience the famous Bass Bennett's food.

"I cannot wait to come in and have one of your amazing steaks."

He eyed me from the stove as he dropped some batter in the skillet. "It's on the house, so get your ass down there, now that you're back in town."

"Count on it," I said as I moved to scramble the eggs. I added a bunch of cheddar cheese and veggies into the skillet.

Cutler took three plates from the cupboard before grabbing napkins and utensils. The three of us settled around the table, just like we'd done so many times before.

"Well, damn. It feels like old times," Bass chuckled. The three of us had been close ever since our undergrad days. And then Cutler went off to architecture school, Bass went to cooking school on the East Coast for a year, and I interned at J&J Interiors in Los Angeles after graduation. "He really has been a grumpy fucker lately."

"I've got no shame in my game. I missed my girl, and everyone knows it." Cutler popped a piece of bacon in his mouth. "I'm not denying it. We've never lived far away from one another. And I didn't like it."

This was one of my favorite things about Cutler. He said what he thought. He was the most confident man I'd ever known, and he never hesitated or held back when it came to saying what he thought or what he felt.

Vulnerability was most people's weakness.

But it was Cutler Heart's superpower.

CHAPTER FIVE

Cutler

Phoenix: *Have we all noticed that Heart is in a much better mood these days?*

Cannon: *No doubt. His girl is back in town.*

Bass: *Glad you brought her home. Sounds like it was a shit situation for her over there.*

Brody: *Which is odd, because you know what they say about French men.*

Bass: *That they eat their bread with cheese instead of butter?*

Bass: *They drink a lot of red wine?*

Brody: *I was going to say that they have sex at all hours of the day, and they always light up a cigarette after.*

Phoenix: *What the fuck are we talking about?*

Me: *From what she's told me, I think that might be a myth. Though the cheese, the bread, and the wine appear to be true. <winky face emoji>*

Brody: *Good to know.*

Brody: *And I'm glad you've got your title back as the only grumpy dickhead in the group, Nix.*

Phoenix: *I wear it with pride. Heading home. Late night for me.*

Me: *Was there a fire?*

Phoenix: *No. But Trudy Lawson decided to bake cupcakes at two o'clock in the morning because she couldn't sleep.*

Cannon: *Is baking cupcakes a crime? I love cupcakes.*

Phoenix: *When you put them in the oven and then fall back asleep and set off all your smoke alarms because you've burned the damn cupcakes—that's where things get hairy.*

Bass: *She couldn't just take them out of the oven before going to sleep?*

Brody: *Seems logical.*

Phoenix: *Not if you take a sleeping pill, and don't hear the smoke detectors, and wake up your neighbors who are pissed about being the only ones awake, so they call us.*

Cannon: *I love when Nix is in a good mood. It warms my heart.*

Phoenix: *<middle finger emoji>*

Me: *I've got to get back to work. I'll see you guys for lunch later.*

I leaned back in my desk chair and picked up the phone when I saw my uncle Bridger's name flash across my cell. He fired off several questions about the house I was building, which I happily answered, and then we moved on to the design that Gracie was working on.

"Yes, Gracie and Emilia have talked through the design, and she's been busy getting orders placed. Floors go down this week, and things are rolling." Gracie had been working with my designer aunt ever since she got here.

"Wow. We should be in by early October?" my uncle asked.

"I don't see why not."

"Great. We're on track."

"We are. And things will move fast now," I said. "We've got cabinets going in next, and then things will really start coming together."

"I'm glad to hear it. And I'm grateful that we've got Gracie taking over the designing and doing all the ordering. It takes a lot of pressure off of Emilia."

"Gracie's happy to be working on this project. I think she missed doing what she loves, and she's already placed a ton of orders. She said deliveries start next week. Hell, she's been here for all of a week, and she's already got sample boards going, and she's been meeting with the subs at the house. She's a beast."

"I'm glad she's back. And I can tell you are too."

"Yeah, it was weird having her so far away. I wouldn't mind keeping her as long as I can. Not thrilled about her moving to New York in three months, but at least we don't need a passport to visit one another."

More laughter, which was a compliment because Uncle Bridger

didn't find many people to be humorous. "You two sure have an interesting relationship. Always have."

"You've never had a female best friend?" I asked, my voice laced with humor because I knew he'd deny it. He loved his wife, his kids, his family, and most of his employees, and he feigned irritation with most other people.

"I'd never had a best friend before marrying Emilia. You know I can't stand most people."

He was full of shit. He liked to play the part of the grumpy asshole, but he was a big teddy bear beneath all that broodiness.

"Well, I didn't like having her so far away. We'll leave it at that."

"Maybe you aren't supposed to be far away from one another," he said as loud laughter came from outside my office.

ROD Construction had grown quite a bit since we'd opened the doors. We had twenty-two employees now, not to mention all the subcontractors we worked with in town, from framers to painters to electricians. A lot of my guys did the woodwork and special projects for homeowners, and we had a real good thing going.

Blue Sky Bay was making a name for itself, and this small town was one that tourists flocked to in the summer and the winter. Blue Sky Lake was a big lure, with its turquoise waters and mountain scenery. Our ski slopes were just as impressive during the colder months, and people were buying up homes and willing to commute to the city, driving forty-five minutes each way every day, just to come home to this beautiful landscape at the end of the day.

I was happy that ROD Construction had played a role in the growth of this town that had become home to me. I loved the locals, and the quaint downtown with all the self-owned businesses. My company did everything from new construction to full renovations where we'd gut a home or business down to the studs and bring our clients' visions to life.

"You might be right, but she's moving to New York to work for her old boss, and we'll just have to visit when we can." I glanced out the all-glass doors to see Gracie standing at the front desk talking with Zoe, who ran our front office. And I didn't miss the way Dirk Roberts had been stopping in every day this week ever since Gracie came to work here. He owned the window company in town, and he handled all of our window and door orders. Suddenly the dude was stopping by every day and hanging all over her. When I mentioned it to her, she just laughed it off and reminded me that she was a grown woman and she could handle herself.

I knew she could.

And I'd never been the jealous type, even with women I was actually dating.

But it irritated me the way he hung all over her.

I'd always been different with her.

"Well, I'm glad she's there now," my uncle said. "Emilia is no longer worried at all about the house, and she said that we're in good hands. So keep me posted, and we'll talk later this week."

"You got it. Talk soon." I ended the call and saw Zoe grab her purse and keys, which meant she was heading home.

Dirk was talking up a storm with Gracie, and I moved to my feet and made my way out to the front office.

"You out of here, Zoe?" I asked.

"Yep. I'll see y'all in the morning." She waved before pushing the door open and stepping outside.

"See you tomorrow," Gracie said, and Dirk just continued gaping at her.

I raised a brow. "I'm guessing you need to get back to your office at some point?"

"Oh, yes. I'm just distracted by a beautiful woman, I guess." He chuckled.

"Well, how about you get distracted at your own place of work?" My lips formed a flat line, and I crossed my arms over my chest.

He smirked. "I'll see you tomorrow, Gracie. Well, if I'm lucky I will."

For fuck's sake.

What kind of shit line was that?

If I had a hose, I'd turn it on and spray him down like a dog.

Gracie just chuckled and waved before turning her attention to me. "I'm making dinner for us tonight."

The last few nights had been busy, as everyone was happy she was back in town. We'd gone to the container park for dinner two of the nights, and last night we'd eaten at Bennett's because she'd been dying for one of Bass's steaks.

"Yeah? Are you sure you feel like cooking? I can grab us a pizza."

"Yes. I picked up some groceries this afternoon and dropped them at the house," she said as we walked out of the office, and I locked up. We'd walked here this morning, seeing as I only lived two blocks from downtown, where my office was.

"Sounds good. It's been a long day." We made our way down to the little dirt trail along Blue Sky Lake that led to my house. The sun was still out, as it was the middle of June and it stayed light fairly late now.

"Well, don't get too tired. We've been so busy this week, you haven't given me any new tips outside of telling me to be confident," she said, glancing over at me and rolling her eyes. "So tonight, I want to get down and dirty."

And there goes my dick.

He was a responsive motherfucker.

"You're serious about this?" I shook my head. "You don't need any tips, Gracie. I think that's obvious, if you consider the way Dirk follows you around like a fucking puppy."

"I'm not talking about getting a guy to flirt with me," she said as we walked up my driveway toward the front door, and she turned to look at me. "I know how to flirt. I'm talking about actual sex. I think it might be a weakness of mine, and that bothers me. I hate sucking at things."

Jesus.

She really just went there.

"First of all, don't say 'sucking' when you're talking about sex and not expect a dude to react." I groaned as I pushed the front door open.

I fucking loved sex.

Loved women.

Loved making them feel good.

But for some reason, talking about sex with my best friend had me on edge.

I'd been going through a bit of a dry spell these last few months. Bass was right: I hadn't been myself ever since Gracie moved to Paris.

We'd never lived far from one another.

And I must've been distracted.

And now I was horny as hell with her living in my house.

But I wanted her here, so I couldn't tell her that.

"Oh, so if I throw out the word 'suck,' it'll earn me some brownie points?" she asked as she followed me into the kitchen.

Gracie paused at the sink and washed her hands before pulling out a pan covered in foil from the refrigerator and popping it in the oven.

"I marinated the chicken when I dropped the groceries off this afternoon. We're having your favorite, Bear. Barbecue chicken, mashed potatoes, and a big salad."

My stomach growled at the mention of it. "You don't want me to throw the chicken on the grill?"

"No. I'll bake it. That way you can grab your shower while it's cooking, because dinner time is lesson time." She chuckled, scooting past me in her dark jeans that hugged her peach-shaped ass perfectly.

Damn. I did need to get laid.

And now I was going to be eating chicken and talking about sex, and my dick was going to have a meltdown.

A shower was a good idea.

I'd relieve some of this building tension and be good to go in no time.

"Sounds like a plan. I'll see you in a little bit."

I could hear country music coming through the Alexa in the kitchen now, and I made my way to my bedroom and into the bathroom. I couldn't get in there quick enough.

My dick was a finicky bastard, and having this pending sex talk on my mind had him on edge.

I turned on the water before stripping down. I always took a shower when I first got home, but tonight I was even more eager to get in there.

And it wasn't because I wanted to wash my fucking hair.

I stepped under the hot spray and leaned my head against the shower wall.

This should not be a struggle for me.

I wanted Gracie to be here.

Hell, I was dreading the day she'd leave, and it was still months away.

But the time I'd spent apart from her had clearly done something to me.

Or maybe it was because I needed to have sex.

I wrapped my hand around my erection and stroked it a few times, immediately feeling my body relax.

I tried to think about the last woman I'd had sex with.

Chanel.

Blonde hair. Big tits. And a filthy mouth.

We'd hooked up a few times while she was in town for business.

Was that really six months ago?

Fuck me.

I'd gotten drunk the night Gracie left and met Chanel at the container park.

One thing led to another, and we'd spent the night together.

And that was the last fucking time I'd hooked up with someone.

No wonder I was struggling.

I squeezed my eyes closed.

"I want you right now," she whispered in my ear.

We were at the container park for line dancing night, which was what everyone in town did on Friday nights.

I followed her to the bathroom and locked the door, and she pushed me up against the wall before dropping to her knees.

"I've been thinking about you coming in my mouth all night," she hissed as she gripped my throbbing erection in her hand and took me between her lips.

I glanced down at her, wanting to watch the way she took my cock.

And then my eyes sprang open when I realized it wasn't Chanel I was thinking about—it was Gracie wrapping her lips around my cock.

Fuck.

No. No. Nooooo.

I tried to stop, but my hand had a mind of its own.

She looked up at me with those big brown eyes. "Is this how you like it? Am I doing it right?"

"Just like that, baby. Just fucking like that." I squeezed my eyes closed, feeling those plump lips closing around me. Taking me all the way in.

Her hand sliding up and down my shaft.

Her mouth wet and warm.

In and out.

Over and over.

Faster.

Harder.

Fucking amazing.

I groaned as I came harder than I had in months.

"Fuck," I hissed as I continued stroking myself, riding out every last bit of pleasure.

I pushed thoughts of Gracie out of my head.

She was living in my house, and she'd just talked about sex—of course she'd be on my mind.

It was an innocent mistake.

It wouldn't happen again. It was a one and done.

And now I'd be fine to give her a few tips, keeping it simple, and then I'd start putting myself back out there.

I'd forget this ever happened.

Fantasizing about my best friend was not an option.

I finished showering and dried myself off before slipping on a pair of shorts and a tee.

I made my way out to the kitchen. Gracie had changed into a pair of denim shorts and a white tank top. She had her back to me, and my eyes trailed up her lean, tan legs just as she glanced over her shoulder.

"Oh, hey. Everything is ready. I set us up at the table out back because it's so nice out." She turned around and walked to the counter, handing me a beer, before motioning toward the back door. Our fingers brushed for a split second, and my brain immediately went haywire. Thoughts of her down on her knees from the shower flashed through my head, and I jerked my hand back, heart thudding, then guzzled the beer like I was dying of thirst.

Gracie chuckled, giving me a sideways glance.

"Wow, someone is really thirsty," she teased, and I forced a laugh, hiding the way my stomach had twisted from that fleeting touch.

What the actual fuck is wrong with me?

"I would have helped you carry it all out there," I said, shaking it off as I followed her outside. I had to literally force myself not to check out her ass.

"It was easy. I actually missed cooking when I was living in that tiny apartment." She took the seat across from me and reached for her glass of wine.

I took a bite and groaned.

"Damn, girl. You are such a good cook. Is there anything you aren't good at?" I asked after I'd finished chewing. She could give Bass a run for his money, though I'd never say that to him, for fear he'd cut off a finger.

"Yes. Apparently, there is something I'm not good at. But I'm hoping you can help me figure it out." She smiled and her cheeks pinked, and I sent a silent message to my dick not to react.

He'd just had an epic orgasm.

Unfortunately, it didn't matter.

The topic of helping Gracie with her sex life was clearly a turn-on.

To both me and my dick.

CHAPTER SIX

Gracie

"Sure. You know I'll help any way I can," Cutler said, completely relaxed, as if this topic wasn't awkward at all.

"This is one of the things I love about you," I said, glancing out at the water in the distance, feeling more at ease than I had in months.

He laughed. "My skills in the bedroom? You don't even know if I'm good."

"Cutler. I don't have to be there to know you're good. I've seen the way women fall all over you. I've seen the way they want more after it's over. I don't have that. I mean, my ex-boyfriend even said I'm lacking in the bedroom."

"I really wish I could have a moment alone with that guy right now. The fact that he's given you a complex about sex pisses me the fuck off."

"He didn't give me a complex. I was already aware that it's not an area of strength." I chuckled. "My inexperience is showing. And I don't take it personally. I've had three serious boyfriends, and let's just say—there wasn't a lot of passion involved in any of those relationships, you know? At least not when it came to—*that sort of stuff.*"

"Listen, Jeege, if we're going to talk about it, you can't be afraid to say it."

"Say what?" I shook my head as I reached for my glass of wine.

"That they were bad in the sack. Shitty fucks. Lame lovers. However you want to word it." He took a long pull from his bottle as his dark gaze locked with mine. "So, tell me what you think was lacking."

"Well, Bowie was a great boyfriend. Do you remember him?"

"Bowie was a boy scout. No way that dude delivered. I offered him a sip of a White Claw when I came to visit you freshman year of college, and he acted like I'd asked him to rob a fucking bank."

I tucked my teeth between my lips to try to keep my laughter under control. "Bowie was the sweetest. But he barely touched me, and we dated my senior year of high school, and then we were long-distance that first year of college. He was just a good guy and a rule follower, but I'd say we both lacked experience. And with him being my first boyfriend, I felt like something was wrong with me, because I was definitely more curious than he was back then. We literally did nothing more than make out, and we didn't even do that all that often. He just wanted to talk and hold hands." I shook my head with a snort.

"Why didn't you talk to me? I would have told you that nothing was wrong with you." He took another bite of his chicken.

"Well, this was mostly all happening the year when you stayed in Magnolia Falls to be with your mom. I certainly wasn't going to talk to you about my concerns that my boyfriend barely touched me."

"It would have been a good distraction at the time." He shrugged and then rubbed his hands together. "How about good ole Carter? I remember I came back to school that year and you were always with him, but you did spend a lot of time in the library together. Were you just studying?"

I rolled my eyes. "You know that Carter was my first. I think I was just happy that I'd finally had sex and could put that behind me."

I'd started dating Carter my sophomore year of college. Cutler had come back to school that year, as his mother was in remission and he'd decided it was okay to leave Magnolia Falls. He was still a bit wild back then, but he was starting to seem more like himself that year.

"Yes. I knew that. And I kind of hated that guy."

"Carter? No one hated Carter. He was the mascot for our university."

"He wore a fucking chicken suit. That did not make me like him more. He was too—" He paused to think it over. "Spirited."

"Too spirited? What does that even mean? You're spirited, Bear," I said over my laughter. "Why is that a bad thing?"

"I'm spirited in a 'Let's grab a beer,' 'Let's jump in the lake and skinny-dip,' 'Let's throw a last-minute party' kind of way… That dude was more about dancing around in a chicken suit. He was relentless at games about getting chants going. It was hard to hold a fucking conversation with him shouting in the stands to sing along with him. And stop avoiding the question. What was lacking in the sack with the chicken?" He smirked, and I sighed.

We were having this conversation, so I knew I might as well just put it all out there. I wasn't going to be able to change anything if I wasn't honest about where I was.

"Fine. Carter was similar in the bedroom to the way he was on the football field."

"He fucked like a chicken?" he asked over a mouthful of food.

"No, Bear!" I said over a fit of laughter. "He was…fast. There was no—you know, *preparty*."

"Do you mean there was no foreplay? Is that what you're saying? Because we can't fix this if you can't be straight with me."

"Yes. There was no foreplay. It was always, fast and—" I blew out a breath. "Missionary. He didn't want to try anything else. And no judgement, it just wasn't very passionate."

"Shit. You dated that dude for three years. And that was after coming off the Virgin King, Bowie. This is what you were dealing with? It never got better with Carter?"

"No. He said our sex life was normal. And he'd had more relationships than me, so I assumed he was right back then." I shrugged, shocked that I hadn't thought to push for more with him. I wasn't comfortable talking about sex back then. Hell, I was just finally starting to talk about it now, years later, and only with my best friend. But my girlfriends would talk about their sex lives, and theirs always sounded much more exciting than mine. But I guess I didn't feel comfortable questioning things at the time.

"Why didn't you ask me? We were together every damn day." He threw his hands in the air.

"Because I knew you were doing things—differently. And with more women."

I tried to hide the hint of jealousy in my voice. Had it always been there? I'd never loved seeing him with different women, but I'd chalked it up to not wanting to become friends with women he'd be moving on from shortly after. But maybe it was more than that? Or maybe I was just protective of him? "So I couldn't ask for relationship advice from someone who didn't have a relationship that lasted longer than a few weeks."

"Hey, hey, now. A few weeks in college is like a lifetime for regular people. And what would I always tell you back then?" He paused as he waited for me to answer.

"That 'the only girl you'd settle down with was me.'" I chuckled. "But you weren't that guy, and we both knew it. It was just your shtick."

"It wasn't my shtick, Jeege. My relationships just sort of fizzled, and the only relationship with a female that ever went the distance was my friendship with you." He wriggled his brows. "But if we'd tested the waters, I would have made sure you felt good every damn day, unlike your shitty boyfriends."

"Well, the good news with my exes, at least the two before Gabriel, was that the lack of passion made for a very drama-free breakup. We ended amicably and there were no hurt feelings, so I'm calling it a win."

"I recall both of them being pretty heartbroken."

"Well, Bowie was sad for a few weeks, and we just talked it through on the phone a lot, but things never got ugly and we're still friends today." I shrugged. "And Carter did try to convince me to stay, but it blew over."

"Didn't he fucking propose to you?" He had a wicked grin on his face, because he'd been with me when Carter dropped to his knee unexpectedly after we'd broken up.

"There was no ring. It was a drunken Hail Mary," I said over my laughter. "And he and I are still very friendly today."

"Okay, so tell me about your final lover, Gabriel. He's a fucking grown man, and he's French, for fuck's sake. Frenchmen are supposed to be born with swagger. He must have known his way around a pussy."

“Cutler!” I shrieked, feeling my cheeks heat with embarrassment.

His head tipped back in laughter. “What? We’re talking about sex. You’ve got a pussy, and you shouldn’t be afraid to talk about it.”

“Oh my gosh. Stop. This conversation is over.” I covered my mouth to hide my smile and glanced out at the water.

I needed a minute.

“This conversation is just getting started, Jeege.” He took the last pull from his beer and waited for me to meet his gaze. “Did he at least make you come?”

I reached for my glass and gulped down the rest of my wine before tipping my chin up confidently. “No. I’ve never had an orgasm during sex.”

I mean, it’s the reason I’m here having this conversation with Cutler Heart.

Because it was time to change that.

I was twenty-eight years old, and no man had ever shown me true pleasure.

That didn’t sit well with me.

I wanted more.

“Fuck me,” he said on a growl, getting up from the table and walking toward the house.

“Where are you going?” I called after him. “We’re done?”

“We’re clearly going to need more booze for this conversation.” He chuckled as he stepped inside the house.

He returned with a new bottle of wine tucked under one arm and a six-pack of beer in his other hand.

He didn’t say a word as he refilled my wine glass. And then he popped the top off his beer and took a long pull.

I watched his Adam’s apple bob in his neck as the liquid moved down his throat.

Why was that so sexy?

Leave it to my best friend to have a sexy neck and an alluring Adam's apple.

He leaned forward, elbows on the table, eyes on me. "He couldn't even make you come with his tongue?"

My heart thudded in my chest, and I reached for my wine glass and took another sip. I swallowed a few times before speaking.

"He never tried. He said oral sex was for college kids, not grown adults. Unfortunately, my college boyfriend was in too much of a hurry, so he never went *downtown* either."

Cutler's eyes widened. "Eating pussy should be every man's pleasure. I plan to do it until I take my last breath. There's nothing better than getting a woman off with your tongue."

Did it just get hot in here?

"Well, it's clearly not for everyone because none of my boyfriends had any interest in it. Or maybe I have an unexciting vagina." I blew out a breath.

"I promise you, you don't have an unexciting vagina." Loud laughter bellowed from him.

"Well, then, maybe it's not for everyone. Maybe it's just a *you* thing."

Why do I sound so defensive now?

"Gracie." His voice was deep and gruff.

"What?"

"It's not a me thing. It's a feel-good thing. And you should feel fucking good when you're having sex. It's not supposed to be a race. It's not supposed to be hurried. A man should never chase his own pleasure before he pleasures his lady."

It was a very Cutler thing to say. Of course he would please any woman he was with. It was his nature.

Anytime over the years that I'd ever said I was hungry, Cutler would appear with a sandwich, or a bag of chips.

If I said that I was cold, he'd come out of nowhere with a jacket.

He was that guy.

So naturally, with my sex life being in the shitter, I'd come to the right place.

"I'm thinking I approach my next relationship differently," I said, tracing my finger over the rim of my wine glass as I thought over my next words. "Maybe I have a fling. Something casual. I've been looking for Mr. Right, and where has that gotten me?"

"Broke in Paris with bad sex," he said, with a mischievous grin on his face.

I tossed my napkin at him and shrugged. "You aren't wrong. So tell me how to attract a man who will be—you know, different from the men I've been dating. No more looking for Mr. Right. I'm going to just look for Mr. Right Now."

"Jeege, you can attract any man you want. It has nothing to do with you. It's about you not choosing these boring dickheads."

"Of course you're going to say it's not me." I looked at him. "Okay, focus. So let's say I go on a date. Instead of trying to find out their life story, or to find out what makes them tick, I need to loosen up a bit. Maybe I say something dirty?" I chewed on my bottom lip, and I could feel my cheeks heat. "You know, to put that vibe out there that I'm looking for some—passion."

He reared back with a laugh, and I glared at him. "This is not a joke, Bear. You aren't allowed to laugh. This is serious. I don't want to die without experiencing good sex."

He covered his mouth as his gaze softened. "I'm not laughing at you, Jeege. You're just fucking funny sometimes. And you know I've got you. But you're twenty-eight years old—your life is far from over. It's just starting. And now you know what you're looking for next. So you need to get comfortable in your own skin. Comfortable with your sexuality."

"I think I'm fairly comfortable with my sexuality."

"Yet, you've never asked a man to go down on you. Never demanded they do what it takes to get you off." He raised a brow. "I don't think you are."

"Fine. How do I get there?"

"That's what she said," he said, cackling.

I pushed to my feet because none of this was funny to me. The wine was kicking in, and I was frustrated. I wanted a simple answer, and I wasn't getting it. He grabbed my hand and pulled me toward him before I settled on his lap, and he wrapped his arms around me. "Don't leave. I'm sorry. No more teasing."

"Thank you. This is serious. I want to use this time to change the things that aren't serving me. And bad sex is no longer serving me."

"Okay, so let's get down and dirty," he said against my ear, and I tried to wiggle off his lap, but he held me there. "Don't get nervous. It's me. You can tell me anything."

I turned the slightest bit to face him. "What do you want to know?"

He thought it over and then tilted his head to the side. "What do you like? What makes you feel good?"

"I don't know—that's the problem."

"Yes, you do." His gaze locked with mine. "When you touch yourself, what do you think about?"

My mouth fell open, and I was certain I was three shades of red. He touched me beneath my chin, pushing my mouth closed.

"How do you know if I even—*you know*? Do that."

"Get yourself off?" he asked. "I assume you must because no one else is doing it for you."

I blew out a breath and looked out at the water as I thought about it.

“There’s nothing to be ashamed of. Hell, I do it all the time,” he said.

My head whipped in his direction. “You do? Even with all the sex you have.”

“I’m not a fucking sex addict, Jeege. For the record, I have a normal amount of sex. And I love feeling good. Hell, I made myself feel good in the shower, right before dinner.”

“You did not!” I gaped at him.

“I sure did. Why do you think I’m so relaxed? Meanwhile, you’re wound tight. There’s one way to take care of that, and it doesn’t require a partner.”

Thoughts of Cutler in the shower, naked, head tipped back with water running down his golden skin as he wraps his hand around his—

Oh. My. Gosh.

I reached across the table for my wine glass, tipped my head back, and finished it off.

He was right.

This conversation required more booze.

CHAPTER SEVEN

Cutler

"Well, I'm certainly not going to touch myself while I'm sitting on your lap, so you can tell your overzealous erection to calm down," she said with a laugh.

Clearly, she could feel him responding to her nearness.

"Hey, you're talking about what gets you off and you're sitting on my lap. I'm only human, Jeege."

"Fine. If I say one thing that I think about, will you just give me a few simple tips, and we'll call this lesson done for tonight?" Her cheeks were pink, and it was cute as hell.

There was nothing I wouldn't talk about with Gracie, but I'd be lying if I said I ever thought we'd be talking about this.

And I'd be lying if I didn't admit that I liked it.

"Yes. Tell me."

She tapped her finger against her lips as if she was deep in thought. Her eyes looked up at the sky for several beats, and then she turned to me. “It could be the wine talking, but I think I might like it if a man took charge, you know? Like not in a way where he rushes things, but in a way that he just knows what I need and what I want, and he tells me what to do so he can please me. That probably makes no sense.”

Holy fuck.

Hearing what she wanted. What she longed for. It was sexy as hell.

How had any man not been able to give her what she needed? She was eager and curious and passionate.

What a fucking privilege it would be to please this woman.

It took everything in me not to react physically, so I schooled my features, not giving anything away.

I placed a hand beneath her chin and turned her until her gaze met mine. “It makes perfect sense. You’ve never had a lover who was tuned in to what you wanted, what you needed. You want a man who can read your signals. A man who can sense what your body needs and wants. And that’s a good thing. But you need to give him those signals so he can do that.”

“Okay,” she said, the word coming out very breathy, which made me even harder than I already was. “So I need to show him what I want with my body language, right?”

“Yes.”

“And how do I do that?”

“Do you want me to show you?” I asked, and now it was my voice that was gruff. “I mean, I can show you without doing anything.”

She’d had a lot to drink, and I was not that guy. Never had been, never would be.

But I could give her something without crossing a line.

She nodded. "Yes. Please show me."

"All right, I'll give you an example." I tucked her long dark hair behind her ear and pulled her closer as I used the tip of my tongue to trace a line down her neck, and then I trailed my lips over the same path before leaning close to speak against her ear. "So if you like this, you show the person by tilting your head back just the way you're doing right now. You've arched into my touch, which tells me you're enjoying it."

Her eyes were closed, and I moved to the other side of her neck and repeated what I'd just done, and she nearly fell against my body. It seemed to startle her, because she sprang forward and nodded before jumping off my lap.

"Okay. I can do that. Arch into it."

I froze for a moment, taking in the way she'd responded, how instinctively her body had reacted.

I'd barely touched her, yet she'd reacted, and it was sexy as hell.

My pulse spiked, and I bit back a groan, unable to think of anything but the way she'd moved, the way she'd trusted me—the way it made me ache to do it again.

She'd liked it.

And so did I.

Her skin was soft and smooth.

Strawberries and coconut flooded my senses.

I shook it off, schooled my features again, and looked up to meet her gaze.

This was my best friend, after all.

"Yes. Little things like the way that you respond to touch. If you don't like something, you let the person know immediately by pulling away. If you enjoy it, you lean into it. You can pull him closer, make a noise that communicates what you're feeling."

"I don't think I did much of that in my past relationships." She started stacking the dishes on the table.

She was done.

This was too much for her, I could tell.

"Well, who could blame you? I don't think anyone was touching you in a way that you liked. So, don't be afraid to take charge, Jeege. You can tell them or show them what you want."

"Dirk asked me out to dinner, but I'm not even remotely attracted to him, so I don't think this plan would work with him." She gathered the plates, and I stood up and took them from her.

Dirk fucking Roberts.

The audacity of this asshole to think he had any business asking Gracie out.

"I'll take these in. And that's a terrible idea. You can't go out with Dirk."

"Why not?" she huffed as she carried the wine bottle and glass while she walked beside me.

"Because it's a conflict of interest. You're an authority figure at the office."

She set the bottle and glass down on the kitchen island, and I placed the plates in the sink before turning to look at her.

"I don't even work there," she chuckled. "How am I an authority figure?"

"Because he's a subcontractor for us, and you're a VP. That causes a power struggle, and we can't have that type of shit going down in the workplace."

"A VP of what?" she asked over hysterical laughter.

"You're my VP of design. You're in a position of power."

"Cutler."

"Gracie," I mimicked her as she placed her hands on her hips. "What's your problem with Dirk?"

"Dirk is a jerk."

"Thanks, Busta Rhymes. He does a ton of work for you. I thought you liked him." She shook her head in disbelief.

"I like him fine. But he's cocky, and he's a player. He's not your type."

I mean, I know…glass fucking houses. I'm not worthy of her either. Maybe no one is.

But she deserved the best, and it sure as hell wasn't Dirk Roberts.

"Well, that's the thing. I don't want to date my type. I don't like the guy romantically, but he's good-looking and he might be good to practice on." She laughed even harder now. She was clearly tipsy from the two generous glasses of wine she'd had.

"That's not you and you know it. And let's not choose some fucker who I'll have to fire because it'll piss me off if he puts his hands on you."

She stepped closer before reaching past me and pouring the rest of the wine into her glass. "Fine. I'll find myself a temporary man, a no-strings-attached hottie, when we go line dancing this weekend. Maybe I'll find me a cowboy," she said, howling as she pretended to toss around an invisible rope.

I was grateful it wasn't real, because she had no clue what she was doing.

Now it was my turn to laugh. "Great. I'll help you choose. I know everyone in town, so I can fill you in."

"Great. You can be my wingman, Bear." Her lips turned up in the corners. "And I think I'm going to find me a cowboy, someone who knows his way around more than a horse."

For fuck's sake. She was being ridiculous.

But I kind of loved it.

Even if a little part of me hated the idea of her meeting someone.

Gracie was a relationship girl. She'd always been in one. And clearly they weren't very good, so picking partners wasn't her strength.

"You know you could be single for a little while."

"That's what the plan is. I'm studying at the school of Cutler 'Bear' Heart." She winked at me. "I'm not looking for a husband. I'm looking for—*a good time.*"

I rolled my eyes. "That's a big stretch from what you're used to."

"That's the whole point. Fresh start. New me. So bring your dancing boots, because we're going to have some fun." She stumbled a little bit, and I caught her by the shoulders.

"Okay, pace yourself, player," I said, my voice teasing. "Let's get you a water and get you to bed."

I wrapped an arm around her shoulder and led her down the hallway to her bedroom.

"I'm tired," she said, pointing to the bed for me to sit, while she grabbed her jammies and walked into her bathroom. She didn't close the door, but I knew she was changing even though I couldn't see her. She walked out wearing little boy shorts and a white tank top, and I tried not to stare. "Thanks for the lesson and for giving me a job and a place to live. I don't know what I'd do without you."

"You'll never have to find out. C and G for life, right?" I stood up and pulled back the comforter, motioning for her to climb in. I had the sudden urge to touch her again. I loved the way she'd reacted to my lips on her neck.

The way she'd tasted.

I wanted more.

What the fuck is wrong with me?

This was Gracie.

My Gracie.

She climbed under the comforter and smiled up at me. "C and G for life."

"Get some sleep, Jeege." I flipped off her light and started to move through the doorway.

"You know you'd be the perfect guy for this temporary gig, right?" she teased. "And there'd be no risk of anyone getting hurt, because we're already best friends. And it would save me the time of finding a suitable short-term lover."

Her laughter filled the room, and I was so stunned by her words that I was grateful she couldn't see my face.

Also, I was now ridiculously turned on at the suggestion.

I adjusted myself slyly, because holy shit.

What the hell was she asking?

"You've clearly had too much to drink. These are verbal lessons." I cleared my throat, but she was still chuckling at the idea.

I was not laughing.

I'd just lived out this scenario in the shower earlier.

This was a dangerous game, and I needed to keep my head on straight.

"Well, you did do the whole tongue and lips thing on my neck," she said with a chuckle, like this was a big joke. "But you're right. That would be too messy. But it would make life a lot easier on me. Because now I've got to find me a man."

None of this was funny to me, though she seemed to find it all to be hilarious.

"Let's just call it a night, lover girl."

She sighed. "Hey, can I ask you something?"

"Always," I said, turning around as the light from the moon made a halo around where she was sitting up in bed. I couldn't see her face, but I knew her eyes were on me.

"I told you what I liked, and now I'm curious. When you were in the shower tonight before dinner," she said, her voice just above a whisper, "what were you thinking about?"

You do not want to know.

"I don't even remember. Probably the last time I had sex," I said, happily leaving off the fact that it may have started that way, but it sure as hell didn't end that way.

She fell back on her pillow. "That makes sense, because it's always good for you, right?"

"Sure," I said as I knocked on her doorframe. "I guess I've got plenty to teach you."

She chuckled. "Good. I've got plenty to learn. Sweet dreams, Bear."

After this talk, I had a hunch my dreams would be plenty sweet.

• • •

On Friday afternoons, if we were all in town, my boys and I always met at Bennett's for lunch. It was where we'd catch up without any distractions. The restaurant wasn't open for lunch, but Bass always had five steaks with wedge salads on the side ready for us as soon as we sat down.

"Hey, hey, look who made it just in time." Brody smirked.

"Sorry I'm late," I said as I walked around the circular table and fist-pumped each one of them. "Gracie and I had a meeting with the Petersons because they are in desperate need of a designer."

"You couldn't handle her being so far away, and you managed to get her back here in Blue Sky Bay, and now she's living at your house and working with you," Cannon said, clapping his hands together twice like the cocky bastard he was. "You are one lucky son of a bitch."

"Says the dude who recently won the world finals event." I laughed at the cocky bull rider as I settled in my seat between Cannon and Phoenix. Bass and Brody sat directly across from me at the round table.

Cannon had just upset the competition with a huge win in Texas that we'd all been present for. The dude was an absolute rock star. A six-foot-tall bull rider wasn't exactly the norm, so he had the odds stacked against him because of his height, yet he just kept winning. He was a natural. He'd been riding since he was a teenager, entering his first competition when we all left for college. His family had a long history of riding bulls, and Cannon had proved himself over the years, but this past season had been his best.

"Well, the goal is to be the overall world champion, win more than just the finals."

"Take the win, asshole. It was damn cool to watch you pull that off." Bass shook his head at Cannon.

"I'm just saying, my biological clock is ticking, because I swear, I have a hard time getting out of bed most mornings." He reached for his beer—there was one already sitting at each of our seats—and we all held our bottles up to clink them together, like we always did.

"To C-dawg and Heart, the two luckiest bastards I know," Brody said as our bottles tipped together and we all took a long pull.

"Have you ever considered that it's painful to get out of bed in the morning because of all the action you get in that bed every night?" Phoenix asked just as Joey walked out with our steaks. He was Bass's assistant chef, and he always made lunch on Fridays. He had five plates displayed across his two long arms, and he set them down in front of each of us. He knew exactly how we all liked our meat cooked.

"I can't be the only one riding the bull." Cannon winked, and I couldn't help but laugh. "How about you, Heart? How are you going to bring women home if you've got Gracie living at your house? That could put a real damper on your sex life."

"I don't give a shit. I'd be celibate to have that girl here." I shrugged, cutting into my perfectly cooked T-bone steak.

I still couldn't stop thinking about what she'd asked me the other night. She hadn't brought it up again, and I was grateful, because obviously she'd had too much to drink.

We couldn't go there.

No fucking way.

Didn't stop me from thinking about it…multiple times a day.

"My dick just flipped you off because we don't use the word 'celibate,'" Cannon said over his laughter.

"You haven't been going out much anyway these past few months. What's going on with you?" Brody asked as he glanced over at me.

I shrugged. "Not sure. I've been on a few dates, but I guess I'm sort of over the hookup scene. Maybe I'm ready for something more."

"I hear you, brother," Bass said, reaching for his beer. "I've only been on a few dates since Celine and I broke up over six months ago, and I fucking hate dating."

He and his girlfriend had been together for a few years before they finally called it quits. He didn't talk about it a whole lot; he'd just thrown himself even more into work after she left town.

"That's your problem," Phoenix said. "You're trying to make it something more than it has to be. Just go out and have a good time. No strings attached. No drama. That's how I prefer it." He forked a cucumber and popped it in his mouth.

"Well, women love a moody firefighter, don't they?" Bass waggled his brows.

"There's only one girl I give a shit about, and she never stops bossing me around," Brody said, laughing.

Clover Stark.

Brody's little girl.

Hell, she was a little bit all of ours.

We'd known her since the day she came into this world, and we all adored her.

"Yeah, well, your girl is four years old, and she bosses all of us around, doesn't she?" Phoenix said, a wide grin spreading across his face when he spoke about his niece.

"Well, isn't this just great?" Cannon said. "I finally make a name for myself as a bull rider, and the women are eating that shit up. And now Heart decides to be celibate just to keep his best friend living in his house, Brody is committed to raising his daughter, so he rarely goes out, Bass is having a love affair with this goddamn restaurant, and the only wingman I still have, Phoenix, works most nights at the firehouse and he's a grumpy asshole. I'm fucked."

"To being fucked." Phoenix raised his bottle, and we all followed suit.

But I didn't feel fucked at all.

I hadn't been this happy in a long time.

CHAPTER EIGHT

Gracie

It felt so good to be working again and doing what I loved. Designing was my passion, and I loved nothing more than bringing clients' visions to life.

Designing Cutler's family home was going to be a breeze, as Emilia had given me very clear and specific direction on the aesthetic they wanted, all while giving me free rein to make choices on their behalf.

It was a designer's dream.

A large budget. Clear aesthetic. And she fully trusted me.

I'd interned with Emilia Chadwick for two summers, so we knew one another well. That helped.

I'd met with Shana Peterson yesterday, and today was our design meeting, as she'd officially hired me.

Shana would be easy in a different way. I got the sense that she didn't want to have to make the decisions on her own, or even at all. She wanted my guidance, and she seemed to trust it.

I understood that. Renovations were huge undertakings. They could be exciting and fun, but also stressful and overwhelming.

That's where I came in.

"I just, I have so much on my plate right now," Shana said. "The three kids and Billy and I are all living in the basement at my parents' house. I'm just spread so thin, but I want to make sure that I get what we want in this house."

I could feel the anxiety radiating from her.

Yesterday we'd met at the office, and she'd hired me on the spot. I'd given her several design books to take home, and several websites for her to look at as well. I asked her to send me any photos of aesthetics that spoke to her, and she'd done a great job with the task, sending me at least a dozen rooms she liked.

So she did have an aesthetic and style all her own; she just didn't know it.

Today we were at their new home, and they'd finished tearing out all the flooring. It was time to get the design locked down. Materials could take weeks, depending on what she chose, and the smoothest renovations happened when things were ready to go, and you weren't waiting around for materials. So it was time to get things locked in, and to choose items that were in stock and ready to go.

"I can imagine how stressful this is. I want to do everything I can to help you." I glanced over at her as she scrolled through my online portfolio of the work I'd done over the last several years. "I wanted you to see these after looking at all the different options, so you could feel confident in my work. If any of these jump out at you, let me know. My assessment after you pointed out everything you like is that you are a mix of French country and traditional. Those two designs marry very well."

"Oh, I didn't even know I had a style." She shook her head, and I could see the stress written on her face.

"Yes. It's sort of a mix of classic, timeless, and comfort, while bringing in some history with vintage pieces. The colors are typically light and earthy, very neutral. We'd bring in texture with fabrics like velvet and florals, mixed with some rustic linen touches."

Her eyes widened. "Wow. I like the sound of that. I felt like I sent you so many pictures of different looks, so I was frustrated that I didn't have one specific style that I liked."

"It's perfectly normal to mix aesthetics. It gives a home personality, and I like that you involved Billy as well. We want this home to represent your family."

"Me too. I was surprised that Billy didn't choose the super-modern photos I showed him," she said, tucking her hair behind her ear.

"Yes, the ones you sent that he'd chosen were very traditional, where your top choices leaned toward French country, but you had a few rooms that were very traditional. The great news is that those are very easy to mesh."

She blew out a breath. "Thank goodness you're helping me. We've gone to the tile store multiple times to choose all the tile for the floors and walls, and I just walk around for hours, and then leave with nothing."

Cutler had come to me because he thought she needed help, and he was right.

Shana Peterson was overwhelmed.

That happened often with renovations.

This was one of my favorite parts of my job. Helping clients create a home that they'd love. Not everyone could visualize the big picture, so being able to help someone bring it all to life was something I really enjoyed.

And I loved design as a whole. I could stare at paint colors and fabric samples for hours and never tire of it. I loved mixing and matching textures and designs and creating something fresh and unique.

This was why I was so excited about moving to New York. It would challenge me both personally and professionally. Moving to a new city would be a little intimidating, but I welcomed it. I wanted to push myself out of my comfort zone. The homes I'd be designing would be different in New York, as city living was very different from living out in the country or in a small town—and I was excited to grow as a designer.

"So what I like to do is make things as easy for you as possible." I chuckled. "I have a great idea from what you've sent me about where to start. I typically go to the tile store and get three to four options for each bathroom, as far as flooring and counters and cabinets and backsplash. I do the same with the kitchen. I know you want wood flooring, so I'd bring a couple different finishes for the wood, and we'd lay it all out, eliminate what you don't like, and start putting together what you do like."

"Really? That sounds dreamy." She let a loud sigh escape. "If I never have to go back to the tile store, I would be very happy."

I smiled and gave her a nod. "We can absolutely make that happen. I will bring everything to you. And if I don't hit the mark on certain rooms, I'll just bring you back some more samples, and that's how we'll start putting the entire design together. Once we have the finishes all selected and ordered, then I'll head over to your storage unit with you, and we'll go through the furniture and décor that you have, and we'll make a list of what you need. You'll give me a budget, and I'll get all the interior pieces, such as furniture, lighting, and artwork, taken care of for you." I squeezed her hand when I noticed that her eyes were watering.

"Gracie, I can't tell you how much this means to me. I just, I can't seem to make a decision, and everyone from my parents to my husband to my kids is asking me a million things at once." She swiped at the tear running down her face. "What color kitchen am I doing? What color bathroom tile did I pick? What kind of flooring am I doing? What am I making for dinner tonight? When can we go to the park? Did I sleep well?"

A laugh escaped her, and I leaned forward and wrapped my arms around her. Sometimes people just needed a hug and to be heard.

"I can't answer the questions about dinner or the park or your sleep habits, but I can take everything else off your plate," I said.

She pulled back. "Okay. I love the sound of this. You've got the budget that we agreed to with ROD Construction, and we'd like to stay as close to that as possible, as far as the flooring and appliances and all of those things. And then we can figure out a separate budget for furniture and décor, but it probably won't be very large."

"Don't worry at all. I can work with any décor budget. I'm quite the deal finder," I said as I pushed to stand.

There was a lot of hammering in the background, and Shana moved to stand beside me. "Sadly, this is the most peaceful place I've been all day."

I laughed. "Yes, I can imagine three kids in a small space is not super peaceful."

"No. But it'll all be worth it, right?"

"It will. I promise." I leaned forward to hug her one last time. "I'll head to the tile store now and have options for you by Monday."

"Wow." Her eyes widened. "You don't mess around."

"Nope. I'm on it."

"Will I see you at country night at Down by the Bay tonight?

Billy and I will be leaving the kids with my parents and getting out for some much-needed line dancing and beers."

"I was just about to ask her the same thing," Dirk said as he came around the corner.

I didn't love that he'd interrupted our conversation, as this was a work meeting for me, and he was here on a jobsite as a professional.

"Yes. I'll definitely be there. I'll come over and say hi." I waved to Shana as she walked out the door.

"She can't make a decision if her life depends on it. It took me four appointments to get her to make a decision on the doors she wanted in the house," Dirk said once she'd walked outside. It irritated me the way he spoke about her.

"I didn't find that to be true at all. She actually has a pretty distinct style. But she's living in her parents' basement with her family, and it's a lot to balance," I said.

He chuckled. "She doesn't even work–I'm sure she can handle it."

I was getting all the red flags of ghosts of boyfriends past with this guy.

"Her children are young, and it's summer break. You've clearly never been a mother." I tugged my purse over my shoulder and blew out a breath.

"Can't argue with that. So, how about you let me take you to dinner before line dancing tonight?"

"I think with us working together, it's best we don't go there. But I'll see you tonight and we can all grab a beer together." I smiled, relieved that I'd thought quickly, and it seemed to appease him.

"No problem. I'll see you tonight."

"See you there." I held my hand over my head and waved goodbye.

I piled everything in the car and was headed to the tile store when my phone rang.

"Hey, Bear," I said.

His voice rang through the Bluetooth speaker. "How did your meeting go with Shana?"

"Really great."

"Was Dirk there getting those doors installed?"

"Yes. And for the record, there will be no fling with him."

"And why is that?" There was a definite edge in his voice.

"You were right. Dirk is a jerk."

"What did he do? Did he upset you?" Cutler asked. The man was ridiculously protective.

I chuckled. "No. He just irritated me."

"Good. Kick his ass to the curb. He's definitely not the guy for you. But we're going to have some fun tonight."

"I plan on it. I just pulled into the tile store. I'll be home in a few hours."

"See you then," he said before ending the call.

I spent the next hour and a half at the tile store, and then made my way to grab cabinet and floor samples before dropping everything at ROD Construction.

I went back to Cutler's house and called out his name, then heard the sound of the shower coming from his bedroom.

I paused for a moment, swallowing hard as I stood on the other side of the door, wondering what he was doing in the shower. I bit the inside of my cheek as my heart raced at the thought.

Get your mind out of the gutter, Gracie.

This was my best friend, and these were not thoughts I should be having.

We'd already agreed it was a line that we shouldn't cross.

This was Cutler.

My Cutler.

What the hell was wrong with me?

I hurried to my room, quickly pulling out a cute outfit to wear before laying it on the bed.

I was going to have some fun tonight.

It was time to get back out there.

No more overthinking things.

No more looking for the perfect guy. I also wouldn't be settling for a man who rubbed me wrong, but something in between would be just fine.

Good-looking. Good personality. No strings attached.

I was sick of always trying to be perfect. Fitting into that box where everyone knew that I was a "good girl."

I wanted to feel wild and alive for once in my life, like I mattered in a different way.

I wanted to know what it felt like to be desired.

Really desired.

Yes, I'd been called pretty by my ex-boyfriends, but I'd never once been told that I was sexy.

The only person who'd ever called me sexy was Cutler, and that didn't count, because he was my best friend. Totally off-limits.

And he was the one to tell me that I should ask for what I wanted.

And I realized that it wasn't all that complicated.

I wanted to experience that kind of all-consuming passion and desire, the kind you read about in romance books. At the same time, it was important to me that I stay in control of my emotions and expectations and walk away unscathed.

This was my time to have a little fun, to be a little wild before I moved to New York and everything got serious again.

And that's exactly what I intended to do.

I added some beach waves to my long dark hair before applying some shimmery bronzer to my cheeks and mascara to my lashes. I finished it off with some pink lip gloss on my lips, then slipped into my white sundress with spaghetti straps that ended just above my knee and my red cowboy boots. When I pulled my bedroom door open, Luke Combs was singing through the surround sound, and I heard Cutler singing along from the kitchen.

I rounded the corner and just took a minute to take him in, as his back was to me. He wore a white tee that stretched across the muscles of his back. His thick dark hair was a little longer than usual, and he wore a pair of faded jeans that hugged his ass just right.

Cutler Heart was all man.

"You checking me out, Jeege?" he asked as he slowly turned around and winked.

"Please. It's not like I haven't seen it all before," I said with a laugh, making light of it.

Because yes, I was checking him out.

But a girl could look and still have boundaries.

I'd been doing it for years.

"You ready to have some fun tonight, Jeege?" he asked as he scooped me up and spun me around before setting my feet back down on the ground.

"Damn straight. It's Friday night. We don't have to wake up in the morning. I'm ready to let loose and have a good time."

He flipped off the lights in the kitchen and wrapped his arms around me from behind.

"Well, being the prettiest girl there means I'm going to have to be watching out for you." He kissed my cheek.

"Don't be scaring off my potential lovers," I said over my laughter, and he just stared at me for a beat, not responding, before he cleared his throat and nodded.

Why is he being so serious now? He knows what my plan is.

I cocked my head to the side, trying to figure out what was going on with him.

As if he could read the questioning look on my face, he shook his head, lips turning up in the corners, though it appeared forced, and he pushed the door open.

"Let's go, lover girl."

I was ready.

It was going to be a good night.

CHAPTER NINE

Cutler

It was one of those nights when the stars just aligned and we were all having a great time. Gracie brought an energy with her that we'd clearly all missed.

Hell, even Phoenix was having a good time, and he rarely had a good time.

We were drinking and dancing and laughing.

It was a warm night, but the breeze off the lake provided enough relief to make it comfortable.

"I missed this girl so much!" Tatum shouted as she and Gracie returned from the dance floor, with Jovi right behind them.

Tatum had grown up next door to Brody and Phoenix, and I'd known her for years. She and Gracie had met many times, and they'd always hit it off.

Throw in some tequila and Michelob Ultras, and it was even more magnified.

Jovi was Bass's little sister, and we all loved her. She was officially twenty-one years old now, so it was her first time coming out with us. She was home from school, and Bass was quite possibly the most protective brother on the planet.

"I think this calls for another shot," Jovi said, wriggling her eyebrows at everyone at the table.

"Hey, let's slow things down. You're barely legal," Bass chuckled as we all sat around the high-top table at Four Clovers.

The center of the container park, which was normally turf, had a large wooden dance floor there on Friday nights during the summer months.

"I've been twenty-one for six months, brother dearest," Jovi said. "I'm also going to be a senior in college, so stop being overbearing." She gave him a look.

Bass rolled his eyes just as Brody walked over with a tray of shot glasses.

"I agree," Cannon said. "We've got our girl Gracie back in town for a few months, and little Jovi is home for the summer and old enough to drink. Does it get any better?" He winked at the girls before joining them with a shot.

"You aren't taking shots, Bear?" Gracie asked, her words slurring the slightest bit.

She'd always been a cute drunk. It didn't happen often, but when it did, I kept my eyes on her even more than usual.

"I'm sticking to beers tonight. I want you to have a good time." I held up my beer bottle, and she just had a goofy smile on her face.

"Who's being overbearing now?" Cannon asked, leaning in close to me so no one else could hear him.

I just laughed him off.

Call it protective. Call it overbearing.

I didn't really give a shit.

Dirk made his way over to the table for the third time tonight, and I'd noticed the way Gracie always shut him down. He seemed to have moved on, and now he was hitting on Tatum.

A local named Justin Loosh walked over to Gracie and pulled up a barstool, and they sat directly across from me. She was laughing and chatting with him, and I turned my attention to Sydney, who'd just wrapped her arms around my neck from behind.

"Hey, Syd," I said as she moved to stand so she was facing me now. "How you doing?"

"I'm good. I was hoping I'd run into you here tonight."

We'd always had a very flirty relationship, though it had been innocent. Nothing had ever happened. And a few months ago, she'd let me know that she'd ended things with her long-distance boyfriend.

I hadn't pursued anything, because I just didn't feel it was a good line to cross.

We were good friends, and I wanted to keep it that way.

"And here we are," I said, my voice teasing.

Our group had grown, with a few more people pulling up barstools at our table.

"Here we are." She placed a hand on my shoulder, stepping closer, and my gaze moved to Gracie as she and the girls headed back out to the dance floor, with a few guys right behind them.

Her cheeks were pink and eyes glassy, as she'd clearly had a lot to drink. She was having a good time.

I watched as Gracie's legs moved from side to side to the music, and the way her hair fell over her shoulders, framing her pretty face. Her laughter was loud and messy and fucking adorable, and I lingered there longer than I should.

I blinked a few times before forcing myself to focus on Sydney.

"How have you been? Can I get you a drink?" I asked as I eyed the barstool beside me, hoping she'd take a seat, as she kept inching closer, and I wasn't feeling it. But I also didn't want to be an asshole.

"Are you going to get me a drink, Cutler Heart?" she purred, and I could tell she'd also had a lot to drink.

"Sure. What would you like?" I asked, just as Brody walked over and set a water down for me, and I motioned for him to take her order.

"I'll take a shot of bourbon and a piña colada."

I tried not to laugh when I saw the confused look on Brody's face.

"Interesting order," he said with a laugh. "I'll be right back."

He moved around the table asking if anyone else wanted anything, and Bass told him to stop serving his sister. Brody nodded in agreement.

"Dude. She's an adult," Cannon said from the barstool beside me as Bree giggled where she stood between his legs. She was a local who'd been after him for a while. Cannon was a playboy and everyone knew it, and he never hurt for female attention, not that any of us did.

"Hey. She's living on my houseboat this summer, and we've got one bathroom. I know her limits. So, unless you want to babysit her and clean up vomit, I suggest you stay in your lane." Bass shot him a warning look.

Bass was serious about two things, and two things only.

His baby sister, whom he'd practically raised, and his restaurant.

Those were his priorities.

It was probably the reason his relationship with Celine had gone south.

He didn't have time for a woman.

He had a sister he financially supported and a restaurant to run.

"Got it, big guy. I'm just saying, you don't want to push her away." Cannon shrugged.

"Well, I hope you won't be pushing me away, because I plan on taking this bull rider home with me tonight," Bree said as she leaned down and kissed him.

He pulled back and winked at me, but I didn't miss the way his gaze kept moving to the dance floor, because mine was doing the same thing.

We were clearly both keeping our eyes on someone, and I had a feeling it wasn't the same person.

Gracie was moving to the left and the right as they danced to Chris Stapleton, and the dance floor was packed as they all sang along, moving in sync.

I laughed when her hands went over her head, and she got everyone to follow her movements.

Justin moved up behind her, one hand snaking around her waist, and I shifted in my seat, ready to pounce if I needed to. But she turned in his arms, head falling back with laughter as they started dancing all on their own.

My chest tightened, and I didn't know what the hell it meant.

I'd always been protective of her, but this was different.

I didn't like the way he was looking at her.

I didn't like that she was smiling up at him either.

And it was fucked up. This is what she wanted, and I was supposed to support her.

Why am I having such a hard time with this?

"Hello, earth to Cutler." Sydney waved her hand in front of my face, and I startled.

"Hey, sorry. I was caught up in the song," I lied.

She tipped her head back as she downed the whiskey and then

reached for her tall fruity blended drink. "So are you ever going to call me?"

"We're friends, right?" I asked, trying to keep things easy.

"Of course we are. But I've also got needs, and I'm guessing you do too? So how about we turn this into a little friends-with-benefits deal, huh?" she asked, her hand finding my knee now.

But my gaze moved back to the dance floor again, just as Justin leaned down to kiss Gracie, and I swear my grip tightened so hard on my beer bottle, I was certain it would shatter.

It took everything in me not to storm out there and haul his ass away from her, which made no sense.

So I forced myself to swallow down my anger. This streak of jealousy was so foreign to me that I didn't know how to process it.

I was being irrational, and I knew it.

She's your best friend. She's your best friend. She's your best friend.

What the fuck was wrong with me?

So I shifted in my seat, and it felt like time came to a stop as I watched everything play out in front of me.

Sydney's voice was a blur of words beside me that I couldn't make out, which she didn't appear to notice because she kept on talking.

Gracie snapped her head back just before his mouth crashed into hers, and relief flooded me.

Why was I relieved?

I can't have her, so now I'm a jealous asshole?

She said something to him, and he looked slightly put off as he nodded and said something back to her. She patted him on the shoulder before turning to her friends.

Atta girl.

She was moving in my direction, with Tatum and Jovi right

beside her, both looking concerned.

"I think our girl has had a little too much to drink," Tatum said.

"I think you've also had too much to drink," Phoenix said, giving Tatum a pointed look. They'd always been very close, and she was one of the few people on the planet who didn't annoy him.

"And I think you've got me mixed up with someone who needs your opinion on how much I can drink." She shot him a glare, which made everyone laugh.

But I'd already moved from my barstool and made my way over to Gracie. "You all right?"

"Yeah. Yeah, of course. I think the booze just caught up with me." She smiled up at me, and her body swayed a little to the left, so I placed a hand on each of her shoulders to steady her. She hiccupped four times, and then her head fell back in a fit of laughter. "Oh my gosh. I had such a good time. I'm going to head home. But you stay and have fun. I'm fine."

Not on a fucking bet.

"Nice try." I reached into my back pocket and tossed more than enough cash on the table to cover our bill before catching Sydney's eyes on me. "I'm going to get her home. I'll see you later?"

"Yeah. Of course. Thanks for the drinks. I'll see you soon," she said before turning her attention to Bass, and I was relieved I hadn't been forced to let her down.

"Come on, Jeege. Let's get you home." I wrapped an arm around her shoulder, and she leaned into me.

"Do you need a ride, Gracie?" Justin asked as he stepped closer.

"We walked here, buddy, but thanks." My gaze locked with his.

No fucking way was he taking her home when she was drunk. And the fact that he'd offered her a ride when he was clearly intoxicated himself did not sit well with me either.

"Thanks, Justin. It's been funnnnnn." Gracie patted him on the chest. “But Bear’s got me.”

I sure as shit do.

“All right. I’ve got your number, I’ll give you a call this week.” He held up a hand and waved goodbye.

Lose her number, asshole.

I was fucking losing it. I’d never been a jealous guy. But here I was losing my shit over a dude she might actually like.

“That was great, wasn’t it?” she asked, leaning most of her weight against me as her legs moved more sideways than forward.

After a block of her swaying even more, I turned and picked her up and tossed her over my shoulder as laughter rang out around me.

“What are you doing?” she squealed.

“We’re never going to get home with you moving sideways and forcing me to go in that direction.”

“Fine.” She smacked my ass, which had me howling out in laughter. “I’ve got a nice view over here anyway.”

I turned at the next street, my house coming into view.

“You like my ass, Gracie?” I smirked, even though she couldn’t see me.

“You’ve got a great ass, and you know it.” She sighed loudly. “Shit. Did I ruin your night with that hot girl who was talking to you?”

“Sydney? No. We’re friends.” I walked up the driveway and dug my keys out of my pocket.

“Oh shit. I think this makes me a sex blocker.” She groaned. “Not only am I not having sex, now I’m making it so you’re not having sex either.”

“It’s called a cockblocker, and you are definitely not one.” I laughed as I pushed through the front door and carried her to her bedroom, where I dropped her on the bed. “And I’m glad you had fun tonight.”

I'm also glad that you came home with me.

She landed with a bounce and laughed some more before pushing up on her elbows and studying me. "I had fun, but it was a little bit of a bust."

I bent down and pulled her boots off one at a time, setting them beside the bed. "Why was it a bust?"

I stood up, shoving my hands in my pockets to keep from touching her.

Her hair was a wild mess as it fell all around her face, and one of the straps to her dress had fallen off her shoulder. Her skin was golden, her eyes sleepy, and she fell back on the bed. "Justin tried to kiss me, but I wasn't feeling it."

I made sure to keep my features unaffected, and I acted as if I hadn't watched the whole thing play out and almost made a complete fool of myself by overreacting. "And did he have a problem with you turning him down?" I asked, an edge in my voice.

"What? No. I just said I was feeling sick, because I was." She sprang forward again. "What's wrong with me, Bear? I want to feel something. But it's just not happening."

"Stop overthinking it," I said, dropping to sit on the bed beside her. "I wouldn't expect you to feel anything with Dirk and Justin. I would have thought something was wrong with you if you did."

A wide grin spread across her face. "Because Dirk is a jerk, and Justin is a—"

She was deep in thought, which made me laugh.

"Did Justin tell you his last name?" I asked.

"No? What is it?"

"Loosh. His name is Justin Loosh."

"Your point is?" She searched my gaze, and her strap slipped down even more, exposing the rise of her breast. I jumped to my feet, needing to put space between us.

"Loosh is a douche."

Loud laughter filled the room as she fell back on the bed again. "That's good stuff. Thanks for making it a great night. And thanks for bringing me home. Sorry again for cocking your block."

"It's blocking my cock," I said under my breath. And the only thing my cock was reacting to tonight was my sexy-as-hell, very intoxicated best friend.

The same best friend who had mentioned us taking our relationship a step further.

And now I couldn't think of anything else.

"Get some sleep, drunk girl. Love you," I said as she pushed to her feet and made her way to the bathroom.

"Good night, Bear. Love you more."

Not possible.

CHAPTER TEN

Gracie

A loud drilling sound filled my head.

Pounding.

Banging.

I tried to pull the covers over my head to stop the noise, but it only got louder.

"What is happening?" I groaned.

"Ahhh…she wakes," Cutler's voice called out from somewhere in the room.

I pushed the covers back and peeked one eye open. "Are you renovating your house?"

My voice was barely recognizable.

Groggy and hoarse.

Loud laughter bellowed from him. "No renovations, Jeege.

That's called a massive tequila hangover. Let's get some ibuprofen in you."

He walked toward me with a bottle of water before handing me two little pills. I swallowed them with some water before falling back on the pillow. "I haven't been hungover since college. And even then, it wasn't this bad."

"Well, you usually don't drink so much."

I nodded as I rubbed my temples with the tips of my fingers. "I did have fun, though. Even if I'm still a woman who's never been pleased by a man."

He had just taken a sip of his coffee, and he coughed a few times before a wicked grin spread across his face. "Well, at least you had fun. And you dominated on the dance floor, so that's a win."

I smiled as I thought about how much fun the girls and I had had out on the dance floor. Cutler hadn't felt like dancing last night, and I remembered seeing him and Sydney all cozy at the table together when I was looking for him, and a weird feeling settled in my chest.

Clearly I was hungover, and the alcohol was affecting me in all sorts of weird ways.

I'd seen my best friend with more women than I could count over the years.

And this was why I didn't like to drink so much. I didn't like feeling out of sorts, which was exactly how I felt at the moment.

I shook it off and glanced beneath the covers. "I slept in my dress? My God, how much did I have to drink?"

"I took off your boots, or I think you would have slept in those too." He smirked.

"I don't think this new carefree life is for me," I groaned, which made him laugh.

"Well, it's not for everyone. And, I hate to say it, but you need to rally. We've got to get to the house to meet the cabinet guy. He wants to go over the layout." He pushed to stand. "Buck up, Jeege. We've got shit to do."

"I thought we were meeting him at noon? What time is it?"

"It's eleven thirty. You slept late. But now it's time to get a move on." He leaned against the doorframe, his bicep flexing as it rested beside his head. He wore a navy ROD Construction polo shirt and dark jeans. How did Cutler always manage to look good? It didn't matter what he wore, or what time of day it was—he just looked good.

I hurried to my feet. "Give me fifteen minutes to rinse off in the shower and get dressed."

"You've got it."

He left the room, and I hustled.

I did a fast body shower, brushed my teeth, slicked my hair into a low chignon, and applied just enough makeup so I didn't look like the walking dead. I pulled on a floral sundress and grabbed my tan cowboy boots.

I glanced in the mirror, grateful that no one would be able to tell that I'd consumed more alcohol last night than I probably had in four years of college put together.

Cutler had a banana for me to take in the truck, and we made our way to the new house. The one his family was building. Emilia and I had the design pretty clearly laid out, and now we needed to get all the subcontractors' designs nailed down.

Once we pulled up, we made our way inside. We had a few minutes before we met Calvin, so we walked the home. They'd just finished painting the interior. The flooring had arrived, and it was stacked to the ceiling in the living room.

"We should be starting cabinets next week, so we need to make sure he's got everything ready to go."

"Wow. Things are moving fast. How do you keep everyone on

track?" I asked, because Cutler was such an impressive man. He could charm just about anyone, and he always appeared really laid back, but when it came to work—he was all business.

"You know, I watched my pops do this my entire life, so it's not new to me. I think most people are surprised how many moving parts are happening at once in this business. So if you want to be efficient, you have to think three steps ahead at all times. Otherwise, you're going to drop a ball, and it'll be a domino effect. If you're staying on top of all the balls, even if one drops, you've got six others in the air."

Like I said. He was an impressive man.

"That's why I really want to start my own business someday, because it's all how you choose to run things, you know?" I shrugged as we paused to look out at the the large French doors that had just been installed a few days ago. The house had gorgeous views of both Blue Sky Lake and the mountains. The scene looked like a painting. "I think in design, it's similar with all the moving parts. And you need to involve your clients and capture their vision, and bring it to life as seamlessly as possible."

"Yes," he agreed. "There are different ways to get there, and when you own your own business, you can choose how you want things to run. My goal is to make it as smooth and efficient as I can. Time is money, and delays are where you run into issues and displeased customers. Sometimes you can't avoid it, but I make damn sure that if it can be avoided, it will be." He turned to look at me. "You've got what it takes to own a business. You know that, right? You've got the design eye, which makes you an amazing designer. But you're also a brilliant businesswoman."

I chuckled. This man had a way of pumping me up when I needed it most. "And how do you know that? I've never run a business."

"Well, for starters, you're organized and smart as hell. And I know you, Jeege," he said, leaning in close to me, his gaze locked with mine, and there was no humor in his voice. "I'd bet the farm on you. Well, if I had a farm."

And now we were both laughing, just as Calvin came strolling through the door.

"Hey, Cutler. Hey, Gracie. Nice to see you again." He extended his arm to each of us.

I shook his hand. "Thanks for coming out on the weekend."

"Not a problem. I'm anxious to walk things one last time with you before we start delivering the cabinets for all the rooms starting next week. I think all of your specific direction has made this much easier." He chuckled. "I usually get notes that aren't very clear. Yours were extremely detailed, and with the notes you gave regarding my drawings, you made things very simple for me."

"Thank you," I said as we walked from room to room. He'd be building custom cabinets for the kitchen, the pantry, and the laundry room. He was building built-ins for the family room and the theater room, and he'd designed all the vanities for every bathroom.

Cutler joined us, which was also impressive, because he wanted to be involved in every area of his business. Normally I did this on my own with the cabinet company, but Cutler didn't pass things off—he hired people who were experts in their fields, and then he observed and learned as much as he could about each facet of the business.

We spent the next two hours discussing the details of each room, the hardware, and the glass cabinets we'd added to bring in some character, until we all felt like we were on the same page and ready to go.

It was a good meeting, and I was feeling much better as far as my hangover went.

Cutler and I ran a bunch of errands and then made our way

back to his house. He'd insisted on ordering us some sandwiches that we were going to take out on his boat. I hadn't been out on the water since I'd arrived in Blue Sky Bay, and I was looking forward to it.

"All right, I've got the food and drinks all loaded. I just need my girl, and we're good to go," he called out, just as I pulled my jean shorts on over my bikini bottoms.

A little sunshine, a good meal, and a dip in the lake was the perfect way to end the day.

"I'm ready." I jogged down the hall and found him in the kitchen wearing nothing but a pair of navy board shorts that hung low on his hips. His muscled back was so defined it made me want to trace every muscle with the tip of my finger.

"All right, let's get out there. It'll be busy on the water since it's the weekend, but I've got a little secret cove where we can park, and no one seems to know about it yet."

"You always know of secret spots," I said, bumping my shoulder against his as we walked through the green grass down toward his dock.

His boat was white and black. It was a gift from his godfathers when he'd built this home a few years back, so I laughed every time I saw the name scrolled down the side.

Beefcake.

He hopped on the boat and turned to face me. "You ready to ride the *Beefcake*?"

My eyes widened at his words, and he laughed loudly. "The boat, Jeege."

"Yes, I know. I'm just moving slow today." I bit my bottom lip. "I haven't been on the *Beefcake* in a while."

"Yeah, how about we make a pact that we never go that many months apart again, all right?"

"That's a deal." I nodded as he extended his hand to help me aboard, just as the boat swayed a little to the side and I lost my footing. I fell forward, slamming into his hard chest. His hand found my waist, steadying me, as he glanced down at me with that wicked grin of his.

Why am I suddenly breathless?

"You okay?" he asked, concern lacing his dark gaze.

"Yes." I stepped back, shaking my head. "Hangovers are not my friend."

He chuckled. "I get it. And I'm glad you're here. I've been dying to take you out on the water. It's been too long."

A pang of something I couldn't place settled in my chest.

A lot would be changing after this summer we were spending together.

I knew with me living across the country, it wouldn't be the same as when I was living in Los Angeles and was only an hour away. I'd come to stay with him at least two weekends a month.

But now I'd be a plane ride away. We weren't even going to be in the same time zone.

I pushed the thought away and glanced out at the water as he fired up the engine. I took the seat beside him as we moved through the water with ease. There were a few boats out in the distance, but as soon as he turned down into this little cove, he slowed the boat and cruised forward until he came to a stop under several tall trees.

He turned toward me and then motioned for us to head to the back of the boat, and he grabbed the bag of food.

"I love boat picnics," I said, chuckling.

"Me too." He handed me a bottle of sparkling water, and I set his sandwich down in front of him where we sat on the bench. "Remember all the times we were out on the water as kids? It was always my happy place."

"Yeah, me too. I love the water."

"That's one thing the city doesn't offer," he said, raising a brow.

"I know. But I'll try to come visit as often as I can. The first few months will be super busy, since I'll be expected to do whatever is asked of me as the newbie there. But we'll talk every day." I groaned when I took a bite of my turkey sandwich. "I was clearly hungry."

He chuckled. "Yeah, I ordered these from the Cozy Griddle. They make some damn good sandwiches."

"I remember when we were kids, you used to tell me how someday you'd grow up and have a boat of your own and a house on the lake." I shook my head at the memory, because it was truly amazing that he'd done everything he'd said he was going to do. "And that you were going to run your pops's business someday, and become an architect at the same time. And here we are."

"Here we are." He winked. "And I do recall you saying you were going to be a girl who decorated houses and owned a farm with pigs and dogs and chickens."

"Ahhh… Bob Picklepants was the best dog ever. And I miss Maxine so much. She was the best pet pig. I still laugh at the fact that my father let me have a pet pig who lived in the house."

"Your dad is the best. We had damn good childhoods, considering all the obstacles we faced at the start." He took another bite of his sandwich and reached for his napkin.

"Do you think that was part of our bond when we were young? That we both had unusual situations with our moms? And then ended up with the best moms around, just a little later in our childhoods."

He took a long sip from his water bottle and nodded.

"I think we both had really strong father figures, and then they both married these amazing women, so we had something unique in common. But I don't know, Jeege." He tilted his head, his gaze locking with mine, as the sound of trees bustling around us filled the air. The sky was clear and the sun was shining, but we had just enough shade to keep us cool. "From the minute I met you, we just fit, you know?"

"Yep. We did. And I agree that we both got really lucky finding our mamas a little later than most." I set my sandwich down on the paper. "It's been a while since you've heard from Tara, huh?"

Tara was Cutler's biological mother. They didn't have much of a relationship, but she'd occasionally reach out unexpectedly every few years. He'd been adopted by his mom, Emerson, whom he was very close to.

"Funny you should ask. She reached out while you were in Paris." He scratched the back of his head, which was always a sign that Cutler was uncomfortable.

"What? Why didn't you tell me?"

"Because you were living in another country, and I knew you were struggling. So I didn't want to bring up something that really doesn't matter."

I knew that his relationship with his biological mother still affected him, even with having a woman like Emerson in his life who had stepped up for him. His mother walking away was something that I always thought had caused him to hold back just the slightest bit in his relationships with most people.

Never with me.

And I was thankful for that.

CHAPTER ELEVEN

Cutler

"We have a deal, don't we? Always brutal honesty. I'm never too busy for you, and you know that."

"Well, you weren't completely upfront about what was happening in Paris with that dickhead Gabriel, so I guess we were both protecting one another in a sense." I glanced out at the water. I hated talking about Tara. Hated thinking about her if I was being honest. But this last time had bothered me more than usual.

"Fine. Moving forward, let's not do that." She popped a grape in her mouth. "What did she say?"

"She asked for money."

Gracie seemed surprised by my words, and she looked up at me. "She asked you for money?"

She'd always just called and said she missed me or wanted to talk to me. She'd never hit me up for cash before, but I guess I'd never been in a position to give it to her before.

"What did you say?"

"I sent her the money," I said without hesitation.

She sighed. "How much did she ask for?"

"Two thousand bucks. She said she couldn't make rent and wondered if I'd help her." I cleared my throat. "It's pathetic, really."

"Her coming to her son who she left as a young boy? Yes. It is pathetic," she said, her voice harsher than usual. But it didn't surprise me. We'd always been protective of one another.

It was that ride-or-die type of friendship I'd witnessed my father having when I was young.

I had it with this girl.

"That's actually not what I meant, although you aren't wrong." I chuckled. "I meant that it's pathetic that I wanted to give it to her, because some twisted part of me still wants her to like me, I guess."

My chest squeezed as the words left my mouth.

I wouldn't say this to anyone but Gracie Reynolds.

It was embarrassing as shit to admit that I still wanted to be accepted by a woman who'd turned her back on me. Turned her back on my pops.

I wasn't looking for a mother, because I had the best one around. Emerson had adopted me, and I loved her fiercely.

But I guess the little boy in me still wanted the mother who'd given birth to me to see me and to realize she'd blown it.

To see some sort of regret in her eyes, or hear it in her voice.

It was fucked up, but it was my reality.

Gracie moved her sandwich to the side and scooted closer to me. She placed a hand on each side of my face, and her eyes were wet with emotion. "You're the most lovable person I know, Cutler Heart. And there's no shame in wanting to be loved by the person who is supposed to love you the most. I get it, you know I do. My biological mother doesn't want to acknowledge me, and I've made peace with that. But that doesn't mean it doesn't sting sometimes."

I tugged her closer, settling her on my lap, because sometimes feeling so much and looking at Gracie overwhelmed me. I wrapped my arms around her, tucking her head in the crook of my neck.

"They both suck, don't they?" I said, and she chuckled.

"I guess we really do share a bond." She smiled up at me. "We got really lucky with our moms the second time around, though, didn't we?"

"We did. That's why I think I spiraled when my mom got sick all those years ago. That fear of abandonment was instilled in me at a young age, no matter how many times my pops talked to me about it. And then my mom came into my life, and she was everything a mother should be—and the thought of losing her? It was more than I could handle back then. Hell, I couldn't handle it now."

"She's been cancer-free for many years, so she's not going anywhere," Gracie said, her fingers stroking the inside of my palm in the most soothing way.

"Yeah. And neither are you, Gracie Reynolds."

"Nope. You're stuck with me forever."

"Wouldn't have it any other way," I said.

"Can I tell you something?" she asked, her voice quieter now.

"Anything. You know that."

"Sometimes I feel things when I'm near you." She quickly sat forward and turned to face me. "Not in a weird way."

I raised a brow. "Okay. In what kind of way?"

"Well, you know I'm in this curious stage, right? Like I want to feel something. Explore things a little bit, but I don't know how to do casual. And I can't force myself to have a fling with someone I'm not attracted to."

"Agreed. You shouldn't be with someone you don't want to be with."

"Right. And I think the problem is that I don't want to be with anyone right now. I need to be single and focus on this new job in New York when I leave in a few months. But I also want to experience things, you know?"

I nodded. "I understand that."

"And obviously you and I are best friends. And that will never change," she said, clearing her throat and looking out at the water to avoid looking at me. "And I know I brought this up as a joke the other day, but after thinking about it, it's not really that outrageous of an idea. I mean, there's no doubt you're abnormally good-looking, and I feel safe with you."

"You should always feel safe with me, because I would never do anything to hurt you."

Where was this going? Because if she went there again, and she wasn't joking, I didn't know that I'd have the strength to fight it.

I wanted her.

I fucking wanted her so bad I couldn't see straight.

It wasn't right and I knew that, but it didn't change the fact that I was struggling with these feelings.

She turned to look at me. "I know that. And that's why I wondered if maybe you could show me a few things, you know, not just tell me, but show me how it should feel. You could make me feel good and I could make you feel good."

Her cheeks flushed pink as the words left her mouth, and I didn't miss the way her chest was rising and falling.

She was asking me to touch her, and she wasn't joking this time.

"I would do anything for you. I just don't ever want to do something that would hurt our friendship. So you're going to have to be real clear about what you're asking, and what you want, Jeege,"

I said, noting the way the sun had started to tuck behind the clouds in the distance.

"Listen, we're both very different when it comes to relationships. And we know that. So there's no mystery. No surprises. No one's pretending to be someone they're not. That's why I thought this might be something that would be okay. Like a one-time thing, and we never talk about it again. And I'm not talking about sex—that would make things too complicated, at least for me. And no kissing, because that's intimate in a different way. But maybe just—other things."

Jesus.

Was she actually asking me to be the first man she allowed to taste her?

Because there was no fucking way I could deny her.

It would be something I'd never forget. No doubt about it.

"Do you want me to make you feel good?" I whispered as I leaned close to her ear.

"Do you think it would be weird for us if we did this? Because I would want to make you feel good too—I mean, just the one time." Her words were breathy, and my dick turned to stone immediately.

Was I really going to do this?

I was doing this.

One time.

One fucking time.

"I think we can make our own rules. Nothing could ever happen between us that would change how I feel about you." I tucked the hair behind her ear. "I know you want to feel something, and I want to be the lucky man who gets to do that for you."

She nodded. "And if I'm terrible at this, you have to tell me what to do differently, right? Promise me that you'll be honest with me."

I hated that this fucker had gotten in her head. Hated that anyone had ever made her feel like she was anything less than perfect.

Because to me—Gracie Reynolds was perfection.

I looked up into her dark gaze before reaching for her hand and placing it over my erection. "You haven't even touched me and look what you do to me."

Her eyes widened as her tongue slipped out and dragged along her bottom lip. She stroked me over my swim shorts a few times, and I groaned.

"So we're doing this?" she asked.

"Yes. No sex. One time. And nothing changes between us."

"Thank you, Bear. This is going to make me feel more confident moving forward. I mean, as long as it all works." A nervous laugh escaped her pretty little mouth.

Thank you?

Was she fucking serious?

I was ready to lose it, and I hadn't even touched her.

Tasted her.

I'd been with my fair share of women over the years, but I'd never had a desire to touch someone the way I did right here. Right now.

"Lean back," I said as I pushed to my feet.

"Wh—" Her eyes were as wide as saucers. "What?"

"We're doing this."

"Here? On the boat?"

"Can you think of a better place?" I said, my voice gruff, as I dropped down on my knees.

"What if someone sees us?"

"No one is out here. It's you and me. And if I get to do this one time, I'm going to enjoy every fucking minute. The sun is just leaving for the day, there's a breeze moving around us, and we're hidden in a cove on the most beautiful lake. Top that off with you coming on my lips—it doesn't get any better."

"Holy shit," she whispered under her breath. "We're really doing this."

She started to unbutton her jean shorts, and I wrapped my hand around her wrists. "Uh-uh. You wanted me to teach you, so your first instruction is to sit back and relax. I want to take these shorts off of you, and then peel your bikini bottoms down and see how wet you are for me."

Her breaths were suddenly coming faster.

She wanted to feel good. Wanted to experience real passion.

And I was going to do that for her.

I wanted that for her.

Hell, to be honest, I wanted it for myself.

I wanted to give Gracie pleasure.

We were crossing a dangerous line, and I didn't fucking care.

Because deep down, I was a selfish prick when it came to Gracie Reynolds.

She was my girl.

I wanted this.

I wanted her.

I reached up for the button on her jean shorts, my eyes locked with hers as I slowly pulled down the zipper.

Damn. I wanted to savor every fucking second of this.

The way her cheeks pinked, and her lips parted slightly.

The way her chest was rising and falling, her nipples pebbling beneath her white bikini top the moment I dropped to my knees.

I was hanging on by a thread. I'd never been so turned on in my life.

My dick swelled, straining against the fabric of my swim trunks.

I could hear my heart pounding in my ears.

She raised her hips instinctually, and I slid the denim down her legs before removing her shorts and tossing them aside.

I ran my hand down her calf, raising her ankle the slightest bit before I leaned down and kissed her there, my lips moving up to her thigh and taking my time as I moved from one leg to the next.

Her skin was warm and soft, and the sky darkened above us as I looked up at her.

She shifted slightly, lowering herself as if she was anxious for me to get where we both knew I was going.

The move made me chuckle. She was so eager, and I fucking loved it.

I ran the tips of my fingers over the center of her bikini bottoms, teasing her a few times before slipping beneath the thin fabric.

My dick was rock hard, and I couldn't believe how much I wanted her.

"You're so fucking wet," I whispered, glancing up at her. "You like this?"

She was soaked. Seeing the way she reacted to my touch was the biggest turn-on.

And all I wanted to do was make her feel good.

Her breaths were labored and she nodded, her teeth sinking into her bottom lip.

I slipped her bottoms to the side and buried my face between her thighs, hiking both of her legs over my shoulders at the same time. I couldn't wait another minute.

Not another fucking minute.

I slid my tongue from one end to the other, and she moaned as her hands found my hair.

Good girl.

She was telling me what she liked with her body.

And I was fucking here for it.

I licked and sucked and kissed every inch of her like my life depended on it.

Devouring all that sweetness.

I couldn't get enough.

Her thighs tightened around my head, and I slowed down.

I did not want this to end.

I didn't want her to come yet, because I was a selfish prick and I wanted more.

She was bucking against me, tugging at my hair as a sexy moan escaped her mouth.

My tongue slipped inside her, and I fucked her relentlessly.

In and out, over and over.

"Cutler. Please," she said, her voice strained and sexy as hell as she begged me to give her what she wanted.

What she so desperately needed.

My thumb moved to her clit as my tongue continued to devour her.

The sound of her labored breaths mixed with her moans had my dick throbbing.

Her legs tightened around my head, and my name was a cry on her lips as she went over the edge.

She continued grinding up against me, and I didn't pull back.

I let her ride out every last bit of pleasure.

And when she finally slowed, and I pulled back to look at her, it nearly took my breath away.

Gracie Reynolds just might ruin me in a way I'd never seen coming.

Pun intended.

CHAPTER TWELVE

Gracie

I couldn't move.

Couldn't breathe.

Couldn't speak.

My body was in a state of euphoria.

It wasn't like I didn't know how to pleasure myself, but this was—next level.

This was completely different.

The feel of his mouth on me.

His lips on me.

His tongue.

I sighed as I pushed up on my elbows and studied Cutler, who was still down on his knees, watching me with concern. Like he thought I might regret what we'd just done. He couldn't be more wrong. "That was amazing. I've definitely been missing out. Thank you."

A loud laugh escaped him. "Sure. Happy to service you. You've got one impressive pussy. Shame on any man who didn't take the opportunity to experience it."

My mouth gaped open, and he took his hand and pressed it closed. "Careful, Jeege. I'm hard as steel right now, so if you keep dropping your mouth open, I'm going to offer to put something in it."

My head fell back with laughter as he adjusted my bikini bottoms and moved to sit beside me on the bench.

I slid down onto my knees. "I have the perfect solution."

"I was kidding." He reached for me, attempting to pull me back up beside him. "Let's sit with this for a minute."

"Nope. I know what you're doing, and it's not going to work."

"What am I doing?" he asked as his lips turned up into the sexiest smile.

"You like to do things for me, but I also like to do things for you. This is a one-time deal, and we each get to make the other one feel good. That was the agreement."

But it was so much more than that.

I'd never felt so alive, so desired.

My thighs were slick, and my nipples ached. I was desperate to make him feel the same way he'd made me feel.

"Gracie," he said, tucking the hair behind my ear, "I don't think you understand how much you already did for me when you came on my lips."

I could feel my cheeks heat. "I want that for you too."

"You sure about that? Because once you put your mouth on me, I won't have this kind of restraint."

I licked my lips with anticipation. "That's what I want."

I wanted to see him come undone.

I wanted to make him feel as good as he'd made me feel.

I reached for the tie on his swim trunks and undid it.

"Lift," I commanded, and he chuckled as he pushed up enough for me to tug down his trunks.

And holy eggplant emoji. Cutler Heart wasn't just larger than life in personality and stature.

He had the largest penis I'd ever seen.

Obviously I hadn't seen all that many—however, I'd read a lot of romance books, watched plenty of sexy movies, and seen my fair share of porn.

And this was—something else.

I shouldn't have been surprised, because everything about him was spectacular.

"He obviously likes you," he said, his voice gruff and laced with desire. "Especially when you're staring at him like that."

"Of course you have the most attractive penis." I threw my hands in the air. "I mean look at it."

"I don't need to look. We're very well acquainted." He chuckled, but I could hear the strain behind it.

He was turned on. Very turned on.

I felt empowered that I was having this impact on him.

I would have thought this would feel awkward or uncomfortable, because Cutler was my best friend—but it was the opposite.

It felt natural and easy, and I was beyond aroused as I took him in.

"I've done this a couple of times, but I'm no expert, so just tell me what you like."

He nodded, a sexy grin spreading across his handsome face.

I wrapped my hand around the base of his shaft and stroked him a few times, and he leaned back against the bench. "Just like that."

I moved forward, pushing his legs apart so that I could settle between them. I glanced up to see the heat in his eyes as he watched me.

It fueled me.

I used the tip of my tongue and swirled it around his tip, and his hips jolted in response.

He liked it.

"Yes," he said, voice gruff.

I leaned forward and wrapped my lips around him, taking him as deep as I could. I bobbed my head up and down as my tongue moved along his long, thick erection.

"Fuck, Jeege. That's so fucking good," he groaned, and I had to squeeze my legs together in response.

I had not expected to be turned on while giving him a blow job.

But here we were.

His fingers tangled in my hair as I continued to slide up and down his shaft.

"Now I want you to slide your hand between your legs. I want you to come with me." His voice was deep and commanding.

I did what he asked.

This was what I was here for.

My hand moved between my thighs, and he gripped my hair harder. His breaths were even more labored now, and I moved faster.

He was panting and bucking into my mouth, and an overwhelming feeling was building between my legs.

I looked up through my lashes and found his intense gaze fixed on me, jaw tight and nostrils flared.

It was the sexiest thing I'd ever seen.

And he just stared down at me before tugging on my hair in warning. "I'm going to come."

It was a warning, and one I didn't want to heed.

I stayed right there as a guttural sound escaped his lips.

"Fuuuucccckkk," he groaned as he unloaded in my mouth just as I went right over the edge with him. "Holy fuck."

Lights exploded behind my eyes as my body shook and trembled. I swallowed every ounce he gave me, and I stayed right there, just as he'd done for me.

He stopped thrusting his hips and I pulled my hand from between my legs, stunned that I'd just orgasmed for a second time in the last thirty minutes.

My mouth made a little popping sound when I lifted my head, looking up at him as I wiped my mouth with the back of my hand. He tucked himself back into his swim trunks.

He reached for me, pulling me onto his lap and wrapping his arms around me.

"That was fucking amazing, Jeege," he said, his voice low and gravelly.

"Really? It was good?" I asked, turning to look at him.

His gaze locked with mine, and for a split second he just stared at me, almost like he was seeing me for the first time. The look in his eyes was intense, and he didn't say a word for a beat. My breath hitched in my throat, but I wasn't certain what it meant.

But I knew he'd been affected as deeply as I had.

And then I saw the shift, as if he'd been somewhere else for a moment and had just pulled himself back together.

"Best blow job I've ever had," he said, and his lips turned up in the corners. "You have nothing to worry about, and if practicing on me is what you need, feel free to help yourself as often as you want. I mean, you did say I had a very attractive dick."

His humor was back in place, and I chuckled. "I can't believe we did that."

"We've shared everything else," he said with a wink. "It only seems fitting."

His hand was on my hip while the other was stroking my cheek, and I was stunned that I had such an overpowering desire to kiss him.

That was not part of the deal.

I slipped off his lap and found my jean shorts before sliding them on.

"We don't want to make things weird or cross any lines that we can't come back from," I reminded him.

A lazy smile settled on his face. "How was that for you?"

"It was so much better than I even expected." I shrugged.

"And you came with my dick in your mouth, didn't you?" he said, reaching for his water as if we were discussing the weather.

"Yes."

"That's because it can be a turn-on when you please your partner. You were responding to me, and that's fucking sexy as hell."

I covered my eyes with my hand for a moment as I processed his words.

This was Cutler.

I'd just had his dick in my mouth and my hand between my thighs.

What universe was I living in right now?

Maybe my favorite universe of all.

He pulled my hand away from my face, and his gaze locked with mine. "No hiding. We don't do that."

I nodded. "I was surprised how turned on I was, especially after I'd just had your head between my legs. I didn't expect that."

"Good. And you liked my mouth on you?"

I nodded. "I did. I'm kind of irritated that I waited so long to do that."

"I'm not. It'll live in my head rent-free for the rest of my life."

He leaned back, glancing up at the sky.

I leaned back beside him. “Is it always like that?”

“Honestly?” He paused to think it over. “No. But it’s always good. But this I would describe more like ‘epic.’”

“Epic,” I said, repeating the word with a laugh. “I like it.”

“Your pussy is as magical as you are.”

We both continued staring up at the sky as it darkened right before our eyes.

“Thank you. I feel more confident now about the future.” I sighed.

He stilled for a moment and I peeked up at him, unsure what I’d said to have him going quiet on me.

And then he leaned forward and kissed the top of my head gently. “Good. You should feel confident about everything, Jeege.”

I was grateful that nothing felt different between us.

There was no discomfort or awkwardness between us.

He’d given me what I needed, and there’d been no hesitation.

I was the luckiest girl in the world to call Cutler Heart my best friend.

• • •

Cutler and I had entered a slightly gray area, yet nothing had changed. We’d gone back home that night and acted just like we always did.

And over the past few weeks, we’d worked together, eaten dinner together, and continued our normal routine.

“Are you excited to see Mel?” he asked.

Melody Chadwick was one of my best girlfriends. She was Cutler’s cousin. She and I met when we were young and had grown really close over the years, especially the summers when I’d interned for her aunt Emilia a few years back when I was in college. She was five years younger than me, and I absolutely adored her.

"I am." I glanced down at my phone to check the time. "She should be here in about fifteen minutes."

"You haven't seen her since you left for Paris, right?" he asked as he took a sip of his beer.

"Yep. She was going to come out this summer to visit me, but obviously I left before that could happen." I chuckled as my eyes zoomed in on his large hand, wrapped around the bottle. I noticed things like this on Cutler now.

The size of his hands.

The edge of his jaw.

The bob of his throat when he swallowed.

"Well, I'd rather her visit you here anyway, because then I get to be with both of you." He smirked.

Cutler and Melody had always been close.

"I've noticed you haven't gone out in a few days. It's not because of what happened, is it?" I asked. "Is it awkward for you now because I'm here? I just don't want to mess up your dating life."

I'd basically asked him to please me sexually, and now I was self-conscious that he wasn't going out with other women because he was uncomfortable that I was here. And I'd be lying if I didn't admit that I was relieved he hadn't brought a woman home, even though I knew that wasn't fair of me to ask that of him. I was the one who'd pushed for this, and I was the one to make the rules.

His eyebrow arched. "Are you worried about me, Jeege?"

"I just, you know, I don't want you to feel weird now because I'm staying in your house, and I, um, we did that stuff, and that might have weirded you out, and now you feel guilty to go out."

I was still speaking when he stepped forward and pressed a finger to my lips.

"I'm not weirded out. I didn't go out when you were in Paris. I hadn't been for a few months before that. I haven't had sex in several months, I told you that. I'm just not feeling it." He shrugged. "So, having you come on my lips was the highlight of my year. Watching you take my cock between your lips was a close second. And I know we have these rules in place, and I respect them, because it's what you want. But personally, I have no desire to be with anyone else right now. I wouldn't mind a few more lessons—you know, to make sure you know what to ask for down the road."

My breath hitched in my throat, and I felt my entire body go very still. For a brief second I couldn't tell if the heavy thud in my chest was shock or something more, something I had no business feeling for him. I searched his gaze, desperate to see even a hint that he was teasing me.

He wasn't.

I was about to speak when the doorbell rang.

It didn't ring once. It didn't ring twice. It rang at least six times, and I knew it was Melody.

This was the longest we'd gone without seeing one another in years.

"Mel's here. Stop worrying. I'm good." He kissed my hair and walked past me to get the door.

Leaving me to sit with what he'd just said.

CHAPTER THIRTEEN

Cutler

My cousin Melody was one of my favorite people on the planet. So she and Gracie both being here with me was as good as it could get.

She'd just graduated with her master's degree in psychology and was working for a practice in Los Angeles, where she'd attended college. I knew her hope was to someday open a private practice, but for now, she was happy to be working in a field she loved.

"I'm so sorry I missed your graduation," Gracie said as we all sat outside at the table overlooking the lake. We'd ordered takeout, and we'd spent the last hour and a half catching up.

Melody chuckled as she reached for her glass of wine. "You came to my college graduation. I didn't expect you to fly home from Paris to see me walk across a stage again and do the same thing."

"A master's degree is a big deal," my best friend reminded her.

"You called. You sent a gift. You went above and beyond. I'm just so happy you're back home." Melody set her glass back down and studied Gracie's face for a long moment. "And now that we're talking about it—my problem was never really with Gabriel. I mean, yes, he could be a pompous ass, no doubt about it. But more than that, I just hated seeing you shrink into yourself for someone who didn't see you the way you deserved to be seen."

"Yes. I've heard some version of this from everyone who met him. I wish I'd realized it sooner." Gracie shrugged.

"You were in love, and you were trying to make it work. No one wanted to step on your choices. You're an adult, making your way in this big world." Melody chuckled, her gaze full of empathy as she looked at my best friend. "But I was worried about you because I love you. We all do."

"Well, I'm glad I figured it out before it was too late to get my job back and get my life back on track," Gracie said.

"Please, girl. You're the most on-track person I know," Melody said, turning to me and wincing. "Sorry, BC, you're the second-most on-track person I know."

I belted out a laugh. First, because I loved that she insisted on calling me "BC" because I'd told her to stop calling me "Beefcake" when I was in high school, and this was what she'd come up with. And second, because I was definitely not the second-most on-track person she knew. "Good save, Mel."

"So, you're going to work here on the family house—which by the way, I can't wait to go over there and see the progress tomorrow morning," Melody said. "And then you'll move to New York at the end of September, back at J&J's?"

"Yes. I just talked to him yesterday, and they're excited for me to be there. He's even got an apartment lined up for the first three months, so I can have some time to check out the areas and see where I want to live. Thank goodness they're willing to take me back." Gracie sighed, and it was clear that it was a sigh of relief. I wasn't going to lie, it stung sometimes that she was so anxious to get out of here, when I was so content having her here. But I sure as shit would never be the guy to hold her back from her dreams, even if I was a selfish bastard internally.

Melody squealed. "I'm just glad you're back. And I will come visit you after the holidays, so we can have a real New York girls' weekend."

They both turned to look at me at the same time as I tipped my head back and took a long pull from my beer bottle. "What?"

"The look on your face is not giving 'I'm so happy for you' vibes." Melody arched a brow. "What's that about?"

"What? You're misreading my face." I laughed, but it sounded forced. "Of course I'm happy for her. I'm just not in a hurry. Gracie was gone for a long-ass time, and I've had her back for a few weeks, so I'm just not ready to start counting down her departure date with you two." Did my voice have an edge to it?

What the fuck is wrong with me?

"Awww… You missed your bestie." Melody scooched closer to me on the bench where we sat and wrapped an arm around my shoulder. "But at least she's in the same country as you now."

I chuckled, looking up to see Gracie watching us with a goofy smile on her face. "Yes. It's a lot closer than Paris," she said.

"Damn straight." I nodded. But it wouldn't be the same and we both knew it.

"So tell me, what's the latest with your dating life? Is Gracie the best wingwoman ever?" she asked, arching a brow again as she waited for my response.

"We've been out a few times, and it's the same ole thing. I'm not really dating at the moment," I said, reaching for a piece of watermelon on the platter in the center of the table. "I've been in a dry spell, and it's by design I guess, because I'm not feeling it at the moment."

"It's tourist season. This is usually your favorite time of year," Melody chuckled before gaping at me. "Is the player tired of the game?"

"I hardly think I own that title anymore. It's been a while since I've been there." I smirked.

"I could dissect the hell out of this. You know I love to deep-dive into people's motives and fears. Shall we?" Melody asked, her tone playful as she reached for the wine bottle and filled her glass.

"Sure. Let's hear it, doc," I said, my heart rate picking up a bit at what she might uncover. Because it was becoming abundantly clear that my lifestyle changes were very connected to what was going on in my best friend's life, and Melody wasn't one to hold back. But I straightened my features as I leaned back in my chair, as if I didn't have a care in the world.

"She's already done a deep dive into my dating life, or lack of it," Gracie said, laughing. "It was actually helpful."

"Okay. I'm down to be dissected. Have at it."

"Well, obviously you have typical abandonment issues, based on your relationship with Tara. Your biological mother was not around and has shown up periodically throughout your life, usually for selfish purposes. She's the epitome of a narcissist, and you will instinctually protect yourself from those kind of experiences moving forward. It's the natural thing to do."

"So I avoid narcissists?" I chuckled. "Got it."

"Maybe I should give that a try," Gracie grumped.

"If only we could all avoid narcissists, life would be much easier. But at the end of the day, Gracie and I have a different experience with our situations. It's probably why the three of us have always been so close, because we've all got something in common. We were all raised by single dads who married women who stepped up for us. However, the big difference between what Gracie and I went through versus what you went through is that our moms were never in the picture. So there was no feeling of loss in that sense. We never knew anything different. No one came in and out of our lives and messed with our heads."

"And that means what?" I asked, taking a drink of my beer as I studied her.

My cousin was brilliant, and she knew her shit, so I actually found this interesting.

"Meaning you're cautious with who you trust," she said, holding her hands up to stop me from disagreeing. "Not on the outside, Cutler. You're this fun-loving, charming, bigger-than-life guy. We all know that. I'm talking about an internal voice that reminds you to be careful. The people you're close to—you're very close to. But that's actually a small group of friends that you fully trust. And then you have a big list of acquaintances. People you enjoy but don't go deep with. Hence your dating life."

"Shots fired," I said over my laughter. "You act like I don't do relationships. I've dated plenty. I just don't have any desire to get serious. I'm content with my life. With my work. It works for me."

"And that takes me to the real reason I think you hold back." Melody sighed and turned to look at me. "You sure you want to hear this?"

"Free therapy? Let's do this." My voice was laced with humor, though I was actually curious about what she was going to say.

"I think these deep-rooted abandonment issues have caused you to always be cautious, while hiding it beneath a very charming demeanor. People trust you, Cutler. You are the cautious one. And when your beautiful mama, Emerson, got sick, it triggered every fear you were trying to keep at bay."

"How so?" I asked, my voice more serious now.

"Well, I think you learned a painful lesson that a person who is supposed to love you, like Tara for example, can walk out of your life by choice. But Emerson getting sick was the first time you realized that someone you loved fiercely could be taken from you. And that's terrifying. And there were a lot of scary moments that year. Moments when I remember seeing you appear as a shell of yourself. As if you'd emotionally detached because it was too much to accept that she might not make it." She reached for my hand and squeezed it. "You didn't go away to college—you stayed back and attended every single appointment with her. But then you went rogue when you weren't with her. Drinking and getting into fights. It was a coping mechanism."

I blew out a breath, my chest suddenly tight as I tried to swallow down the emotion lodged in my throat. I glanced across the table to see Gracie's eyes wet with emotion, as if that time in my life had been just as painful for her.

"And then she got better," I said. "Little by little, she fought like the badass warrior she is. And she came out of it even stronger, and thank fucking God, because I can't imagine a world without my mother in it." It was the truth. I loved her with everything I had.

"Right. But I think that's when you changed the way you look at relationships."

"Really?" I shrugged. "I feel like I went back to school that next year, and got back on track."

"Do you remember when you were young, you used to always say you were going to grow up someday and marry Gracie Reynolds." She chuckled. "And I know you were just a kid and it was all in good fun. And you two became the best of friends and never went there—but Emerson got sick before your first year of college, and after that—you never spoke of long-term relationships with women again. Everything was light and casual. I think there's a reason for that."

"Not that I'm just a dude who changes his mind too quickly and hasn't found anyone who knocked him on his ass yet?" I tried to keep it light and playful, but she was definitely hitting a nerve.

"No. I think the reality set in." Her voice grew even more serious and her gaze locked with mine. "You can control who you let into your life, into your heart, by being cautious, choosing people who aren't selfish, who you trust—but you can't control if someone is taken from you unfairly. You can have all the trust in the world in them, and they can still get sick. They can get in an accident and be taken from you. And I think that fear has caused you to put a guard around yourself. You don't want to find a partner, a girlfriend, a wife, because if you loved someone enough to go there and they left you, you couldn't survive it."

My eyes widened and I reached for my beer, drinking the last of it as her words set in.

"Well, look at my relationship with Gracie. I wouldn't survive it if she got sick and left me, but here we are. So how do you explain that? I have many friends and family that I couldn't handle losing, but I don't cut them out of my life." I raised a brow, challenging her.

"Correct. But those were all people who were already in your life. Most of the people you are super close with were in your life before Emerson got sick. And building a future with someone is different. Take Gracie for example," she said, looking between us. "She'll most likely find a partner and start a family with someone at some point. You aren't setting your life up to do that. I think it's fear that's holding you back."

"Not everyone wants that. Gracie and I want different things, and that's okay. I don't think I'd be a great husband or father, if I'm being honest," I said, surprised by the words that had left my mouth.

"I thought you just didn't want those things because you get bored quickly," Gracie said. She appeared offended by what I'd said. "You've never told me you don't think you'd be a good partner or a good father."

"It's never really come up. Everyone wants different things. I like focusing on work. Surrounding myself with family and good friends. Dating and getting to know different women, at least when I'm in a place where I want to do that." I rubbed a hand over the back of my neck. "I'm good at those things. The idea of failing someone I love doesn't sit well with me."

"Boom. There it is." Melody pretended to drop the invisible mic. "It's all fear-based. I think you want things that you're afraid to want."

"And what if we all just want different things?" I pressed. "Not everyone wants the fairytale ending. Some of us have different ideas of what that is."

"You know I support whatever you want, Bear," Gracie said. "But if it's fear that's holding you back, you're robbing yourself of something great. And I can speak with complete confidence that there is no one who would be a better husband and father than you. And that's the truth."

"Look at you two trying to marry me off." I shifted in my seat, avoiding Gracie's gaze, before forcing a laugh. "You need not worry. I'm good, I promise. I'm happy with my life and the way that I've set it up. But I hear you, and I appreciate the insight."

There was a lot of truth to what Melody had said.

I knew that a part of me had changed when my mom got sick. I wasn't in denial about that.

At the time, the thought of losing her was more than I could process.

And sure, I was fairly certain those feelings would cause me to look at life differently.

I was aware of that.

But changing it was a whole different story.

Because I never wanted to feel that again.

CHAPTER FOURTEEN

Gracie

Melody was excited about being here for the Fourth of July, because the celebrations were endless this weekend. This town of ours loved any reason to throw a party, and tourists were out in droves. We'd gone to country music night at Down by the Bay, and the place was going off. It was packed with all the locals mixed with all the tourists who were currently here for the holiday weekend, and to spend time on the lake.

Blue Sky did not take holiday weekends lightly. The entire town was decorated with red, white, and blue ribbons wrapped around all the streetlights on Bay Avenue, and red flower baskets hung from up above. We'd just watched an amazing fireworks show, and now we were out on the dance floor having a good time.

I'd learned my lesson a few weeks ago, so I was not drinking shots tonight. Melody and Jovi were having a good time drinking, and Tatum and I were sticking to beer this time around.

My gaze kept moving to where Cutler sat back at the table. I swear the man didn't need to move off his barstool, and women just flocked to him.

It had always been that way.

He rubbed his hand over his jaw, and I had a flashback of the feel of his scruff between my thighs. It was all I'd thought about over the last few weeks.

His head tipped back with laughter when Sydney said something to him as she sat on the stool across from him.

And I had this sudden, overpowering urge to walk over and interrupt them.

I hated this weird jealousy that I was feeling.

His words last night just before Melody arrived were playing on repeat in my head.

Having you come on my lips was the highlight of my year. And watching you take my cock between your lips was a close second.

He'd also said he had no desire to be with anyone else right now, which had caught me off-guard. I was terrified that I'd made him uncomfortable, but apparently, he was totally fine with what we'd done.

He was a guy who was used to casual relationships.

I was the one with all the hang-ups.

Tatum bumped into me when she shifted to the right. I quickly pulled myself out of my daze and moved along with the group as Tyler Childers belted out lyrics about whiskey easing his pain and everyone sang along.

Jovi and Melody were completely off the beat, which made me laugh.

When the song came to an end, Tatum hooked her arm through

mine as we walked off the dance floor. It was a perfect night, with warm weather and a light breeze moving around us.

"Don't worry about Cutler. He's not interested in Sydney," Tatum said as she leaned close to my ear, making sure no one else heard her. "I've watched her try time and time again ever since she and her ex broke up, and he never bites. I think he only sees her as a friend."

I startled at her words. "I wasn't worried. He's my best friend. He can do whatever he wants. I've seen him with plenty of women over the years."

She studied me for a long moment. "So you'd be fine if he went home with her?"

A pit settled in my stomach, and I pushed the thought away. "Of course I would."

"Oh, okay. I thought I was picking up on something, but maybe I misread it." She pulled out her stool, and I took the seat beside her. My gaze moved around the table to see Sydney standing between Cutler's legs, her hand on his chest.

Why did that bother me?

I had no right to be bothered.

I shook it off and took a sip of my beer as Melody came up and leaned her head on my shoulder. "I had too much to drink. I think I'm going to be sick."

I pushed to my feet, reaching for my crossbody purse. "I've got you. Can you make the walk home?"

"Yes. I just think I probably need to leave now so I don't hurl in front of everyone."

I nodded. "Let me just tell Cutler."

I walked over to him and stood beside his stool, feeling like I was intruding on a moment.

"Hey, sorry to interrupt—" I cleared my throat, and he turned to look at me, a lazy smile on his face. "I'm going to get Melody home. She's had a little too much to drink and she's not feeling great. Just wanted you to know."

"I can come with you," he said as he started to move, but Sydney put her hand on his chest.

"You promised me a dance, Cutler Heart. They are two grown women—I'm sure they can walk a block or two alone," Sydney said before wincing when she looked at me. "No offense."

"None taken. She's right, enjoy yourself. We're totally fine on our own." I held my hand up to wave, and I saw the struggle in his eyes, but he nodded.

He'd had more to drink tonight than he'd had since I'd been back. I'd felt like he was a little distant this morning, and I think whether he wanted to admit it or not, the things Melody had said last night had affected him.

And tonight, he was going to drink and have a good time and probably go home with Sydney to prove a point that he was fine with the way that he lived his life.

And maybe he was.

We all wanted different things, and that was okay.

But I wasn't going to lie—I didn't love seeing Cutler with a woman.

I really never had.

Even when I'd been in relationships, I'd always felt a weird heaviness in my chest whenever I'd see him leave a bar with a woman. It was selfish and it made no sense, but I'd never liked it.

I said a quick goodbye to everyone, and Tatum, Jovi, and I made plans to meet for lunch tomorrow.

"Come on, Drunkody," I said as I wrapped an arm around Melody, and we started walking home.

"Drunkody!" Her head fell back with a laugh. "I'm going to

regret this tomorrow when I have to drive home, aren't I?"

"You're still young enough that you will probably rebound just fine." I chuckled as we walked along the dirt path along Blue Sky Lake.

"I hope you're right," she said with a sigh. "Do you think Cutler will go home with Sydney?"

Her words were slurring a bit as we walked toward the door. "Probably."

"I heard her call him out, and she was irritated, but I guess she got over it." She followed me inside the house, and I filled a large glass with water and grabbed her some Tylenol.

"Called him out for what?" I asked.

"Let's have leftover pizza. I'm hungry, and I'll fill you in," Melody said as she hopped up on the stool at the island.

I pulled out the leftover pizza and put a slice on a paper plate and popped it in the microwave for her. "She can't be too bothered, because she was all over him."

"Well, I think that's the problem." She leaned forward with this goofy smirk on her face. "She's. All. Over. Him."

I chuckled at her theatrics as I gave her a hot slice of pizza, popped one in the microwave for me, and dropped to sit on the stool beside her. "That's not unusual for Cutler."

"Well, she noticed that *he's* not all over *her*." She groaned after taking a bite. "This is what I needed."

"This will help your hangover too. It's good to get food in your stomach."

"Good point. Anyhoo," she said as she reached for her water bottle, and her gaze locked with mine, "remember when I went back to the table to ask Cutler to order me and Jovi another shot?"

"Yes. The one that probably put the final nail in your coffin," I said with a laugh. I grabbed my slice from the microwave when it dinged.

"True. But my point is…she was giving him a hard time that he kept watching you on the dance floor, and his eyes should've been on her." Melody tossed her hands in the air, all fiery and bothered. "If I'm with a man and he's watching another woman, I'm not demanding his eyes be on me. I'm walking the hell away because his eyes aren't on me."

My chest pounded a little faster at the thought of him watching me, but I played it off. "She's being ridiculous. He was not watching me. And we were all out on the dance floor, so how does she know who he was watching?"

"Well, from what I heard before I walked away, she felt like he'd been watching you all night, and she made it sound like it wasn't the first time." She shrugged as she pushed off her barstool. "He always has been slightly obsessed with you. He was such a sad sack when you moved to Paris."

We finished eating our slices, and I stood and carried our plates to the trash.

"He's my best friend. I missed him too. I can't believe that I actually thought Gabriel was going to be my person, you know?" I shook my head, still stunned by how badly everything had gone.

"Maybe your actual person has been right under your nose all along," Melody said, the booze still making her words slur slightly.

I didn't comment.

Most people didn't understand my relationship with Cutler.

I didn't care, because it worked for us.

"Let's get you to bed, Drunkody," I chuckled, and her head fell back with loud laughter as I walked her down to the opposite side of the house to the guest room. After we got her changed and her teeth brushed, I set a glass of water beside her bed, and I swear she was already snoring when I turned the light off and pulled the door closed.

I made my way to my room and took a quick bath, then tied my hair on top of my head before slipping into my pajamas. I glanced at my phone to see it was after midnight and Cutler wasn't home. He might not be coming home at all.

I cringed at the thought as I slipped beneath the covers.

What if he brought Sydney home with him?

What if I heard them having sex?

Now my stomach wrenched.

I didn't close my door, because we never slept with our doors closed and I wanted to hear him come in.

I blocked out all those thoughts of Cutler and Sydney together and squeezed my eyes closed.

But I was wide awake, my mind reeling from what Melody had shared with me.

And that's when I heard the door open and close, and heavy feet coming down the hallway.

No way he could have slept with her that quickly.

Well, if he was like my college boyfriend, Carter, it would've been possible.

I chuckled internally at the thought, because I knew Cutler wasn't that guy.

I kept my eyes closed, pretending to be asleep when I heard his feet stop moving outside my door.

"You awake, Jeege?" he whispered as his footsteps came closer, and I could feel him bend down beside my bed. "Did I wake you?"

I chuckled and opened my eyes. "No, but it's not for lack of effort."

He smelled like whiskey, and he had a goofy smile on his face highlighted by the little bit of light from the moon coming through the sliver in the blinds on the window.

"I wanted to leave when you left." I could tell that he was drunk by the way his words slurred.

"We were fine. Did you have fun with Sydney?" I asked, feeling my throat tighten as the words left my mouth, because I wasn't sure I could handle his response right now.

It made no sense that I was feeling this way, but we'd entered a gray area, and I was trying to work through it without making things weird.

"No. I told you I don't want anyone else. And fuck, I tried. I tried to get into it. I'm just going through something," he said, and I could hear the struggle in his voice.

I sprang forward, putting my hand on his cheek. "Hey. It's okay, Bear. You don't have to try to do anything. I'm not forcing myself to like anyone right now either."

"I missed you when you left."

"I missed you too. But we only left about forty minutes ago," I chuckled.

"I meant when you were in Paris. And I guess I meant tonight too. I like you being here, Jeege." He shifted where he was squatting beside the bed and fell down on his ass, laughing in the process.

"You're drunk. Let me get you to bed." I sat up and tossed my legs over the side.

"Can I sleep in here with you? I don't want to be alone tonight." He had this lazy smile on his face that was so sexy I had to squeeze my thighs together in response.

"Of course you can. It's not like we haven't slept in the same bed hundreds of times. You just shared a bed with me in Paris." I leaned down and pulled off his boots, one at a time, before extending my hand to him and pulling him to his feet. He walked around the bed, and I lifted the covers and he climbed in. He was fully clothed.

This wasn't weird at all.

We were best friends.

So why did it suddenly feel so hot in here?

I moved to the other side of the bed and climbed in, rolling on my side to face him.

"I never want to lose you, Jeege," he said in a slurred whisper.

"You never will."

"I hated being so far away from you." His hand moved to my hip.

"I'm right here." I scooched closer, loving the feel of his big, warm body against mine.

"Do you know what I like to fall asleep dreaming about?" he asked.

"Tell me."

But the sound of his breaths told me he wasn't going to finish that thought.

He was already asleep.

And I closed my eyes and breathed him in as sleep took me.

CHAPTER FIFTEEN

Cutler

I opened my eyes to see Gracie sound asleep beside me. Lucky for me, I rarely got hangovers.

She stirred the slightest bit beside me. Her long hair was in a knot on top of her head, with long black lashes framing her closed eyes. Her lips looked like pink rosebuds, and the strap of her white pajama top had slipped down her arm, exposing her golden skin.

My chest squeezed as I took her in.

Goddamn, I loved this girl.

I climbed out of bed and pulled her bedroom door closed behind me. I looked up to see Melody at the end of the hallway, coming toward me with a cup of coffee.

The big smile on her face made it clear that she'd noted what room I'd just stepped out of. "Well, good morning to you, BC."

I chuckled, keeping my voice low. "It's not what you think."

She handed me the coffee mug. "This was for Gracie, because I assumed you spent the night out. But obviously, you did not."

"Get your mind out of the gutter," I said as I followed her down the hallway toward the kitchen. "I slept with my clothes on. I came home drunk, and we were talking and I fell asleep in there. It's not like we haven't shared a bed many times."

But that was all before I buried my head between her thighs a few weeks ago.

And now that was consuming my thoughts day and night. The way she'd looked while down on her knees with her lips wrapped around me. The little groans she'd made before she came on my tongue. Her dark eyes sated as she'd met my gaze, her lips parted the slightest bit, before a lazy smile settled on her face.

Fuck me.

This was my best friend, and I was currently doing everything in my power to stick to the plan. I never wanted to do anything to mess up our friendship. The ball was in her court, and she was making the rules right now, and I needed to respect that.

"You're very lucky I'm currently fighting the worst headache, or I'd have a lot more questions for you." She moved to sit on a barstool, and I took the one next to her.

"You can ask me anything. There are no secrets here. You're reading into it."

"Okay, I've got a marching band currently performing a full concert in my head, and I need to get on the road because I have a meeting later this afternoon in the city. But I'll leave you with this to ponder," she said, taking the last sip of her coffee and walking her mug to the sink. "Do you think there's a possibility that the reason you don't have any desire to hook up with other women is because your best friend is here in town? Could those two things be related?"

"I'm proud of you, Mel. You're an impressive therapist. Clearly you're always working." I chuckled. "And of course the two could be related. I missed my best friend. So much so that I wasn't even going out when she was living in Paris. This isn't new—it started months ago. And now that she's here and staying with me, why would I want to go out when I can hang with her? It's really not that deep."

"Keep telling yourself that, BC." She came around the island and kissed my cheek. "I'm going to go jump in the shower. Love you."

"Love you," I said as she disappeared down the hallway, leaving me with my thoughts.

I sat there sipping my coffee and thinking about my night.

Sydney had offered me a no-strings-attached night in her bed.

An offer I normally wouldn't have been opposed to.

But I couldn't do it.

I couldn't fucking do it.

I didn't want to.

I'd wanted to get home. Where I knew Gracie would be.

I didn't know what the fuck any of it meant. I knew that she was my best friend. I knew that we had crossed a line. And I knew that I wanted to do it again.

I was self-aware enough to know that I was going through something, and it was making me look differently at my life.

This was Gracie.

I could say anything to her.

I was going to talk to her. Maybe she was feeling the same thing I was feeling.

"Bear!" she yelled, and I heard her feet running down the hall.

I turned on my stool as she lunged right into my arms.

"You are not going to believe this," she said, stepping back with a big smile on her face as Melody came running out of the room because she'd obviously heard the excitement.

"What's going on?" Melody and I asked at the same time.

Gracie held up her phone. "I had a missed call from Johnny this morning, so I just called him back."

"What did he say?" I reached for my coffee and took a sip when she stepped back.

"They just signed a huge client that he's been telling me they were dying to sign. Apparently, he bought two huge condos in a high-rise, and he wants to knock the walls down and make it one big place," she said, shaking her head with disbelief. "Well, he not only signed with J&J, but they also gave him the links for all the designers in the New York office, and they included mine because this project won't start until the beginning of October. And guess who he chose?"

"Could it be you?" I asked, my voice laced with teasing.

"It's me. He picked me." She had the biggest smile on her face, and it was a reminder that she was leaving, and she was excited about it.

"That's my girl. Already have your first client and you aren't even there yet."

"So proud of you," Melody said as she locked eyes with me, and I forced a smile. I'd never do anything to dim Gracie's light.

I pushed to my feet and wrapped my arms around her. "Congrats, Jeege. This is amazing news."

Melody came over and pushed her way into the hug. "I can't wait to come visit so we can live our *Sex and the City* dreams. You are going to crush it in the Big Apple, Gracie girl!"

We all laughed, but mine felt forced.

Because now I definitely wouldn't be telling her about the way I'd been feeling.

That would just confuse her.

And I wasn't a selfish prick. Not where she was concerned.

• • •

Another week had gone by, and I'd been swamped at work. Gracie had taken on a few more jobs with our clients, because Blue Sky Bay was a small town and word traveled fast.

Everyone knew she was doing design for ROD Construction temporarily, and they all wanted her guidance.

She was busy with my family's home (which was moving along quickly), the Petersons' place, and a few small jobs for local homeowners who wanted to do updates on different rooms in their houses.

We grabbed a late lunch at the Cozy Griddle to talk about all the projects we had going. We ate burgers and shared a milkshake before Gracie dragged me to an antique store in town for some pieces for the Peterson project.

"This is what I'll miss most when I leave for New York," Gracie said as she perused the back of the large store. Personally, I'd never come in here before now. I knew Wanda Waters, the woman who owned the place, but antiquing wasn't really my thing.

"Not me? You're going to miss Wanda's antiques?" I laughed as I reached for the very aged cowboy hat sitting on a table and placed it on my head.

"Of course I'll miss you most." She paused to meet my gaze. "But I'm talking about design. It's a different vibe there. Modern. Sophisticated. It's cool and chic and I love it, but my heart is truly in this sort of old-world style with lots of history and character pieces."

So then don't leave.

It wasn't a crime to think it. It was a crime to say it out loud.

But I could think it as much as I wanted to.

"You'll be fine. You'll be the queen of sophisticated design."

"I can adapt to any type of design. But designing a style that you connect with is always the most fun. That was the whole point of owning my own business when I moved to Paris. I could take on my own style, you know? But this is the next-best thing, so it's a step in the right direction." She reached for a mask on the table, and she glanced around to make sure no one was looking.

I chuckled. Obviously no one was looking, because we were the only people in the place, aside from Wanda, who was currently out front taking a smoke break.

She pulled the mask over her eyes, and I kid you not, my dick went rock hard at the sight of Gracie wearing a sexy-as-shit black cat mask.

She picked up the whip beside it and swung it around.

"What kind of antiques store is this?" she asked with a wicked grin on her face.

"The kind I actually like. In fact, let's take two to go. This is my new favorite store." I tugged her close and rubbed my scruff on her neck as her head fell back in a fit of laughter.

She peeled the cat mask away and set it on the table before putting the whip beside it.

"I actually wanted to talk to you about something," she said as she bit her bottom lip.

I took the hat off my head and set it on the table. "What's up?"

"Well, I'm leaving at the end of September, right?"

Don't fucking remind me.

"Yes. I'm excited for you." I crossed my arms over my chest.

"Are you excited to get your house back to yourself?"

"You know I love having you there." I kept my voice even, making sure I hid all the things I was feeling about her plans to go to New York.

"So, here's the thing, Bear." She stepped closer. "You're in a weird place, right? It may or may not have something to do with me shacking up with you and making you uncomfortable to bring women home, but either way, you haven't been dating or seeing anyone."

"Correct. And I'm good with that."

"Well, I had all these plans for a fling, but there just isn't anyone I'm interested in."

Ouch. Tell me how you really feel.

"Slim pickings here, huh?"

"I mean, I told you that night on the boat that no one else makes me feel anything, outside of you. You know, because of our connection."

"Right. It's a strong connection," I reminded her.

"And I'm leaving in a few months, and this was sort of my time to, hmmm…explore things." She cleared her throat.

"And so far you haven't gotten to explore more than my lips between your thighs," I said, my voice teasing.

Her eyes went wide once again, and I fucking loved how easy it was to get her all flustered.

"Be serious, Bear." She swiped her tongue out along her bottom lip, and I couldn't help but stare at her mouth.

"Continue," I said.

"What if we extended our deal. You know, we're already living together, which makes it very convenient. We're both always home at night, so it's not like we're seeing anyone else. Unless you are and you aren't telling me?"

"When would I be doing that? Of course I'm not." I shrugged, keeping my voice even, though my heart rate spiked at the suggestion to extend our deal.

It shocked me that she wondered if I was hooking up with anyone else. It was obvious that she didn't have a clue how fucking difficult it had been for me to be sleeping across the hall from her, wanting her the way I did.

"So we could maybe agree to continuing with Operation Exploration," she said, her cheeks turning a darker shade of pink than usual. "And if you decide you want to see other women, we just end the agreement immediately, because that's where we'd run into problems."

Other women?

When I was with Gracie, no one else even existed. I didn't think about anyone else. Only her.

"Let me make sure I'm understanding the agreement. We can fool around, like a friends-with-benefits type of thing, as long as neither of us are seeing other people? Because that works both ways."

"That's not a problem for me. You're the one with a shorter attention span." Her eyebrows shot up playfully, but I wasn't paying attention to her teasing at the moment.

"I assure you my attention is focused on you right now. And that means I'm all in. And for you? No other men," I said, voice low, deliberate. "Not while I have this time with you. When I'm with you, I want all of you—every kiss, every touch, every taste, every inch. You're mine…for now."

My God, even saying it didn't quiet the image of her in my mind.

Her lips parted, her chest rising and falling. "So we could do this for as long as we feel like it's working, and when I move away, we just pretend it never happened and go back to being besties without the benefits."

"Fair enough. But I have some stipulations," I said, reaching for the whip on the table and running it along the inside of her thigh as she sucked in a breath.

"Tell me," she whispered.

"Tits and lips. I want both." My eyes roved over her chest,

trailing slowly up to her mouth.

"What does that mean?" she asked, words strained and breathless.

"It means that I want to kiss you. I can't fool around without kissing. It's not intimate." My hands flexed as I fought the urge to pull her close and kiss her right here, right now.

"I thought that was the point?" she asked as she bit her bottom lip.

"Well, we're changing the rules. And this is a deal-breaker for me." I met her gaze head-on. "I get to kiss you when we're together."

I moved the point of the whip higher up beneath her denim skirt and stroked along her core as she gasped. "Okay. We can kiss when you want to. As long as you don't think it will make things weird between us."

"Gracie. We're in an antiques store, negotiating our friends-with-benefits contract, while I'm stroking a whip between your thighs. I'd say we passed 'weird' when we walked through the door."

"Fair enough. So kissing is on the table. And what is it that you want with my boobs?" she asked, a little moan escaping her lips when I used the edge of the whip to stroke her clit.

I already knew the answer to that question.

Because I'd be eating Gracie Reynolds's pussy for dinner if we could get these terms ironed out.

"It's open season with your tits. I get to see them. Kiss them. Lick them. Fuck them." I pulled the whip from between her thighs and moved it to her breasts, where I circled each of her perfect tits.

Again, with her mouth dropping open.

And she clearly noted the expression on my face, because she clamped it closed immediately.

"Okay. Deal. But I think we should keep sex off the table. That might be pushing things too far. But maybe we decide as we go on that one?" she asked, her voice husky and laced with need.

"We can leave it off the table for now. We've got plenty to work with." I leaned forward, speaking against her ear. "Let's go."

She nodded, her gaze lingering on my hand when I set the whip down.

CHAPTER SIXTEEN

Gracie

"Do you think we should write the terms down so that we don't cross any lines?" I asked as I pulled a notebook and a pen out of my backpack on the bench in his mudroom and followed him into the kitchen.

I. Was. Freaking. Out.

Yes, I'd suggested we continue with this arrangement of ours, but I hadn't expected his response to be so…sexy. So detailed. As if he'd been thinking about this every day, just like I had.

And now it was happening.

It. Was. Happening.

So, my nerves were on edge thinking about what we were going to do, and I needed some form of control in this situation.

A notebook and pen were usually the answer.

His lips turned up in the corners. "I don't know, Jeege. I usually just sort of go with it. I've never written up terms before hooking up with someone."

"Well, you aren't hooking up with *someone*. This is me and you. That makes everything different, right?" I sat on a barstool and flipped to the first page in my notebook, noting the way my hand trembled the slightest bit. "Rule number one, there is an expiration date. That's important, right?"

"Obviously." His heated gaze took me in, and his tone was laced with sarcasm, making it clear that he thought I was being ridiculous about writing up the rules.

I was going to enter the grayest of gray areas with my best friend. We needed to have clear lines in place. It was only logical.

"September thirtieth will be the last day of our agreement; however, we can terminate the contract at any time before then if we choose to." I tapped my pen on the pad of paper a few times before jotting it down, looking up to find him watching me. Dark eyes, and a sexy-as-sin smirk on his lips. I forced myself to stay focused. "That means, if you happen to meet someone you're interested in, and you'd like to explore things with another woman—our deal ends immediately. We don't want to complicate things."

"All right. Same goes for you. I won't be sharing you with anyone else."

"Okay. That works for me." I felt my cheeks heat, and I could swear my palms were suddenly sweaty, so I quickly turned my attention back to the notebook and jotted down number two. "But I do think it's important to be very clear. Everything is on the table, aside from sex, right?"

He leaned back slightly, and my pulse skipped a beat when his lips curved into that slow, deliberate smile that always made my stomach do strange things.

"I mean… Are you asking me?" His gaze held mine, and I could feel the warmth in his eyes. The way that he was entirely focused on me. "You know I'm a fan of sex," he said, but there was a softness there too. "But I'm more interested in what makes you comfortable. What makes you feel good. Everything else—every inch of you, every thought, every desire, every moment—if you're feeling it, I'm all in."

My breath hitched in my throat, and I was suddenly desperate to lean closer, even though I was nervous. Everything about him right now—the tone of his voice, the heated look in his eyes, that slight movement as if he could close the distance at any second—had me thinking in ways I wasn't supposed to.

My hand was shaking so bad that I settled my other hand over it to make it less obvious. I'd thought making this list would calm my nerves, but looking at him now, hearing the words coming from his mouth, it was impossible to think straight.

Focus, Gracie.

"I think sex would complicate things. At least for me it would." I blew out a breath, because the thought of experiencing good sex for the first time in my life was definitely intriguing. But we were already playing with fire. Rules were put in place for a reason, and my gut told me this was one I should stick to.

"Then it's definitely off the table. But everything else is fair game." His lips lifted in a teasing curve, and I squeezed my thighs together in response. He was ridiculously sexy. Unfairly sexy. He pushed to his feet, his movement fluid, confident, and my eyes couldn't help but follow. He walked to the door and looked outside at the night sky, tilting his head back, letting the moonlight catch the edge of his jaw. "Let's go for a swim," he said, and there was that low, intoxicating edge in his voice. "I love jumping in the lake before bed."

My stomach fluttered—every glance, every word from him felt like it was meant just for me.

And that was dangerous.

I desperately tried to keep it together, clearing my throat before holding up the pen for him. "Okay, let's just both sign this, and we can make changes or additions as we go if we see fit."

He walked toward me, showing all the confidence in the world with each stride as he closed the distance between us. He took the pen from my hand, his fingers grazing along mine and lighting a fire in me just from the simple touch.

He signed it without hesitation, and I signed my name beneath his before he motioned for the back door.

"I need to go grab my swimsuit," I said, turning toward the hallway, but then he wrapped his large hand around my wrist.

"My backyard is completely private. No swimsuits. Everything is on the table, remember? So let's start with a little skinny-dipping." He dropped my wrist and walked backward toward the door. "Isn't this what Operation Exploration is all about?"

"You want to go skinny-dipping?" Why did my voice sound three octaves higher than usual?

"I do." His voice was gravelly. "Trust me. You'll enjoy it, Jeege. Unless you're afraid to be naked with me?"

For a moment I thought I'd stopped breathing, and I blew out a breath to pull myself together. My pulse raced, and my body heated in a way I'd never experienced.

I was going to do this.

I was going to skinny-dip with Cutler, and allow myself to do whatever I wanted.

I cleared my throat, tipping my chin up. "I'm not afraid. I just don't love cold water."

His tongue swept out to wet his bottom lip, and I had to force myself not to react. "Trust me. You won't be cold for long. Come on."

I followed him outside. The leaves on the large trees in his backyard were rustling in the slight breeze, but it was still warm outside. It was dark, and I tipped my head up, taking in all the stars in the sky.

It was so peaceful out here—something I'd miss terribly when I moved to New York. Los Angeles was always loud and bustling, and I'd craved the quiet that I'd grown up with when I'd lived there. The quiet that you usually found in a small town where there wasn't traffic and the sound of horns blaring at all hours.

We made our way down to the dock, and the dark blue water looked almost black. The only light was coming from the stars and the moon, along with a few of Cutler's patio lights in the distance. He didn't hesitate as he tore his tee over his head, giving me a perfect view of his muscled chest and chiseled abs. And then, before I could process anything, he tugged his shorts off right along with his briefs, kicking them to the side as he stood completely naked in front of me.

He just grinned and raised a brow as if he was waiting, and I stood there gaping at him.

My God.

The man was just—not normal.

His body was complete perfection.

And his penis was as impressive as it had been a few weeks ago.

"I'll meet you in the water, Jeege." He turned, giving me a spectacular view of his hard, muscled ass, just before he dove into the water. He came up to the surface and shook his head and howled. "It's great. Get in here."

My breaths were shallow, and I forced myself to pull it together as I yanked down the straps of my tank top, then shimmied out of my jean skirt as it fell in a puddle on the deck beneath my feet. I unsnapped my bra, glancing in the water to see Cutler standing with his elbows resting on the deck and his eyes on me.

Watching me.

The heat and want and desire impossible to miss in his gaze.

I let my bra fall and then used my thumbs to tug my panties down my legs, kicking them to the side.

I am really doing this.

I wanted to experience things that I hadn't experienced, and jumping in the lake at night naked with a man was definitely not something I'd ever done before.

A ladder was attached to the deck, and I turned around, chuckling internally that my ass was just a foot away from his face. As I took the first step down, his hands found my waist and he pulled me down, submerging us both beneath the water. I used my arms and surged to the surface as I gasped and laughed at the same time.

"Not nice, Bear." I splashed water at his face as I moved my arms and legs in circles to keep my head above the surface, while he stood with ease. I pointed my toes and tried to touch the bottom, but Cutler had almost a foot on me, so only one of us could reach the bottom, and it certainly wasn't me.

"Listen, Jeege. You tried to enter the water the same way you write contracts. Very slowly. I'm an impatient man."

He looked ridiculously sexy with the top of his chest exposed, his dark hair pushed away from his handsome face as water droplets fell down his cheeks.

I was working hard to stay afloat, and he stepped closer. "Stop being stubborn and hold on to me."

"I'm not being stubborn," I said, my breathing labored, because yes, I was being stubborn. "I thought I would try to get some exercise in. You know I love to multitask."

I reached for his shoulders, still keeping my body a few inches away from pressing against him as I locked my gaze with his.

He smirked. "I think you're afraid to be naked with me."

"Why would I be afraid to be naked with you? I'm the one who came up with this plan."

"I don't know. You tell me," he said. His voice was smooth like silk, and he oozed confidence. "Are you afraid of the way that I make you feel?"

I sighed. "No. I like the way you make me feel. We've just never been naked in front of one another since we were kids."

His hands moved to my hips, his tongue moving slowly along his bottom lip. "Can I touch you?"

"Yes," I said, and it came out all breathy and embarrassingly needy.

He pulled me against his body slowly, my breasts pressed to his chest, and my legs wrapped around his waist on instinct.

Wow. This was proving even better than I'd imagined, and we hadn't done anything yet.

So why am I breathing so heavy?

His hands moved up my back before tangling in my long wet hair. He wrapped the ends around his hand and gently tugged my head to the side before his lips found my neck. My body immediately came alive, but I forced myself to breathe.

And then he moved his lips to the other side of my neck, taking his time as he gently trailed across my skin. He moved along my collarbone, his breath warm, as if his lips were cataloguing every single inch of me. I was desperate for his mouth to be on mine as my head fell back and my breaths grew more labored.

But he took his time, and I'd never been more turned on in my life. When he pulled back to look at me, his eyes searched mine, and I felt like he could see every thought I'd ever tried to hide. As if he could see just how badly I wanted him right now. My heart thudded against my ribs, loud enough that I was certain he could hear it, feel it.

He leaned in slowly, just a whisper closer, and I couldn't breathe. My lips tingled with anticipation, and I felt it as every single nerve came to life. His nose brushed against mine, tentative, gentle, like he was testing the water. I could feel the warmth of his face against mine, the soft rise and fall of his chest. My hands hovered on his shoulders as I hesitated. Unsure where I should touch him, my pulse racing as the world around us melted away.

His hand came up to the side of my face, pushing the wet hair behind my ear as his calloused fingers traced along my jaw.

"I want your mouth on mine. Now," he said, his voice commanding and gruff.

I leaned forward, and his mouth crashed into mine. It was frantic and needy, my lips parting as his tongue slipped inside, tangling with mine.

Cutler definitely knew how to kiss.

It was urgent and needy as our teeth clashed, tasting, exploring, as if we couldn't get enough.

My fingers tangled in his hair, tugging him closer.

His hands found my hips, shifting me the slightest bit as he glided me slowly at first, up and down his erection. I was basically dry-humping this man in the water, and I was too turned on to be embarrassed about it.

I nipped at his mouth and moaned as I ground against him shamelessly.

My body was acting of its own volition now.

He pulled his mouth from mine, and I missed his lips immediately.

He just watched me with this heated gaze in his eyes as he

continued guiding me up and down.

Over and over.

It was the most erotic experience of my life.

"Look how fucking sexy you are grinding up against me," he said, his voice deep and gravelly. "Use my cock, just like that."

I leaned down, needing to feel his lips on mine again, and I moaned into his mouth as I moved faster. Greedily chasing my own pleasure.

Our tongues tangled, lips desperate to get closer, and this building pressure between my legs was almost overwhelming.

My head fell back on a gasp as I exploded, nails digging into his shoulders as bright lights exploded behind my eyes, and I continued grinding against him as I rode out every last bit of pleasure.

My body was still tingling when my breathing finally slowed, and I opened my eyes and looked down at him.

"Hey," I said.

"Hey, beautiful. How do you feel?" His lips turned up in the corners, and he looked so incredibly sexy it nearly took my breath away.

"I'm a big fan of skinny-dipping, Bear," I whispered.

"Yeah, me too, Jeege. Me too."

"I'd say this first lesson was a big success," I chuckled.

"Agreed." He wrapped his arms around me tighter. "If I can make you come once a day while we're doing this, then it's a win."

"I want to return the favor," I said.

"You don't even realize how much pleasure I just got out of that. Tonight isn't the night for returning the favor. But trust me, Jeege. We're just getting started."

I smiled at the insinuation.

Because I was here for it.

I was here for all of it.

CHAPTER SEVENTEEN

Cutler

Brody: *Are you still good to pick up Clover today, Heart?*

Me: *Yes. Gracie and I are leaving here in ten minutes to come pick her up.*

The guys and I took turns spending Saturdays with Brody's daughter, Clover, because he typically needed to be at the container park on Saturday afternoons, and it was the one day that he didn't have his nanny. I looked forward to spending the day with her once a month.

Brody: *Appreciate it.*

Bass: *I'm at the restaurant today, so stop by with the little nugget if you're downtown.*

Me: *Gracie and I are going to take her to the diner and then stop in Snow Balls for her favorite ice cream. We'll drop by and see you.*

Phoenix: *Bring her by the firehouse too. I miss my girl. I don't miss any of you fuckers, but I always miss Clover.*

Cannon: *She's a chick magnet too. But seeing as Heart is always with Gracie, I don't think women are going to be hitting him up.*

Brody: *Way to use my daughter to get women.*

Cannon: *Hey, Clover's my girl. But if women find it sexy that I've got the cutest girl in town hanging out with me, so be it.*

Bass: *It's slightly opportunistic but it works for you.*

Cannon: *I'll take that as a compliment.*

Phoenix: *I don't believe that was a compliment.*

Bass: *Heart, can you stop by my place this weekend? The shower keeps backing up and I think it's a plumbing issue, probably due to Jovi's fucking hair clogging the drain. But I tried pouring shit down there, and it's not working.*

Cannon: *Wow. I just pictured Jovi in the shower naked. Not a bad way to start my day.*

Bass: *Fuck you. Get your filthy fucking thoughts away from my sister.*

Cannon: *Did you not just tell us that she was naked in the shower?*

Phoenix: *Quit while you're ahead, dickhead.*

Bass: *Dude. Do not fucking joke about Jovi. The girl is going places, and it's not here in Blue Sky Bay.*

Me: *I'll stop by tomorrow and take a look at the pipes.*

Phoenix: *You live on a houseboat. Your pipes are probably shit.*

Cannon: *I think you've all got shit pipes. Fairly certain I'm the only one that has a pipe that works really well. <eggplant emoji> <winky face emoji>*

Bass: *You set him up for that one, Nix. <head exploding emoji>*

Me: *My pipe has always been solid. <winky face emoji>*

Cannon: *You just don't use it anymore? Or are you keeping secrets from us?*

Phoenix: *I was kind of wondering the same thing, I'm just not a dick so I didn't want to ask.*

Brody: *Don't flatter yourself. You're a complete dick. But I think we're all wondering the same thing.*

Bass: *Have you crossed into a gray area, my man?*

Me: *I don't know anything about a gray area, boys. I'm just living my best life over here.*

Phoenix: *What kind of bullshit answer is that?*

Cannon: *It means he's definitely in a gray area. He and his pipe are up to no good.*

Brody: *Since when do we keep secrets?*

Bass: *There's only one person he would keep a secret for, and we all know who that is.*

Me: *You're all ridiculous. On my way to your place now, Brody.*

They weren't being ridiculous. I was being secretive, and they fucking knew it.

We didn't keep shit from one another.

But I was in a very gray area.

We weren't having sex, so it wasn't as gray as it could've been.

"Why do you look perplexed?" Gracie asked as we walked side by side. Brody's house was close to downtown and not far from me, and it was a nice day, so we were walking.

Clover liked to walk, and when she got tired, she loved for me to pop her up on my shoulders. Gracie knew her, but she hadn't seen her since she'd been back in town, as the last few weeks had been busy for both of us. She was anxious to see her, since Clover had grown so much over the last year.

"I'm not perplexed. I'm actually very relaxed," I chuckled, glancing over at her with a smirk.

She laughed and shook her head. "I think we're both relaxed. We've got ourselves a nice little arrangement."

"Don't use the word 'little' with our arrangement," I said with a loud laugh.

"Fine. We've got ourselves a nice big arrangement."

I glanced down at her, not able to hide the smile on my face. "You surprised me when you came into my shower after we got out of the lake last night."

"It only seemed fair. I mean, I had a feeling I knew what you were going to do in that shower, so I thought I'd give you a hand," she said, smiling up at me as her cheeks turned a dark shade of pink.

"Literally and figuratively."

She'd shocked the shit out of me when she'd knocked on the bathroom door and asked if she could join me. And she'd used her hand to do exactly what she'd known my hand was about to do.

She was a quick study.

Because skinny-dipping with Gracie Reynolds was beyond any fantasy I'd ever had, and I couldn't wait to get in that shower after we'd come back inside.

The way she'd glided up and down my dick, all desperate and needy.

Dry-humping with this girl was better than sex with anyone else.

And kissing her—fuck me.

We probably shouldn't have gone there, because I wanted my lips on hers any free moment I had now.

But I had to be careful: I couldn't push too hard. I wanted her to call the shots and feel in control of this situation. So we'd watched a movie after the shower and kept our hands to ourselves, which took every bit of restraint I had.

We turned the final corner, and she peeked up at me, her teeth sinking into her bottom lip. "I liked it. The lake and the shower."

"Good. We can do that as often as you want."

"Well, now I feel like I'm the desperate one. Do you want to do it, or are you doing this as a favor?" she asked, and I could hear the doubt in her voice. I reached for her hand to stop her from moving forward and pressed her back against the side of the tree beside us.

"A favor? Are you fucking serious? Did it seem like a favor when I groaned your name in the shower last night?" I said against her ear, nipping at her lobe.

I pulled back, and she searched my gaze. "No. But why am I the one who initiates when we—you know, do stuff?"

"Because I'd have bent you over the kitchen counter already if you'd been down for that. You're the one who wants a contract and rules. I'm the one who's following your lead."

She tucked her lips between her teeth and then blew out a breath. "So you'd have sex with me without hesitation?"

I caught myself smiling before I could stop it. God, did she really think I was just some horny asshole, ready to throw myself at anyone? Did she not know that it was just her?

Only her.

The thought made my chest tighten in a way I couldn't explain.

I didn't want to read too much into it. Didn't want to scare her with how much she occupied my thoughts. So, I played it off, letting a playful grin spread across my face.

"Without hesitation?" I echoed, voice light, teasing. "My only hesitation is you, Jeege. I don't want to do anything that doesn't feel right to you. But yeah, I mean, we were dry-humping in the lake, and you gave me a hand job in the shower. And we had a whole lot of fun on the boat a few weeks ago. So, sex wouldn't be a big jump for me personally. Do I want it? Do I think about it every fucking second I'm around you? Fuck yes." I chuckled. "But I'll do whatever you're comfortable doing, because you're my girl, and that's how this works."

I realized how often I'd found myself taking her in, without even thinking about it. Not in a lecherous way—it was never about that. But in the quiet, impossible-to-ignore way she moved. The way she laughed.

The way she existed.

The tilt in her head when she smiled, the little gestures she didn't even notice. It had become a habit, these stolen moments I took, each leaving my chest tight, my heart a little heavier with something I didn't fully understand.

I'd catch her looking my way sometimes and wonder how I'd

gotten so damn lucky that she was in my life.

It terrified me that I was having these feelings. Feelings that I wasn't supposed to have.

She just wanted me to show her a good time.

This was a recipe for disaster.

She nodded. "I'm going to think this over. I just don't want to get attached, you know, physically. We're best friends. I'm leaving in a few months."

There she went again. Reminding me about the expiration date on our arrangement.

But I watched her, trying to catch the little tells, the flicker in her eyes, or the slightest quiver in her voice. Her hands rested casually, her expression neutral, yet I could swear there was something behind her words that she wasn't saying.

"All right, let's go get Clover and stop talking about sex," I said. "I can't be all horned up when we're picking up my goddaughter."

All four of us were godfathers to Clover, and I loved it because my dad's best friends had done the same thing for me when I was young.

They were family, and I'd grown up with them, and I wanted to do the same thing for Clover.

When we arrived, Brody thanked us both profusely before hurrying out the door to get to work. Clover Quinn Stark was four years old, and quite possibly the cutest child on the planet. Her light brown hair fell around her shoulders in ringlets, and I chuckled as she sat on Gracie's lap, telling her about her favorite ice cream.

"My uncle always gets me all my favorite ice creams from my Snow Balls if I eat my lunch real good," she said. "Right, Uncle Cutty?"

"Yes, ma'am, Lucky Clover. Should we get walking?" I asked as she pushed off of Gracie's lap, and I took her hand and led her out the door.

They both happened to be wearing yellow sundresses and sneakers, and Clover had already gasped and chuckled about the coincidence. They looked cute as hell, and I couldn't wipe the smile from my face.

"Gracie, I like your name, do you like my name, because it's Clover. Clover Quinn Stark but Uncle Cutty calls me his Lucky Clover, 'cause sometimes I'm his lucky girl. And I think you're a lucky girl too, 'cause you're uncle Cutty's bestie, like my bestie is Pippa, and I calls her Pippa Mint because my favorite ice cream is peppermint," she said, all in one breath.

The girl hadn't talked much until she turned three, and once she started, she had a lot to make up for.

Gracie and I each held one of her little hands in ours as she walked between us, and I chuckled at how much she'd just shared because she was cute as hell.

"I love your name so much, and I love peppermint ice cream too," Gracie said. "And yes, Uncle Cutty is my bestie for sure."

"Well, I feel like I won the lottery spending the day with my two best girls," I said as we walked into the Cozy Griddle, which was her favorite place to eat.

We ate lunch, and she told us all about her plans to go kayaking with her daddy tomorrow, which was her favorite. And then we stopped at Snow Balls for ice cream, and I was always grateful that the owner, Sandra, allowed Clover to put three flavors into her one scoop.

Peppermint. Lemon. Strawberry.

Not a combo I would choose, but she was very passionate about her three choices.

We then walked around downtown and stopped by to see Bass

and Phoenix, and it was a full afternoon.

"Do you gots any kids, Gracie?" she asked as we walked toward her house.

"I don't. But someday I hope I do."

"You feels like a mama," she said. "My uncle Cutty isn't a daddy, so he says I'm his little girl too."

"Yeah, he talks about you all the time." Gracie smiled down at her, and I could swear my fucking chest tightened. Because I could watch these two all day long.

"He talks abouts you too," Clover said, giggling. "I wish you could stay here with us forever."

Me too.

"I promise I'll visit a lot."

"Uncle Cutty is gonna be's sad. But he can be my bestie with Pippa Mint." She looked up at me with those big green eyes.

"Thanks, Lucky Clover. I've got my two girls. That's all I need." I winked at her as the front door pulled open, and Brody filled the doorway.

"How much ice cream did they give you?" He raised a brow, his voice filled with humor.

Brody was a damn good father, and if I ever did decide to have children, I'd take a lot of what I'd learned from him, mixed with the fact that my pops was the best dad I could have ever asked for.

"Just one scoops, daddy. With three flaveys." She held up four chubby little fingers instead of three and then concentrated hard until she figured out how to push one down.

We all laughed, and I scooped her up and nuzzled her neck. "Love you, Lucky Clover."

"Love you, Uncle Cutty," she said over a fit of giggles.

And then she reached for Gracie, who pulled her into her arms. "Thanks for the best day ever, sweet Clover."

"You're my bestie too, Miss Gracie." And she kissed her cheek.

Gracie shook her head and smiled. "Besties forever."

Brody took her into his arms and thanked us several times, and we made our way home.

I could get used to this.

Just hanging with my girl.

Lunches and friends and making memories.

Working together and creating beautiful homes.

Laughing until my stomach hurt.

Skinny-dipping in the lake together.

Yes. I could definitely get used to this.

CHAPTER EIGHTEEN

Gracie

I was setting out the appetizers when Cutler came around the corner and picked me up off my feet before setting me on the counter. "It's game night. You don't need to do all of this."

"I love a good party—you know that."

He studied me for several beats, as if he was trying to memorize every line and curve on my face. "You're so fucking beautiful, Jeege. You really do take my breath away, at least when you stand still long enough for me to look at you."

My breath hitched in my throat. It wasn't like he didn't tell me he thought I was attractive often, but it was the way he'd said it.

The way he was looking at me.

For a man who didn't do serious relationships—he was all sorts of green flags.

Thoughtful. Passionate. Funny. Attentive.

I mean, I was going to have my work cut out for me finding a serious boyfriend to compare to my temporary lover and best friend when I left here.

"You take my breath away too, Bear." It was the truth. "The women in Blue Sky Bay would hate me if they knew they were being deprived because of my temporary needs."

He chuckled, stepping between my legs. "No one else matters when it's you, Jeege."

Our gazes locked, and then he leaned down and kissed me. It wasn't fast or needy this time. It was slow and tender.

And then he pulled back and walked to the refrigerator and grabbed us each a beer.

I tracked his movements with my gaze.

The way his arms flexed as he popped the tops off the bottles.

The way he handed me my beer and then tipped his head back as the cool liquid moved like silk down his throat.

We were careful when it came to our relationship, all while staying true to his promise to make me feel good every night, and I stayed true to mine to return the favor. We'd make out until our lips ached most nights. Explore one another's bodies. Shower together occasionally. Skinny-dip when we felt like it.

But we always ended in our own rooms, and we hadn't discussed taking things further and crossing that line and having sex.

But I thought about it all the time.

It consumed my thoughts.

I worried about bringing it up because I'd told him that might make things complicated for me, and he'd probably worry that I'd grow too attached to this situation.

This very temporary situation.

If we could walk away from this, and remain best friends, and not have any weirdness afterward—it would be a win.

My goal was to have something casual. A no-strings-attached, hot, sexy fling.

I'd managed to do it with a man I trusted immensely.

Would it make me greedy to ask for more?

I knew he'd said he thought about it often too, but he'd never asked for it. And we both knew he was used to having a lot more sex than I was. Sure, we fooled around every night, but I was sure he had needs that he'd been neglecting for me.

"What's going through that head of yours, Jeege?" He grabbed a carrot stick off the platter I had sitting on the counter and popped it in his mouth.

"I was just thinking about your needs."

He tipped forward a bit with laughter and then flashed me that sexy smile. "My needs, huh?"

"Yeah. I'm sure you have needs, right?"

"Sure." His tongue swiped out along his bottom lip. "And they're all being exceeded at the moment."

"But you must want more? You must be dying to have sex, right?" I shrugged. "I mean, you don't appear moody or irritable, but maybe you're struggling on the inside."

"I'm not struggling on the inside." He chuckled and then raised a brow, stepping closer. "Are you struggling, Jeege? Do you want this cock inside you?"

I gasped, just as the doorbell rang, and I heard him chuckling as he walked away.

Maybe I was struggling.

He'd been the best teacher I could have asked for.

I'd had enough orgasms to set me up for a lifetime. At least once a day since we'd started this agreement, and on several evenings he'd doubled down and given me multiple orgasms in one night.

Maybe it was time to make an amendment to our contract.

I hopped down off the counter, just as Jovi, Bass, and Tatum walked into the kitchen.

"You're not sick, are you?" Tatum asked. "Your cheeks are all flushed."

Jovi placed her hand over my forehead. "You don't feel feverish."

Cutler had a wicked grin on his face as he moved past me and grabbed beers for everyone.

"No, I've just been running around, getting everything ready." I cleared my throat before hugging them one by one, just as Phoenix, Cannon, and Brody walked in.

We all got our drinks, and we brought a bunch of appetizers outside as we settled around the big outdoor table. Game night was one of my favorite things to do, and back when we were in college, I'd tortured most of these guys and made them play many times. Jovi, Tatum, and Cannon were new to my favorite pastime, but they were excited about any excuse to get together, drink beer, and sit outside by the water.

"So the first game is Taboo," I told them. "We need to get into groups of two, and then your partner has to give you clues, but you can't say any of the words on the card you choose, so you have to be creative."

"I'm a visual learner," Cannon said over a mouthful of nachos. "I need to see someone play."

"Yes. His listening skills are less than impressive," Phoenix grumped.

"Are you still pissed off about the raincoat mix-up?" Cannon rolled his eyes, and all the guys fell back in laughter.

"Dude. I asked if you had a fucking raincoat that I could borrow for a hike for a team-bonding thing for the firehouse. You brought me a box of condoms." Phoenix shook his head in disbelief.

Cannon's lips turned up in the corners. "Lots of people refer to condoms as 'raincoats.'"

"Why would I need condoms to go on a hike with my fucking coworkers?"

"I never hike without condoms." Cannon shrugged and then winked at Jovi, who was sitting next to him laughing, and Bass glared at him. "You never know who you'll run into. And I brought you the magnums. A little ego booster. So, you're welcome."

"I'm done talking about this. The guys had a field day with it, and I'm sure that's why I ended up in bed with the flu last winter, because I'd been forced to hike in the rain without a fucking raincoat." Everyone was laughing now, aside from Phoenix, who took a pull from his beer and then glanced at me and Cutler. "Let's have the pros do a round, and then everyone can see how it's done."

"Great." I pulled out the buzzer and glanced at my best friend. "I'll read and you guess?"

"Sure. Tatum can do the buzzing," he said, and we explained that she needed to make sure I didn't say any of the words that were listed on the card, and if I did, she'd hit the buzzer.

She nodded. "I've got this."

"Okay, I'm starting the timer." I cleared my throat and pulled the first card. "Your uncle Ro won the title in this sport."

"Professional boxer."

I smiled. One down. I pulled the next card.

"I had one of these growing up, and her name was Maxine."

No hesitation at all as Cutler smirked at his friends. "Pet. Pig."

Cocky, but justified.

Next card. Hmmmm… This one was a bit more tricky, only because the clues listed on the card limited what I was allowed to say. I took just a beat to think, and it came to me quickly. "First part of your nickname growing up."

"Beef." His gaze locked with mine.

"Name you called Dirk when he flirted with me."

"Jerk." He smirked. "Beef jerky."

"Yes." I pumped my arm in the air. I pulled the next card. "Okay…happiest place in the world?"

"Disney World."

"And what is my favorite thing to eat there?"

"Cotton candy, Jeege." He smiled. I wasn't allowed to say 'theme park' or 'Disney,' so this was a way around that.

Next card. "This was a famous man, and his last name is my mom's first name."

"Elvis Presley."

I nodded as we got a few whistles and laughs.

"Damn. Could these two be any more in sync?" Cannon laughed.

We still had time on the clock, and I reached for another card.

"First concert I ever went to." I raised a brow at my best friend.

"Backstreet Boys."

I was laughing hysterically as I reached for another card because the time hadn't run out yet.

We were absolutely killing it.

"'Show me the money!'" I said in my best theatrical voice.

"Jerry fucking McGuire," Cutler shouted, just as the timer rang and he jumped to his feet and high-fived me.

"They got seven on the first try." Jovi was shaking her head and smiling at me. "I don't think that's the norm."

"Boom. That's how it's done, my friends." Cutler sat back down and reached for his beer.

"Well, shit. None of us are going to be this good at it." Brody threw his arms in the air.

"Phoenix is your brother, so I'm guessing you two would do

pretty good," Tatum said as she pursed her lips. "And Bass and Jovi have that sibling advantage, so I'm guessing Cannon and I are going to be the weak links."

"Speak for yourself, Tater Tot. I'm never a weak link. I've got you, girl." He winked, and Tatum fell forward laughing.

Cannon was a serial flirt, and Phoenix rolled his eyes and glared at him. "She's too young for you. Get your filthy thoughts out of the gutter. I say we split the teams up so no one has an advantage like what we just witnessed."

Tatum only laughed harder. She and Phoenix had grown up together, and she was one of the few people that I'd noticed he wasn't a total grump to.

"For the record, Nix, I'm a year younger than you." She shot Phoenix a warning look.

"And he's older than me."

"I'm a year older than you, you wanker." Cannon howled in laughter. "Always so protective of Tater Tot."

Phoenix shot him the bird as Cutler came up with a plan.

"Let's break up the teams. I'll write everyone's name down, so pick a name, and as long as it's not your own, that's your partner." He tore some paper out of the notebook, and I quickly helped him write everyone's name down and folded them up.

We broke into teams.

Me and Bass. Cutler and Tatum. Phoenix and Cannon. Jovi and Brody.

And I'd never laughed so hard in my life over the next hour and a half.

Phoenix and Cannon were up one last time, and they'd already fought endlessly on their last few turns.

"I'll ask the questions this time," Phoenix said.

"Good. I'm better at answering than asking," Cannon said, and

I tried not to laugh because Phoenix was already annoyed with his partner.

"I'll do the buzzer for you," I said.

Cutler started the timer, and Phoenix pulled the first card.

"When you were a sophomore in high school, this happened to you."

"I had sex with Sophie Miller," Cannon said, leaning back in his chair confidently with a wicked grin on his face.

"How would the card know that you had sex with Sophie Miller?"

"No clue, but it was a good year."

"Focus, dickhead. Try again," Phoenix grumped, and we all laughed because they were hilarious together.

"I won my first bull riding title that year." He nodded.

"Again. The game would not know that."

"You said it happened to me sophomore year," Cannon said with a smirk. "So the game knows something."

"It is not that. Should I pull another card?" Phoenix asked, clearly agitated.

"Fuck that. We're not quitting." Cannon stroked his thumb and pointer finger over his jaw. "I also had sex with Taylor Walters. I got suspended for streaking on the football field on a dare. Thank you very much for forcing me to do such an offensive act, Brody, you big dickhead."

The buzzer rang.

"We got no points." Phoenix threw his hands in the air. "Not one fucking point."

"Your clues were lame, my dude. Step up your game. What was the answer?"

"Bee sting. You got stung by a bee your sophomore year of high school." Phoenix glared at him.

"Big fucking deal. Lots of people get stung by bees. I hardly remember it."

"You had an allergic reaction. I was with you," Phoenix snapped. "I had to call 911, you fucker. It was a big fucking deal."

"When did you get so sensitive?" Cannon stuck his finger in his mouth and then shoved it in Phoenix's ear, and before I knew it they were wrestling on the ground.

Two grown men.

One was laughing, and the other was trying to feign annoyance, but he finally gave in and laughed before he pushed to his feet.

We spent the next hour playing Pictionary before we decided to call it a night.

And every time I looked up, I found Cutler's eyes on me.

We had a conversation to finish, and I knew he wasn't going to let it go.

And I had no intentions of letting it go either.

It was time to adapt our contract.

CHAPTER NINETEEN

Cutler

I was still laughing when I closed the door, because Phoenix was still pissed off about Cannon and him getting last place in Taboo.

"That was fun," Gracie said as she set the plates in the sink.

Did she really think we were going to make small talk after what we'd discussed just before everyone arrived?

I sidled up behind where Gracie stood at the sink, my hand moving around her, brushing against her side as I dropped a few glasses in the sink. My mouth grazed against her ear as I spoke. "Yeah. It was a good time."

"We crushed it in Taboo, didn't we?" she said, her words sounding a little breathless now.

"Yep. We're clearly in sync." I smirked when I stepped back. "Even our bodies are in sync."

“Is that normal for you?” she asked as she turned off the water and dried her hands.

“Nothing that we’re doing is normal for me.” I shrugged, because it was the truth. “And I fucking love it. I wouldn’t change a thing.”

“You wouldn’t change any of the rules?” she asked, her voice teasing, and it was sexy as hell.

I tugged her against me, stroking the hair away from her face. “Well, if I’m being honest, there wouldn’t be any rules if it were up to me. But you’re calling the shots right now. This is your time, Jeege. I support that.”

“Leave it to me to have something casual and make a ton of rules anyway.” She shook her head with a laugh. “What’s the point, if it’s supposed to be light and fun?”

“Listen, I love everything we’ve got going. I know you aren’t staying. I know what this is. You know what this is. So maybe you just stop trying to control it and do what you want. We’re best friends. Nothing we’ve done has changed anything, right?”

“Right.” She chewed on her thumbnail. “So do you want to remove the no-sex rule?”

Damn, I loved this girl something fierce.

“I would love to burn the rule book and bury myself deep inside you for the next few months until you leave,” I said, my voice gruff.

“I want that too,” she sighed. “It’s not like we both haven’t done it before. And it’s not like we haven’t showered together and been naked together almost every night since we came up with this plan.”

“Agreed.”

“I think everyone already suspects something is going on after the way they acted tonight,” she said, teeth sinking into her bottom lip.

This was Gracie.

She was working through the idea.

She wanted it. She knew I wanted it. But it terrified her because this wasn't what was supposed to happen.

My girl liked a plan.

And I understood that, because I understood her.

I chuckled. "They definitely know something is up. And I know we agreed not to tell anyone, and I do understand not sharing this with our families because it would be a big fucking deal—but our friends are different."

She studied me. "What do you mean?"

"They aren't going to put pressure on us or ask a million questions. And it's getting uncomfortable when we're all out, you know, keeping this secret."

"Why?" she whispered, eyes wide and curious.

"Because I don't want to pretend to talk to random girls or watch some dude dance with you. You're here right now. We're always together. And then we go out, and everything has to shut off. I don't like it."

"That's fair. I just didn't want to add any pressure to the situation." She blew out a breath. "But I'd be lying if I said I didn't want to scratch out Sydney's eyes when she was all up in your business the other night when we were out."

"So how about we change the rules," I said. "We do whatever the fuck we want while you're here. We're good with the arrangement and we don't need anyone else's approval."

"Agreed. But I do think keeping this from our parents is smart, because that's where we'd feel the pressure. They'd have a lot of questions." She chewed on her thumbnail some more as her gaze locked with mine.

She was right. They'd have a shit ton of questions. Questions I sure as shit couldn't answer, because I didn't know what was happening between us.

This was not familiar territory for me.

But this was Gracie, so everything was different.

"Okay." She tipped her head back and smiled. "Have your way with me, Cutler Heart. Show me what I've been missing."

"Isn't that what I've been doing?" I smirked.

"Yes. But no more holding back. No more rules. I'm all in." She sank her teeth into her bottom lip, and her cheeks flushed.

That was all I needed to hear. I reached behind her, my hands covering her perfect little ass, and I lifted her up. Her legs came around my waist, hands tangling in my hair as she chuckled.

"Get ready to have your world rocked, Gracie Reynolds."

A wide grin spread across her pretty face. "You've been rocking my world since I got here. I would expect nothing less."

I carried her down the hall to my bedroom and dropped her on the bed, and she bounced the slightest bit, her hair falling all around her. I climbed onto the bed, hovering above her.

"You know you're my best friend and I love you, right?"

Gracie Reynolds was the only girl or woman outside of my mother that I'd ever said those words to. And I'd been saying them to her for over two decades.

I felt it.

I meant it.

"I know you do. And you're my best friend and I love you too. Always have. Always will." She smiled, her eyes wet with emotion.

"Same. And this isn't too much for you?" I had to make sure. This was Gracie, after all.

She was my person.

The girl I loved most in the world.

I'd never forgive myself if I did anything to fuck this up.

She shook her head no. "You're my best friend, Cutler. And

I want this. I want you. I know it's not forever, and I'm okay with that because that's the last thing I want right now. And in our own way, we're forever. And right now, we're filling something for one another, and I don't want to question that."

My mouth crashed into hers.

Tasting and exploring and claiming.

My hand slid behind her neck, tipping her head back the slightest bit to take the kiss deeper, our tongues tangling in a desperate dance of need and desire.

I'd never wanted anyone more.

Needed anyone more.

I pulled back, kissing my way down her neck.

My fingers moved to the straps of her sundress, and I slid them down her silky skin.

I paused when I realized she didn't have a bra on, and I pulled the fabric down, tracing over her pretty pink nipples. "If I'd known you didn't have a bra on, I would have dipped my hand into your dress hours ago."

"This dress has built-in cups," she said, a mix of labored breaths and humor.

"Do you know how much I love these tits?" I asked as I leaned down and flicked her hard peak with the tip of my tongue before circling one and then the other.

"Tell me," she said as she arched her back, making it clear that she wanted more, and I fucking loved it.

I couldn't get enough.

I made my way down her body, taking her dress, which was pooled around her waist, with me. I slipped it down her legs and dropped it on the floor as I reached for the edge of her white lace panties and slowly removed those as well.

I leaned down and buried my face between her thighs.

I'd done this enough times now that I knew exactly what she liked. I flattened my tongue, pressing it against her core, and slid it slowly back and forth as she groaned.

Her fingers tore at my hair, tugging as she writhed beneath me.

I fucking loved it.

The way she wanted me.

The way she needed me.

I could stay right here for the rest of my life, and I'd be a very happy man.

I slipped a finger inside her as I leaned down and sucked her clit hard.

"I want you inside me right now," she moaned.

I pulled back to look at her, and I nearly came undone just at the sight of her lips parted as her breaths came hard and fast. Her heated gaze met mine, and I saw it all right there. Her passion. Her desire.

She wanted this as much as I did.

"I want you to come on my lips and then you'll get my cock." I added a second finger and then leaned back down and covered her clit with my mouth and sucked hard.

She bucked against me.

Over and over.

"Please," she begged, and I smiled against her as I pumped my fingers in and out faster before flicking her clit with my tongue, just as her body started to tremble and shake.

Her thighs tightened around my head, and I savored everything she gave me as she went over the edge. I stayed right there until her breaths had slowed and then pulled back, slipping my fingers into my mouth and moaning.

"Holy shit," she whispered.

"You know what, Jeege?"

"What?" A sexy grin spread across her gorgeous face as dark hair fell all around her.

"If I found out my life was going to end tomorrow, and I was asked to choose my last meal… I'd just park myself between your thighs and leave this earth a happy man."

Laughter bellowed from her, and she reached for the button on my shorts. "I want you naked. Now."

"I love when you take charge," I said. I pushed to stand, tugging my shirt over my head and dropping my shorts and briefs on the floor before moving to the nightstand to grab a condom.

Gracie propped up on her elbows and whistled. "I could look at you like this all night, Cutler Heart."

I tore off the top of the foil packet and rolled the latex over my throbbing cock. "Yeah? You like the look of me right before I bury myself inside you?"

She bit her bottom lip and nodded.

I climbed back on the bed with her and quickly maneuvered her to settle on top of me, so I was lying on my back, and she was straddled above me.

Her hair was a mess of wild waves tumbling over her shoulders. Her plump pink lips parted just slightly as my hands flexed on her hips.

I catalogued every curve of her face, the way her eyes were heated and flanked in long black lashes. I wanted this image, right here, right now, burned into my brain for all eternity.

She gasped, eyes wide as she looked down at me. "What are you doing?"

"You're going to set the pace, baby." I tucked her hair behind her ear. "We're going to do whatever feels good for you."

She smiled, eyes heated. "I want it to feel good for you too."

"I already feel good and I'm not even inside you yet." I tugged her head down, and our mouths fused in a red-hot passion that I'd never experienced.

Need and desire so fierce that I struggled to stay in control.

Our naked bodies pressed together as I kissed her senseless.

I needed her like I needed my next breath.

Our tongues tangled as she ground her heat up and down my erection. I was so hard, my dick threatened to explode. But I stayed right there, my hands tangled in her hair.

We kissed until our lips ached, and she pulled back, hair falling down over her perfect tits. She wrapped her hand around my dick and lifted up just enough to settle the tip at her entrance.

And then she slid down.

Slow.

Inch by inch.

Her breath hitched, and I covered her breasts with my hands. "Breathe, baby."

Her eyes opened and locked with mine and she did as I asked.

Taking me in even further.

Nothing had ever felt this good.

Nothing compared.

I groaned when she pushed down, and I filled her completely.

I didn't move. She didn't move.

She reached for my hands, our fingers intertwining as she adjusted to my size.

And then she did the sexiest move of all. Her lips turned up in the corners, teeth sinking into her juicy bottom lip, and she started moving.

Up and down my shaft.

It was pure ecstasy.

This woman was made for me.

I sat forward, my lips sealing over her hard peaks as I moved from one breast to the other.

Our bodies were covered in a layer of sweat as we found our rhythm.

"That's it. Set the pace," I said, my voice so gruff it was barely recognizable.

She leaned back, dropping her hands to the top of my thighs and arching her back.

So fucking sexy.

Faster and harder.

She rode me like it was her life's mission.

Like my cock was made for her.

Our breaths were coming hard and fast, and I groaned when she tightened around me.

I knew exactly what she needed as my thumb found her clit, and that's all it took.

She gasped, and I watched her fall apart as she cried out my name.

I thrust into her once.

Twice.

"Holy fuck," I grunted.

And I followed her into oblivion as we rode out every last bit of pleasure.

She fell forward in a heap on my chest, her breaths labored, her body warm against mine.

And I knew I was fucked.

Because nothing would ever compare to this.

CHAPTER TWENTY

Gracie

It was amazing what good sex could do for a person. I'd most definitely been missing out, and I was making up for lost time.

Cutler and I had taken advantage of every free moment we had over the last week, ever since we'd changed up the rules, which of course I'd adjusted in the notebook and had us both re-sign.

Once a type A girl, always a type A girl.

Crossing the line with Cutler proved to be the best decision I'd ever made. And he'd added a new rule of his own that I'd agreed to. When we had sex, he wanted us to sleep in the same bed together after. So, I was now sleeping in his bed every night as well.

My casual fling was proving to be full of surprises.

A small part of me worried that the lines were graying more than we should allow—but I pushed the thought away.

Because right now I was having the time of my life and I just wanted to enjoy it.

Enjoy him.

So I was going to allow myself this time with Cutler and not overthink it.

I came over to the Four Clovers to meet Jovi and Tatum for a drink and an appetizer because Jovi was leaving to head back to New York for her last year of college this week. I'd grown close to both of them. Work was crazy busy, and it was nice to get some girl time.

"I can't believe you're heading back to school this week," I said, turning my attention to Jovi. "I'm going to miss you."

"Me too. And we'll get to hang out when you move there in September."

"At the end of September," Tatum said, making a pouty face. "Don't rush it. I'm losing you both, so I'm going to hold on as long as I can. I'm so happy we've had this summer together, though."

"It's been such a good summer—I mean, aside from living on a small houseboat with my overbearing brother." Jovi shook her head and chuckled.

Tatum's head fell back with laughter. "He's so protective when it comes to you. I'm sure it's a pain in the ass, but it's actually kind of sweet."

"I love him so much," Jovi said. "He's the best brother a girl could ask for. But come on, I'm almost twenty-two years old and graduating from college this year. He treats me like a child."

"Dinner of champions, ladies." Brody set down our three martinis along with a big basket of Tater Tots. "Let me know if you need anything else. I just got a few customers I need to check on, so I'll be back."

We thanked him and I turned my attention back to Jovi. "He

means well, and it's definitely sweet, but I'm sure it's hard living in such close quarters, especially with him treating you like you're still a kid."

"Yes. I've been on one date since I've been here, and that was a total bust." She reached for her glass and held it up. "To the single girl life."

We all clinked glasses, and I felt a tinge of guilt that I hadn't told them what was going on with Cutler and me. We'd agreed we wouldn't keep it a secret from our friends, but it had only been a week since we'd decided that, and I hadn't seen them before now.

It felt weird to just bring it up at this point.

"Well, I don't think we're all single girls." Tatum smirked, and then turned to me and waggled her eyebrows. "Do you really expect us to believe that nothing is going on with you and Cutler?"

"Agreed. The way he was looking at you at game night?" Jovi said as she coughed over her drink, and we all chuckled. "If a man looked at me like that, I'd be climbing him like a tree."

The table erupted in more laughter.

I raised a brow. "And how does he look at me?"

"Like he wants to lock you down for life," Tatum said. "It's that certain look that says 'I want to put a ring on it.'"

My thoughts raced at her words, and it surprised me when a flicker of hope warmed my chest.

This is temporary. A fling that you agreed to. Don't romanticize it.

"Yep. That man is all in. And I've known him a long time, and I've never seen this side of him." Jovi reached for a Tater Tot.

"Well, you're wrong and you're right." I set my glass down.

"Do tell, little sneaky one." Tatum leaned in closer.

"We've sort of got an arrangement going."

"What kind of arrangement?" Jovi asked, eyes wide.

"You know, a friends-with-benefits sort of thing," I whispered as I glanced around to make sure no one else was listening. "I've never done anything like this before, but it was time for a change. The relationships I've had before now have been an absolute bust. And after ending things with Gabriel, I just do not want to go down that path again. I want to focus on my new job, and not worry about finding a long-term partner. I wanted something casual, and seeing as Cutler is my best friend, and he doesn't do the serious relationship thing, it's worked out perfectly for both of us."

My chest tightened as the words left my mouth, because even though I knew what this was, even though I'd been the one to ask for it—it felt so much deeper than the way that I was describing it. I'd never felt so connected to anyone before, but considering I was having sex with my best friend, it was normal to feel this way, right?

"I knew it. You've got that good sex glow going. How long has this been going on?" Tatum asked.

"The sex is new. It started on game night, actually." I chuckled as they gaped at me. "But we were doing—other things, just no sex. We've kept things all very official so that there won't be any misunderstandings."

Jovi's mouth was hanging open. "How did you make it official?"

"You know, we wrote it down, we have rules in place. It was anything on the table aside from sex at first. But then we decided to add the sex in on game night." I reached for my glass. "And I'm not sorry about changing things up."

"Stoooop." Tatum clapped her hands together. "So what part were we wrong about? It sounds like we were spot-on with what we picked up on."

"The other part. Yes, we're having a besties fling. But no one is putting a ring on anything. He's not that guy, and I know that." I shook my head and shrugged. "And it's totally okay. I feel like my entire life I've been following these certain rules. You know, I've always been in serious relationships with the goal of them leading—somewhere. And it's all led me nowhere. So, when I left Paris, I made a conscious decision to have a fresh start in Blue Sky Bay. I'm leaving for New York in two months, and I'm having the time of my life with my best friend. I think he was probably worried I'd romanticize things, but surprisingly, I'm totally okay with what we have. It works for us."

Jovi took another sip of her martini and smiled. "I'm so impressed. You're evolving into this powerhouse woman. You don't need a man bringing you down. You just needed to have your world rocked, and who better to do that than your best friend, who happens to be hot as hell?"

"Damn. I could use a hot guy bestie, but I'm afraid I'm fresh out." Tatum smirked. "I'm happy for you. Sometimes we put so much pressure on ourselves as women. It's exhausting."

"Right?" I agreed. "I had this sort of self-inflicted biological clock ticking last year. Like I took this leap with this man, against everyone's advice, and moved to Paris. So I felt like he had to be the one, you know? And when it ended in a huge disaster, I felt like I'd failed. And why would I feel like I'd failed? The guy was a complete narcissist. It wasn't my job to make it work. He doesn't feel like he failed. So I'm in a new phase of life. I'm not settling. I'm doing what feels right in the moment, and I'm not looking beyond that, at least not in my romantic life."

"You are so right. And you shouldn't have to feel that way." Jovi shrugged. "You've got plenty of time."

"I know. And then I did a deep dive into why I've had the relationships I've had. None have been very exciting or passionate, and I just fell into a comfort zone where I didn't think about what I actually wanted. I thought more about what I was supposed to want."

"Amen, sister." Tatum held up her glass, waiting for us to clink ours with hers. "And now you're getting exactly what you want."

They both had goofy smiles on their faces, and I couldn't help but smile.

Because they were right.

I was getting exactly what I wanted.

• • •

"Oh, Gracie, I can't get over how gorgeous this is," Shana said as we stared at her bathroom tile that had just been laid.

"Yes, this beautiful stone is hard to beat. And all the coordinating marble you chose for the shower and the backsplash is going to complement the look so well."

"I can't believe how quickly you got it. I thought we were going to be delayed because I couldn't make a decision before working with you." She chuckled.

"Nope. Luckily everything that you chose was in stock, so we're still on track for your move-in date." I had only selected options that were in stock for her to choose from, but she needed a win, and this felt like one that I could give her.

She wrapped her arms around me and hugged me tight. "I'm just so grateful for you. I'm finally sleeping again, and I've hardly even been here, because I know you've got it."

"That's exactly how it should be." I glanced down at my phone to check the time. "And you have a soccer game to get to, so you better get going. I just wanted you to see the progress, and give you something to be excited about with this project."

She blinked a few times, and I noticed her eyes were wet with emotion. "I'm so grateful for you," she said again.

She gave me one more hug and hurried out of the room, just as

I heard someone calling my name. I sighed, because I recognized the voice.

You can do hard things. You survived a relationship with Gabriel.

"What's up, William?" I asked as I came around the corner and found one of our subcontractors in the laundry room. He was installing the wallpaper for me, and he'd already had some run-ins with the other subcontractors.

I didn't know how Cutler handled all the moving parts and personalities in this business. And he never seemed bothered by it. He was even-keeled, yet he knew how to get things done. They all respected him.

"Well, your painter did shit work, and I can't work under these conditions." William tossed his hands in the air.

"This guy has some nerve talking shit about my work," Carl hissed as he came walking out of the pantry, startling us both.

"Oh. I didn't know you were still here," William said.

"Well, here I am, asshole." Carl placed his hands on his hips and stepped forward.

"And I here I am speaking the truth, asshole."

Please make it stop.

"Listen, you little diva. You had a problem at the last project with the cabinet guy touching your work, and now you have a problem with me," Carl shouted, and they stepped closer to one another.

"I don't want any of you assholes touching my paper!" William's voice bounced off the walls in the small space, and my heart raced at how heated this was getting.

I moved forward to step between them because I had a feeling they were ready to throw blows, and I hoped like hell they wouldn't do that if I was standing between them.

"Your paper? Did you make the wallpaper? Are you the artist?

I don't believe you are." Carl's sarcasm was impossible to miss.

"You son of a bitch!" William shouted.

"What is going on in here?" Cutler's voice came from behind me, and my shoulders relaxed immediately.

"Oh, hey, Cutler." Carl cleared his throat and shoved his hands in his pockets.

"'Oh, hey'?" Cutler asked. "I hear shouting on the jobsite, and all you have to say is 'hey'?"

Cutler stepped in front of me, and I instinctually stepped back, which I assumed was the purpose. He placed himself between the two men and crossed his arms over his chest. "You know I don't tolerate that on my jobsites. Period. You have a problem, you come to me. You don't get into it here while you're working. And I don't appreciate you putting my girl in the middle of your mess either."

They both turned to look at me and winced.

Cutler glanced over his shoulder and winked at me, and William and Carl both apologized at the same time.

"Now apologize to one another. You're brothers, for fuck's sake," my best friend said, and now it was me who was gaping at them.

"You're brothers?" I asked, not hiding my surprise.

"Of course. Do you think I'd talk to a stranger like that?" William shrugged.

"I've been dealing with this prima donna my entire life," Carl grumped. "He thinks he's an artist and the rest of us are talentless."

"Your words, not mine, brother," he chuckled as he picked up his roll of wallpaper. "I guess this wall is prepped as good as it's going to get. I'll get this going right now, Gracie."

"Thank you," I said.

"Unbelievable. You made that whole scene and for nothing." Carl shook his head and stormed out of the laundry room.

Cutler motioned for me to step out of the room, and he placed his hand on the small of my back as we walked down the hallway into the kitchen.

Another subcontractor, Jackson, was there, laying the floors, and he and Cutler were discussing the timeline.

The electrician, Coby, was waiting for him as soon as he finished talking to Jackson. I didn't know how he handled being pulled in so many directions all the time.

Cutler Heart wore a lot of hats.

And right now, while I stood there watching him do his thing, it nearly took my breath away.

His shoulders strained against his navy tee as he listened intently to Coby's questions.

I watched as he put fire after fire out.

Everyone came to him, and he never lost his cool or got frustrated.

He was the most confident man I'd ever known.

The sexiest man I'd ever known.

And it took everything in me not to pull him against me and kiss him right here in the middle of this kitchen, in front of all these people.

The irony was not lost on me.

I'd come to Blue Sky Bay to have a fling and keep things casual.

But this felt like anything but casual.

This felt terrifyingly real.

And that was not supposed to happen.

CHAPTER TWENTY-ONE

Cutler

"I can't believe that this is what you wanted to do before your parents arrived," I said, wrapping my arms around Gracie a little tighter under the hot water.

"I love baths. I've never bathed with a man. You've covered a lot of firsts for me, Bear." She rolled onto her stomach, her chest now pressing against mine, as water splashed all around us.

"I've never taken a bath with a woman. You've covered some firsts for me too." I nipped at her bottom lip.

"That was really nice of you to insist that they stay here at your house this weekend. You know they were more than willing to stay at a hotel."

"Of course they should stay here. Although I didn't think about the fact that it would mean that you wouldn't be in my bed." I leaned forward and ran the tip of my tongue along her bottom lip. I had this unwavering need to touch her anytime she was near.

A little moan escaped and her eyes fluttered closed as she moved forward, grinding against my rock-hard cock.

I traced a finger through the bubbles on her skin, water sliding down her arm. Her hair was piled on her head, her smile soft and trusting, eyes sparkling in a way that made my chest ache. She looked at me like I was the only person in the world, and something settled inside me—a warmth, quiet and steady, filling a space I hadn't known was empty before now.

It was undeniable.

I didn't just love this girl.

I was in love with Gracie Reynolds.

"Why do you always have to make everything feel so good?" she whispered.

"Do you want another first?" I asked as I leaned against her ear before kissing down her neck.

Her dark brown eyes opened, locking with mine. "What did you have in mind?"

"Well, seeing as we've both never taken a bath with anyone else, I'm guessing neither one of us has had sex in a bathtub."

"You want to have sex with me in here?" she asked, her voice so sexy I felt myself grow beneath her.

"I do."

"What if the water makes a mess?" she asked, a wicked grin on her face.

"I'm a contractor. I'm happy to repair any damage from our sexual escapades."

She tucked her lips between her teeth and pressed her breasts against my chest. Her nipples were clearly hard enough that I felt them.

"I mean, I did ask for lessons, and this is a new one."

"I'm nothing if not a good teacher of sexual pleasure," I said, tucking the loose strand of hair that had broken free behind her ear. Her hair was tied up in a messy bun on top of her head, and her face was clean of makeup. She looked fucking stunning.

She pushed up, positioning my tip between her thighs, and then she froze. "We don't have a condom."

"Fuck me," I groaned, gripping her hips to lift her out of the tub.

We were going to have to move our party to the bedroom.

"Wait." She pressed down on my shoulders. "Have you ever been with anyone without a condom?"

"Never. No." I had no hesitation, because I'd never considered it.

"Neither have I," she said, the words breathy, and I could see the way her chest was rising and falling. "And I've been on the pill since I moved to Paris."

"What are you saying, Jeege?" I asked, my voice gruff.

Because the thought of fucking my girl with nothing between us?

It was more than I could wrap my head around.

Pun. Intended.

"I want to feel you without a condom."

I wanted to feel every inch of her. Experience everything with her.

I nodded. "Me too."

The sexiest smile spread across her face. She'd gotten her confidence back since being here. She was asking for what she wanted. What she needed.

She wasn't adapting her needs for someone else.

I fucking loved it.

Lucky for me, we wanted the same things most of the time.

She pushed up just as I sank down lower into the water and gripped my dick to make it easier for her.

She slid down, taking me in slowly, gaze locked with mine.

It was early in the morning, so the sun was just coming up, and the little bit of light illuminated the bathroom.

I filled her completely, and I had to squeeze my eyes closed for a minute because I'd never experienced anything like this.

She was wet and tight and warm.

She had my dick in a vise, one I never wanted to break free from.

She started moving.

And holy shit.

Holy motherfucking shit.

Feeling her around my bare cock was overwhelming.

Nothing had ever felt better.

I just watched her in awe.

My girl.

My fucking girl.

The most beautiful girl in the world.

She rode my cock like her life depended on it.

And I never wanted her to stop.

"That's it, baby. Look at you riding me like you were made for me," I grunted as she smiled down at me, moving faster.

Water was splashing over the sides of the tub, and I didn't give a fuck.

I couldn't get enough.

I gripped her hips, driving her up and down as I thrust into her over and over.

She was panting and moaning, and it was sexy as hell. I moved my thumb to her clit, and I'd barely touched her when she gasped.

"Cutler," she cried out, and I jolted forward one more time and came so hard I couldn't see straight.

Unloading myself into her.

The sound that escaped me was barely audible.

I tugged her mouth down to mine, and she moaned against my lips as my tongue slipped inside.

When we stopped riding out our pleasure, she fell forward, tucking her face beneath my chin as her breathing slowed.

"I love you," she whispered.

"I love you too."

We'd said it hundreds of times over the years.

But this time it felt different.

And I was fairly certain we both knew it.

• • •

We'd taken a shower after our bathcapades and laughed our asses off at the mess we'd made. We'd gotten everything cleaned up, and now Gracie was standing at the stove making breakfast when the doorbell rang.

I wrapped my arms around her from behind and tipped her head back to kiss her one last time before we'd have to keep our distance for the next few days.

All of this public affection would be toned way down.

Letting Gracie's parents or my parents know that anything was going on between us would be a disaster.

The expectations would be outrageous, and they wouldn't understand what this was.

Hell, I was having a hard time wrapping my head around it.

"I'll get the door," I said as I smacked her on the ass and walked toward the entryway.

When I pulled the door open, I found Cage and Presley Reynolds standing on the other side, with big smiles on their faces and two suitcases. They were family to me. I'd grown up with them. I wrapped my arms around Gracie's mom first, and then Cage pulled me in for a big hug.

They'd been to my home a few times over the last few years, but they'd never stayed with me.

"Hey, guys, come on in," I said, and we set their bags to the side, because I knew they were anxious to see Gracie.

She came running around the corner and threw herself into her father's arms, and then into her mother's embrace.

They'd always been very close.

She took them to the kitchen, and I grabbed their bags and rolled them down the hallway to the guest room.

Gracie would be staying in her room this weekend, one she hadn't stayed in over the last few weeks.

We'd both be sleeping alone, which I wasn't thrilled about.

But it was definitely the right move with her parents staying here.

They wouldn't understand, as our families were just too connected.

This is why friends don't typically cross the line—or so I've been told...by my very own type A best friend, whom I just had sex with in the bathtub less than an hour ago.

Involving our families was a can of worms neither of us wanted to open.

We were talking and catching up, and Gracie set down a stack of pancakes and a large bowl of scrambled eggs in the center of the table, and I pulled the bacon out of the oven and set it down as well. I made sure everyone had a fresh cup of hot coffee, as they'd gotten up early to drive here.

"You look so much happier than when we saw you in Paris," Presley said. "I'm so grateful you came here, and that you two got to spend this time together before you leave for New York."

I felt my chest tighten at the mention of her leaving. I knew it was coming. I knew it would suck.

But I felt it physically, which surprised me.

Like a deep, heavy pain moved into the center of my chest every time I thought about it.

"It's been great having her here," I said, taking a sip of my coffee.

"You two have always been thick as thieves. Everyone needs a best friendship like the two of you have," her mother said.

"I'm grateful she's got you looking out for her," Cage said. "I don't think there's another guy on the planet that I'd be comfortable letting Gracie stay with other than you. As a father, I can't even tell you how much it means to have that peace of mind." His gaze locked with mine, and I suddenly felt like he could read my face. Like he was aware of what had just happened in the bathtub right before he arrived.

I jumped to my feet and moved to the coffeepot.

"Of course. You know I've always got her back." I cleared my throat because I was certain it was closing. "Does anyone need a topper?"

My God. This was Cage Reynolds. I loved this man.

And I'd totally crossed the line. What was I thinking?

He'd never look at me the same if he knew what we'd been doing.

What I'd been doing to his little girl.

I filled their mugs and then topped off Gracie's, and she looked up at me with wide eyes, as if she could tell that I was freaking out.

Well, guess what.

I am freaking the fuck out.

"That's plenty," Gracie squeaked, and I realized I'd filled it so high that she'd have to lean down to take a sip because it would spill over if she tried to raise it.

I put the coffeepot back on the counter and sat down at the table. They asked us both a bunch of questions about how work was going and how the family house was coming along, and of course they asked if either of us had been dating at all.

"No. I'm taking a break from men, remember?" Gracie chuckled. "I've sworn off them so I can focus on my career. No more distractions."

Apparently, I was not a distraction. It shouldn't have bothered me, but for whatever reason, it did.

"I think it's a good idea for you to focus on yourself and your career right now, sweetheart," Cage said. "New York will be a fresh start for you. You don't need to tie yourself down to some asshole here, when you aren't staying. Gabriel was enough for a lifetime." He winked at his daughter, and a sick feeling settled in my stomach.

I am the asshole here.

"Trust me, Dad. It was a tough lesson, and I won't be changing my plans for any man ever again, so you need not worry. I'm excited for this opportunity in New York." Gracie sighed, and she glanced over at me.

I would normally be adding to the conversation, but I was at a loss for words.

I needed to pull my head out of my ass.

"Nothing is stopping our girl, and I'll make sure of it. I've had to fight off all the single dudes in town to keep them away from her." I reached for a piece of bacon and took a bite.

"I knew I could count on you, Beefcake," Cage said with a smirk. "Sorry. Couldn't help myself. Feeling a bit nostalgic right now."

Gracie laughed and shook her head. "Why? What is happening?"

"Dad and I were so worried about you in Paris. And we wanted you to come home, but once we knew that you were going to stay with Cutler, we completely relaxed." Presley turned to look at me. "She's a grown woman, but she's still our little girl, and just knowing that she was with you, someone we fully trust, I can't begin to tell you the peace of mind it's given us."

I was the fucking devil.

I deserved a one-way ticket to hell.

I'd completely betrayed them.

As if Gracie could read my mind, she clapped her hands together. "This is a bit theatrical, isn't it? I'm a grown woman. I don't need anyone to take care of me, including my best friend. I'm grateful that he opened his doors to me and offered me a temporary job, but I don't need rescuing."

"I know you don't, sweetheart. But from a father's perspective, it's just nice to know that a kid, one whom I consider to be a second son to me, is watching out for you." Cage cleared his throat, as if he was overcome with emotion.

A second son.

I deserved any karma that came my way.

The doorbell rang, and I jumped to my feet, anxious to get away from the conversation, but Gracie's father clearly had the same idea.

"I'll get that," Cage said, stepping in front of me.

Presley had a big smile on her face. "We have a surprise for you. You've done so much for us, and for our girl, Cutler. We couldn't resist."

"Surprise!" I heard my mother's voice before she even came around the corner. I froze for a second, my chest tightening. Then I saw her—my mom smiling at me, and everything hit at once: relief, joy, and definitely shock.

She and my father walked into the kitchen with wide grins on their faces.

"We came to have a big family weekend with the six of us," my mother said, a big smile spread across her face.

"Hey, Mama," I said, pulling her into my arms.

My Sunny.

The woman who'd been the brightest light in my life from the time she entered it.

"Surprise, son," Pops said as he wrapped his arms around me.

We had both sets of parents under the same roof with me and Gracie.

Karma was definitely here for me.

CHAPTER TWENTY-TWO

Gracie

This. Was. A. Lot.

We'd spent the day out on the boat, and I'd had to shoot Cutler multiple warning looks to pull himself together.

I think my father referring to him as a second son, and basically saying he trusted him with his life, was a bit much for my best friend to handle, considering all that was going on between us.

Especially after we'd just had epic sex in the bathtub without a condom this morning.

Was that really this morning?

It felt like a hundred years ago now.

Apparently, my parents, who were friends with Cutler's parents, thought it would be the ultimate surprise to have them all come on the same weekend.

And stay at the house together.

"With Gracie being here, and then Cage and Presley coming, we wanted to join in the celebration," Emerson said as she leaned her head on my shoulder where we all sat on the couch eating pizza. "I'm really proud of you for taking this leap. It's a great move for your career. I can't imagine the design experience you'll get living in such an amazing city."

"Yes. Thank you. I'm excited," I said, but I felt like I'd been going through the motions lately. I didn't even know if I was actually excited about it anymore, but I knew I was supposed to be. It was the right thing to do after the dumpster fire my life had been just a few months ago.

This is me getting my life back on track.

"Well, I can tell you that all the Chadwicks are very happy that you had this stopover here in Blue Sky Bay, because Emilia wouldn't trust anyone else to design this home," Nash said, tossing me a wink.

He and Cutler had so many similar mannerisms, and everyone teased them about it.

"Yeah. We'll take you over to see the house tomorrow. It's really coming along," Cutler said.

"That sounds great," Emerson said. "And we thought maybe tomorrow night we could cook out and sit out back and have dinner. Presley and Cage have some friends who have a place here, and we were hoping it would be okay if they joined us." She and my mom had been giving one another strange looks. "Presley and I will go grab the groceries and do all the cooking."

Something is definitely up.

"Who is it?" I asked.

"Oh, it's Jana and Grant Langford," my mom said. "Apparently, they have a place here now, and they come up in the summer. Jana came by the spa when she was in Cottonwood Cove visiting her parents. She mentioned that they were going to be here this weekend, and I said we were going to be here as well."

My mother and her best friend, Lola, owned the cutest day spa in the small town where I'd grown up, Cottonwood Cove.

"Yes, I think I met them once," I said.

"That's right. Their parents are close friends with my parents." My mother turned her attention to Cutler and his family. "I don't know them all that well, but they've always been nice."

"I think I met them at one of Grandma and Grandpa's holiday parties when they were in town," I said. "And I think they had a daughter who was a little younger than me, but I only met her briefly."

"Yes. I've only spoken to them a few times, but I've known them for years, and their daughter Britani is three years younger than you," my mother said, and then she gave me that look.

You know the one.

The one that lets you know that something is going on.

And I immediately knew it was not something I would like.

"Sure, of course. The more the merrier," Cutler said.

"Let's go get the fire started out back." Nash stood up, and my dad and Cutler followed him outside.

Mom, Emerson, and I moved to clean up the plates and put the leftover pizza in the refrigerator.

Once the guys were out back, my mom turned to me. "Okay, we've got a slight situation, but we don't want to tell Cutler."

"Definitely not. He'll be against it. He hates setups." Emerson chuckled.

"So when I ran into Jana, she was asking about you, and if you were still in Paris, as she'd obviously gotten updates from her parents, via Grandma and Grandpa." Mom blew out a breath. "I said that you'd moved back to Blue Sky Bay for a few months and you were staying with your best friend, Cutler. And she immediately asked if he was single, because apparently Britani is considering living here full-time in the home they bought, and she's single."

"I mean, Cutler is pretty clear about not wanting to settle down, but it can't hurt to introduce them," Emerson said. "When I met Nash, he didn't have any intention of settling down either." She laughed. "And look at us now. I think men tend to have less of a plan than women do when they're younger. It takes a good woman to kick a man's ass in gear."

My mother laughed as Emerson slipped the last few pieces of pepperoni pizza into a freezer bag and set it in the refrigerator.

Oh. My. Gosh.

They were setting him up with a family friend?

I kept my face completely relaxed as I forced a smile and listened.

"Listen, there are different stages of life, right?" Mom looked at me. Eyes always tender and understanding whenever they met mine. "You needed to go to Paris and give it a shot. I think that's part of being young. And now you've come to a place where you want to focus on yourself and on your career. There is nothing wrong with that. I'm glad I was able to do it when I was young too. But sometimes you just meet the right person, and it turns your world upside down in the best way."

"Well, I've had mine turned upside down in the worst way, so I'm not in any hurry to have my world even remotely shaken." I chuckled, and Emerson came over to stand beside me and she squeezed my hand.

"I'm so proud of you. And I can't wait for you to start this next adventure," she said. "But I do think it's going to be difficult for Cutler when you move across the country. Nash and I were actually worried about him when you were in Paris. He just wasn't himself.

Your friendship is so special, and we're just really grateful that you have each other."

Oh, we have each other.

"Yes. I think you struggled being that far away from him too. You two have just always had such a special connection," Mom said, turning to look at me and tucking my hair behind my ear. "But, I think this is such a good opportunity for you. The fact that they wanted you back so badly, it speaks volumes about the faith they have in you. And what could be a better résumé builder?"

Owning my own business, which is what I was supposed to do in Paris.

"And who knows, when you're ready, you just might find your Prince Charming in New York City." Emerson grinned at me. "But I know Cutler's going to have a hard time when you leave, so as much as I don't think it's a great idea to do a setup without him knowing, maybe they'll hit it off and it'll be a good distraction. At the very least, they can be friends, as she probably doesn't know many people in town."

"Exactly," my mom said. "There's no pressure. I told her that I wasn't big on doing setups, but that I'd be happy to introduce them because it would be nice for her to know a few people here. But I am a little anxious about it," she admitted, chewing on her thumbnail, something we both did when we were nervous.

"Why?" I asked.

"Well, Jana just ignored me when I said I wasn't really comfortable doing a formal setup, but that I could definitely introduce them. She asked me multiple times if he was single, so I think she has her heart set on this being more of a romantic thing. I just hope I didn't get us into an uncomfortable situation." Mom rinsed her hands in the sink and reached for some paper towels.

I nodded. Jana Langford clearly wanted to set her daughter up with Cutler. A huge lump formed in my throat at the thought of having to sit through a dinner tomorrow night and watch Britani Langford flirt with him. I had a memory of her being very pretty.

And now she was moving here.

I shouldn't have cared. I was leaving.

But Cutler wasn't supposed to settle down.

He didn't want that.

But what if they were right, and he'd change his mind?

"We're ready," Cutler called out from where he stood in the doorway, his gaze finding mine, and I quickly looked away.

"I'm going to go grab a sweatshirt," I said as both of our moms followed him out the door.

I walked into my bedroom and shut the door, placing my hands on the dresser and blowing out a breath.

Having both sets of parents in the house and acting like nothing was going on between us was already challenging.

And now Britani was coming here in hopes of a love connection with Bear?

My Bear.

This was too much.

This was all too messy.

My bedroom door opened, and Cutler stepped inside before closing the door behind him.

"This is a fucking mess, Jeege," he whispered, moving toward me and pulling me into his arms.

"I know. This thing tomorrow night is a setup with Britani Langford," I hissed, because I couldn't let him be blindsided.

"I know. Pops and your dad filled me in outside." He shook his head in disbelief. "Even if this wasn't happening between us, I would not be okay with this. I don't need our parents setting me up with women. But what the fuck can I do about it now?"

"She's really pretty." The words left my mouth before I could stop them.

His gaze softened, and his lips turned up in the corners. "And you're always the prettiest girl in every room I've ever been in."

"Oh my gosh. I sound so jealous. I hate this. I just—I don't want to see everyone pushing her on you tomorrow. Maybe I can fake sick." I kept my voice low, nervous that someone would come looking for us.

"Hell no, Jeege. You are not ditching me to deal with this alone."

I sighed. "We'll figure it out. Where do they think you are now?"

"I said that I had to use the restroom." He stroked my cheek. "Should we just tell them?"

My jaw dropped. "Are you serious? How do you think that would go over?"

"Well, your father would probably kill me, so I'm guessing not very well."

"Right. You and me together," I said, motioning between us. "It would have to be a forever thing to ever be okay for them. They would never understand our temporary arrangement. They're old-school. They'd freak out and assume that I wouldn't be going to New York. It would be a whole thing. They would analyze it to death, and all of our extended family would get involved."

Did I even understand our temporary agreement anymore?

Here I was feeling an overwhelming sense of jealousy about them setting Cutler up with another woman. I doubted this was a normal feeling for a casual fling.

What the hell was I doing?

"Hey, don't spiral, Jeege," he said, as if he could read my thoughts. His voice had a way of settling me. Calming me. "You're right. They wouldn't understand the situation. I'll just have to play along tomorrow night. It's not like I'd be open to being set up even if you and I weren't doing whatever the fuck it is we're doing."

Because what the fuck are we doing?

I raised a brow defensively. I needed to pull it together. Stick to the plan. "We're having fun. Maybe not at the moment. But this morning we were."

He leaned down, grazing his lips over mine. "I can still feel the way your pussy tightened around me when you came on my cock."

"Cutler!" I gasped, trying my best to keep my voice low. "Do not start with the dirty talk when we have both sets of parents on the other side of the door."

He chuckled. "Okay. I'll let you go out first."

I pushed up on my tiptoes and kissed him hard and then groaned when I pulled away. When I got to the door, I turned around before opening it.

"Hey, Bear," I whispered.

"Yeah?"

"If you like her tomorrow night, I don't want you to feel bad. She's moving here, and I'm leaving. She's probably going to be great. I mean, at some point in your life you might want to have an actual relationship, and she might be the one to knock you on your ass." I reached for the door handle, a pain hitting my chest as the words left my mouth.

"Don't do that, Jeege. I'm not thinking about when you leave," he said, his gaze tender. "I'm thinking about our time together right now. Let's stay right here, okay?"

A lump formed in my throat, and I pushed it away before nodding. "Yeah. Okay. I'll see you out there."

I pulled the door open and walked out, grabbing my beer bottle off the counter before I stepped outside.

Loud laughter mixed with the sound of the trees rustling above, and the water slapping against the shore filled the air around us.

It was so peaceful here. I loved it.

"Come sit with us, sweetheart," Dad said.

I dropped into the chair beside him and set my drink down on the ground. "I'm so glad you guys are here."

I truly was so happy to see everyone. The circumstances were definitely awkward, but that was on me and Cutler. Not them.

"I think Cutler seems like he's mellowed out. The timing might be perfect for this setup," Mom said.

"He does seem very content and relaxed," Emerson said. "I think it has a lot to do with Gracie being here. You've always grounded him in a way no one else ever has. You two really balance each other out." She smiled as the fire crackled in front of me.

It was probably all the good sex that had him so relaxed, but I certainly couldn't say that.

"Yeah, I'm very lucky to call Cutler my best friend." I nodded as I watched him walk outside and drop to sit in the chair across from me.

His father started asking him questions about the boat, and everyone joined in. I just sat there watching him for a moment as all these feelings started rushing in at once.

I was absolutely jealous at the thought of him being set up with another woman. About the thought of him with any other woman. I liked waking up in his arms every morning, so much so that I was reluctant about leaving for New York. I liked working with him, cooking dinner together each night, and jumping in the lake at the end of the day.

His laughter startled me from my thoughts, and I glanced over at him again, really taking him in. Cutler Heart was not only the most attractive man I'd ever laid eyes on, but he was also loyal and fearless and real. He was so much more than just my best friend. He was my person, my other half.

And that's when it hit me.

I was madly and irrevocably in love with my best friend.

Leave it to me to fall for a man I couldn't have. He wasn't a relationship guy by nature, and I sure as hell was not in a place to be looking for a relationship.

It was the last thing I needed.

And trying to make this more than it was supposed to be was a terrible idea. There was too much to risk.

I couldn't exist in a world where Cutler Heart wasn't at the center of it.

Loving him scared the hell out of me.

But losing him—that would be the worst thing that could ever happen to me.

CHAPTER TWENTY-THREE

Cutler

If you looked up the term "shit show" in the dictionary, I was fairly certain it would refer you to this exact moment in time.

My parents were here.

Gracie's parents were here.

Gracie was here.

And we'd now tossed in the Langfords, who no one seemed prepared for, most of all me.

They were definitely on a mission to marry their daughter off, and I appeared to be the front-runner for that position at the moment.

A man they didn't know jack shit about, other than the fact that I was friends with the Reynolds family.

"I don't know how committed you are to construction, but I'll be looking for someone to take over my company someday," Grant Langford said, and my father spewed beer from his mouth, causing us all to startle.

Yeah, welcome to my life, Pops.

You brought them here.

"I'm so sorry. It must have gone down the wrong pipe." Pops used his napkin to dab his face as my mother gaped at me.

I'd been grilled throughout the entire dinner.

I'd been asked about my profession, which he'd shown no interest in.

I'd been asked how long I'd owned my home.

If I had a 401k.

Did I use a financial planner.

What my ten-year plan was.

I was surprised he hadn't asked me the last time that I'd had sex, but I had a feeling this night was far from over.

"I'm very committed to building homes and expanding the company." I cleared my throat, glancing over at Gracie, who'd tried multiple times to interject and change the subject—though she'd had no luck.

"Ohhhhh. I like a man who wants to get his hands dirty," Britani said, scooting closer to me for the third time, which meant the arm of her chair was touching mine where we sat outside. She covered my hand with hers, which caught me completely off-guard. I barely knew this woman. And this was all going down in front of Gracie, and no one knew how incredibly awkward this was for both of us.

I glanced over at her and noted the way her hand gripped the arm of her chair, knuckles white. She took another long sip of her wine, and I knew she was just trying to get through this night.

We both were.

I pulled my hand away and settled it on my lap. "You didn't

mention it, what do you do for a living, Britani?"

We'd heard about her father's business. He owned several car lots, and he'd let it be known that he was very successful. Extremely successful. Presley appeared horrified, and she kept shooting me looks of apology. I did my best to keep my smile easy, because there was nothing we could do at this point.

The crazy train had left the station, and we were on it right now.

"I'm my mother's personal assistant." She blinked up at me with what I assumed were fake eyelashes because they were so thick it was difficult to see her eyes. She was pretty, no doubt about it. Long blonde hair, curves for days, and a nice smile. I could appreciate a beautiful woman and still have zero romantic interest in her.

Case in point.

"Oh, I didn't know that you worked for your mom," Presley interjected. "What do you do, Jana?"

"I'm a homemaker." She smiled. "I keep the big guy well fed and well dressed. It's a full-time job."

Apparently so, if it required an assistant.

"Enough about work. When was your last relationship?" Britani asked me, her hand finding my knee now, and I was trying hard not to show my irritation. But this was probably the hardest sell I'd ever experienced from a woman. And her father was equally relentless.

Not exactly how I wanted to spend my evening.

"I haven't had a long-term relationship ever, if I'm being honest. I date quite a bit, and I'm content with the way things are going," I said, taking a long pull from my beer. My gaze found my father's. We'd always been able to communicate without words.

You're going to owe me big for this.

"I actually love that," Britani said, wiggling her eyebrows at me. "That means the right woman hasn't come along yet."

She couldn't have been more wrong. The right woman came

along so long ago that I couldn't remember a day when she hadn't been in my life.

The timing had just never been right.

I pushed to my feet, forcing a smile so I wouldn't appear rude. "I need to use the restroom. Excuse me."

Gracie's eyes flickered to mine, and I saw the concern there.

This had been a complete disaster.

I walked inside, stepping into the guest bathroom before splashing some water on my face.

How the fuck was I going to get out of this?

And she was moving here.

There was a knock on the bathroom door, and before I could reach for the handle, it opened.

It was not who I was hoping it would be.

Britani Langford rushed inside, pushing the door closed behind her before lunging herself at me.

I was so caught off-guard, I fell back against the wall, knocking the picture down as it shattered on the floor.

What the actual fuck was happening?

"I want you, Gunther," she said, tilting her head up to look at me.

Who the fuck is Gunther?

I wrapped my hands around her wrists before pushing her back as gently as I possibly could. "What the fuck is going on?"

Her eyes were wild, and I hadn't noticed her top being unbuttoned when she first walked in, but it definitely was now. I let her hands go and stepped back, bending down to pick up the broken glass.

"Were you not giving me signals out there?" she asked, completely unfazed by how insane this was.

"I don't know what signals you were picking up on, but I don't recall sending a single one," I said through gritted teeth. I needed to be crystal clear with this woman before things got even more awkward.

"Seriously? Are you the first man in history not to want this?" she asked, using her hands to motion down her body.

"Apparently so. Gunther isn't interested in more than a friendship," I said, not hiding my sarcasm. "Come on, Britani. You don't even know my name, which is Cutler, by the way. But why do you feel the need to come on so strong? We don't even know one another."

"I thought that was your thing? You haven't had a serious relationship, right?" She crossed her arms over her chest. "I'm guessing you like to fuck, and I wanted to show you how good it could be with me."

With our parents sitting outside? Is she serious?

"I date. We have conversations. We go out a few times. It's not like I'm banging people in bathrooms while having dinner with my parents."

She narrowed her gaze, which was difficult to make out because of the lashes weighing down her eyelids. "'Gunther' was my nickname for you, by the way. You don't look like a Cutler. You look like a Gunther."

I tossed the broken glass in the trash and leaned the photo of my favorite tree in the backyard against the wall for now.

"Listen, let's just go back out there and call this done, all right?"

"You're rejecting me? Look at me!" she gasped. "You really don't want this?"

She wasn't lacking in self-confidence at the moment, but I would put money on the fact that it was probably to mask a deep-rooted insecurity, because this was just too much.

"I do not. I'd like to be friends." I started to walk past her, in hopes she'd let me get to the door without any more theatrics.

I needed to get out of here.

But before that could happen, she shocked the shit out of me again by stomping her foot down hard before breaking out into hysterical tears.

No warning. No sniffling. No eye blinking.

Just a complete meltdown.

We're talking about this girl going from zero to one hundred in a matter of three seconds.

She wailed and cried, and I was fairly certain she'd left a mark on my wood floors with her heel.

If my parents and Gracie's parents weren't the ones who'd set this up, I would've assumed the guys were punking me, and one of them was going to jump through the window laughing any minute now.

No such luck.

"Why? Tell me why!" she sobbed. "Why would you not want me?"

"Hey. Hey," I said, placing my hands on her shoulders. "What is happening here? We don't even know one another."

"My therapist says that rejection is a trigger for me." She gulped in a few breaths. "And I am fucking triggered, Gunther!" she shouted so loud that I wanted to cover my ears with my hands.

I needed to get the fuck out of here.

I needed to come up with something that would appease her.

"Listen. It's not you. I wasn't honest with you earlier, and my family doesn't know this, because I'm not ready to share it with them. But I'm actually seeing someone. That's why I can't do this." It was partially true. I was seeing someone. The woman sitting outside, probably wondering what the fuck was going on in here. But Britani was most definitely not my type, regardless, and I was desperate to get out of here unscathed and without making this dinner party any more uncomfortable than it already was.

Her tears stopped instantly. This woman could be a trained actress with the way she could turn on and off her emotions. “Oh. So you feel guilty because you’ve already committed to someone else? But I thought you didn’t do relationships?”

“I don’t normally. But I met someone, and I’ve been with her for a while now. I’m just not ready to tell my parents, because I’m not sure where it’s going. I don’t want to complicate things.” I was fucking spitballing now, although in all honesty, I didn’t know where things were going with me and Gracie. Her plan had a shit ton of holes in it, but I wasn’t ready to press the matter just yet.

She wiped her cheeks, and I reached for some tissues and handed them to her. I startled and jumped back when she looked up at me before realizing it wasn’t a spider on her face, but one of her fake lashes, currently stuck to her cheek. I motioned for her to look in the mirror, and she quickly reattached what I thought was a tarantula to her eyelid and then smiled at me.

“I’m sure it’s difficult for you to stay faithful, and I’m probably the worst temptation imaginable,” she said. She pulled the door open, stepped out, and then glanced over her shoulder to speak to me. “So do you have any single friends you could introduce me to, Gunther?”

“I’ll have to get back to you on that,” I said, trying to keep my tone even. “I’d like to keep my personal life private at the moment, if you don’t mind. Do you think you could keep the conversation we just had between us? I think we can say that we’ve both agreed to be just friends.”

She ignored me as we made our way to the backyard.

Everyone was staring at us, and it was awkward as hell, and I had no idea what she was going to do.

This girl was completely unpredictable.

“Everything okay?” Gracie asked, and I didn’t miss the concern in her eyes. It wasn't jealousy or anger; it was pure concern.

For me.

My girl knew me well.

"Um…not really. We've been duped, Daddy," Britani said, and now she appeared hostile toward me.

"Duped?" Grant said, his eyes finding mine. Everyone sitting around the fire was now staring at me.

"Gunther has a girlfriend." She threw her hands in the air dramatically.

Thanks for the discretion. Gunther will not be telling you any more secrets.

"Who the fuck is Gunther?" my father asked as he looked around in confusion.

"Apparently, I don't look like a Cutler. I look like a Gunther." I shrugged.

Gracie's head fell back in laughter, and our parents covered their mouths with their hands to try to keep themselves from doing the same.

"So how exactly did you dupe my daughter?" Grant pushed to his feet, his face bright red as he stepped toward me.

"I'm as in the dark as you are. Britani walked into the restroom uninvited and she demanded an answer about us starting a relationship and she forced me to tell the truth."

"Which is?" Jana asked, and now she was glaring at me.

Was I missing something?

Was this a prearranged marriage that I hadn't been informed of?

"I'm seeing someone. I have been for the last few months." I didn't look over at Gracie to see her reaction, because I didn't want anyone to catch on to who I was talking about.

My mom's eyes widened. "Oh. Why didn't you tell us?"

"Because I didn't know where it was going. It's still new. And I guess I hadn't realized you'd promised me to a woman I'd never met."

Now it was my father's and Cage's turn to fall forward, burying their faces in their hands and laughing so loud I could swear Pops snorted.

"I don't believe we promised anything. I think there's been a huge misunderstanding," Presley said, her eyes filled with apology when she looked at me. "I said that I'd introduce you to Cutler. There were no promises made."

"Did you think we were coming here because we actually like cheeseburgers and corn on the cob? I don't do anything without an objective. You've wasted our time, Presley," Britani hissed, and there was a whole lot of venom in her tone.

"I'm only going to tell you once not to speak to my mother like that," Gracie said, pushing to her feet, which had everyone doing the same the minute she stepped forward. "I think you owe both her and Cutler an apology."

"That will not be happening." Britani glared at Gracie.

"Well, needless to say, I think it's a good thing you like construction, because if you can't be honest about your relationship, then you are in no position to run my company," Grant said, spewing his anger at me.

Really, dude? That's the best you've got?

"I think it's time we call it a night," Jana said.

"I think that's a very good idea." Presley crossed her arms over her chest. "I'd offer to walk you out, but I just don't want to."

My mom laughed, which was apparently contagious because we were all laughing now as the Langfords stormed away.

My gaze found Gracie's, and she smiled. And just like that, everything was better.

CHAPTER TWENTY-FOUR

Gracie

When I woke up Sunday morning, I was relieved the weekend was coming to an end. Not because I didn't love my parents. Not because I didn't love Cutler's parents.

It was because I missed being in his bed.

In his arms.

We'd all stayed up last night and laughed for a few hours after the Langfords had left, because it was the most bizarre night ever.

Cutler had surprised me when he'd stuck to his story about seeing someone. I figured after they'd left he'd say that he'd just made it up to let Britani down.

But instead, he'd doubled down. He'd said he'd met someone he was crazy about.

He and I hadn't gotten to talk about it, but he'd texted me last night once we were in bed and told me that he missed me, and I'd said I missed him too.

There was a knock on my bedroom door. I called out that it was open, and my mom and Emerson walked in.

"You slept late," Mom said. "The guys are making breakfast, but we came in here to grill you."

I rubbed my eyes and sat forward. "You can ask me anything, just never set me up on a date, because that was—a lot."

My mom climbed onto the bed on one side, and Emerson took the other.

"I promise, my matchmaking days are over." Mom shook her head in disbelief. "I called Grandma this morning, and she said she wasn't surprised at all. Apparently Britani is a handful, and they don't know what to do about it. I feel so bad for putting Cutler through that, though."

"He'll be okay," I said. "I still can't believe she followed him into the bathroom, and that she was so unhinged."

"Agreed. I was pretty shocked from the minute they walked in the door," Emerson said.

"In hindsight, I guess I really don't know them at all. Lesson learned." My mom sighed.

"So, we came in here to ask if you've met Cutler's lady," Emerson said.

"I have, and she's fabulous." I could feel the biggest smile spread across my face, and it took everything I had not to laugh.

"Really?" Mom pressed. "Why didn't you tell us when we told you about Britani coming over?"

"Well, first off, it isn't my story to tell. It's his personal life. And I didn't know that she thought he was betrothed to her. I thought it would be a casual dinner. No big deal. But clearly that did not happen."

Mom's head fell back with a laugh. "I think when Grant was asking him about taking over his company, I realized something wasn't right."

"How about when Jana asked if he was available to join them on their family vacation over Thanksgiving?" Emerson said over a fit of laughter. "It took all I had not to let her know that he always comes home for Thanksgiving. And that I was offended that she wanted my boy for Turkey Day, not even bringing up the fact that they literally just met."

"He's easy to love, isn't he?" I said, and they both stopped laughing and turned to look at me. I cleared my throat. "I mean, people just love him. He's that guy."

"Yes. He really is." Emerson smiled down at me. "And so are you, beautiful Gracie."

"Ahhh…slumber party in Gracie's room, huh?" Cutler said as he pounced onto the bed and then tickled me until I couldn't breathe from laughing so hard. "Come on. Breakfast is ready."

He stood up and helped both of our moms up from the bed, wrapping an arm around each of them.

"I just need to brush my teeth, and I'll be right out," I said.

"You got it, Jeege." His eyes scanned me from head to toe.

"Can I ask you one thing?" Emerson said as they walked toward the door.

"Ask away, Mama."

"Is this girl a good one?" she asked.

"This girl is the best girl." He glanced over his shoulder and winked at me.

My stomach fluttered and I scooted out of bed, escaping to the bathroom before they caught on.

I splashed water on my face and brushed my teeth before pulling on a sweatshirt and making my way out to the kitchen.

Everyone I loved was here, and the laughter made my chest squeeze.

I wished my brother was here, but we'd all be home for Christmas, and I was looking forward to it.

"There she is," my father said, and I made my way over to him and kissed his cheek.

"Good morning." I took my seat between Cutler and Nash and glanced around at the spread on the table. Waffles and fried eggs and sausage. "That was nice of you guys to cook for us."

"Cutler was the first one up today. I think he probably woke up early because he was a little traumatized by his unexpected date last night," my father said, raising a brow at my mother and Emerson.

"Hey, she just asked if he was single. It wasn't like I promised him to their family." My mother shook her head in disbelief. "Okay, let's talk about Thanksgiving and Christmas, Gracie girl. I know you'll be living in New York then, but you'll be home for the holidays, right? Burke will be done with his semester abroad, so he'll be home from Italy in early December. I'll be happy to have both of my children back in the same country as us."

"I know. I'm ready for him to be home too. And of course I'll come home for both holidays—I wouldn't miss it." I glanced over at Cutler, who was watching me.

The realization was hanging over our heads like a dark cloud.

When would I see him next? I was leaving at the end of September. I'd be flying home to Cottonwood Cove in November and December. I didn't know when I'd be able to come visit him.

The thought made my heart heavy.

A sick feeling settled in my stomach.

Everything was going to change when I left.

And I didn't want to think about it.

"Are you guys going to celebrate Christmas in the new house

here with everyone?" my father asked Nash, Emerson, and Cutler.

"That's the plan," Cutler said, smiling at his mom, but it appeared forced.

I knew exactly what he was thinking, because I was thinking the same thing.

It would be a while before we'd see one another again.

"Any chance we'll get to meet your special lady friend when we come for the holidays?" Emerson asked, and Nash laughed.

"His 'special lady friend'? That's very fancy, baby." Nash tugged her chair closer and kissed her cheek.

Our parents had such great relationships.

It was what I'd always wanted, but I'd failed immensely in that area of my life. Maybe having examples that were so amazing made it even more challenging to find.

"We'll see. If we're still together, I'll definitely bring her to Christmas dinner," he said confidently.

He sure was playing this game well.

Maybe he was planning to start dating for real when I left.

Maybe I'd awakened something in my best friend.

Because he'd definitely awakened something in me.

• • •

It was staging day at the Chadwicks' amazing home. When I worked for J&J Interiors, we had a team in place for move-in days. I didn't have that here, as this was a temporary situation. But this house was done and ready to be furnished, and everything I'd ordered and kept in storage was being delivered today, and boxes were already stacked in the living room for items that had recently arrived.

I would be fine on my own, minus moving the furniture. But the movers would be bringing in all the furniture and setting the items where I wanted them. The only issue would be if I didn't like where they'd put something and later needed it moved.

But I was hopeful that my vision of where everything would go was solid. I was thrilled that the Chadwicks had agreed to be surprised, and Emilia and Bridger would be flying here tomorrow afternoon to see it.

Today would be a very busy day. I didn't ask Cutler for help, because the man had four large projects going at the moment, so he had his hands full. I knew he had to be on-site today to meet the owners at a commercial project he'd just taken on. I also knew that he'd drop everything to help me, but he shouldn't have to.

I did, however, call Tatum and ask her to meet me here after work to help unpack the boxes and décor. She only worked half days at the senior living center on Saturdays, so she was happy to come help. She'd turned down the offer of money, after we'd argued profusely, but she'd agreed to let me feed her while she was here.

Just having a second set of hands would make a big difference. This was a large home.

I'd started unpacking boxes over the last week and I'd been setting things on the counter in the kitchen, and today I would hyperfocus and get it all done.

This morning was deliveries, so I made sure to get the area rugs put down before the furniture arrived.

There was a fifty-fifty chance the rug placement wouldn't be quite right, but hopefully it would be close enough that I could shift things on my own if I needed to.

I'd arrived here early this morning, and I'd already gone through a bunch of the décor I'd ordered. I didn't know for sure where each piece would go, but I knew that they would work somewhere. I loved the flexibility in design. A stack of vintage books or a gorgeous vessel could go in a kitchen or a living room or even a bedroom.

So I always found a bunch of those types of pieces to have on hand. Candles and antique vases were staples as well. Picture frames and lamps and floral arrangements brought in a ton of character.

I always loaded up on those items, all in the correct color palette, and then I'd find them a home once the furniture was all in place. I'd started to place items on the built-in bookshelves that I'd had built and painted in a sage green color. I couldn't wait for Emilia to see them, because most of the décor and furniture was going to be a surprise to her.

I walked through the home one last time before the chaos started. The wallpaper was absolutely stunning. William was a bit theatrical, but he was very talented and precise, and I appreciated it. Carl had done an amazing job painting, and he'd stayed late last night to get the trim work done.

The walls were a soft off-white and the trim was a crisp white, so the contrast brought some visual elements to the space. We'd added some really gorgeous wood accent walls throughout the home, with wainscoting in the dining room and hallways, and feature walls in all the guest suites.

I stopped in the primary closet and smiled as I tipped my head back to admire the dusty rose and cream floral wallpaper on the ceiling, along with the three antique gold pendant lights. I'd had a lot of fun choosing the light fixtures for this home, and they all looked so great together.

The doorbell rang, and I jogged downstairs.

It was game time. This was my favorite part of my job. Seeing a space completely come together.

Seeing your vision come to life.

The delivery guys showed up with the couches and tables, and bedroom furniture for each room. I'd gone with a lot of natural oak and some antique black and antique white pieces, with pops of color in the accent furniture and décor. There were beautiful reading chairs and end tables, and I'd already had the curtain rods hung. I couldn't wait to get the curtain panels up.

Everything was going as smoothly as I could have hoped, and I was thrilled. Several art pieces and mirrors that I'd ordered were heavier than I'd realized, and I wasn't quite sure if Tatum and I were going to be able to hang those on our own, but I was determined to figure it out.

By the time all the furniture had been delivered, Tatum showed up, along with the sandwiches I'd had delivered from the Cozy Griddle. A guy in town named Sammy had started a delivery service, and he was a life saver. There were no apps for the service—you just texted him and asked him to go pick it up, and you paid him cash. He'd even picked up a big box of cookies from Blue Sky Baykery that I wanted to put out on the island for Emilia and Bridger tomorrow.

This was what I loved about small towns.

"Ummm…wow," Tatum said as she gaped at the space filled with décor and several boxes stacked against the wall that still hadn't been opened. She nodded at a trio of nine-foot faux potted trees that we'd have to somehow move throughout the house until we found the right space for them. "I didn't expect there to be this much stuff."

"Yep. It's a big house and it's staging day," I said, handing her a bag with her sandwich and some chips. I unscrewed the top from a water bottle on the counter and took a gulp. I'd been hustling all morning, and even though the fall weather had arrived, I'd worked up a sweat. I pulled the elastic off my wrist and tied my long hair in a messy bun on top of my head. "You don't have to stay the whole time at all. You can help for a few hours and then take off."

"No way. I'm excited to do this with you."

I opened my sandwich and took a bite before setting it down and moving to open a large box that had just been delivered.

"I take it we don't sit down and eat?" she chuckled, her long blonde hair pulled back in a ponytail.

I laughed. "You can totally sit and eat. I just get overstimulated, and my adrenaline is on high alert on staging day, so I tend to graze and work. But you just got off your shift, so take a break for a little bit. How was work today?"

I cut the top of the box open and pulled out two gorgeous white-and-blue ginger jars that were just what we needed to bring some character into the kitchen. I walked over to one of the long cabinets with glass doors, then opened it up and placed the smaller jar on a higher shelf and the larger jar on a lower shelf. I stood back to admire how gorgeous they looked in there. I ran my fingers along the cremone bolts that I'd added as the hardware on the two long cabinets on each end of the kitchen.

Damn. This was really coming together.

"It was great. I really love my job," she said after she'd finished chewing. "I mean, some days are exhausting, but it's very rewarding at the same time."

Tatum was the activities director at Blue Sky Senior Living, an assisted living home, and she planned all the activities and events for their residents. I could tell how much she loved her job whenever she talked about it because she was always smiling and laughing when she'd tell me about her day.

"That's the best. How was Stan today?" I asked as I unpacked a bunch of wicker baskets that I'd use to organize the walk-in pantry.

"You know, he's my favorite. But that man is such a flirt. Bernice called him a 'dirty dog' today, and it took everything in me not to laugh in front of them." She reached for her water and took another sip. "But Captain doesn't seem like he's doing well, and that worries me. He's the retired veteran I told you about. He's the sweetest man, and I think I finally convinced him to let the nurse come evaluate him next week."

"Oh, that's a relief. You said he's been losing a lot of weight and looking really pale, right?" I asked as I broke down a few more boxes, and then studied all the lamps I'd set on the table.

"Yes. But hopefully it's just the flu or a bug." She crumbled up the paper that her sandwich had been wrapped in and tossed it in the trash bag. "Okay, put me to work."

"All right, if you can start opening those boxes there, and just start pulling out all the décor I ordered, we'll get it all unpacked, and then we'll start figuring out where to put it. It's the hanging stuff that I'm concerned about. Some of those mirrors are really heavy."

"We'll figure it out, don't worry at all." I gave her some scissors to open the boxes, and she got down to business while I started hanging the curtain panels on the rods. Window coverings made such a difference. They brought so much warmth to a space.

Tatum gasped from where she sat on the floor. "Oh my gosh, those are stunning. And the cream velvet panels with that crystal chandelier are just breathtaking."

We'd gone with a wire-brushed white oak, and I absolutely loved mixing the sort of rustic woods with a crystal chandelier. It just screamed French farmhouse, which was my favorite vibe.

"Yeah, it's gorgeous, right?"

"It is," she said as she gaped up at the chandelier with wide eyes. "So tell me, why aren't we asking your strong muscled lover to help us hang the heavy stuff?"

I snorted. "Of course he would do it if I asked, but he's got his own stuff to do. He had an important meeting today, and I told him that I had this covered. I don't want to start pulling him away from his work to help me with mine. Normally you have a team that you bring in on staging day, but seeing as I'm doing this as a little side gig while I'm here, I can't really hire people for such a short time."

"I totally get that. But I do have a question for you." She held up the faux floral arrangement that she'd just pulled out. "Wow. This is stunning. It looks so real."

"Yes. There are good faux florals and bad faux florals. You have to know where to order from." I reached for the arrangement and admired it myself before setting it on the kitchen counter for now. "What's your question?"

"So what happens when you leave here? I know you and Cutler are best friends, but do you just go back to being friends, and dating other people? It won't bother you if he's back on the market and hooking up with women after you leave?"

I was staring at the curtain panels I'd just hung in the dining room, and I blew out a breath.

The thought actually made me sick to my stomach. My hope was that the distance would make it less painful.

I wouldn't be happening in front of me and I wouldn't have to see it.

"I haven't fully thought that far, but it'll be fine. I'm the one who came up with the arrangement, so I have to accept the aftermath," I said. "There's no other option."

"No other option for what?" His deep voice had me whipping around to see Cutler walk through the door.

And he wasn't alone.

I don't know how he did it, but he always showed up when I needed him most.

CHAPTER TWENTY-FIVE

Cutler

"What? Oh, um," she said, eyes wide as if she didn't expect to see me here. "There is no other option for where to put the floral arrangement."

She quickly shrugged it off and then tilted her head to the side as if she was waiting for an explanation about why I was here.

"I figured you'd need help, so I brought backup." I eyed the barely touched food on the counter. "Is this your sandwich?"

"Yes. Are you hungry?" she asked, and I chuckled.

"No. I ate lunch. I'm wondering why you aren't eating—you've taken one bite, and you've been here for hours."

"Ahhh...you're becoming a real wet nurse, Heart." Cannon clapped me on the shoulder. "Put us to work, Gracie."

"You going to eat those chips?" Phoenix asked Tatum when she moved to the counter to take a sip of water. "I assume those are yours?"

She rolled her eyes and handed him the bag. "Some things never change."

"Hey, you were always more prepared with lunch than I was." He tore the top open and shoved a few chips in his mouth.

"You just ate at Four Clovers. How are you and Heart always hungry?" Brody asked with a laugh.

"Hey, this body is a work of art," Phoenix said over a mouthful of food. "I need to keep it well fed. Thanks, Tate."

"You're looking good, per usual, Tater Tot," Cannon said as he winked at her, and I noticed the way Phoenix's hands fisted at his side.

I could swear Cannon flirted with her just to get under his skin. Phoenix and Tatum had grown up living next door to one another, and he'd just always been protective of her.

Bass added, "I've got two hours before I have to be at the restaurant, so let's stop with the flirty banter and get our asses moving."

Gracie laughed, and she started directing us. The place was an absolute disaster, and I had no idea how she'd possibly have this ready to go by tomorrow morning, when my aunt and uncle were set to arrive.

I'd offered to move their arrival back by a day or two, but she'd turned me down. She had to get the Petersons' house staged next, and she said she worked best under pressure, and she never missed deadlines.

But looking around the place, I didn't know how she was going to pull this off.

We all spent the next few hours moving furniture, breaking down boxes, and carrying tall potted trees from room to room. I unpackaged more throw pillows than I'd ever seen in my life, and Brody and I were assigned to hanging things on the walls, with Gracie directing us like a fucking boss.

She was badass.

I loved watching her in her element.

Bass had to take off and get back to work. Tatum stayed until it got dark, when Gracie insisted she head home. Brody and Phoenix and Cannon stayed for another hour and hung floating shelves and carried all the broken-down boxes out to the recycling bin on the side of the house.

"All right, you think you two can handle the rest?" Brody asked.

"Yeah. We've got it. Thanks so much for coming," I said, giving each of them one of those half bro hugs that dudes did.

These were my brothers in every way.

We always showed up for one another.

Always had. Always would.

"You guys are life savers," Gracie said, pausing to give them each a hug. "I will be baking you all cookies and any other treats you want."

And then it was just the two of us. I made my way out to the backyard to help her place the outdoor furniture she'd ordered.

I had no idea how she would have done all of this herself, but I had a hunch she would've just stayed and worked through the night.

She was impressive, no doubt about it.

When we stepped back inside, I whistled as I took it all in.

It looked like something out of a magazine.

She hadn't stopped since we'd arrived, continuing to move things around on the built-in bookshelves until she'd gotten things just right.

I plopped down on the couch and watched her do her thing.

Seeing it all come to life with her design was next level.

"Damn. This looks fucking amazing, Jeege. You are unbelievably talented."

She turned to look at me, the corners of her lips turning up. "Thank you. I thought I'd be here until the sun came up, but we're almost done. This is unbelievable. Thank you so much for bringing everyone over. How did you even know I'd need help?"

"Maybe I did it for selfish reasons." I tugged her down onto my lap, wrapping my arms around her. "Maybe I wanted to make sure you were in my bed tonight."

She tipped her head back. "Thank you, Bear. You always know what I need."

"Yeah?" I leaned down and nipped at the lobe of her ear. "And what do you need right now?"

She sighed, and her warm breath tickled my cheek. "Let's go home and take a shower together."

"I could get on board with that. But I'm feeding you first because you never ate your sandwich."

She tipped her head back and chuckled. "What did I do to deserve you?"

"Exist. That's all you ever have to do."

And I fucking meant it.

Her eyes were wet with emotion, and she looked away briefly, as if everything we were feeling was too much.

Hell, I understood it, because I felt it too.

Somewhere along the way, our relationship had shifted.

And once again, the timing wasn't right for us.

• • •

I sipped my coffee after taking the last bite of French toast at the Cozy Griddle with Brody and Bass.

“So what’s the plan here, brother?” Bass asked, one brow raised.

“The plan with what?” I looked between them, because they were both staring at me with concern.

“Ummm…the woman who lives with you. Your best friend and now lover,” Brody chuckled.

I rolled my eyes just as Stanley, who owned the café with his wife, Margo, walked over to the table with a pot of coffee. “Refill?”

“Please. Apparently, I’m going to need it for this conversation.” I blew out a breath as the older man topped me off.

“Where’s your girl? She’s much better company than these two,” Stanley said with a smirk.

“Hey, I’m great company,” Bass snipped.

“Well, you’re not as pretty to look at.”

“We can’t argue that one.” Brody shrugged.

“Leave these boys alone and let them be,” Margo said as she swatted a towel at her husband.

“Just saying. He doesn’t look this grumpy when he’s with Gracie.” Stanley followed his wife back into the kitchen.

“My point exactly.” Bass turned to look at me, his tone all business now.

“Seriously? Are you guys worried about this? We’re fine. Everything is good. What’s the problem?” I asked, my voice coming off more defensive than I meant it to.

“Dude. You’re in the most serious relationship you’ve ever been in, and she’s fucking leaving,” Brody said. “This is not a fling. This is not a friends-with-benefits situation. This is a disaster in the making.” He shook his head in disbelief, as if I should have known this.

“We’ll be fine. We’ll figure something out.”

But I knew he was right. I was trying not to let myself even go there. Not to admit that I was clearly headed for exactly what I’d always avoided. Because I was in love with this girl, and when she left, it was going to shatter me. We had no idea what the future held, and she might leave and never look back. I mean, of course we'd always be best friends, but this was so much more now. And the idea of it ending scared the shit out of me.

"Have you discussed it? I mean, you could try the long-distance thing," Bass suggested.

"She's moving to New York. That's on the other side of the country. How would that possibly work?" Brody leaned back in the booth and reached for his mug.

I scrubbed a hand down my face. "Listen, things got a little more complicated than we planned. I know that. I didn't expect this to turn into what it has. Maybe it's because we have a history. Maybe it's because we were already best friends. I don't fucking know. But we have a plan, and I'm fairly certain she wants to stick to it."

She'd made that clear. She was the one who was leaving. The ball was in her court.

"I don't know that it's going to be that simple, Heart." Bass did not hide his concern. "I've never seen you like this. And you've always been the happiest dude I know. But you're just—happiest when you're with her. So I don't know how you're going to handle being away from her."

"It's not like you can pack up and move to New York. You have a business here. Have you guys discussed it?" Brody pressed. "Does she know how long she wants to stay in New York?"

"No. We don't talk about it. We're just—aware that it's coming, you know?" I tried to keep my tone calm, but I knew this was not going to be easy. "And she's excited about New York. So I don't want to fucking dim her light. I would never do that. But I'm not sure how this works when she leaves. We had rules in place, rules that I laughed about because she insisted on writing them down in her notebook. But it was always clear that it would end, and we'd just go back to being best friends."

These guys knew me well, and they were right to be concerned. I was concerned.

The only person who didn't seem concerned was Gracie.

She was confident about our plan, or at least she acted like she was.

She never talked about what would happen when she left. We were just always in the moment, but also very aware that there was an end date.

"Will it bother you if she starts dating when she moves to New York?" Bass asked.

My jaw clenched at his question.

"That's a fucked-up question. Don't ask me that," I hissed.

"Well, I guess I just got my answer." He gave me a look. "This is a wake-up call, Heart. You need to get yourself in check. Because she's leaving in less than a month, and you two are shacked up like you're in for the long game. We're just worried about you, brother. Hell, we're worried about her too."

I glanced down at my phone to see a text from my mom.

Mama: *Hey, sweetheart. I was just talking to Uncle Bridger about Christmas, and I told him you might be bringing your girlfriend. Is that still going strong?*

I groaned and set my phone down.

"What's wrong?" Brody asked.

"My mom is obsessed with meeting my mystery girl. She asked me if I was in love yesterday." I rubbed my face.

"Are you?"

"What? I mean, of course I love Gracie. I always have. But this is—different. At least for me it is. But I'm more than aware that this wasn't supposed to be her end-game. She doesn't think I'm that guy. She's also made it clear that she doesn't want to be in a serious relationship right now. That's why this works. For the first time in her life, she wants to focus on her career and herself. I know that. So what am I going to do? Fuck it all up for her and tell her I'm madly fucking in love with her?"

"Well, yeah. That's kind of how it works when you fall in love with someone. You're supposed to tell them." Bass smirked as he picked at the fruit on his plate and popped a piece of cantaloupe in his mouth.

"And what if I'm not that guy? What if I put it all out there and then I fuck it up? This is Gracie. I can't risk that."

"Has it ever dawned on you that you probably haven't ever been in a serious relationship because you've always been in love with your best friend?" Brody asked, tipping a shoulder up and pursing his lips. "You just weren't ready for it before now."

Bass nodded. "He's right. You're in a fucked situation."

"Thank you. I'm more than aware. And there's a lot at stake. But at the end of the day, I know she wants to go to New York. I know this is important to her. And if I tell her how I feel now, it's going to confuse her and make her feel bad for choosing her own dreams over me. I'm not that fucking guy. I won't do that." I blew out a breath.

"So what are you going to do?" Brody asked.

"I'm going to suck it up and stick to the plan. I owe her that much. And we'll see how it goes." I cleared my throat. "But for now, I'm going to enjoy my time with her, all right?"

"Of course, brother. I get it. It's a shit situation." Bass shook his head. "But I do think you're going to have to tell her how you feel at some point."

"I'm going to let her take the lead on how we handle it when she leaves. Some things aren't meant to be said. Sometimes loving someone means not being a selfish prick." I tossed my napkin on the table and shrugged.

Brody chuckled. "Damn. You really are in love with the girl. It's worse than I thought."

"You're a smart guy," Bass added. "You need to trust your gut. And we'll be here for you regardless."

"Thanks. Don't worry, it'll all be fine." I got up. "I need to stop wallowing and get my ass to work."

I wanted to enjoy these last few weeks and not worry about what would happen after.

I'd pick up the pieces and figure it all out when I had to.

What other option did I have?

CHAPTER TWENTY-SIX

Gracie

"So you like the apartment?" Johnny asked from the other side of our Zoom call. "It's in a great neighborhood. Fully furnished. Walking distance to the office."

"I love it. It's perfect," I said.

He'd sent me over a listing for an apartment that the company had sublet for me for the first three months after I arrived. It belonged to a client he'd done work for in Los Angeles, and she had several homes, and apparently she never used her Manhattan apartment. So she'd offered to rent it to J&J for three months, and she'd consider extending the lease at that time.

Seeing as I didn't even know where I wanted to live there, I was thrilled that he'd come up with a reasonable solution. I had three months to figure out where I'd rent permanently after that.

And this was the best area possible, according to Johnny.

He'd grown up in New York, and then moved to Los Angeles to open J&J Interiors with his cousin Jenna before moving back to the Big Apple to focus on that office.

"Are you ready for this move? The countdown is on. Three weeks to go. Everything is falling into place." He smiled and leaned back in his chair. "I posted all those photos that you sent me of the Chadwick home on the website, so clients could see your recent work. That project was truly spectacular, darling."

Johnny was the most exuberant, enthusiastic person on the planet. He always dressed to the nines in his designer suits, and his personality was larger than life. He'd been the most amazing mentor to me when I'd started at the firm, and we'd formed a close friendship.

"Yes. It was a great project to dip my toes back into design. The budget was the largest I've worked with, and they really gave me creative control for all the interior furnishings, which was wonderful."

"Well, we've gotten so many messages about the design. You really nailed it. It was very unique. Very you," he said. "And that's what you bring to the table. This very special design aesthetic, along with the ability to know what your clients want, and then to be able to give it to them. It's a gift. And I'm so thrilled to have you back at the firm, and we're going to be in New York City together. It doesn't get any better."

"It really doesn't," I said, but it felt forced. "But I'm sure I'll be doing a lot more modern, contemporary designs when I get to New York."

"Yes. It's a different vibe here for sure. I had to pivot a bit from what I was used to out west. The sort of organic, boho vibe was popular there, and it's darker and moodier here for the most part.

You'll get your occasional client who wants a European vibe, or a very traditional aesthetic—but modern minimalist is a popular trend on the East Coast right now." He chuckled. "I believe in you. You're a very talented woman."

"Thank you, Johnny. I'm so honored that you trust me to work for you." I sighed. I was thrilled about this next adventure, but it was a weird mix of emotions for me. I didn't realize that I could be excited about something while dreading it at the same time.

How could I feel such strong feelings that completely conflicted with one another?

"What am I picking up on?" he asked, leaning forward now. "Is there hesitation in your voice?"

"What? No. Of course not. I couldn't be more excited. This is the opportunity of a lifetime. And it means the world to me that you believe in me and that you want me back. And at the New York office. It's an amazing opportunity. Especially after the way I left the first time." My words were strained, my stomach in knots every time I thought about leaving.

"The way that you left?" He chuckled. "You gave me a month's notice, you apologized profusely, you made sure all of your clients' needs were met before you left, and you took a shot at love, darling. Mind you, he was a wanker, but you needed to find that out for yourself. I believe it's all part of being a creative individual. Look at me: I've been in love three times in the last four months."

Now it was my turn to laugh. "You do have all the big feelings, don't you?"

"Always. And I wouldn't change a thing. So tell me, are we worried about leaving the big teddy bear? I know how close you two are. And you've been living there and working together since you left Paris. I'm sure it will be hard to leave your bestie again. And he is one beautiful man, isn't he?" He clasped his hands together and rested his chin there.

"He's the best." I shook my head, blinking several times, because even thinking about leaving Cutler made me emotional. "But he knows I'm leaving and he supports me."

His mouth dropped open, eyes wide. "What aren't you telling me?"

"Nothing. I just said that he supports me."

"It's in your eyes, darling. Oh boy." He fanned his face. "You took a trip to Dicktopia, didn't you? You went to Pleasuretown with your best friend, and you liked it. I mean, who could blame you after your last lover. Gabriel is what I like to refer to as a cockissist."

"A what?" I asked over my laughter.

"A cocky-narcissist. I can spot them a mile away. He was arrogant. Wealthy. Self-focused. I'm sure the sex was terrible."

"You aren't wrong."

"There you go. So you went back to the small town that probably felt like home and you fell into the big, strong arms of the handsome bear who's loved you your entire life. Of course you'd want to experience the good life. That man is all man. All. Man." He raised a brow. "But now things are…complicated? We're in a gray area?"

"Have you ever considered writing a romance book? You've got quite the imagination."

"If I wasn't so busy managing this business, I would definitely write erotica. I love me a sexy alpha." He wriggled his eyebrows.

"Don't we all." I smirked. "But I'm fine. He's fine. Everything is fine."

"He certainly is."

I covered my mouth with my hand to try to slow my laughter. "I just mean that we'll figure it out. It'll all be okay. We'll just need to find our new normal. It's been really nice here, and I've needed this. But I'm ready to take on this next challenge. You can count on me."

His gaze softened, and I saw the empathy there. "You're always so hard on yourself, Gracie. Listen to me. You come to New York, and I'll be here guiding you. We have a great team in place as well. You design your ass off for a few months and you live in that gorgeous apartment, and you have your Carrie Bradshaw moment, living in the most amazing city in the world. And if it doesn't make you happy, and you see something different for yourself, I am the first person who will support you. You know that, right? No one is ever stuck, darling. Not at J&J Interiors. I will keep you for as long as you want to be here. But I've always known that you'll branch off on your own someday. It's what the most talented people do. Look at me?"

I couldn't hide the smile on my face, because I was very lucky to have a mentor like Johnny. I also knew that I needed to do this.

I needed to stand on my own two feet after losing my stride for a while.

Being in Blue Sky Bay, being with Cutler—it was a safety net.

He had always been my safe place.

And I needed to prove that I could handle challenges.

I could face my fears.

Paris had been a huge setback for me, both in my career and emotionally. I'd lost my confidence, my mojo. I'd doubted myself more than I wanted to even admit.

And I desperately needed to reclaim that on my own.

To prove that I was still that girl who could do whatever she set her mind to.

I would regret it if I let this opportunity go because I was afraid of failing.

Because I was afraid of leaving Cutler.

"Love you, Johnny. Thank you for everything."

"I'll see you soon, darling. We'll be sipping martinis and swapping fabric swatches in no time."

• • •

"This is amazing," I said as we walked through downtown toward the town square. I'd never been in Blue Sky Bay at the start of fall, and to say that this small town rose to the occasion was a massive understatement. Tonight was the grand opening of the fall festival, and the entire downtown along Bay Avenue was decorated with hay bales and pumpkins, with corn stalks wrapped around every light post. Every store window was decked out, and it was so festive and fun. But the town square at the center of everything was where they'd put the pumpkin patch, and the place had been completely transformed. Normally the square had a large grassy area where people sat and had picnics. They'd set off the fireworks for the big Fourth of July event here as well. It was across from the container park, so everyone could go back and forth between the two.

"They go all out, right?" Cutler said as his large hand covered mine.

My gaze moved around at the maze of hay bales and pumpkins and gourds. Carnival games had been set up around the perimeter, and music played through the speakers downtown.

"They really do. I knew they went all out at Christmastime, but I've never been here at the end of September."

He smiled down at me, and I loved how proud he was of the town that he lived in. He'd felt the same way about Magnolia Falls, the small town where he'd grown up. But I remembered him telling me back in college that he wanted to expand his father's business someday and move to Blue Sky Bay.

And Cutler Heart was a man of his word. He always did what he said he was going to do.

I loved that about him.

"Gracie, Cutler," a familiar voice called out, and we both turned to see Shana and Billy Peterson walking toward us.

"Hey, how are you guys?" I asked as I gave them both a hug, and Cutler greeted them as well.

"I mean, look how relaxed I look." Shana motioned to her face and laughed. "We're so happy in the new home. Truly, you both exceeded our wildest dreams."

"We could never thank you enough for what you did for us," Billy said, looking between us. "You turned that fixer-upper into our dream home."

"That's so nice of you to say." Cutler clapped Billy on the shoulder, and I couldn't help but smile at the overwhelming pride I felt. The reveal had been beyond what I could have imagined. Shana had cried multiple times, which in turn had made me cry.

Creating a home for clients was the best job in the world.

It was about bringing their vision to life, in a place that they wanted to grow old in.

How do you beat that?

"I'm so happy you love it." I sighed. "It's the best compliment ever."

"You two make quite a team," Shana said. "Too bad you aren't sticking around, Gracie. I think you could make a real mark on this town with your talent." She started blinking rapidly, and her husband laughed as he wrapped an arm around her.

"She gets this way pretty much every day when we wake up in the morning," he said. "This was a long time coming, and having a place for our boys to call home means everything to us."

"Speaking of our rugrats, we should probably go find them." Shana hugged me one more time.

I waved and then turned to look at Cutler as I blew out a big breath. "That was sweet of them to say."

"You're more talented than you know, Jeege. Let that sink in," he said, stroking the hair away from my face. "Making dreams come true for people is a gift."

"She was talking to you too." I arched a brow. It was getting cooler with each passing day, and I was grateful that I'd worn a heavier sweater tonight, because the breeze off the water bustled around us.

"I know. But I'm confident about my skills." He smirked. "I know my talent. I know I'm where I'm supposed to be, building new homes and renovating old ones, and changing this town one home at a time. But you're just getting started on your career journey. And I want you to recognize your talent and your worth, because there's no one like you, Gracie Reynolds."

My heart thumped against my chest as a large lump formed in my throat.

"You've always seen me, haven't you."

"Always. Even when you couldn't." He tugged me against him and kissed my hair.

"There you are," Phoenix said as he came jogging over. "I just got off work and thought I'd meet you here before we head over to Four Clovers."

"I wouldn't have guessed you to be a pumpkin patch guy," I teased as the three of us started walking toward the fun.

"I'm not. But Margo Burns always sets up a stand with her famous hot chocolate, and she adds all sorts of toppings, and that shit is addicting." He motioned to the booth in the corner, and we followed him over there.

"I saw that the firehouse window was all decorated with pumpkins wearing fire helmets," I said with a laugh, and he shook his head, a wide grin spreading across his face.

"Yeah, the rookies have to do the windows for the holidays, and they had a little too much fun doing it this year." He paused when Margo clapped her hands together.

"You never could resist my hot chocolate, Phoenix. And Cutler is always nagging me to serve it earlier every year at the diner." She winked at them. "Gracie, are you ready for the best hot chocolate you've ever had?"

"I sure am." I moved closer to Cutler when a gust of wind blew past me, and his arm came around me like it was the most natural thing in the world. He rubbed my shoulders as Stanley filled the cups with cocoa, and then Margo added the whipped cream and sprinkles.

"They don't make it this good in New York City," Stanley said as he handed me a cup. "You know what they say about Blue Sky Bay, don't you?"

"Tell me," I said, wrapping my hands around the cup of warm cocoa.

"'Once you give your heart to Blue Sky Bay, you never get it back.'" He smirked.

And I had a feeling he was right.

But Blue Sky Bay wasn't the only one I'd given my heart to.

And I feared I'd never get it back.

Because I knew in my gut that it was exactly where it was supposed to be.

CHAPTER TWENTY-SEVEN

Cutler

There was this looming cloud hanging over our heads, and I could tell it was weighing on Gracie.

We'd need to have the talk that neither of us wanted to have. She was leaving in three days. We couldn't avoid it anymore.

It felt like a cruel joke in some ways. Everything was so good right now. We were happy. And it was all going to come to an end.

We'd have to find our new normal, and I didn't have a fucking clue what that would look like.

I rolled on my side, where she was snuggled up against me, sleeping soundly.

Long black lashes rested along the top of her cheek, and her plump pink lips were parted the slightest bit, her hands drawn together just beneath her chin. Her long hair was a wild mess of waves falling all over the white pillow.

She looked like a fucking angel.

I could look at her forever and it wouldn't be long enough.

I wanted to memorize every single curve of her face so I'd never forget this moment.

Waking up with Gracie Reynolds in my bed was not something I took for granted.

I knew that I was the luckiest man in the world at the moment, but I also knew that it wasn't forever.

And that was a tough pill to swallow.

To know in your gut that this was your person, that this was the other half of your soul—but to also know that you had to let her go.

You had to let her spread her wings and fly.

Because you loved her that much.

She started to stir, and the corners of my lips turned up. Because we didn't have anywhere to be this morning.

No work.

No meetings.

There was a talk that needed to happen between us, but something else needed my attention first.

I moved to the foot of the bed and lifted the covers before slipping beneath them, and I crawled up ever so slowly as I gently moved her legs apart.

She stirred some more, a little moan of pleasure escaping her, and I couldn't help but smile.

I knew what she wanted. What she needed.

And she knew I was going to give it to her.

I kissed my way up the inside of her thighs, which was easy to do, seeing as we both slept naked now. Her legs fell apart even further, as she tangled her fingers in my hair tucking me closer. I chuckled as I pressed my mouth to her core.

All that sweetness.

My tongue swiped along her seam, licking and sucking as a groan escaped her.

"You're so wet," I whispered against her. "So sweet."

Her fingers tangled in my hair, tugging and pulling, and I fucking loved it.

I loved everything about her.

Her heart. Her body. Her mind. Her laugh.

Gracie Reynolds really was my forever girl.

She was it for me. Always had been.

I flattened my tongue and slid it up and down her heat as she bucked wildly beneath me.

I'd bring her right to the edge and then pull back.

Letting that desire build.

That need.

"Please," she begged, and I fucking loved it.

I fucking loved the sound of her begging me for pleasure.

I sucked hard on her clit, flicking my tongue there, giving her exactly what she wanted.

Her body shook, her legs tightened around me, her fingers tugged hard at my hair as she fell apart on my lips.

And I stayed right there.

Wanting her to ride out every last bit of pleasure.

When her breathing slowed, I raised my head, and she lifted the edge of the blanket.

"Good morning, Bear," she said, her voice sated and sexy as hell.

I crawled up her body and moved beside her, adjusting her so that her head rested on my chest. "Good morning, baby."

Her fingers traced along the muscles on my stomach. "Not a bad way to wake up. I'm going to miss this."

It was the perfect segue.

"Yeah? We haven't really talked about you leaving, and it's only a few days away. Do you think we should discuss it?" I asked as I rubbed her arm.

She didn't move. Didn't turn to look at me. But I could suddenly feel the tension radiating from her body. "We knew it was coming, but I didn't expect it to be this—complicated."

"I didn't either." It was the truth, the sad reality that was waiting for us.

"You're not a relationship guy, remember?" she chuckled, but it wasn't genuine, and we both knew it. She wanted to make light of this, but that wasn't going to work.

"Maybe I didn't realize the right girl was there in front of me the whole time. I'm not proud to say I didn't let myself see what this was until now," I said, laying it all out there.

She pushed herself up, taking the sheet with her, then wrapped it around herself so she was sitting up facing me, her legs tucked beneath her.

"I don't think either of us knew what this was. It was supposed to be casual. Friends with benefits, remember?" she said, her bottom lip trembling. "That's what I expected it to be. Because I already fell on my face giving up everything for a man before I came here, and I've made all these plans to restart my life. To focus on my career. This wasn't supposed to happen, Bear."

I reached up with the pad of my thumb and swiped at the tear rolling down her cheek. It nearly broke me to see that tormented look in her eyes.

"What wasn't supposed to happen?" I sat forward, wanting to pull her onto my lap and kiss her senseless, but I knew we needed to have this conversation.

"I wasn't supposed to fall in love with you," she whispered, and when she looked up, I saw so much pain in her eyes.

It wasn't the right time for us.

It never had been.

I knew it. She knew it.

But that didn't make it any easier.

Hearing those words—it did something to me. I wanted to hold on to this moment, memorize it and savor it.

She loved me too.

It was fucking ironic that we were here.

Both admitting our feelings. And now we were going to be living on opposite sides of the country.

"Sometimes you can't plan these things. I've never been in love, Jeege, not until now. Obviously, I've always loved you, but this is different. And I sure as shit didn't plan it. But I don't regret one damn thing about this. Not one thing, Jeege."

"You don't?" she croaked as tears streamed down her beautiful face.

"No. Because I've loved you my whole life, Gracie Reynolds. I loved you when I was a kid and I didn't know what it meant. I loved you when I didn't even believe in this kind of love. I loved you when I was in meaningless relationships that meant nothing to me. I loved you when you were in serious relationships. And I will love you for as long as I'm on this earth."

"Cutler," she sniffed, the word barely audible. "How am I supposed to leave now? I'm moving to the other side of the country. A different time zone. A long plane ride away. This isn't like I'm going to be living in Los Angeles, and we can drive back and forth. I don't know how this is going to work."

Her anxiety was palpable. Thick and real and overwhelming.

I'd always been able to feel Gracie's pain, and I felt it more than ever now.

"Hey." I used the pads of my thumbs to swipe her tears away before placing my hand beneath her chin and tipping it up until her gaze met mine. "This isn't our time, baby. But that doesn't change the way we feel. Nor would I ever ask you to give up your dreams for me."

This was the most difficult thing I'd ever done, and I'd had some difficult days in my life.

But convincing the woman I loved that it was okay to leave me—that would forever be the hardest thing I'd ever done.

But that's how much I loved her.

I loved her enough to let her go. To set her free. To watch her fly.

I had to believe that our time would come.

But right now, we didn't have options. I was in the middle of several large projects, and she had the opportunity of a lifetime waiting for her in New York.

"So we just say goodbye?" she croaked. "That's it?"

"It's never goodbye with you. You're a part of me. And I'll be here, Gracie. I'm not going anywhere." I sighed as a heavy feeling settled in my chest. And I knew it had to be said, because I would not be another shithead who robbed her of her happiness. "And if you go to New York, and you meet someone, and your life is everything you want it to be—I will love you regardless. That will never change. This is your time, Jeege, and I want you to go do whatever it is that you need to do. I will always be your biggest fan. So you go do your thing. Don't worry about anything else, okay?"

"What if I'm gone for years?" she asked, throwing her hands in the air.

"Then you're gone for years." I kept my voice calm and steady so she wouldn't see the panic behind those words.

"I'm going to miss you." She sniffed several times as tears streamed down her beautiful face. "I'm going to miss you so much."

"Listen, it'll all work out. We're C & G for life, right? We'll be fine. Just go and spread your wings, and don't worry about me or about us. We will always be okay." I pulled her onto my lap and wrapped my arms around her, and she just stayed right there, tears falling and sobs escaping.

I squeezed my eyes closed because I felt a sense of finality.

And she was crying because she felt it too.

"I love you, Cutler Heart. And if you fall in love with someone else, I'll understand. I want you to be happy. And whoever gets to be loved by you is the luckiest girl in the world." She cried as the words left her mouth.

I didn't want to tell her what I knew to be true.

She was the only girl I would ever love.

And time was just playing a cruel joke on us.

CHAPTER TWENTY-EIGHT

Gracie

"I don't know why you're insisting on doing this when you only have two days left until you leave," he groaned when we pulled up at the pound and got out of the truck.

"Because I don't want you to be lonely." It was the truth. He was so busy supporting me that he didn't stop to think about himself and how he would feel after I left. He'd just acted all stoic and brave, after pouring his heart out to me and telling me to go chase my dreams.

This was the kind of love story that you read about in a book, or watched on the big screen.

Who'd have thought my epic love story would be with the boy I'd known my whole life?

The man I felt safest with.

The man I was walking away from in two days.

"Jeege, I've lived alone for a long time. And the guys will be so far up my ass after you leave that you won't have to worry."

"Listen," I said as I came to a stop before opening the door. The brick building had large windows with paw print decals on them with a worn sign hanging above. "I came here earlier this morning while you were working, and I had no intention of finding a dog. I just felt this need to come look. And what happened, you ask?"

"I didn't ask."

"Well, I'm going to tell you anyway," I chuckled. "I met the dog you're supposed to have. He even kind of looks like you."

"He's undeniably handsome?"

"Well, he has your coloring. The hair. The eyes. The muscular stature."

"You have the same coloring as I do," he said. "Does he look like you?"

"Oh gosh, I hope not." I laughed as I tugged the door open. "Hey, Jeanette. Tell me you didn't let anyone take Meatball home."

"Meatball?" he said, gaping at me, and I just laughed.

"Trust me. It suits him."

Jeanette chuckled. "Oh, sweetie, no one has been in here today aside from you. He's exactly where he was when you came by this morning."

"See. It's meant to be," I told Cutler with a look.

"Interesting name," he said as we followed Jeanette to the back.

"You're going to love him. He's gentle and sweet, like a meatball."

"He really is the sweetest," Jeanette said as she pulled out her keys. "He's a chocolate English bulldog, and he's four years old, so he's fully potty trained, and he's just a great dog."

"If he's so great, why is he here?" Cutler grumped, and I knew he wasn't thrilled about this, but I had to do something. I hated the idea of him being lonely after I left.

"We don't know," the older woman said as she pulled open the door. "He wasn't chipped, and someone found him sitting outside the Cozy Griddle a few days ago. I searched all the usual places, and no one reported him missing. Sometimes tourists just decide to leave their pets after they visit. I just can't imagine leaving a family member behind like that."

I glanced over at Cutler and then back at Meatball, who moved at a snail's pace and came up to me and then immediately walked over to Cutler, where he dropped to sit on his feet.

Cutler bent down and scratched the back of his head. "Hey, buddy. Did someone leave you behind?"

Meatball dropped all the way down before rolling on his back, and Cutler laughed. Jeanette said she'd give us some time alone with him and excused herself.

I dropped down to sit on the floor as well, and Meatball pawed at Cutler to keep rubbing his belly.

"He's pretty fucking cute," he said.

"I told you. Can you see the resemblance?" I asked, which made him laugh again.

"Yeah, Jeege. I can see it. He's got a big head and a wide chest. I'll take it as a compliment." He dropped to sit beside me. "And what about you? Are you going to get a dog?"

"Well, I'll be living in a small studio apartment in Manhattan, so that's a hard no. And I'll be working long hours in the beginning. You can take Meatball to work with you, and he can go to Four Clovers with you. It'll be great."

"You know I've lived alone for a long time, right?" he asked as Meatball fully climbed onto his lap.

"I know," I said with a sigh. "I just don't like the idea of you being alone."

"I'll be fine."

"Well then, do it for me." I shrugged. "If you have this big guy in your bed, I don't think there will be room for anyone else."

I kept my voice light, but I think he saw through me. I wasn't just nervous about leaving; I was heartsick over it.

Heartsick because I'd finally found what I'd been looking for my whole life, and now I was just going to walk away from it?

Why was life so damn complicated?

First, I left a great job and a great apartment, for the wrong man.

And now I was leaving the right man, for a job and an apartment that wouldn't mean anything to me if I wasn't with him.

"Hey. Look at me." His voice was commanding and firm.

I looked up. "I'm looking at you, Bear."

"Stop worrying. We'll talk every day, and we'll see how it goes, all right?" His gaze locked with mine.

I nodded. "Yeah. I guess it's time for a new plan, since the original plan really went to shit."

He laughed, and Meatball made a weird howling sound as if he were trying to mimic Cutler. "The plan is that we don't have a plan. We just roll with it, Jeege. It'll be okay."

"Okay. Sometimes no plan is a plan." I shrugged.

He kissed the top of my head. "So do we know what Meatball needs to have at the house?"

"Does this mean you're taking him home?"

"I mean, he's a slobbery fucker, and there's a very foul smell coming from him, so I'm guessing he's also gassy."

"Like father, like son," I said, and he cackled before pushing to his feet.

He offered me a hand and pulled me up. "I'm doing this for you."

Jeanette came around the corner. "What do we think?"

"We think whoever left him behind was an asshole," Cutler said. "We'll take him."

"Meatball is a lucky boy, I can tell." She walked us to the front and set us up with all sorts of stuff: a crate, dog treats, a week's worth of dog food, and a booklet about being a new pet owner.

We piled into Cutler's truck, and Meatball sat between us, as if he'd done it a hundred times before. Cutler turned on the radio, and we sang along with Benson Boone all the way home.

And I'd never been happier than right here in this moment. Completely content.

When we got home, we set up the crate and took Meatball out in his new yard.

"Do you think I can take him out on the boat?" Cutler asked.

"I don't know, do all dogs know how to swim?"

"These are probably things we should have found out before adopting a dog." He looked at me as my phone vibrated in my back pocket again.

I pulled it out and glanced down to see four missed calls from Johnny. "Johnny's called a bunch of times. Let me try him back real quick."

He nodded as he sat in an Adirondack chair, watching Meatball wander around the yard. I stepped inside and dialed Johnny's number.

"Finally," he said, his voice sounding even more enthusiastic than usual. "I've called you multiple times."

"I'm so sorry. Cutler just got a dog, so we were distracted."

"Damn. A sexy man with a dog is even more attractive," he said, his voice laced with humor. "I digress. I have news."

"Okay. What is it?"

"Well, you know our firm is very well known, and has been

written up in many design magazines over the years."

"Yes. It's the best. That's why I want to work there," I said, chuckling.

"Let's just say our website gets a lot of exposure." He paused, and I could tell he was drinking something. "I just received a call from *Design & Décor* magazine. You know, only the top design magazine out there."

"Yes. I'm a subscriber. It's my favorite."

"Well, buckle up, darling. They want to feature you because they fell in love with the photos of the Chadwick home. They'll fly out to New York and interview you, and if the Chadwicks are okay with it, they'd like to schedule a shoot at their home."

"What? Are you kidding me?" I gasped. "*Design & Décor* wants to interview me?"

He was laughing hysterically now, and Johnny had one of those laughs that made you laugh when he laughed.

"Darling. You're a star. I just emailed you the information to send to the Chadwicks to ask if they'd be okay with having their home featured in the most popular interior design magazine on the planet." He chuckled. "I'm sure it's a yes, especially since Emilia Chadwick has been featured in this magazine before. The fact that she gave you creative control over their family home also speaks volumes. And we'll go shopping for you when you get here, and pick out something fabulous for you to wear to your interview."

"Okay. Yes. Oh my gosh. I need to go tell Cutler. Thank you. I'll see you soon."

"You will. I'll be waiting for you with bells on when you get to the airport."

We ended the call and I ran out the door into the backyard, surprised when I didn't see him there or Meatball in the grass where I'd left them.

"Bear?" I shouted as the sun was just starting to go down.

"I'm in the lake. And no, Meatball does not know how to swim. He thought he did, when he jumped in with no warning, and he just sank." Laughter came from the edge of the yard down by the water. Meatball was lying on the wood dock soaking wet, not a care in the world.

I ran to the end of the dock and gaped down at Cutler. "*Design & Décor* magazine wants to feature me for the photos they saw of your family home."

"You're a fucking rock star, baby," he howled, and once again, Meatball let out a howl of his own. "That's my girl."

I was laughing as I moved closer and realized he was in his clothes. "Why are you in the water fully clothed?"

"Because that dog you convinced me to get decided to jump in, and he literally made no effort to fight for his own survival. He actually glanced over at me as I ran toward the water, and he just surrendered and started to sink. So I had to fucking jump in and save his lazy ass."

I covered my mouth with my hand and shook my head. "Look at you, Bear. Jumping in the water and saving Meatball."

"Well, come on, girl. Get your ass in here. We've got to celebrate. You're going to be in a magazine."

I dropped my phone and kicked my boots off on the dock next to Meatball, and I didn't even think twice before jumping in the water with my clothes on. I didn't care that it was cold enough to be wearing two layers. I wanted to be in the water with him.

The immediate shock of the cold water had my body tensing and my skin prickling when I broke through the surface.

Cutler was right there to catch me as I grabbed onto his shoulders, gasping a few times.

"I'm proud of you," he said.

"Do you think your family will be okay with having their home featured?" I asked.

"Are you kidding? They'll be fucking thrilled." He pulled me closer, and my legs came around his waist. "They're all going to be so proud of you."

"They're sending someone to New York to interview me next week." I shook my head. "I can't believe this is happening."

"I never had a doubt. Keep chasing those dreams, baby, and I'll be cheering you on the whole way." He tugged me down and kissed me.

And we sat in the water as the sky darkened and the stars sparkled overhead, with Meatball lying there watching us make out like teenagers. We laughed and talked and kissed some more.

It was interesting to me that I'd known Cutler most of my life, yet we never ran out of things to talk about. There was just a comfort and closeness that made it so easy to talk with him about anything.

And that's exactly what we did.

I wished I could freeze time right here.

Because I never wanted this moment to end.

Blue Sky Bay felt like home, because the truth was…

Cutler Heart was my home.

CHAPTER TWENTY-NINE

Cutler

I woke up with a sick feeling in my stomach. It was Gracie's last day here. I hated the thought of not waking up with her after tomorrow.

I glanced over to the side of the bed, where loud snoring had woken me up multiple times during the night, to see Meatball in his crate, sound asleep on his back.

This dog was a character, no doubt about it.

Maybe she was right, and having him here would be a good distraction.

I'd offered to fly with her to New York, but she'd shipped her personal items there already, and she was only bringing clothing, as the apartment was fully furnished. She'd come back and get the rest of her stuff once she found something permanent, in a couple of months.

She'd told me it would be more difficult for her if I came with her.

I wasn't sure why, but I'd nodded and agreed.

A loud snort came from the crate, and Gracie chuckled from where she slept beside me. Her eyes were still closed, and she'd rolled on her side to face me, but she was obviously awake now.

"He's quite the vocal guy," she said, her voice sounding sleepy.

"He sure is. I think he was wiped out from his two-second swim where he literally exerted no energy and just threw in the towel," I said, and she laughed some more as her eyes slowly opened.

"Hey."

"Hey," I said. "How'd you sleep?"

"I slept great. Your bed is so cozy." She intertwined her fingers with mine.

And we both just lay there quietly.

Everything had already been said.

We stayed there, listening to the sound of Meatball snoring, and she scooted closer so I could wrap my arms around her as I breathed in the smell of strawberry and coconut.

A loud howl came from the crate, and we both laughed as we moved to our feet. I pulled on some pants and took him out back while Gracie got dressed.

We decided to walk Meatball downtown, as Gracie wanted to stop by Blue Sky Bay-kery for some croissants and walk along the water.

"The reason I didn't want you to come with me to New York for the move isn't because I don't want you there with me," she said, peeking up at me as the breeze moved around us.

"I know you want to go do this on your own. I get it." It had been a bit of a punch to the gut when she'd initially told me—but I understood her need to do this at the same time.

"That's not it." She blew out a breath. "It's hard for me to leave you, Bear. And if you come with me, I won't want you to leave. So I just think we need to rip the Band-Aid off all at once."

"I understand. I don't disagree." I ran a hand through my hair, Meatball staying right beside me on his leash, walking at a snail's pace.

"I hate goodbyes."

"Then we won't say goodbye because it's not goodbye," I said, exhaling before continuing. "Come on. I wanted to show you this piece of land that just came on the market. I'd love to get your opinion on it."

Meatball decided to just sit down when we moved off the path along the water to take a detour through the trees. I tried to get him to move, but he was just dead weight, and Gracie's head fell back in hysterical laughter when I picked his lazy ass up and carried him the rest of the way.

I set him down on the plot of land that had one of the best views in Blue Sky Bay.

"Wow. This is spectacular. And it's a large piece of land."

"I thought you'd like it." I dropped Meatball's leash because he was not going anywhere, and he appeared to be a happy camper to just stay right there under a tree. Gracie turned in a circle, taking it all in.

"It's the perfect mix of mountain and water views. It's so peaceful out here too, yet it's just a short walk to downtown."

"Yeah, I've had my eye on it for a while, and it just came on the market this week."

A few months ago, I wouldn't have hesitated. I would have put an offer on the land the minute it hit the market. It was the perfect place to build a custom home.

But I was hesitant because I didn't know what the future held anymore.

If I'd have a reason to leave.

The only reason I'd consider leaving was standing in front of me.

She bit her bottom lip. "It's pretty dreamy. I can see why you had your eye on it. Would you build a home for yourself? Or a home to sell?"

A home for us.

"I don't know. Both are options."

"Well, I think this has to be the best location in Blue Sky Bay. You can walk to downtown, you've got the most incredible view of the lake, and look at those mountains. Can you imagine those in the winter when they're covered in snow? It's really magical. I love it."

I nodded. "Yeah. It's a special piece of land."

She spent the next thirty minutes walking the property and telling me everything she would do if she designed this home. The entire back of the house would be windows. The view would be the focal point. She'd have courtyards in other areas of the home, because the surrounding forest would offer gorgeous views if you had sitting areas off the home. I loved her creativity. Her vision.

We both shared a love for taking nothing and creating something special.

She continued talking about it on our walk home. I carried Meatball, because apparently, he was done with physical exercise for the day.

He curled up in the dog bed that we'd grabbed for him on the way home, and I sat on the edge of my bed and watched as she packed up one of two large suitcases that she'd be taking with her on her flight to New York early tomorrow morning.

And before I realized it, it was time to get dressed and ready for Gracie's goodbye party down at Four Clovers.

I chuckled as I realized we were color-coordinated when she strolled out of the bathroom. She wore a white flowy skirt, black cowboy boots, and a cream sweater that hung off her shoulder.

"I mean, we didn't even plan this." She smiled as she walked over to where I was sitting on the bed after just pulling on my work boots. "I like your tan polo shirt. We match well."

"Did we plan it, though? You did buy me the shirt."

"I love a neutral aesthetic." She leaned down and kissed me. "We definitely need to get some photos tonight."

We decided to leave Meatball at home after feeding him and taking him out. Tonight would be busy at the container park, since it was line dancing night.

Once we arrived, the place was already going off. "Busy" was an understatement. I could swear, everyone in town had come out to say goodbye to Gracie. She'd made a mark on this town and the people who lived here.

She and Tatum had dragged Stanley and Margo out on the dance floor, and all the guys and I were laughing our asses off as we watched. Everyone from my office, and even some of the subcontractors, William and Carl and Jackson, had stopped by to wish her well. The Petersons were there, gushing about how much they loved their home.

"Holy shit. Even Wanda Waters is here. That woman doesn't leave her antique store," Bass said as he reached for his beer.

"Well, she does live in the apartment above it, so that's pretty convenient for a homebody." Brody laughed.

"Gracie's a special woman," Cannon said, glancing over at me. "Sorry, brother. I know it sucks for you."

"Nah. Don't be sorry. I'm proud of her for doing this." I took a long pull from my bottle and looked out over the dance floor, where Gracie was leading everyone in her favorite line dance.

"She doesn't strike me as a city girl," Phoenix said. "She'll be back."

"Agreed," Bass said. "You can take the girl out of the country, but you can't take the country out of the girl. Look at her."

She held up the hem of her long skirt and moved her feet left and right, a big smile on her face as she sang along with Chris Stapleton. She was in her element.

"Agreed." Cannon clapped me on the shoulder just as Gracie looked up, and her gaze locked with mine. She and Tatum walked over to the table, and she was still catching her breath.

"Hey. Tatum said she'd take a photo of us. I want a recent one to take with me." She reached for my hand. "Let's go over by the tree."

I followed her over and quickly dipped her back, and we both laughed as Tatum took some pictures.

"These are great." Tatum glanced down at the phone before handing it back to Gracie.

"Gracie," Shana Peterson called out, and Gracie jogged over to her as Tatum and I started walking back to the table.

"Hey," Tatum said to me. "How are you doing with everything?"

"I'm good. Happy for my girl, but of course I'm going to miss her like crazy."

I didn't want to wallow. Not when everyone was acting like I should be. I was trying to keep it together. Stay positive.

Maybe we'd be fine.

I wasn't a big complainer, so I was doing what I could to appear unfazed.

"You don't have to be stoic for me, but I'm glad you're putting on a brave face for her," she said. "She's really freaking out."

I narrowed my gaze. "She seems all right. I think she's ready."

"I mean, it's all perspective, right?"

"Meaning?"

"Meaning…" She paused and glanced over her shoulder to see Gracie deep in conversation with Shana Peterson. "I'll just give it to you straight, so you know where her head is. Because I don't think she'll tell you."

"Okay."

"She's got to do this, Cutler. She has something to prove to herself and maybe to everyone else, because she's really beaten herself up over what happened in Paris. But she's struggling with leaving you, and she won't admit it, because she doesn't want to make it harder on you." She shrugged. "Just be patient with her. She loves you."

I nodded before rubbing my face. "I'd wait forever for that girl. I understand that she needs to do this. I understand that she might love it there and start a whole new life. And it's not for me to stop her from doing that."

"So you need to let her go and see what happens." Her gaze was sad, and she forced a smile. "Who knew you were such a romantic guy? You've totally ruined your playboy reputation."

I laughed. "All it takes is the right girl to change everything."

Gracie came walking back over and took both of our hands in hers. "Come on. I just convinced all the guys to get out on the dance floor with us. Let's go."

"Phoenix is going to line dance?" Tatum gasped. "This is definitely a first."

We all lined up, and Brody, Bass, and Cannon all had shit-eating grins on their faces.

Phoenix looked like he was being tortured, which made it even funnier.

And Gracie led as we moved across the dance floor listening to Kenny Chesney, with the whole crowd singing along now.

I wrapped my arms around her from behind as we moved

together, and she tipped her head back, her lips grazing my ear.

"I love you, Cutler Heart."

Yeah. I love you too, Gracie girl.

We ate. We danced. We laughed. And we stayed late into the night.

She was leaving on a flight before the sun would even be up.

But we didn't care.

Almost like we didn't want the night to end.

When we finally got home well after midnight, we found Meatball still sleeping on the bed, just where we'd left him.

"I'm going to get him outside real quick," I said.

"Let's both go. We could even jump in the lake again." She followed me outside.

"Baby, you were freezing last night after we jumped in."

She shrugged. "I don't want the night to end."

"Then the night doesn't have to end. But you don't have to jump in the lake to keep me awake." I chuckled. "I'm all yours."

She nodded and said she'd go get ready for bed. I quickly got a fire going before I took the dog outside, which took all of three minutes because he'd barely stepped onto the grass before he lifted his leg and then wandered back inside to his dog bed.

I decided to let him sleep there because he was happy, and I couldn't wait to get to my girl.

I stepped into the bedroom. The firelight danced in the background, and all the lights were off. Gracie was sitting on the bed, propped up on her elbows, completely naked.

"What took you so long?" she asked, her voice teasing.

I tore my shirt over my head and kicked off my boots before shoving my jeans and briefs down as quickly as possible. "If I knew you were in here waiting for me like this, I would have let Meatball pee in the house."

Her head tipped back with laughter. “Last time together for a while, Bear.”

“So, let’s make it count.” My voice was gruff as I leaned down and kissed her.

I wanted to savor every last second with her.

I made my way down her body, kissing every inch.

If this was our last night together, I was going to make sure she remembered it.

CHAPTER THIRTY

Gracie

Even though my heart was breaking, I couldn't help but smile when my alarm went off, and I realized I was sleeping between Cutler and Meatball. We knew it was our last night together and had stayed up most of the night, falling asleep about an hour ago.

I didn't care.

I could sleep on the flight.

We'd had sex three times, taking advantage of every last moment.

"You up?" Cutler's voice was sleepy and gruff, and I sat up and rubbed my eyes.

"I'm up. But we have a visitor." I crawled down to the end of the bed, and Cutler chuckled when he realized Meatball was with us.

"Come on, buddy. Let's get our girl some coffee before I take her to the airport."

I got dressed quickly, brushed my hair and teeth, and that was as much as I was willing to do this morning. I tossed the last few things in my suitcase and wheeled it out to the front door, where he'd rolled the other one out last night.

I was a weird mix of completely relaxed from hours of fabulous sex and sick to my stomach about saying goodbye.

I dreaded it.

"Coffee." Cutler handed me a to-go cup and grabbed my bags to take them to his truck.

I bent down and said goodbye to Meatball before hurrying out to join him. The sun was just starting to come up, and he'd loaded my luggage and had my door open.

When I climbed in, he reached over and buckled my seat belt.

"Hey," he said, pausing and waiting for me to look at him.

"Hey."

"We're not going to do this big sad goodbye, all right?" He kissed my hair and then closed the door and got in the driver's seat. He was quiet as he drove toward the airport.

"So are we just going to say nothing?"

He chuckled. "Of course not. I'm just saying, let's not make it harder than it has to be. We'll talk all the time, and we'll see how it goes. There are airplanes, we can visit. No need for goodbyes."

I nodded. "Okay. And of course we'll talk. We've always talked every day. Why would that change now?"

"It won't."

How is he so calm?

I was freaking out on the inside, and ready to fall apart, and he appeared to be completely…unbothered.

"You're doing it, Jeege." He pulled into the passenger pickup area at the airport.

"Doing what?"

"Overthinking. Spiraling. I know you well, and that's what's happening."

I was tired and grumpy and sad. I was in no mood to be analyzed.

"I'm not overthinking. I'm thinking a normal amount. And you don't seem to be thinking at all," I grumped when he put the car in park.

"Is that what you want? Would it be easier for you if we get in a fight right before you leave?" He raised a brow, the corners of his lips twitching the slightest bit.

"Is this funny to you?" I hissed, pushing the passenger door open.

He beat me to the back of the truck and grabbed my bags. Was he in a hurry to get me out of here now? A few days ago he'd pushed to come with me to get me settled in, and now he was basically dropping me at the curb and telling me that we weren't going to say goodbye.

"It's not funny. I'm trying to make this easier for you."

"Easier for me? Or easier for you?" I gave him a look as a whistle blew from behind me.

I whipped around to see an older man in a security shirt watching us.

Seriously? Hardly anyone was here this morning—it was completely unnecessary.

"It's not easy for me, Jeege."

"Well, it'll be easier to date with me out of your hair," I said, feeling a lump form in my throat as tears blurred my eyes.

"Okay, you really do want to pick a fight, don't you." He placed his hands on my shoulders. "I love you. I fucking love you. I'm trying to do the right thing here for you. Not for me. For you."

I blew out a breath. "Well, you don't have to do the right thing now. You're a free man. I don't live here, remember?"

This surge of emotions had me completely off-kilter.

His gaze locked with mine, and he didn't speak for a few beats. "Call me when you land, Jeege."

"Fine," I huffed.

What was happening to me?

Was this a coping mechanism? Was he right?

I was overthinking.

I was spiraling.

He wrapped his arms around me as the whistle blew again from behind me.

"You need to move that truck now," the man called out, and I turned around and glared at him before looking back at Cutler.

I couldn't handle this.

It was too much.

"Okay. I should go." I took a few steps back, my bottom lip wobbling, and he stood there looking as steady as an oak tree.

He exhaled. "I love you. I'm proud of you. Go chase your dreams, baby."

"I love you. Take care," I told him.

Take care?

What?

I hated everything about this goodbye.

Hated it.

I turned around and walked toward the door, because I just needed it to end.

I was sleep-deprived, though it had been worth it.

I would probably never have good sex again.

But that wasn't really my fear.

My biggest fear was that I would never truly love anyone the way I loved Cutler.

And that was my burden to bear. I was the one who was leaving.

I turned around and watched him drive away.

He was gone.

It was over.

At least this version of us was over.

I walked inside and checked my bags, going through the motions in a blur.

Once I'd made it to the gate, they were already boarding.

I was grateful that Johnny had insisted on flying me first class for the move, because I'd have a roomier seat to sleep in.

Or at least I imagined so: I'd never actually flown first class.

I boarded the plane and slipped my carry-on beneath the seat in front of me and buckled myself in.

I reached into my purse for my phone, just as a man who appeared to be a few years older than me slipped into the seat beside me.

I wasn't in the mood for awkward pleasantries, but I smiled and nodded before glancing down to see a text from Cutler.

Bear: *I love you. It doesn't matter where you live, or how far apart we are. That doesn't change.*

People continued boarding as I stared down at my phone. I kept doing so while the flight attendant gave us the little spiel about how to survive if we crash-landed on a farm somewhere.

The lump in my throat was so thick it was difficult to swallow.

I quickly typed a message back before we took off.

Me: *I love you too. But everything is going to change. It's inevitable.*

Bear: *I wouldn't change a thing.*

Really? Not a single thing? We'd now be living on opposite sides of the country.

Was this sleep deprivation causing me to be so irrational?

"Ma'am, would you like something to drink before we take off?"

Wow. First class was no joke. When I flew home from Paris, my lips were chapped from dehydration, but here we were still on the ground and I was being offered a beverage.

"I would love a water," I said, and it sounded more like a croak.

I would not lose my shit on an airplane.

I wasn't that girl.

"If you'd like something else, we can bring it out for you."

I shook my head frantically. "No. No. The water is great."

My voice cracked on the last word, and her eyes widened, but she hurried off to get our drinks.

"Are you all right?" the man beside me said, and he looked at me as if he was concerned.

"Oh, don't worry. I'm just sad, I'm not going to lose it," I said, my voice wobbling, and he chuckled.

"I'm not worried you're going to lose it. Just making sure you're all right."

"Thank you. I'll be fine," I said as the flight attendant set down my water and a hot coffee for him.

"Goodbyes are tough sometimes. I get it." He winked.

Goodbyes were tough. And this one was the worst goodbye of all time.

I'd just acted like a complete asshole to the man I loved. The man who'd supported me when my life had spiraled. The man who had supported me when this opportunity presented itself.

He'd been completely selfless, and I'd acted like a child when I'd said goodbye.

I reached for my phone and sent another text just as we prepared for takeoff.

Me: *Sorry for acting ridiculous when I said goodbye. I'll text you when I land. Love you.*

"Please make sure all of your devices are in airplane mode," the flight attendant said, and I was fairly certain she was talking directly to me from where she stood up front talking into a microphone.

I tucked my phone away and reached for the tissue in my backpack.

"Yes. I hate goodbyes." I blew my nose, and it was much louder than I expected, and I gave the man next to me an apologetic look.

My chest ached.

My head was pounding.

And I just wanted to make it all go away.

I stared out the window until my eyelids were so heavy that they finally closed.

And I'd slept for what felt like hours when a hand on my shoulder startled me from my slumber.

"You might want to start waking up," the deep voice next to me said. "We're about to land."

I'd slept the entire flight.

I felt slightly out of it, but much more rested and less—on the verge of a meltdown.

The flight attendant asked us to put our seat backs up to the original position, and I did so.

"Sorry if I startled you," he said. "Just figured you'd want a few minutes awake before we landed. I'm Tripp, by the way."

I rubbed my eyes and yawned. "No. Thank you so much. I appreciate it. I needed the sleep."

"Do you live in New York?" Tripp asked.

"I'm moving there."

Nope. The waiting meltdown was still there in the form of a gigantic lump in my throat.

"Ahhh…big move. I'm sure it's scary and hard, but trust me when I tell you, you're about to experience the most magical city in the world," he said confidently. "Born and raised there."

I nodded. "I'm excited to be there. It's just hard to say goodbye to the people I love."

He turned to me and smiled now. "Trust me. If they're your people, it won't matter where you live. They'll stick around."

"I hope you're right."

We were quiet as we made our descent into JFK.

This next chapter was about to begin.

Once we landed, I waved goodbye to Tripp, then grabbed my luggage where Johnny was waiting for me.

"Hey, thanks so much for picking me up," I said as he wrapped me up in a hug.

"I couldn't wait to see you, darling. And I want to take you over to your new place. I live just a few blocks from you, so we're practically neighbors." He chuckled.

I smiled, though it felt forced.

We made our way outside to the waiting car, and we chatted the entire way to my new home until the driver pulled up in front of my building.

The driver stepped out of the car and pulled open the back door, and we both stepped out onto the street as the sound of horns blasting made me jump the slightest bit. He pulled my luggage from the trunk as I tipped my head back to take in the gorgeous building, and we both thanked him for the ride as we walked toward the entrance.

Johnny used a key before pulling the exterior door to the building open. It looked like a hotel in here, with people bustling around, and the lobby was absolutely stunning.

"All of the keys are color-coded. This blue key is for your

exterior door. You can buzz people up from inside," he said as we wheeled my two suitcases onto the elevator.

He pushed open the door to my apartment, and I couldn't help but gasp once I stepped inside. It was small but quite possibly the most charming apartment on the planet. The photos hadn't done it justice. The place had a stone fireplace, and French doors that opened to the street. It was decorated like a French flat, and I knew I'd be comfortable here. The furnishings were gorgeous and completely my style.

"You've got thirty minutes to freshen up, darling," he said. "The team is meeting us at the restaurant downstairs for a drink and dinner to welcome you here on your first night."

I wanted to fall in a heap on the floor, but I nodded. It was time to rally. This was what I'd come here for. "Sounds great. Thank you so much. The restaurant is right downstairs?"

"Yes. It's in the entrance of the building. We'll get a nibble and a cocktail, and then I'll give you a tour. There's a gym and a coffee shop and the restaurant as well." He kissed my cheek. "Welcome home, darling. See you soon."

I opened my luggage, noting the four boxes stacked in the corner that I'd shipped here ahead of time. I grabbed some dark jeans and a black sweater and my boots and quickly changed.

I thought about the last words Cutler had said to me.

I'm proud of you. Go chase your dreams, baby.

It was time to pull up my big girl pants and do what I'd come here to do.

CHAPTER THIRTY-ONE

Cutler

Gracie had left two weeks ago. We talked daily just like we always had, but most days we were rushed. It was tough with the three-hour time difference and both of us being buried at work.

I was struggling with how much I missed her.

I couldn't say that to her. I knew she was overwhelmed the day we'd said goodbye, and I was trying to put on a brave face. We could do this.

But it sucked already.

My house was quiet. I'd never minded alone time before, but everything was different now.

I was grateful that I had Meatball, because the dude never left my side.

But I still hated this house without her in it.

When Gracie was here, there'd been constant music playing and she was always dancing.

Always laughing.

We played board games, we cooked, we'd jump in the lake and end up in the shower at the end of the day.

Fuck.

I fucking missed her.

I rubbed a hand over my chest, desperate to make the ache go away.

Hence the reason I'd come home and gotten shitfaced on whiskey.

I sat on my couch, the room dark and quiet, only the sound of Meatball's snoring filling the space around me.

I tipped my head back and downed the amber liquid, relishing the way it burned going down.

I ran a hand over my face, a reminder that I hadn't shaved in days. I was a fucking mess.

I picked up my phone and pulled up my group chat called "The Godfathers."

Romeo, River, King, and Hayes.

They'd been in my life since the day I was born.

I typed in the words that I'd only used one other time in my life, when my father had sunk into a dark place back when my mother was sick.

And here I was typing those words again.

ME: *ROD 911.*

ROD was the name of my company, which my father and my uncle Kingston had started back in Magnolia Falls. It stood for "Ride or Die," words my father and my uncles took very seriously.

Words I'd grown up living by.

Uncle Ro: *Hang tight.*

Uncle River: *We've got you.*

Uncle Hayes: *Got you, buddy.*

Uncle King: *We'll figure it out, Beefcake.*

I chuckled, though there was nothing genuine behind it. But the memory of my childhood name comforted me in a weird way.

We had a bond. I knew they wouldn't tell my father that I'd sent it. I figured I'd get a call in the morning, and they'd help me figure things out. It was well past midnight, so I was surprised that they'd all responded so quickly.

They'd given me this code back when I was in high school. They'd told me to send this text if I ever needed them, and they knew I wouldn't use it unless it was important.

We'd set the code up without my father's knowledge, though I knew he'd be happy that they had it in place.

I was close with my dad.

With both of my parents.

I spoke to them daily.

But this was complicated, because it was Gracie. We were connected by our families. I didn't want this to be any messier than it already was.

Gracie and I had agreed to keep our relationship a secret until we figured things out.

But we were living on opposite sides of the country now, so how the fuck were we supposed to do that?

I thought about calling Gracie, but it was three o'clock in the morning there. She'd be alarmed. It was my job to make this easier on her.

Not harder.

And I was drunk as hell and needed sleep.

"Come on, Meatball." I scratched the top of his head and stood up, stumbling a bit. He did some sort of dramatic yawn before hopping off the couch and following me to my bedroom.

I hated the way I felt. The guys had been nagging me to meet them out tonight, but I just didn't feel like it.

I brushed my teeth and stripped down to my briefs, rolling my eyes when I saw my big beast of a dog lying on his back, sprawled in the middle of my bed.

I was too drunk to care.

"What kind of bet did I lose?" I climbed beneath the blankets as the room started to spin. "There used to be a beautiful woman lying there. And now she's gone. It's just you and me, Meatball."

I squeezed my eyes closed, begging sleep to take me from my misery.

And thankfully, the booze and exhaustion kicked in all at once.

And darkness took me.

• • •

A jackhammer pelted me in the head numerous times before Meatball howled so loud that I thought my head would explode.

What the fuck is happening?

I sat up, my head spinning, as nausea climbed my throat.

The pounding continued, but I realized it wasn't in my head; it was coming from outside.

I walked to the bathroom, took a piss, and then realized the noise was actually coming from my front door.

I pulled on my gray joggers and stumbled down the hallway as the world's worst hangover dominated my movements.

I pulled the door open, startled when I saw them standing there.

My four uncles.

My godfathers.

As they clapped me on the shoulder one by one and stepped inside, I rubbed my face, trying to process what was happening.

"You look like shit," River said, humor lining his tone.

"This is obviously bad," Romeo said. He put an arm around my shoulder, walking beside me toward the kitchen. "Come on. Let's get some coffee on."

"There better be something to eat here," Kingston said. "I'm starving, and we didn't want to stop because we were anxious to get here." He pulled the refrigerator open and started pulling food out.

"I think our boy probably needs food in his stomach too." Hayes started the coffee and pulled out several mugs from the cupboard.

Meatball howled again, his new form of communication when he was hungry. He wasn't much of a barker, but he sure knew how to howl.

"And what the fuck is this?" River held out a hand, motioning to my new four-legged best friend.

"This is Meatball," I grumped as I stood at the kitchen island and set my forehead down on the cool porcelain. "He needs to eat."

"I've got it, you go sit. You clearly went big last night," Romeo said, ushering me to the kitchen table.

"Thank you. He eats the moist food in the bag in the refrigerator. He gets half a bag." I picked my head up when Hayes brought some coffee over.

Kingston was cooking up some eggs, and River put some toast in the toaster, and I just sat there, sipping my coffee and replaying the evening.

ROD 911.

"Fuck. I texted you last night." I sighed as I moved to the laundry room and grabbed a hoodie and pulled it over my head.

"You did." River set a plate of toast down in the center, handed me a piece, and took the seat across from me. "Get some bread in your stomach."

I nodded and took a few bites, just as Romeo set Meatball's dish down on the floor beside the island, and he came to sit in the chair beside me.

"I shouldn't have sent that. I was just having a moment."

"You've sent that text two times in your life," Hayes said. "I don't think you were having a moment. I think something is up, and you're trying to deal with it on your own." He set down five plates and forks, and then Kingston walked over and scooped the eggs on a plate for each of us.

I was actually hungry, which was a good sign.

I took a few bites of food as they waited for me to fill them in.

"Is there a reason your dad isn't here?" Kingston asked.

"Fuck. I don't know." I blew out a breath and looked up. "I don't want to involve my parents right now. I don't know where this is going, and we didn't want to add pressure to the situation."

"Pressure?" River asked, setting his fork down. "Are you in trouble? Legal trouble?"

I snorted. "No. Why would you think that?"

Romeo said, "You sent the first text years ago in the middle of the night when your father was spiraling. He'd fallen apart in front of you for the first time in your life, and you were worried. Things were bad. None of us knew if Emerson would be okay, and we rallied around them, and thankfully she came through it like a champ. And then you sent the text last night. Everyone's healthy as far as we know, so we were worried you were in some sort of trouble."

"Ride or die, Beefcake. We don't judge." Kingston raised a brow, and I saw the loyalty in each of their gazes as my eyes moved around the table.

"Jesus. No. I'm not in trouble with the law," I chuckled, this sarcastic sound coming from me. "I'm in love with Gracie Reynolds."

Romeo whistled. "It's about damn time."

"Why is this a bad thing?" Hayes asked as he popped some more eggs in his mouth.

Why did none of them seem surprised that I'd just shared that I was in love with Gracie? Clearly, I was the last one to figure this out.

"Well, it's complicated. She was just staying here after getting out of a shitty relationship when she returned from Paris. She didn't want to date anyone, so it started out as a casual thing that we kept between us," I admitted. "We had a plan, and it was working well at first."

River looked at me. "You're lucky Cage didn't hear about that, or he might've been the one to get in trouble with the law when he kicked your ass."

"That's the thing. It was never casual for me. Hell, I think I've loved her my whole life. But I was following her rules." I rubbed my face. "She knew she was leaving. It wasn't supposed to turn into something."

"Well, it never is," Romeo chuckled. "But you can't stop the way you feel about someone. So what's the problem? Did you tell her that you love her?"

"Yes." I filled them in on all the details. How we'd decided to just see what happened after she'd left for New York. No rules. No plan. "And I'm fucked, because I'm miserable. And if I tell my parents what's going on, and this doesn't work out, they'll be really upset. So I'm keeping it in. I mean, my friends know, but I'm trying to put on a brave face. But at the end of the day, it is a big fucking deal. I love her. She lives on the opposite side of the country, and we have no fucking plan. She might never come home. She might love it there. She might meet someone else and forget about me. Who fucking knows? I'm not the safest bet, so I wouldn't blame her for moving on. I've never even had a serious relationship. I'd probably fuck it up."

And there it was.

Was I going to press her to make things official when I knew she doubted I could be that guy?

That I could be the forever guy?

Romeo turned to face me. "Don't say that. You are that fucking guy. You may have dated a lot of women over your adult life—hell, we all did. But this girl has always been the one. You called it back when you were a kid. You just had to let go of some of those fears, and allow yourself to love her. And you're the most loyal dude I know, Cutler Heart."

"Agreed," Kingston said as he reached for his coffee. "No one is that guy until they meet that girl, you know?"

"Oh, we all know. And you had to go and pick my sister, didn't you?" Hayes said to Kingston with a smirk.

"Fuck yeah. Best decision I ever made." His tone turned serious, and he said to me, "If you love her, don't let fear keep you from going all in."

"And how do I do that?" I shrugged. "This is her dream job. She already followed the wrong guy to Paris. She wants to make this work. I'd be selfish to ask her to come back for me. I'm trying to do the right thing. Let her chase her dreams and hope she still wants me when she's done chasing them. But what do I do in the meantime? Just sit around miserable, waiting to see what happens? I'm going out of my mind."

"You're not a sit-on-the-sidelines type of guy, Cutler. It's not who you are." River's gaze locked with mine. "No more secrets. No more holding back. You love her, right? She's your girl?"

"Yes. No question about it."

"Then you support her dreams, but you don't hold back for one second," River said. "It's not about pressuring her to come back, because that's not your decision to make. If you want this, if you want her…" He paused and took a sip of his coffee. "You put it all out there. You let your family know, and you tell her you aren't holding back. If she wants you there, you fucking go there."

I nodded. "What about my business?"

"What about it?" Hayes said. "You start something in New York, if that's what it takes. You don't have to do it right away. Just tell her you're willing to. You're willing to visit as often as she wants. You're willing to move there if that's what she wants. You're not going anywhere, because she's it for you. This isn't a wait-and-see; this is the real deal. So you figure out how to make it work. End of story."

"Yep. That's some damn good advice. You're not asking her to choose you or her job," Kingston said. "You are choosing her. And whatever she needs, you're going to do it."

"And if right now, she says that she needs to do this on her own," Romeo said as he set his fork down, "then you tell her you'll be right here waiting for her. You aren't playing it by ear and dating other women. You're here waiting to see what she wants. That's what you say."

"And what if she doesn't know what she wants? What if she wants to do this on her own?"

"Well, that won't be because you didn't shoot your shot," Hayes said. "But doing nothing, and letting the woman you love go without a fight—that's a sure way to lose her." He shrugged.

Kingston reached for a piece of toast. "What's that saying, 'If you love someone, you need to set them free, and if they love you, they'll come back.' And if they don't, they were never yours."

"What kind of philosophical bullshit is that?" River chuckled. "She's always been yours. You just have to tell her you're all in."

"She's always been mine, and I've always been hers. We just

didn't know it before now." I leaned back in my chair.

"Boom. Mic drop," River said, laughing.

"We don't let fear keep us from going after what we want, Beefcake." Romeo clapped me on the shoulder.

"Thanks. I can't believe you guys are here. I needed this." I rubbed my face again in relief.

"Always. Ride or die," River said, looking around the table.

I smiled as we all said the words together: "Ride or die. Brothers till the end. Loyalty always. Forever my friend."

They were right.

I couldn't just sit back and wait for things to play out.

It was time to come up with a plan. It might not mean things would happen today, or tomorrow, or even in a couple of months.

I'd get things squared away at the office so I could fly there and talk to her in person.

But Gracie Reynolds needed to know that I was all in.

It didn't matter where we lived or how often we saw one another.

She was my girl, and I didn't want anyone else.

And if I had to wait a lifetime, she'd be worth the wait.

CHAPTER THIRTY-TWO

Gracie

I'd been in New York for a month now, and the city was taking some getting used to.

It was both fabulous and overwhelming.

It was louder and more crowded than I was used to.

The energy was amazing, and business was booming and very busy. I loved my job, though it was a very different vibe here as far as design.

It was an amazing mix of styles, which reflected the city well. The two clients I'd taken on so far were definitely on the contemporary side. One of the projects was a modern loft, and the other was what I would call industrial chic.

Both were very minimalist, whereas my preferred design was definitely not that.

I loved floral arrangements and pottery and area rugs and curtains and artwork.

I loved to show life in every room I designed.

But you had to be adaptable as a designer.

I stepped out of our office building and strode down the street toward my favorite café. At moments like this, I did feel like I was channeling my inner Carrie Bradshaw.

But I missed the mountains and the lake and the peacefulness of small-town living.

I'd grown up in a small town. I'd gone to college in a small town.

And then I'd lived in Los Angeles for a few years, and I remembered liking city living so much more in my early twenties than I did now.

I'd also be lying if I didn't admit that what I missed most was Cutler.

We talked every day and texted as well. But it wasn't the same.

I wanted to ask him if he was dating anyone, but I never let myself go there, nor did he.

We were just going to play it by ear.

That was the plan, or the lack of a plan.

I cried myself to sleep most nights because I missed having him beside me. I couldn't tell him that, because he was a fixer, and he'd want to make it better.

But this was something that I needed to do.

I needed to take on this challenge and give it a fair chance.

I pulled the door to the café open, and Jovi waved at me. She was going to school not too far from here, and we'd been trying to meet for a glass of wine at least once a week.

It helped me feel like a piece of home was here with me.

"I ordered you your favorite chardonnay," she said. "And happy Halloween, by the way."

“Is it Halloween? How did I not know that?” I chuckled. “I swear the days are blurring together.”

“Well, that will happen when you put in sixteen-hour workdays.” She smirked. “I’m proud of you, though. You’re doing your thing, girl.”

I snorted. “I’m trying.”

I worked long days, which kept me from stopping to think about how homesick I was.

Could you be homesick for a person?

Yes, apparently I can.

“Are you and Cutler still talking every day?” she asked as she sipped her wine.

“Yes. But we’ve always talked every day, so we’re in a weird place. I don’t know what we are.”

“Are you dating anyone?”

“No.”

“Do you want to date anyone?”

“No. How can I date someone when I’m in love with Cutler? It doesn’t matter where I live,” I said with a shrug. I took a sip of my chardonnay. “I don’t want anyone else.”

She leaned closer and smiled. “So why not just tell him that and make it official?”

“Because it’s selfish. I’d be asking him to be committed to me, when I live on the other side of the country and I don’t know how long I’ll be here. The man has needs.”

“You have needs too, and you aren’t tempted to be with anyone else. Maybe he feels the same way.”

“I don’t know. He sounded very distracted when I spoke to him yesterday, and I haven’t heard from him today. He’s probably tired of this arrangement. I can’t blame him. That’s why I didn’t put any sort of plan together. It’s just—harder than I thought it would be. But at the same time, I’m proud of myself for doing this. I need to give this a shot. The experience is incredible, and I'm being challenged every day."

She smiled. "I'm proud of you too."

"Okay, tell me your plans for tonight."

"Do you want to go with me and my roommate to a Halloween party at a frat house tonight?"

My head fell back with laughter. "Absolutely not. I'm far too old for that. But tell me, is that cute guy from your economics class going to be there?"

"Yes. He's the one who asked me to come. But I can't tell if I like him yet. He's giving me player vibes."

"Well, trust your gut. But go and have some fun. It's your last year of college. What are you wearing?" I asked, taking a sip of my wine.

"Do you promise you won't laugh?"

"Never."

"I'm going as Jane Austen." She shrugged as a wide grin spread across her face. "She wrote my favorite book, and I'm channeling my inner Regency era. I love the way they dressed back then. I found something at this secondhand store, and I'm adding a vintage-looking brooch that I have from my grandmother, and then a cute headband. So, if the playboy is looking for a sexy kitty, he'll realize quickly I'm not that girl."

"Well, you are a business major with an English literature minor—that makes you the most interesting girl in the room at most parties."

She chuckled, and we sat there talking and drinking wine for the next hour while her phone kept vibrating with missed calls.

"It's my roommate. I should get going—I need to get my costume together."

"Okay. You have to send me a pic of this magnificent costume. And if you get drunk and you need me to come get you, just call me.

I'll be home working." I stood up and hugged her.

"You don't have a car," she pointed out.

"I'll Uber to you and get you home safely, because being dressed as a woman from the 1800s is going to attract a lot of attention." We both laughed.

"Love you, Gracie. I'll text you later. Don't work too late. You're young and you're hot," she added with a chuckle. "You need to have some fun."

"Love you. Be safe." I waved as I stepped out onto the sidewalk in front of the café, and she turned in the opposite direction.

I pulled my coat tighter and glanced down at my phone to see if Cutler had replied. I hadn't heard from him today, which was very unlike him.

I walked toward my apartment building and smiled when a group of kids ran by in costumes. A woman in an elegant white trench coat strode in my direction, and I glanced down at her dachshund, who was also wearing a white coat. I covered my mouth to keep from laughing. I'd sent Cutler a Halloween costume for Meatball, and I'd insisted he put it on him when he received it two days ago and then send me a photo.

He was a giant candy kiss, wrapped in faux foil with a tag coming out of the top of his head. I'd requested a selfie of the two of them, and it was now my screen saver.

My chest ached when I thought about Cutler.

I missed him in a way that I couldn't explain.

I tipped my head back and looked up at the gray sky as a breeze bustled past me. Then I crossed the street and arrived at my building, where I came to an abrupt stop.

A tall man wearing a gray hoodie and a navy blazer with a pair of dark jeans was sitting on the bench outside the high-rise where I lived.

No. It couldn't be him.

My pulse pounded in my ears as my eyes widened with disbelief when I took in his dark hair and chiseled jaw—and I just started running.

"Bear?" I shouted from about forty feet away, my heart racing.

He stood up and opened his arms, just as I launched myself into him.

I wrapped my arms around his neck, panting from the short sprint. "What? How? What are you doing here?"

"Hey, Jeege. Fancy meeting you here," he said as a sexy grin spread across his handsome face.

"What are you doing? How are you here?"

"I missed my girl. Wanted to come see you and didn't want you to tell me all the reasons why I didn't need to do that."

I gaped at him. "I wouldn't have told you not to come."

"No? You wouldn't have worried about me missing work?"

"Well, maybe. I know how much you have on your plate right now." I chuckled. "But I'm so happy to see you."

"Listen, I know we said no plans, but I wanted to talk to you about that, so here I am."

"Here you are. You're full of surprises." I pushed up on my tiptoes and kissed him. His hand tangled in my hair, and he kissed me right back.

Someone whistled from behind me, and I quickly pulled back as Cutler laughed and reached for my hand.

I led him inside, and as we rode the elevator up to my floor, I just stared at him. "I can't believe you're here."

"Is it a good thing?"

"It's the best thing. I was struggling a little bit today," I admitted, because he was here, so it seemed fair to just tell him how I was feeling.

And by "struggling a little," I mean "struggling a lot."

He nodded slowly. "I've been struggling too."

I didn't expect that. Cutler was always so calm and together, so I'd just imagined him back home living his best life.

What if he was here to tell me that he couldn't handle the way we'd left things? What if he wanted to just call this done? Maybe he felt guilty about the idea of dating other women unless he officially told me first?

Or maybe he was here to tell me that he'd met someone.

Was this the "We should go back to being just friends" speech?

I'd understand if so. He must be lonely. I was lonely.

I was painfully lonely.

But I didn't want anyone but him, so how was I supposed to fix that?

"Don't go deciding why I'm here before you hear me out," he said as the elevator door opened to my floor.

"How do you always know what I'm thinking?"

"Because I know you, maybe even better than I know myself." He walked beside me as I pulled out my keys and opened the door.

He'd seen my place when we'd FaceTimed, so he knew what it looked like, but I thought it was even cuter in person.

"Johnny sure knows what you like, huh?" He smiled as he pulled his blazer off and dropped it on the barstool in the kitchen.

"Yeah. And I'm fairly certain this is the only apartment in the city that looks like this. Everything is very modern here, typically."

"Well, he knew how to make sure you'd be comfortable, and I appreciate that." He paused to glance around at the cozy sofa covered in throw pillows and the charming white kitchen with natural wood accents.

I walked to the kitchen and grabbed a bottle of wine and two glasses. "He left me this bottle of wine the day I arrived as a welcome gift, and I've never had any desire to drink it until now."

I handed Cutler the bottle opener. After he'd filled both of our glasses, we took them to the couch.

We settled on the white sofa, which had views of the city through the large window on the wall in front of us.

"Where's Meatball?" I asked.

"He's at the firehouse with Phoenix." He chuckled. "He didn't look too thrilled when I dropped him off dressed as a big candy kiss."

I fell forward with a laugh, imagining the grumpy Phoenix with this big dog dressed in a Halloween costume.

"Why didn't you tell me you were coming?" I took a sip of wine and set my glass down on the table beside me.

"I wanted to surprise you," he said, his gray hoodie stretched across his muscular chest, and it took everything in me not to slip my hands beneath the fabric and crawl onto his lap.

I wanted to touch him. To burrow into him and never let go.

But I needed to know why he'd shown up without telling me.

"And you said that you had something to talk to me about?"

He did that sexy slow nod as the corners of his lips turned up the slightest bit. He extended his arm and set his glass down on the coffee table. "I don't like that we don't have a plan."

That wasn't what I was expecting. "Since when do you like a plan regarding a relationship?"

"Since starting a relationship with you."

"I'm guessing you want some form of closure, since we left things sort of in limbo. I get it. There's more at risk, right? You don't want to mess up our friendship. We can't stay in this weird no-man's-land. It makes sense, and I understand." I cleared my throat, preparing myself for the blow to come.

"I'm not worried about our friendship. That'll never change."

"So, what are you worried about?"

"Well, your 'no plan' theory means we can date other people, right?"

"Sure. Are you dating other people? Is that what you came here to tell me?" I forced a smile, making an effort to keep my tone even and unaffected. "Because we didn't have any rules about that, so you haven't done anything wrong."

"Jeege."

"Bear," I said, keeping my voice light, even though I was freaking out on the inside.

"I am not dating other people. I don't want to date other people. And I don't want you to date other people."

"You don't?"

"I don't."

"If you change your mind, you just need to tell me first, so no one gets blindsided." I blew out a breath.

"There is no changing my mind. I know what I want, and I came here to tell you exactly what that is."

"What do you want?"

"I'm looking at her."

My heart pounded in my chest.

He wanted me. And I wanted him.

"Are you sure about that?" I bit my bottom lip.

"Never been so sure about anything in my life."

I smiled up at him. "Sounds like we have a new plan."

He pulled me onto his lap and wrapped his arms around me.

And though I was terrified of this blowing up in our faces, I was willing to do whatever it took to make it work.

Because the love of my life was sitting right in front of me.

And he wanted this as much as I did.

CHAPTER THIRTY-THREE

Cutler

"I want to say something to you, and I need you to hear me," I said.

"Okay." She searched my gaze.

"We will figure this out. It's not about where we live, it's about how we move forward." He tucked the hair behind my ear and traced the pad of his thumb along my cheek. "This means no more secrets. We tell our parents. The people in our lives should know that we're together."

Her eyes widened. "Okay. You don't think that will add extra pressure?"

"Jeege, I don't feel pressure about being with you. I *want* to be with you. I've been miserable ever since you left. Fucking miserable. And I'm not saying that because we can't make it work if we don't live in the same state. But we can't make it work if we don't at least admit that we want it to work. Does that make sense?"

"Yes." She nodded, eyes wet with emotion.

"So, we don't hide it. We don't avoid it. We face it head-on." I reached beneath her chin, tilting her face up so she was facing me. "I love you. Not like a best friend. Not in a way that I want to play it safe. This is a my-life-doesn't-work-without-you kind of love. A nothing-else-matters kind of love."

She nodded, bottom lip trembling now. "I love you the same way."

"Then it doesn't matter where we live. And we don't have to decide today. You stay here and kick ass and see what you think of living in the city. If you love it here, and this is where you want to be—then I will sell my company and move here. I'll start a new company here with you if that's what we decide is best. It doesn't matter where I work. What matters is that we're together."

"You would move here?"

"I would absolutely move here."

She sniffed a few times, and I swiped my thumbs beneath her eyes. "And for now, we can visit each other. I get weekends off sometimes."

I chuckled. "Yes. It was ridiculous to think we wouldn't visit. We'll talk every day, and we won't be afraid to tell one another how much we miss each other. We'll make this work, because we want it to work. I'm not afraid to say that. I want this to work, Gracie Reynolds. You and me. We're end-game."

A smile spread across her gorgeous face. "Very smooth, Bear. Did you just say we're 'end-game'?"

"Damn straight."

"We've always been end-game, haven't we?" she said, a single tear streaking down her cheek.

"We have."

I leaned down and covered her mouth with mine. It was frantic and needy, and I couldn't get enough.

I wanted everything with this girl.

And I wanted it to start right now.

She pulled back and searched my gaze. "So we're really doing this?"

"Yes."

The sweetest smile spread across her gorgeous face. "Thank you for fighting for us."

"There's nothing more important to me in the world." I intertwined my fingers with hers and glanced at the coffee table to see the pink faded wooden heart sitting there. "Does that go with the décor?"

She chuckled. "It goes with me wherever I go. It's like I have a piece of you here when we aren't together."

"Damn. That heart has some miles on it." My gaze locked with hers. "CH plus GR. I even knew it back then. It just took me a while to get my shit together."

"You were worth the wait."

"Yeah?" I ran the tips of my fingers through her silky hair. "So, I had this plan that as soon as you agreed that this is what you wanted too, we would call our families immediately. No more waiting."

She tilted her head to the side. "And that's not the plan now?"

"Well, I'm struggling with the fact that I want to strip you naked and bury myself in you, but I also want to insist we tell everyone that we're together immediately, because I want everyone to know that this is real."

She placed both hands on my cheeks. "This is as real as it gets. And I love that you want to make it official with our families, and so do I. But what if we just change the order that we do it?"

"I like the sound of that," I said as she pushed up a bit and unbuckled my jeans. I shifted forward and slid them down my legs, along with my briefs. Gracie hiked her skirt up so it pooled around her waist, and she reached down to take off her heels, but I stopped her. "Leave those on."

Her cheeks flushed pink as she raised herself up and wrapped her hand around my erection and slowly slid down.

Inch by fucking inch.

Taking me all the way in.

"Goddamn, I missed you," I hissed as I gripped her perfect ass and guided her up and down my shaft.

Her head fell back, and her sweater fell off one shoulder. I tugged it down, exposing her lacy cream bra. I sealed my lips right over the fabric and sucked, using my tongue to flick her hard peak.

"Yes, don't stop," she whispered, her voice laced with need.

"Never fucking stopping, baby," I grunted before pulling her bra down so I could have access to her beautiful tits.

She arched her back, hands resting on the tops of my thighs to support herself as she rode me into oblivion.

Over and over.

I could feel her getting closer as she tightened around me.

Needy and desperate.

I pulled back so I could watch her.

My girl.

Her hair fell down her back as she rocked up and down my dick like it was her day job.

I was in awe of her.

Tits bouncing, lips parted, cheeks flushed.

I'd never seen anything more beautiful.

I pressed my thumb to her clit in little circles, knowing just what she needed.

A gasp left her lips as she shattered around me, and I pumped into her once more.

And again.

A guttural sound escaped my throat as I went right over the edge with her.

She fell forward, and I buried my face in her neck as our labored breaths filled the air around us.

She was mine and I was hers, and I felt it in every inch of my body.

I wrapped my arms around her as her body fell limp against me and her breathing slowed.

And I just held her there for a few minutes until we both came back to reality.

She pulled back to look at me, and I tucked her hair behind her ears.

"I'm glad we went with that first." She smirked, and I laughed.

"It was the better plan."

"It really was." She chuckled as she slowly lifted up, and she got up and made her way to the bathroom. I followed her in there, and we cleaned ourselves up.

"What are you smiling about?" I asked as I moved behind her where she stood at the sink, and my gaze met hers in the reflection of the mirror.

She turned around to face me. "I'm smiling because I just realized we get to do that whenever we're together, and there are no more rules in place to say that we have to stop."

"I like the sound of that. I'm all yours, Jeege."

"I think in a way I've always been yours." She shrugged. "We just had to wait for the right time."

I wrapped my arms around her. "The irony is not lost on me."

"What do you mean?" She tipped her head up to look at me.

"We've finally figured it out, and now we live on opposite sides of the country. But once you realize that you love someone so intensely that you can't live without them, distance is no longer an obstacle. Because this," I said, motioning between us, "this is unbreakable. You and me—we're unbreakable."

"I couldn't agree more. So let's go make those phone calls," she said, pushing up on her tiptoes and kissing me. "And then I'll feed you."

We settled at the dining room table with Gracie sitting on my lap, and we propped the phone up as we FaceTimed her mom first.

"Hey, sweetheart," Presley said, her eyes going wide when she realized I was here as well. "I didn't know Cutler was visiting this weekend!"

"Yes. He surprised me. And I have a surprise for you. Is Dad nearby?" Gracie asked.

"He is," she said, calling out for Cage to come join her.

"Hey, Gracie girl. Is that Cutler with you?" He squinted at the phone.

"He surprised her," Presley said. "And Gracie has a surprise for us."

"You're moving back to Cottonwood Cove?" Cage asked, his voice filled with hope.

"No, Dad, that's not it," she chuckled. "But Cutler and I have news."

"Okay," they both said at the same time.

"Shall I?" I asked, and Gracie nodded. Was I suddenly nervous? The Reynolds were like family to me, but this was a big deal. A big fucking deal, and I knew it. And I wanted them to know that I took it very seriously. I shifted in my seat, and the moment she threaded her fingers with mine and smiled, I completely relaxed. "Well, do you remember when I said that I was seeing someone when I saw you last?"

"Yes. I was horrified for trying to set you up with Britani." Presley shook her head, as if she was still shocked by the way that had all played out.

"Well, I wanted you to know that I'm crazy in love with this girl right here. She's been my best friend my whole life, and we realized it was more than just a friendship a few months ago, and then she had to go and move across the country." I chuckled. "But when you love someone the way I love her—the way I love your daughter—then you fight like hell to make it work. And that's what we're going to do."

They were both staring at the phone with their mouths hanging open, as if they'd been completely caught off-guard.

"You're in love with Gracie? Our Gracie? Your Gracie?" Cage asked, his voice calm and even.

"Yes. I'm madly in love with our girl. And we didn't want to tell you when you visited, because we weren't sure what we would do when she left for New York."

"Oh my gosh." Presley burst into tears. "Oh my gosh. Cage. Did you hear that? They're in love. Cutler and Gracie. This is the best news I've ever heard."

"Baby, I'm sitting right next to you," Cage said with a laugh.

"I'm sorry we didn't tell you, but we weren't sure how we'd make it work, or what we'd do when I moved here. But we're going to figure it out, because I'm madly in love with this guy right here," Gracie said as tears streamed down her face now too.

"Why the hell are my wife and daughter crying?" Cage asked, scratching the back of his neck.

"Because they love each other," Presley said, and her voice cracked as the words left her mouth. "I always knew they belonged together."

"And that made you cry?" he asked, and I couldn't help but laugh.

"They're happy tears, Dad." Gracie sniffed a few times, a sweet smile settling on her face.

"Have you told Nash and Emerson yet?" Gracie's mom asked. "Because she and I are going to get on the phone immediately about this to celebrate."

"We're calling them next," Gracie said.

"Man, I'm really happy about this. I've never liked anyone you've dated, if I'm being honest," Cage said, a wide grin on his face. "But this is as good as it gets. We love you both."

"Love you," Gracie and I said at the same time before ending the call. We quickly dialed my parents before Presley beat us to the punch.

It was the same reaction with my mom and dad. My mother cried. My dad pumped his fist. They asked a dozen questions, and we answered each one the best we could, my arms wrapped tight around my girl.

"So you were together when we were in Blue Sky Bay?" my mother asked for the fourth time.

"We were, Mama," I said. "But we didn't want to add any pressure to our relationship, as we didn't know how it would all play out once Gracie moved."

"And you've got it figured out now?" my father asked.

"We do," I said. "We'll be long-distance for a while and give Gracie some time to see if this is where she wants to be. And if this is the city she needs to live in, then I'll be closing down the business in Blue Sky Bay and moving here and building something new in New York."

I didn't know how my dad would respond to my plan, but I wasn't going to lie about what I was willing to do to make this work.

His lips turned up in the corners. "Proud of you, son. You already know the secret to life."

"What's that, baby?" my mother asked, smiling at my father like he hung the moon.

"That you should always put the people you love in your life first. There's nothing more important than family, and he's always understood it. But his romantic life had me a little worried for a while," my father said, and his gaze locked with mine. "I wanted you to experience that life-changing kind of love, the kind that I have with your mother. Because not everyone finds it. And looking at you two right now, I know that you have it. And as a father, there's nothing that I want more for you. You can build a business anywhere, Cutler. You can make money anywhere. But you can't find your person anywhere. So you fight like hell for that when you find it."

And now my mom and Gracie were both crying.

I chuckled and wrapped my arms around her a little tighter. "We know how lucky we are, and we'll do whatever it takes to make it work."

And I knew that we would.

C and G for life.

CHAPTER THIRTY-FOUR

Gracie

The next few weeks had been a blur. Work was insanely busy, and then I'd flown back to Blue Sky Bay for the long holiday weekend.

"So you had a great Thanksgiving?" Johnny asked as we sat across from one another at the cute café that was downstairs in the building below our offices.

"I did. Since my brother Burke is still in Italy until next month, my parents agreed to come to Blue Sky Bay for Thanksgiving, so we got to spend it with both Cutler's family and mine. And we had Thanksgiving dinner at the house that was featured in *Design & Décor*, and the article came out while I was there." I still couldn't get over it. The article had been released this past weekend in stores everywhere, so everyone had bought copies, and Emilia had framed the first page of the article and displayed it at their home.

"Stop it. That's as good as it gets." He shook his head before taking a sip of his cappuccino and setting down his tiny cup. "You end up falling in love with one of the family members of the home that you designed, and you celebrated the holidays in said home. Darling, this is a fairytale in the making."

I chuckled. "Well, I have known the family most of my life, and I've done many holidays with them, but yes, this one was extra special for a multitude of reasons."

He clapped his hands together twice. "Yes, you were featured in the magazine, and you and Cutler had your big debut as a couple. How did it go?"

"It was amazing. We'd been so worried that everyone would have expectations or there'd be added pressure, but that wasn't the case at all. Everyone is just really happy for us. I think my mom and Cutler's mom must have cried at least a dozen times while we were there."

He sniffed a few times. "This is so romantic. I just love love, you know? My problem is that I just love too many people, and I get bored easily and then I'm ready for a new lover," he said with a wicked grin on his face.

"I can't wait for the day when you get knocked on your ass."

"You and me both, darling." He wriggled his eyebrows. "So, update on the Dumont project and then we can head over to take a look."

"I'm really excited for you to see it. It's going to be spectacular. We've made it through demolition and framing and all the behind-the-walls stuff. Now that the walls are in place, you can really see how large the space is."

"I mean, they joined two massive condos together, which must have made the view even more spectacular," he said, and I loved that Johnny truly enjoyed design the same way I did. We connected about our mutual love for our profession.

"Yes. I can't wait for you to see it. We changed the layout, moving the bedrooms to the back side, and now it's just all view when you walk in. You're going to love it."

He studied me for a beat. "And I know they wanted a very industrial vibe. How have you been feeling about that?"

"I mean, of course it kills me because I want to put long linen draperies on the sides of the windows to add some drama. I'd love a few chandeliers in the open space." I chuckled. "But I'm adapting."

"You sure are." He stood up. "Let's go see your soon-to-be masterpiece, and you can walk me through it and tell me what your plan is."

"Perfect. Let's do this." I zipped my coat all the way up, since it was snowing outside and the temperatures had dropped quite a bit over the last week and a half.

The swanky high-rise was only two blocks away. I was grateful once we'd stepped inside the building and the noise of the city had quieted.

"Wow. This view is…breathtaking. The way you reconfigured this is truly brilliant," Johnny said as he strode to the floor-to-ceiling windows and whistled.

"I made suggestions, and they were open to them. It was a group effort."

He turned around to face me. "Always so humble. You were just featured in a major design magazine—it's okay to brag a little, darling."

I chuckled. "You brag enough on my behalf."

"Good point." He tapped me on the nose and then asked me to share my vision as we went from one room to the next. I pulled up photos on the iPad where I'd saved my mood boards for each space, and he appeared to be very impressed. This design style was definitely new for me, but I'd spent a lot of time researching all the elements. I'd presented my ideas to the client, who'd loved them.

Hopefully that would be the case when it all came together.

Design could be tricky, because oftentimes I'd choose finishes based off smaller samples, and I had to be confident that it would all marry well together to become a cohesive aesthetic.

I knew confidence was gained through experience, but it also came down to having an eye for design and being comfortable in that.

This was an area of my life where I felt like I'd really come into my own shortly after I'd started working for Johnny, several years ago. I would wake up at all hours of the night thinking about the homes I was designing. That creative side of me had come to life, and with that, I had a newfound confidence.

This feeling that I was doing exactly what I was supposed to be doing.

I'd lost that for a little while after I'd moved to Paris.

But I already felt like I had gotten my mojo back, and it wasn't about moving to New York, or proving anything to anyone. I'd gotten my confidence back in Blue Sky Bay, but I hadn't realized it.

It wasn't about what firm I worked for, or even being featured in a magazine, although neither of those hurt. It was more about creating something that I was proud of. And I'd felt just as fulfilled when I'd completed Cutler's family's home and the Petersons' home as I'd feel about completing this project.

I'd been lost when I was living in Paris.

But I'd found my way again back in Blue Sky Bay.

Coming to New York City was the right decision. I'd stepped out of my comfort zone in design. I was surrounded by some of the most talented designers in the industry. I was living in the most amazing city, and it would be something that I would forever look back on and be grateful for.

But did I see myself living here forever?

I didn't.

Cutler and I had agreed not to make any decisions just yet, as we wanted to give it some time. The fact that he was willing to walk away from the company that he'd built without hesitation—that meant something to me.

And anytime I complained about the noise and the traffic here, he was the one who'd tell me to be patient. To give it time. To enjoy the experience.

So that's what I was doing.

"I think this is going to be spectacular. You're really making a name for yourself." Johnny wrapped an arm around my shoulder, and I thanked him.

And I held my chin up a little higher when we stepped outside, because he was right. I was working hard and making a name for myself in a career that I loved. I was putting in long hours and growing as a designer, and I was proud of that.

And it felt good to feel proud of myself again.

Johnny and I made our way back to the office, where I spent the next few hours placing orders, and then I jumped on a Zoom call to meet with a new potential client. On days like this, the hours just blurred together and I lost track of time, and I was embracing it.

"Please say you'll come to happy hour for just one glass of wine?" Whitney asked as she stood in my doorway. She was the office manager at J&J Interiors, and we'd hit it off immediately after I started working here.

Over the last two months, I'd turned down Whitney's many invitations to office happy hours because I worked long hours—and I was more of a lunch girl, if it was up to me—but I decided I was going to branch out a bit.

"I'll come."

"Stop it!" she shrieked. "Get your purse before you change your mind. We're just going to the wine bar next door."

I chuckled at her enthusiasm, and we walked the short distance over to the wine bar. Whitney was quite a bit taller than me, and her black hair was cut in a sharp A-line bob just below her ears. She always wore red lipstick and exuded confidence. Justine, Mara, and Talia waved us over to where they were sitting at a high-top table.

"I'm so glad you came," Mara said, her long blonde hair pulled back in a neat chignon as she leaned forward and hugged me. She was a designer who'd been with the company for two years.

Talia was her assistant, and Justine ran the marketing team for both the New York and Los Angeles offices. They were all good friends, and we ate lunch together a couple of days a week. We'd all grown close.

"Me too." I set my purse down and took a seat. "I guess work will be waiting for me tomorrow."

"So how was your long weekend home with your hot contractor?" Talia asked, tucking her red hair behind her ears as she smiled.

They'd met Cutler on FaceTime during lunch at the office a few times, and they'd loved him, of course.

"It was great. It was hard to leave," I admitted, pausing to order a glass of wine, and Whitney did the same.

"Damn. I wish he lived here and had a sexy single friend you could introduce me to," Whitney grumped.

"I take it your date didn't go great last night?" I asked.

She was a serial dater who was on multiple dating websites, and she was constantly showing me the guys she was going out with. But she was quite possibly the pickiest woman on the planet. She found something wrong with every single one of them.

"Guess why she won't be going out with Stewart again?" Talia used her hand to cover the wide grin on her face.

"Do tell," Mara said. She took a sip of her wine and set her glass down.

"Keep in mind that last week she went out with the neurosurgeon who looks like he could be on the cover of *GQ* magazine, and she thought he had too much chest hair." Justine's head fell back with a fit of laughter, her brown ringlets bouncing on her shoulders.

"Dude. His chest hair was so overgrown that it was bunched up beneath his chin, and looked like a beard." Whitney's eyes were wide as she shook her head.

The table erupted in a fit of laughter.

"And tell them about your problem with Zed, the beautiful artist from last night," Talia said with a smirk.

"I can't wait." I rubbed my hands together.

"He's a spitter, and I'm not in the market for receiving a saliva shower. Five minutes in, I knew it had zero chance of working." Whitney shrugged.

"How much did he spit to be labeled a 'spitter'?" Mara asked, a wicked grin on her face. "How bad could it have been?"

"Listen, if I need an umbrella to have dinner with you, it's not going to work. Zed and I are donezo." She sighed. "So, the more important question is, how do you make the long-distance thing work? Is there a lot of phone sex involved?"

I shook my head, feeling my cheeks pink. "I can't give all my secrets away."

"I'm guessing that means there's a lot of phone sex." Whitney chuckled, and Mara waggled her brows.

We continued talking and laughing as we ordered a second glass of wine. Justine filled us in on her new boyfriend, and Talia told us that she'd run into the ex she'd dated all through high school, and the sparks were stronger than ever.

I was really glad I'd come, but I was happy once I pushed through the door to my apartment and kicked off my stilettos.

It had been a long day but a good day.

I saw a missed call from Cutler and FaceTimed him as I dropped to sit on the couch.

"Hey, baby," he said, a big smile on his handsome face.

"Hi. Where are you, and why aren't you wearing a shirt? It's almost December and there's snow on the ground."

He laughed and turned his phone to Meatball, who was wearing a life jacket, before giving me a view of the large indoor pool behind him. I smirked to keep from laughing.

"Apparently, the indoor pool allows dogs to come swim one day a week, so Meatball just got his first swim lesson, because I can't allow him to just sink if he jumps in the lake. I can't handle Meatball having no life skills, Jeege. I told him that we love to go out on the boat, and he needs to get his shit together." He propped his phone up and pulled his hoodie over his head.

"Damn. I liked the view with no shirt," I chuckled as I watched him take Meatball's life jacket off and attach the leash. He started walking and picked the phone back up so I could see him.

"I like any view that I can get of you." He winked.

"So how many dogs were there tonight with you and Meatball?"

"Exactly zero. But Charlie runs the place, and he said that I could bring him once a week. You know I prefer the lake, but it's fucking cold outside right now, and Meatball is a lazy fucker, so I figured an indoor heated pool would be better," he said as he helped the dog into his truck and then sat in the driver's seat and continued talking.

We'd learned to take the moments we had to talk, because with the time difference it could be hard to always be available at the same time.

But we made it work.

I couldn't stop smiling. "I love my boys."

"We love you more." He turned on the car when Meatball tried to climb onto his lap. "I need to crank the heat, or he will insist on cuddling."

"Such a good Papa Bear." I shook my head in disbelief. "First you're giving him swimming lessons, and now you're cranking the heat for him."

"Well, my girl is crazy about her little Meatball, so I'm just trying to keep him alive." He flashed me that toothy grin that I loved so much. "Did you work late?"

"I actually went to happy hour with the girls."

"Atta girl. Getting yourself out there. Did you have fun?"

"I did." I sighed. "I had a lot of fun. But I miss you."

"I miss you too, baby. But remember, this will just be a blink in time in the grand scheme of our life. You are where you need to be right now, and so am I. We've got this. And I get to see you in a few weeks for Christmas." He leaned back in the driver's seat, his gaze so tender it made my chest ache.

What did I do to deserve this man?

"I can't wait." I stood up and walked to the bathroom, where I turned on the water in the bathtub. "Okay, you drive home and I'll hop in the tub. Call me in an hour so we can talk until I fall asleep."

"I'm going to drive fast so I can FaceTime you while you're still in the tub."

I chuckled and ended the call.

I closed my eyes after I'd slipped into the hot water, grateful that this long day had come to an end.

I laughed when the phone rang a few minutes later and Cutler's name lit up my screen.

He was definitely a man of his word, and I couldn't answer the phone fast enough.

CHAPTER THIRTY-FIVE

Cutler

"I'm just so happy that we got to spend Christmas Eve with you both," my mother said as we all sat around the big farmhouse table at my parents' house. All my uncles and aunts and cousins who lived here in Magnolia Falls had just left after we'd had dinner together, like we did every year.

My mom lived for Christmas, so every square inch of our home was decorated in garlands and lights and holiday décor, and it smelled of fresh pine. She put up six Christmas trees every year, and there was even one in my childhood bedroom, which Gracie was thrilled about because that's where we were staying.

"It was so good to see everyone," I said. "And you know anytime you make unicorn Krispies, I'm going to come running."

"I remember being obsessed with these when I was younger."

Gracie tore off another piece of my mother's famous Rice Krispie Treats covered in rainbow sprinkles and popped it in her mouth.

I was so fucking in love with this woman, and I'd missed her like crazy, so I was savoring every second we had together this week.

The distance was challenging but manageable. Now that we'd made the decision to be together, we talked a couple of times a day and planned when we'd get to see each other next. And it was working well for now.

But I was already taking action in case she decided she wanted to stay in New York. I'd started studying for the Home Improvement Contractor License for New York City, but I hadn't told Gracie yet. I'd have to do a few things if I wanted to move my company across the country, which would take time.

So I'd get the ball rolling and be ready if the time came for me to do it.

"I can still picture you as a little girl, with those big brown eyes, asking me how I'd caught a unicorn to get all the sprinkles." Mom chuckled.

"I remember that." Gracie shook her head with a huge smile on her face. "I used to love when we'd come to Magnolia Falls. We'd go to Demi's coffee shop for the best pumpkin lattes, and then my dad dragged me to Romeo's gym a few times to try to teach me how to box."

"I still love going to Uncle Ro's gym," I said. "Man, it's just always good to be home."

"It is. And tomorrow we're heading to Blue Sky Bay when you two leave for Cottonwood Cove," Pops said. "I guess we've got a lot of homes now. And it sounds like we might have to start coming out to New York too, if you two end up there."

"I love big cities," my mom said. "I mean, I don't know if I'd want to live there, but I love visiting." She was still scrolling on her iPad, looking at Gracie's recent designs. "Are you loving it there?"

"I'm happy that I did it. It's still an adjustment, and personally I like small-town living a lot. But it's a once-in-a-lifetime opportunity right now, so I'm where I'm supposed to be, I guess," Gracie said, and our gazes met.

She struggled with what she wanted to do, and I tried to be supportive, because at the end of the day, it didn't matter where we were. All that mattered was that we were together.

"You've got to take those opportunities," Pops said. "We're proud of you for doing it. And we support Cutler if he decides to open up ROD there and close the office in Blue Sky Bay. Because what matters most is that you two do whatever you need to do to be together."

I was lucky to call these two my parents. They'd always been supportive and loving, no matter what was happening in my life.

"I haven't said anything, because I've got it handled, but Tara called a few days ago," I said, catching them all off-guard. It wasn't something I talked about often, but I'd realized I didn't need to keep it to myself. My parents had dealt with her manipulative behavior when I was young, and Gracie was very familiar with her popping in and out of my life over the years.

"What did she want this time?" Pops asked.

"She wanted more money," I admitted as I scratched the back of my neck. "And I realized that I'd given her money a few months ago for the wrong reasons."

"What do you mean?" my mom asked, her eyes wet with emotion.

"I was doing it for myself. I'm not proud to say that I think in a way I wanted to impress her. To show her that I'd done just fine without her, and that she'd messed up by walking away all those years ago." I shrugged, and my gaze locked with Gracie's as she smiled the slightest bit. She'd reminded me many times that I didn't need Tara's approval, which wasn't something that I could buy. "And I realized that I don't resent her for leaving, because look where I am. I've got the most incredible family and the most incredible girl. I'm not lacking in any area of my life, and I don't need the approval of a woman who doesn't know anything about me."

"That's very true," my father said, his eyes filled with compassion as he looked at me. "And if you keep giving her money, I don't think it'll ever stop, unfortunately. But I don't judge you for having a big heart, Cutler. I'm proud as hell of you. But you sure as shit don't need anyone's approval, least of all Tara's."

"Agreed. And it's a tricky situation, because she's your mom too," my mother said.

I took her hand in mine. "That's the thing, Mama. I don't feel that way at all. And it hit me when she called the other day, because she told me that she has COPD from years of smoking. And I didn't feel the way I thought I would. Instead, I felt irritated, like she'd never taken care of herself, nor cared for anyone else. But when you were sick, I felt like I'd lost a limb. I was angry at the universe because it wasn't fair. Because you're the most amazing mother and friend and sister and wife. You are my only mother. My Sunny. I love you so much it hurts."

Tears were streaming down her face, and I glanced over to see the tears moving down Gracie's cheeks as well.

"It's been the honor of my life to be your mother." She sniffed a few times.

My dad wrapped his arms around Gracie and chuckled. "Nothing like Christmas Eve with the Hearts, huh? We're a sappy bunch."

"I wouldn't change a thing," Gracie said. "So, what did you end up telling Tara?"

"I told her I couldn't give her money in good conscience again, because she's just going to use it for drugs and alcohol, and I wouldn't take part in that. But I sent some groceries to her house, so she'd have food in her refrigerator. And I didn't do it to prove anything. I did it because I'm able to, and that was reason enough." I shrugged.

"How did I get so lucky to call you mine, Cutler Heart?" Gracie said, her teeth sinking into her bottom lip.

"I'm pretty sure I claimed you when we were five years old, and you finally got on board after all these years." I winked at her.

"I don't know about that, but I'm definitely on board," she said.

My parents both chuckled. "Well, seeing you two together is the best Christmas gift you could have given us," Mom said.

We stayed up late into the night opening presents and making new memories.

And tomorrow we'd be doing the same thing with Gracie's family in Cottonwood Cove.

And I wouldn't have it any other way.

• • •

Gracie's family was large and loud and lots of fun, and I'd always felt like I was home when I was here. My uncle Bridger had offered us his helicopter so we could make it there much quicker this morning, so we'd made it here to open gifts at her grandparents' house. Gracie had always been close with them, and they adored her.

They'd made a big deal about us being together, as I'd grown up around all of them.

"So our little Gracie finally ends up with the right guy," her uncle Finn said as he gave me a pound with his fist. "Welcome to the family, Beefcake. Well, I guess you were already a member, but now it's more official."

"He's always been part of the family," Hugh, another uncle, said as he looked between us with a big grin on his face.

"I always knew you'd end up together," Gracie's aunt Brinkley added.

"I'm the one who told you that I thought they were more than friends." Georgia, another aunt, let a loud laugh escape before turning her attention to her niece. "Remember when you confided in me in high school that you had a big crush on Cutler?"

"What?" I feigned surprise and tugged my girl closer to me. "You had a crush on me in high school? Was this before you were dating Bowie, the Virgin King?"

"Hey now," Cage said, pretending to cover his ears as everyone laughed.

"I'm actually the one who predicted they would end up together," Burke said, and Gracie smiled at her brother, who was home from school in Italy.

"You also predicted that Cutler would go on *The Bachelor* and become a famous reality star," Gracie said with a smirk.

Burke laughed. "Hey, that could have happened during his college years. Listen, this is a dream come true for me, because I've never liked any of the dudes you've dated, and now you've hit the jackpot." Her brother high-fived me.

"I'm the one who hit the jackpot," I said as I wrapped my arms around her a little tighter.

We spent the rest of the afternoon watching football and hanging out with family. When we got back to her parents' house, Gracie helped her mom unload all the leftovers that her grandmother had sent home with us.

Burke said he needed to go lie down, as he was jet-lagged and still on Italy time.

Cage and I each grabbed a beer, bundled up in our coats, and went out back to light a fire.

"Is this a good time to talk to you about something?" I asked, clearing my throat.

His expression turned a bit more serious, and he leaned forward in his chair. "Of course. Is everything okay?"

"Everything is great," I assured him.

Why am I suddenly nervous?

"Yeah? I'm sure the distance isn't easy, Cutler. But I want you to know that I appreciate you encouraging Gracie to do this," he said, giving me a steady look. "I know she regretted her choice to go to Paris, but I really think she's gotten her confidence back now. It was too good of an opportunity to turn down. And you guys are young, and you've got your whole lives ahead of you."

"I agree. And I'm proud as hell of her for doing this." I intertwined my fingers, resting my elbows on my knees. "She doesn't know it yet, but I've started the process to get licensed in New York City. I don't want to wait until she tells me it's where she wants to stay permanently and then have to start the process. I want to be ready. The ball is in her court, and when she says jump, I'll just ask how high." I chuckled.

"You'd really close down your business and move across the country, wouldn't you?"

"It's not even a question. I'd do it right now, but she's not certain she wants to stay there. So we've agreed to give it six months, and see how she feels," I said. Gracie's lease had been extended for three more months, so she'd make the decision in the next few months.

"You're a good man, Cutler Heart."

"Well, not sure about that, but I'm certainly a lucky man." I exhaled. "And what I wanted to talk to you about is my commitment to your daughter."

“I don’t have one bit of hesitation about your commitment to one another,” he said confidently.

“That’s good to hear, because I need you to know that I’d walk through fire for that girl. She’s the first person I want to talk to when I wake up in the morning and the last person I want to talk to before I go to sleep. She’s always completed me in a way. I want to give her everything her heart desires, and then some. She’s my girl. Always has been. Always will be.” I looked him in the eyes, and I mean I really looked him in the eyes. Wanting him to see all the love that I had for his little girl. “I want to propose to her in the near future, and I want to make sure I have your blessing. You know how much respect I have for you, so knowing that you’re on board with this would mean a lot to me.”

“I thought Presley getting me a new set of golf clubs was going to be the best Christmas gift this year.” He pushed to his feet and tugged me up to stand. “But you just made me a very happy man.”

He clapped me on the back, and we just stood there hugging for the longest time.

Cage Reynolds had always felt like family to me. And now we were going to make it official.

We both sat back down. “Do you know how you’re going to do it?”

“I’m working on that right now,” I said. “We’ve been through a lot together, so I’ll need to make it really special.”

“Well, damn. You’ve got me all choked up, so I think you could just speak from the heart like you did tonight, and you’ll be just fine,” he said. “But knowing you the way I do, I have no doubt it’ll be something we’ll all talk about for years.”

“That’s the plan,” I said.

“What’s the plan?” Gracie came walking outside wearing her white ski jacket and white hat with a big pompom on the top of her head.

"The plan is that we wake up tomorrow and go get some pancakes at the Cottonwood Café," Cage said, thinking quickly on his feet.

"Oh, I haven't seen Mrs. Runither in a few months, but Mom said she's still working there on the weekends. And you know how much she loves you, Cutler." Gracie settled on my lap and chuckled.

"She was a big fan of the Beefcake."

"I've yet to meet anyone who isn't," she said as she rested her head in the crook of my neck.

"Sounds like a plan," I said, my gaze locking with her father's again.

"It sure does," he said with a smirk.

Because now that he'd given me his blessing, I was putting this plan into action.

CHAPTER THIRTY-SIX

Gracie

Johnny and I were having dinner tonight to celebrate the completion of the Dumont project. The reveal was today, and they absolutely loved it. The project had been a huge stretch for me creatively, because I'd been so out of my normal comfort zone. And I'd fully enjoyed it.

I'd wrapped up two other smaller projects over the last two weeks, and I had one large loft in Brooklyn that was getting close to the finishing stages.

I'd been living in New York City for almost five months. My lease would be up next month with the extension they'd given me, and it was time to make a decision. Cutler and I talked about it daily, and he was on board to do whatever I wanted.

And I'd really thought long and hard on it, and I felt like I should speak to Johnny before I flew to Blue Sky Bay to spend Valentine's Day with Cutler.

"You leave tomorrow, right? You'll be home with your handsome Bear." He chuckled.

"Yes." I nodded as our server set down our two martinis and a basket of warm bread. We were dining at the restaurant downstairs in my building. I loved this place, which was the first restaurant I'd eaten at after moving here. "I'm excited to see him."

"I'll bet you are. And he was just here two weeks ago." He sighed. "The distance must be getting old. And I know your lease is up next month, so tell me what you're thinking."

"Well, you know that Cutler's been getting things aligned to apply for his license here in New York City, and we've been looking at apartments to purchase, and considering all of our options." I'd found a booklet he'd been studying, and he'd admitted that he'd started the licensing process, since he knew it would take some time.

"I love that he's willing to uproot his life for you, darling. That man really loves you." He reached for his drink and took a sip, popping his lips when he set the glass back down to show his approval.

"He does. And I love him just as much." I blew out a breath. "I've really put a lot of thought into this. I'm actually talking to you about it first, and I'll speak to him when I go home this weekend."

He smiled, folding his hands together and resting them on the edge of the table. "Tell me what you're thinking."

"First and foremost, I could never thank you enough for the opportunity to work for you. Having you as my mentor has been a dream come true. Honestly, I have the most respect and admiration for you, Johnny."

He reached across the table and took my hands in his. "The feeling is mutual, darling. And I have a feeling our time together is coming to an end."

Our server approached and set down our salads, and Johnny pulled his hands back as we reached for our utensils.

"So, I haven't spoken to Cutler yet, because I've gone back and forth many times about what I wanted to do. But last night I just had clarity, and everything just seemed to be crystal clear."

"That's what I was hoping would happen. I didn't want you to second-guess your decision," he said as he popped a cherry tomato in his mouth.

"Same. But what I realized is that I needed this time here, to learn and to grow and to get my confidence back. And New York City did not disappoint." I shook my head and smiled. "This experience will stay with me for a lifetime. And this has definitely been a step in the direction I want to go in. It just isn't the final step."

"I'm truly honored that I got to be part of the journey."

"You were such a big part of the journey, and I love this company and all the people I've worked with so much. But I'm ready to create something of my own, you know? I'm ready to invest in myself. Build a company that's mine, put a stamp on my name and my design style." I shrugged. "And though I love the energy here, I miss the mountains and the lake and the peaceful serenity that you find in a small town. It's where I feel the most content, which in turn feeds my creative juices."

"I get that. The buzz of the city, the hustle and bustle, the tall buildings and changing seasons get my adrenaline pumping. I'd lost that when I lived in Los Angeles, as it was a different vibe there. So I understand wanting to be in an environment that inspires you. You're all about nature and country music and homes with history and character. I knew that when I hired you, and I also knew I wouldn't be able to keep you forever."

A tear broke free and moved down my cheek, and I quickly

swiped it away. "I am so appreciative of everything you've done for me. You hired me twice and you didn't judge me for leaving the first time. And then you invited me back and you let me spread my wings and try something new. Something so far out of my comfort zone."

"You've shined like the brightest star, darling. And here's the truth. I have a keen gift for recognizing talent when I see it. You have an abundance of it. If you called me in six months or a year or five years from now and you said that you wanted to come back to the firm—I wouldn't hesitate. But I'm also excited to watch you build something of your own, because you're ready now. You needed this place to land and get your footing before you really believed in your potential. And if I have any part in fostering that, it's my greatest honor. I can't wait to see what you do when you open the doors to your own business. You're ready." He tilted his head to the side and smiled as our waiter cleared our salad plate and then set our steaks down in front of us.

"I feel ready. And I'll be here to wrap everything up over the next month, but I wanted to give you plenty of notice, so you could find my replacement."

"Darling, you're irreplaceable, hence the reason your Bear was willing to move here for you." He set his martini glass down after taking a sip. "You haven't told him about your plans yet?"

"No, because I honestly wasn't certain what I wanted to do. I found out he'd been studying for the test that he'd need to get licensed here, and then he started sending me apartment listings in areas that we both liked. He was completely on board to move. And we would have been happy here, I don't doubt that. But at the end of the day, we both love small towns. We like to jump in the lake after dinner, or take out the boat on the weekends, or go line dancing in town. That's our happy place, you know? And I want to start my life with him there. But I'm glad he respected this time that I needed to be here, and that he was willing to move here if this was where I wanted to be."

"You've got a good one, darling. Hold on tight." He sliced a piece of steak and groaned before chewing.

"I intend to."

And we spent the rest of the evening discussing a few of Johnny's projects and what all I would be doing my last few weeks here in New York.

He didn't make me feel guilty or question my reasoning. He understood it, and that meant a lot to me.

I felt very confident with the decision I'd made, and I couldn't wait to talk to Cutler when I flew home tomorrow.

• • •

Cutler and I sat down at the table to eat dinner. I'd arrived in Blue Sky Bay an hour ago, and he'd met me at the airport with Meatball, who was now lying in front of the roaring fireplace.

"Happy Valentine's Day, Jeege. I'm happy you're here," he said. "I've got gifts for you, but we'll save those for after dinner."

"I've got a few things up my sleeve for you too," I said with a grin. "But I did want to talk to you about something important while we eat."

"Okay. What's up?"

"I know you've been studying for that exam and getting the process started to get your New York City contractor license." I exhaled. "I don't think you should do that."

Why was I suddenly nervous?

His brows cinched together. "You don't want me to move there with you?"

I shook my head and smiled. "I don't."

He nodded. "Okay. Tell me what's going on."

"I'm really proud of myself for going there, Bear. And I'm so grateful about the way that you encouraged me to embrace my new life there, and you supported me every step of the way. I promise you, I did embrace my new life. I went all in, and I've enjoyed pushing myself out of my comfort zone."

"But you like being there by yourself," he said, and it wasn't a question; it was a statement. I heard the hurt in his voice, and it was obvious that I was doing a crappy job of telling him what I wanted.

I stood up and moved to where he sat across from me, and I bent down in front of him, taking his hands in mine. "I'm not being clear. I actually hate being there without you. But that's not why I don't want you to come there. I went there, and I did what I set out to do. I grew as a designer and a person. But I realized that I have nothing to prove to anyone anymore, nor do I have anything to prove to myself. I've made some mistakes along the way, but that's part of living."

He wrapped both of his large hands around mine, and I saw the confusion in his gaze, but it was surrounded by love. "It's absolutely part of living."

"At the end of the day, I'm just a girl in love with a boy, and I want a life filled with that love. I can build my career anywhere. And I don't need to live somewhere just to prove that I can do it. I want to live in a place where I wake up every day with you beside me," I said.

"I get that. And we can do that anywhere." He searched my gaze, and all I saw was empathy and understanding.

"I don't want to do it anywhere. I want to do it here, with the water splashing against the shore in the morning. I want to go out on the boat and watch the sun set for the day. I want to walk Meatball down a country road, and line dance on the weekends. I want to start my own business right here in a town that feels like home. A town that I can help you transform, one house at a time. I want to build a life with you here."

His lips turned up in the corners. "We can do that, baby."

"Yeah?"

"Yeah." He pulled me onto his lap and wrapped his arms around me. "Are you sure?"

"I've thought about it a lot. And I appreciate that you were willing to give up everything you have here, everything you've built—all to support me." I shook my head, the tears falling down my cheeks. "I don't know what I did to deserve you. I don't know how to even express how much I love you."

He turned my body the slightest bit, placing a hand on each side of my face. "You deserve everything, Gracie Reynolds. I knew it the first time I met you when I was just a little kid, and I've known it every day since. And I understand not knowing how to express this love that we have between us, because it's hard for me to put it into words too."

I sniffed a few times and nodded.

He reached for my hand and placed it over his heart. "This belongs to you. It always has and it always will. I would follow you to the moon if that's where you wanted to go. And if you want to start our lives here in Blue Sky Bay, nothing would make me fucking happier. But know this—all I need is right in front of me. You. Are. It. For. Me."

I leaned forward and kissed him, wrapping my hands around his neck, before pulling back. "You're it for me too, Bear."

"So you're really moving back here. Did you talk to Johnny?"

"I did. He understands and he supports my decision. I gave him a month's notice, and I'll wrap up my projects there and then move back when my lease is up."

"New plan, huh?" he asked with a smirk.

"You know how much I love a plan."

"This is good because you know I bought that piece of land, and I didn't feel right building a spec home on it to flip and sell. It feels more like a forever home for my forever girl."

"Oh, really? Do you have a designer in mind who could make it everything you want?" I asked, my voice teasing.

"I sure do. I hear she's starting her own business here soon, and she's a hell of a line dancer."

I laughed and Meatball let out a loud howl, which made me laugh harder. "She sounds fabulous."

"She really is. And she's the love of my life."

"Wow. Maybe she'll give you a good discount then?" I said with a smile.

"We make a great team, Jeege."

"We sure do." I ran my fingers through his hair as my gaze locked with his.

He stood up, taking me with him. My legs came around his waist, and my arms wrapped around his neck. "Where are we going? We barely ate our dinner."

"I've got something better in mind. Food is overrated." He chuckled as he carried me down the hallway toward the bedroom, where he dropped me on the bed. He hovered over me, a wicked grin spreading across his handsome face. "I can't wait one more minute to bury myself in you."

"You do remember carrying me to the bedroom as soon as we got home from the airport, right?" I smiled up at him.

The man was ridiculously sexy.

"I just can't get enough of you," he said, his voice gruff.

"I hope you never do."

"Count on it. I plan to spend the rest of my life loving you, Gracie. It doesn't matter where we are, as long as we're together."

"As long as we're together. C and G for life, remember?"

“Those are words I plan to live by.” He had this lazy smile on his face that always did crazy things to me.

And he leaned down and claimed my mouth.

Kissing me like I was his last breath.

Like I was his forever.

EPILOGUE

Cutler

"When do you think we'll break ground?" she asked as I held her hand and walked toward the plot of land that we were going to build our dream house on.

"Well, seeing as the drawings are done and permits are in place, we can start anytime. But there's something I wanted to run by you first before we can officially start."

"Okay, but it's getting dark, so I don't know if we'll be able to see much in a little bit," she said.

Gracie had been back in town for a couple of weeks, and she'd already filed for a business license and gotten things up and running. My girl was one hell of an impressive woman.

She came to a stop when she saw all the candles forming a path. The guys had helped me put this together earlier today, and I couldn't wait to bring her here. To make it official.

"What's this?" she whispered.

"This is forever, baby." I placed a hand on her lower back and guided her forward. "Come on, let me show you."

Glass jars with taper candles lined the path, and at the end was a gigantic pink heart made out of flowers standing upright on a stand so it would be eye level. Pink roses filled the heart, and white roses inside spelled out "CH + GR," just like the heart I'd made her all those years ago.

She didn't speak; she just stood there with tears streaming down her face.

I thought I'd feel nervous when this moment arrived, but I felt completely calm. This was Gracie—and I'd never been more certain about anything in my life.

I dropped to one knee and took her hand in mine. "I met you when I was five years old, Gracie, and I knew you were special even back then. I claimed you that day, and I swear I've claimed you every day since. And what started as a friendship grew into something I never even knew I could have. You are my best friend, my lover, and my favorite person on the planet." I swiped away the tears rolling down her cheeks. "I've watched you these last few months, and I've been so damn impressed and inspired by you, pushing yourself outside of your comfort zone and kicking ass every step of the way like a goddamn warrior princess."

She chuckled, looking up at me with those gorgeous dark brown eyes, wet with emotion.

"And I had all the faith in you, Jeege. I knew you'd figure it out, and I knew I'd follow you wherever you wanted to go, because I realized the only dream that I'm chasing is right in front of me. She's been in front of me my whole life." I smiled, pushing away the lump in my throat. "We've been through everything together, and you were always right there beside me. *My girl.* And through all the storms that we've faced over the years, you were always the one standing there in the rain with me, pulling me through. You have my heart. And I want to spend the rest of eternity loving you. Building a home together and a family together. I want you to be my wife. Gracie Reynolds, you are my forever. My forever girl. Will you make me the happiest man and be my wife?"

"You had me at 'warrior princess,'" she said, her words breaking with a sob.

"I'm going to need a more specific answer," I said, smirking. "Will you marry me, baby?"

"Yes. Of course. I'd marry you right here, right now," she whimpered. "I've loved you my whole life, Cutler Heart."

I pulled the ring box from my shirt pocket and slipped it onto her finger. It was a large round diamond on a platinum band. Classic and elegant, just like her.

"Oh my gosh, Bear, it's stunning," she said, gaping down at her hand and then blinking up at me. "I love it so much."

I pulled her up to stand and leaned down and kissed her.

When I pulled back, I placed a hand on each side of her neck. "I'm so ready for you to be my wife."

"I'm so ready for you to be my husband." She sniffed a few times.

I took her hand in mine. "And we're going to build our dream home right here."

"Yes, we are. And Meatball definitely shouldn't be an only child," she said with a grin. "That would be very lonely for him."

"Are we talking about puppies or babies?" I asked, my voice laced with humor.

She smiled. "We're talking about everything. Thanks for giving me the fairytale, Cutler Heart."

"Thanks for showing me that it exists." I stroked my thumb along her bottom lip. "Are you ready to go celebrate with our friends?"

"They know about this?"

"There may or may not be an engagement party over at Four Clovers waiting for us."

A wide grin spread across her face as we started walking. I was grateful at the moment that the candles were all battery-operated, at the insistence of Pheonix, who'd told me he was not okay with open flames.

So we could just leave these going until they ran out of charge.

"This is why I love small-town living. Everyone knows what's happening and celebrates the big and the small moments," she said, glancing up at me. "I can't believe we're getting married."

"Yep. Time to start planning a wedding," I said as the Down by the Bay Container Park came into view, and we could see that the place was packed. Country music boomed through the speakers, and as we approached, the music turned off, and everyone shouted at once.

"Congratulations!"

We both laughed and started making our rounds. A large cake was sitting on a table, and the drinks were flowing. Gracie answered a bunch of questions about the proposal, and I found my way over to the table with my boys.

"So I'm assuming she said yes?" Phoenix asked.

Brody laughed. "Of course she said yes. Would they be here if she didn't?"

"I mean, there's drinks and a cake and dancing. I was coming either way." Phoenix used his hand to cover his smile, but I saw it there. This was his way of congratulating me.

"Man, I love weddings," Cannon said. "There's always an open bar and lots of horny single women there. It's the best."

"Well, glad to hear it, because you're all going to be standing up there with me when we do it." I held up the beer bottle that Brody had just handed me, and they all raised their bottles.

"To Heart," Cannon said. "I would not have guessed you to be the first one to get married, but I can't say I'm surprised that you ended up with the girl we all knew you should be with. I will miss my wingman, but I'm happy for you, brother."

We all clinked our bottles together, and I took a long drink. My gaze moved to the dance floor to see Gracie out there dancing and smiling and having the time of her life.

"Do you think you'll get married here or in Magnolia Falls or Cottonwood Cove?" Bass asked.

"I don't know," I said. "I'll let her pick whatever she wants. I don't care about the wedding. I'm just ready to make it official."

"I'm happy for you, brother." Brody clapped me on the shoulder. "And who would have thought you'd end up with our Gracie girl? She's been right there in front of you the whole damn time."

"Me." Phoenix held up his hand. "I always thought they had something secretly going on, and they'd end up together."

Cannon raised an eyebrow. "I'm with Nix. I was shocked they didn't get together sooner. The sparks were sparking."

"Did you just say 'the sparks were sparking'?" Bass bellowed out in laughter.

"Hey, Jovi told me that's a thing the kids are saying these days," Cannon said with a laugh.

"Dude. Do not quote my sister or even look at her, you got me?" Bass glared at him before turning back to me. "I also thought you two would end up together eventually. I mean, you barely functioned when she moved to Paris. She's your girl."

"Yeah, he never has been happy with anyone other than Gracie, has he?" Brody shrugged. "I think you were just waiting for the right time."

"I'm just glad we finally figured it out, because I can't wait to marry that girl." I held up my bottle again, and we all tipped our heads back at the same time.

"Meatball is one lucky bastard," Cannon said over his laughter. "His parents are making it official. That dude gets private swim lessons, and Bass keeps sending leftover steak for him."

"I bet he gets to attend the wedding too," Phoenix said.

"Damn straight," I said as I caught Gracie's eye as she moved down the dance floor with a big smile on her face.

I just sat there watching her while they all made fun of me, and I didn't give a shit. Because I could sit here watching her all night.

"For fuck's sake," Bass hissed beside me, pulling me from staring at my future bride.

"What's wrong?" I asked.

"I keep getting these emails from this woman named Briar Sinclair telling me that her company wants to buy the land beneath Bennett's. She's called me multiple times over the last few weeks, and I just ignore the calls. And now she keeps fucking emailing me, and she says she's going to come to town and meet with me in person. I've told her that I'm not interested in selling." Bass rubbed his face.

"Why does she want that land?" Brody asked.

"Apparently, they want to build a hotel on the corner, and they already purchased the two empty surrounding lots beside my restaurant, which is why I couldn't expand when I'd attempted to do so last year. They're obviously trying to force my hand."

"I do love a persistent woman. Is she hot?" Cannon asked, and Bass flipped him the bird before Cannon threw his hands in the air in surrender. "I'm kidding, dude. We'll figure this out."

"Can't you just ignore her? You own the place," Phoenix said. "She's going to have to find another piece of land to purchase."

Bass exhaled. "That's the thing. I own the building, but I don't actually own the land beneath it. The subsurface rights were sold separately, so it's a little more complicated than just telling her to fuck off. And they obviously have big money if they're buying up multiple pieces of land."

"Do you want to talk to my uncle River and get some legal advice?" I asked, because I could tell he was stressed about it.

"That might not be a bad idea." Bass sighed and then shook his head and smiled, though I could tell it was forced. "All right, let's take a shot. This is a celebration, and I didn't mean to bring the party down."

Brody added, "Let me grab us some celebratory shots, and we'll deal with this Briar Sinclair bullshit tomorrow." He walked to the bar and grabbed us five shot glasses of whiskey.

"Cheers to the first man to fly the coup," he said as he held up his glass.

"May the rest of us stay single forever." Cannon tipped his head back, and we all laughed.

"Hey there, fiancé," Gracie said as she sidled up beside me.

"Hey, beautiful." I tugged her closer before leaning down and kissing her hard.

"Damn. Get a room," Phoenix said, and Cannon whistled.

"I think that's actually a great idea. I'm taking my future wife home, and I'll talk to you guys tomorrow."

"What about the cake?" Phoenix shouted.

"You guys have at it," I told them with a laugh.

I had other things on my mind.

We said our goodbyes as we made our way through the party, everyone in town congratulating us on our way out.

Once we were on the path to the house, I turned and picked her up and tossed her over my shoulder.

“Bear!” she squealed over her laughter. “What are you doing?”

“I’m going to carry you over the threshold, baby,” I said as she smacked my ass from where she was hanging over my back.

“We aren’t married yet—we’re engaged. You do the threshold thing on our wedding night,” she said with a chuckle.

“Well, I guess I’ll be doing it multiple times, because I like carrying you. Get used to it.”

“You’re ridiculous,” she teased as I pushed the door open and set her down on the counter, moving to stand between her legs.

“I’m crazy in love with you, Gracie Reynolds.” I tucked her hair behind her ears.

She smiled. “I’m crazy in love with you too. Thanks for the swoony proposal.”

“Thanks for saying yes.” I stroked my thumb over her bottom lip. “This is just the beginning. Forever starts today.”

“Forever started the day I met you, Cutler Heart,” she whispered.

She tangled her hands in my hair and kissed me as I lifted her off the counter, her legs coming around my waist as I carried her to the bedroom.

She was right.

Forever started the day I met her.

I’d loved this girl my entire life, and I’d love her till I took my last breath.

She was my forever girl.

EXCLUSIVE BONUS CONTENT

BONUS SCENE

Cutler

Twenty Years Earlier

"You ready for this?" My father asked as I settled in the chair at Wayne's Ink Palace.

"Hell yeah, I'm ready for this. I've been waiting to turn eighteen to get this inked on my arm." I chuckled, glancing at my best friend, who looked a little less certain than I was.

"Gracie looks like she's about to puke, so we might need a bucket for her, Wayne," Uncle River said, unable to hide his concern as he glanced at where she sat beside me.

Uncle Kingston pulled a can of Sprite out of his jacket, popped the top, and handed it to her. "I thought our girl might need this."

"Where the hell did that come from?" Uncle Hayes barked out a laugh.

"Coat pocket, boys. You know I like to be prepared," he said.

Gracie had driven to Magnolia Falls last night, just so she could come with me to get my first tattoo. We always showed up for each other for the important things—it's just the way it had always been.

Gracie took a sip of her soda and sighed. "I'm fine. I got my ears double pierced, remember?"

"Yep. It's just like getting your ears pierced." Uncle Romeo's head tipped back, and he chuckled. "And of course you're okay, Gracie Girl. I've seen you in my boxing gym a few times, and you hold your own."

"Your left shoulder, right?" Wayne asked, as he'd been the man to ink my Pops's and my uncles' tattoos many years ago.

"Yes. Right here." I clapped a hand over the top of my shoulder.

"Are you nervous?" Gracie whispered.

"Not even a little bit." I winked at her.

I'd been waiting to get this Ride or Die tattoo since I was a kid. It was a motto that I'd grown up hearing. Words the men that I looked up to most in my life lived by.

Ride or die. Brothers till the end. Loyalty always. Forever my friend.

Wayne took the piece of wet paper with the stencil reading *Ride or Die* and pressed it over my shoulder.

My father's cell phone rang, and his eyes found mine as the corners of his lips turned up. "Doesn't matter how old you are, your mom never stops worrying about you."

He answered the call and put her on speaker. "Hi, baby. Did you make it to your doctor's appointment yet?"

"I just got here. Can he hear me?" she asked.

"I can hear you, Mama." I chuckled, and Wayne made no attempt to hide his smile as he settled on the chair on my left side, while Gracie sat on my right.

"I just wanted to tell you that I love you. And Gracie, don't let those men give him a hard time if he changes his mind," my mother said, and hysterical laughter sounded around me.

"I won't." Gracie smiled even though my mom couldn't see her. They'd always been close.

"Wayne, I'll trust you'll take good care of my boy." Her voice was all business.

"I got you, Dr. Heart. You've taken the best care of all three of my little rugrats, so I promise to do the same with yours." Wayne turned on a light above his head and moved closer.

"He's a grown man, baby. He's leaving for college in a few months. And he's getting the same ink we've all got. It's not a big deal."

"Well, it's a big deal to me. I swear you planned this on the day you knew I had my mammogram scheduled so I wouldn't come with." Her voice was laced with humor, but I knew she was disappointed she couldn't be here with us.

"I promise I'm fine, Mama. We'll see you in a few hours. Love you."

"Love you more," she said, and my father ended the call and shook his head, just as Wayne got to work.

It didn't hurt nearly as much as I'd expected it to, aside from Gracie squeezing my hand so hard I was probably losing the circulation there, which made me laugh.

"Hey, it doesn't hurt," I said, giving her a little squeeze, and she relaxed.

Wayne looked between us and smirked. "Ain't young love the best?"

"It's not like that," I said when I saw Gracie's eyebrows shoot up. "She's got a boyfriend. He's a little boring, if you ask me. But she likes him."

"Bowie is not boring. He's just a little shy." She shot me a warning look and rolled her eyes. "And Bear is torturing all the girls in his class because he hasn't decided who he's taking to senior prom yet."

"I've only got one girl, and you're going with that snooze fest boyfriend of yours, so I may just go solo and have a good time." I waggled my brows.

"We don't even live in the same city." Her head fell back on a laugh.

"Well, we'll be living in the same city soon." I smirked as my uncles and my father laughed.

I had a plan of my own, and it included officially making Gracie Reynolds my girlfriend. Living in different cities had hindered that plan for years, but once we were together at school, I was determined to get my ass out of the friend zone. Because she was the only girl I'd ever really wanted.

"Well, I for one can't believe you two are leaving for college so soon," Uncle Kingston said, then popped a few M&M's in his mouth. "It seems like you were both just five years old last week."

"Ahhh...you're going away to school together, huh?" Wayne asked.

"Yep. That's always been the plan, and now it's all becoming very real." Gracie studied the ink Wayne was drawing on my shoulder. "Just like he always said he'd get this tattoo once he was old enough to do it."

"Well, I'm not as formal as Jeege over here. She writes every plan she has down, so there's no getting out of it once we agree to it," I said. My voice was all tease.

"And you love it." She smiled.

"I feel like Gracie should be getting the Ride or Die tattoo with you," my dad said, studying the fresh ink as Wayne continued darkening each letter. "She's always been your ride or die."

"You're right about that. She's my girl. Always has been. Always will be."

"C plus G for life." Her teeth sank into her bottom lip.

"For life."

And I meant it.

ACKNOWLEDGMENTS

Greg, Chase & Hannah, You are my reason for EVERYTHING! Love you so much!

Nat, I am ENDLESSLY grateful to be on this journey with you. So thankful for your friendship and for all that you do for me. Love you!

Mom, thank you for reading everything that I write the minute I finish it! It means the world to me. Love you!!

Georgie, I'm truly so grateful for you. Thank you for being an endless support system to me. Love you so much!

Willow, you are the brightest light, and I love you endlessly! So thankful to be on this journey together!

Catherine, my shmoops… thank you for seeing me through all the ups and downs. Endlessly grateful for you. Love you!

Kandi, Thank you for being YOU! I'm so grateful for your friendship and I love you so much!

Liz and S.J., I cannot even begin to thank you enough for celebrating this release with me! I'm so thankful for your friendship!!

Pathi, Endlessly thankful for you! Thank you for all of your support and encouragement! Love you so much!

Jessica Turner, I'm so incredibly grateful for you. Thank you for believing in my words, and these characters, and cheering me on. Seeing my books in bookstores is a dream come true, and I'm so thankful for you!

Sarah Rifield, Thank you for working so hard to get my books out in the world, and being an amazing cheerleader and support system. I'm so grateful for you!

To the amazing team at Entangled Publishing… thank you for making my wildest dreams come true! I appreciate you all so much!

Nicole McCurdy, I am so grateful for your input and feedback. I love working with you so much! So thankful for YOU!

Bill Siever, Thank you for working your magic, always jumping in to help me and being so supportive. I'm so grateful!

Katie and Kim at Lyric Audio Books, thank you so, so much for all that you do to help bring these books to life! So grateful for you!

Kim Cermak, Love you my Bravo sister! Truly, my world is so much better with you in it! Thank you for all that you do for me, I'm so grateful for YOU!

The most amazing VPR team, thank you for all of your support and encouragement! Christine Miller, Kelley Beckham, Tiffany Bullard, Sarah Norris, Valentine Grinstead, Charlie Grinstead, Josette Ochoa, Ratula Roy, Jill McManamon, Jaime Guidry, and Emma Walczak! I am so thankful for you

Tatyana (Bookish Banter), thank you for being such a support, and such an amazing friend. Love you!

Paige, I adore you. So grateful to have you in my life. I love our decorating DM's and being on this journey with you. Love you my sweet friend!

Abi, thank you for beta reading, and cheering me on, and stepping up whenever I need help! Love you so much!

Stephanie Hubenak, thank you for always reading my words early and cheering me on. Our daily chats are my favorite. And the GRAPHICS!! You are endlessly talented my friend! Love you!

Kelly Yates, Thank you for always stepping up and reading my words early! So incredibly grateful for your friendship!

Logan Chisholm, I'm so grateful for you and all of your support. Thank you for creating the most gorgeous videos for me!

Kayla Middlekauff, Thank you for making amazing content! I

am so thankful for YOU!

Janelle (Lyla June Co.), thank you for your support and friendship! I'm so grateful for you!

Hang Le Design, I am incredibly thankful for you. Thank you for working your magic and creating the most beautiful cover! I love working with you and am so grateful for you!!

Crystal Eacker, Thank you for your audio beta listening/reading skills and for always coming through for me every single time! So grateful for you my sweet friend!

Erika Plum, thank you for the adorable bookmarks! You nail it every time!

Jennifer, thank you for being an endless support system. For running the Facebook group, posting, reviewing and doing whatever is needed for each release. Your friendship means the world to me! Love you!

Rachel Parker, So incredibly thankful for you. My forever release day good luck charm! Love you so much!

Dad, you really are the reason that I keep chasing my dreams!! Thank you for teaching me to never give up. Love you!

Sandy, thank you for reading and supporting me throughout this journey! Love you!

To all the bloggers, bookstagrammers and ARC readers who have posted, shared, and supported me—I can't begin to tell you how much it means to me. I love seeing the graphics that you make and the gorgeous posts that you share. I am forever grateful for your support!

To all the readers who take the time to pick up my books and take a chance on my words...THANK YOU for helping to make my dreams come true!!

Doubling the Trees Behind Every Book You Buy.

Because books should leave the world better than they found it—not just in hearts and minds, but in forests and futures.

Through our Read More, Breathe Easier initiative, we're helping reforest the planet, restore ecosystems, and rethink what sustainable publishing can be.

Track the impact of your read at:

CONNECT WITH US ONLINE

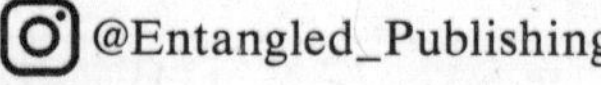

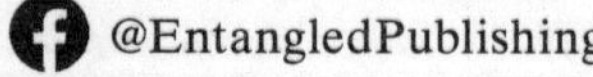

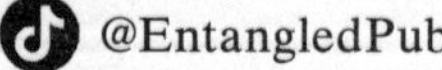

Join the Entangled Insiders for early access to ARCs, exclusive content, and insider news! Scan the QR code to become part of the ultimate reader community.